SHADOW RUN

SHADOW

ADRIANNE STRICKLAND &
MICHAEL MILLER

RUN

Delacorte Press

Text copyright © 2017 by Michael Miller and AdriAnne Strickland
Jacket art copyright © 2017 by Raphael Lacoste

All rights reserved. Published in the United States by Delacorte Press, an imprint of Random House Children's Books, a division of Penguin Random House LLC, New York.

Delacorte Press is a registered trademark and the colophon is a trademark of Penguin Random House LLC.

Visit us on the Web! randomhouseteens.com

Educators and librarians, for a variety of teaching tools, visit us at RHTeachersLibrarians.com

Library of Congress Cataloging-in-Publication Data
Names: Miller, Michael. | Strickland, AdriAnne, author.
Title: Shadow run / Michael Miller and AdriAnne Strickland.
Description: First edition. | New York : Delacorte Press, [2016] | Summary: "The captain of a starship and a prince are forced to revise their ideas of family and loyalty, with the fate of their worlds hanging in the balance."— Provided by publisher.
Identifiers: LCCN 2015044876 (print) | LCCN 2016023307 (ebook) | ISBN 978-0-399-55253-3 (hardback) | ISBN 978-0-399-55255-7 (glb) | ISBN 978-0-399-55254-0 (ebk)
Subjects: | CYAC: Science fiction. | Princes—Fiction. | Families—Fiction. | Adventure and adventurers—Fiction. | BISAC: JUVENILE FICTION / Science Fiction. | JUVENILE FICTION / Action & Adventure / General. | JUVENILE FICTION / Family / Alternative Family.
Classification: LCC PZ7.1.M583 Sh 2016 (print) | LCC PZ7.1.M583 (ebook) | DDC [Fic]—dc23

The text of this book is set in 12-point Bembo.
Interior design by Ken Crossland

Printed in the United States of America
10 9 8 7 6 5 4 3 2 1
First Edition

To Eirin Arthur Strickland (1988–2014): brother-in-law, true friend, occasional foe, and lifelong inspiration. My aliens can only hope to be as good as yours. See You, Space Cowboy . . .

—AdriAnne

Dedicated to Cord Kruse, who taught me how to write with another person. VLR, my friend.

—Michael

I

NEV

THE FIRST TIME I HEARD THE CAPTAIN'S VOICE WAS OVER THE SHIP'S comm: "Hold on, it's going to be a rough run."

She wasn't wrong. The young man across from me, Arjan, grinned as I took a wide stance and braced myself against the g-forces of the good ship *Kaitan Heritage* hurtling out of orbit.

"I see you've flown before," he said.

He knew I was a stranger to this business, so his acknowledgment was of the condescending sort. I hoped Arjan wouldn't get in my way. Well, he was already in my way, literally blocking the stairs. He was around my age, nineteen, or maybe twenty-one at most, tall with black hair that fell to shoulders that were broader than even my own. In spite of his size, I would have happily tried to brush by him if I could have succeeded with minimal fuss.

We were alone in the cargo hold, a large space dominated by pallets of canisters and an industrial panel with a maglock that I guessed connected to the containment hold on the other side. High on one wall was a display showing a feed from outside the ship. Clouds streaked by, while the walls themselves were caked with old space scum built up over time from condensation and dirt.

I nodded in response. I was definitely no stranger to space travel, which was how I could tell that we were leaving Alaxak in a hurry. Even if a ship was too utilitarian to be equipped with the best gravitational dampeners, most pilots attempted to escape the pull of a planetary body with a little less violence than what we were currently undergoing. The captain had either a great deal of faith in the *Kaitan* or a completely different way of assessing risk. The entire ship was shaking with the strain, and the thrusters roared loudly enough that I felt compelled to raise my voice to speak.

"I've been around, thanks. Where are we headed?"

"You really haven't done this before?" Arjan gave me a sympathetic shake of his head.

I did my best to hide my annoyance at the gesture, biting back a retort. Being uppity as the new hire wasn't likely to endear myself to anybody, and my agenda was worth sacrificing my ego. More than that, Arjan was the captain's brother. I hadn't met her yet, but she was the reason I was here.

I had traveled what felt like the length and breadth of the frozen planet of Alaxak to find someone specific: a captain with phenomenal abilities. Rumors, speculation, and a great many purchased drinks had led me to the village of Gamut, and then to here, a ship called the *Kaitan Heritage,* and to Captain Qole Uvgamut. "Of Gamut," in their dialect. She and Arjan belonged to one of the old native families that had originally settled the planet. One of the families, perhaps, whose long exposure to the unstable energy source known as Shadow yielded more than just sickness and death.

And yet, even though she'd technically hired me onto her crew, I hadn't been able to get close enough to even say hello, let alone place a biometric sensor on her.

I wasn't sure how I would even manage an introduction like that. *Hi, my name is Nev, and no, I can't tell you my last name or quite what I want with you, but would you please come with me?*

But rumor also had it that Arjan was nearly the caliber of pilot she was. So when I'd shaken his hand, I'd placed a biometric sensor on his forearm. And based on the miniature readout displayed on my wrist feed at the touch of a button, the data was now uploading to Uncle Rubion through their Quantum Intersystem Network, thanks to the hack I had infiltrating it. Normal comm links didn't work at such distance, but the QUIN did.

I didn't know how long it would take my uncle to interpret the data, but whatever his conclusion, my time on the *Kaitan* was limited. My pickup was coming in two days' time, and I had to be on it with at least one of the Uvgamuts.

I already hoped it would be Qole, and not just because of the incredible rumors regarding her Shadow affinity.

"I'm afraid I'm new to this particular venture," I said, "but I'm a quick study. Can you give me a brief overview of my duties?"

Arjan gave me a teasing smirk. "Your duties? Well, my good sir," he said, mimicking my accent, "here's the abbreviated explanation: once we start the run, Qole and I net the Shadow and get it into the containment hold"—he pointed at the maglock—"you load it into these canisters as quickly as possible"—he pointed at the stacks and stacks filling the cargo hold around us—"and then you try not to die."

Shadow. The thought of getting so close to it made me nervous. Speculation that it had caused the Great Collapse aside, I'd only seen it used as fuel in cutting-edge industrial facilities before now. In spite of that, it was the reason most of us were here. Well, everyone else was here to "fish," as the locals called it, for the volatile substance, while I was here to see what someone with the right biological makeup could do with it. Not that Arjan knew that, and in the meantime, I apparently had a job to do in order to keep up the pretense.

I had to resist grimacing at him. "What happens if I'm less than quick?"

"Shadow will eat through the lining of the containment hold, and then we'll all die."

Nice. "Shouldn't the lining be resistant to such degradation? Unless it's old, that is."

Arjan's face hardened. "Why bother paying an astronomical amount for new lining when you have a *fast* loader to get the Shadow into these safer, *cheaper* containers?" He patted a canister, and the noise rang out metallically. "It's how everyone does it out here."

I wanted to quote a proverb my mother used to repeat about not standing under a landing ship just because my friends did, but I refrained. I liked to think I wasn't new to danger, but the longer I spent in these cold fringes, the more I learned that the term *acceptable risk* meant something quite different from what I was used to.

"And about how long will I be at it?"

Arjan simply laughed in my face this time. "Oh boy, you *really* haven't done this. You stop when she stops." He pointed at the ceiling, presumably toward the bridge and Captain Qole. "If you're not a dead man walking by then."

Blasted hell, I thought. But I smiled. "I'm sure I'll manage."

He only grinned back at me.

"What about the rest of the crew?" I asked, to give him something better to do. "What are their jobs?"

"Come on." To my relief, he turned to leave the hold, waving me on with him. "I'll give you the free-fall tour while you can still move."

A flight of stairs just about as wide as I was, a hallway flanked by doors, and then more stairs brought us to the crew stations. A walkway bisected four recessed consoles that were ringed with monitors.

The *Kaitan* wasn't what I was accustomed to. Unlike the ships of the inner subsystems, it wasn't all glowing walls and hovering displays. Instead, mechanical parts and pieces were used wherever possible, in what I assumed was an effort to simplify repairs, while some of the displays were decades old. And the crew was just as atypical. Laughter surrounded us as we entered the space, and I caught the last part of a conversation.

"You should have seen his face, Basra, when you told him you'd never planned to sell to him. I thought you'd make someone cry in record time." The speaker, a young woman, was one of two occupants in the stations. A striking slash of black hair covered part of her face, the strands parting just enough to show an intricate tattoo around the hidden eye. Like Arjan, she had the darker hair and skin tone that still characterized native Alaxans, their population having remained mostly undiluted on their isolated planet. She cut her words short, and we surveyed each other.

After a second of silence, the other crew member stood up easily and reached out a hand. "Basra," came the introduction,

5

and I shook a beat longer than I should have. He definitely wasn't from around here, though I couldn't place where. Nor could I discern whether the pleasantly modulated voice or slender frame belonged to a man or a woman, and the hairstyle—an unabashed crest of brown curls rising from a shaved scalp—combined with simultaneously soft and angular coppery features, was no help at all. I settled on thinking of him as male for the sake of convenience.

"Nev. Nice to meet you," I replied, stupidly late.

Basra retreated just as smoothly back to his station, shoulders slightly curved, never giving me the once-over I had been expecting. I wasn't sure if the assessment had happened faster than I could notice, or if he just didn't care.

The young woman, in contrast, did not get up. She remained in her seat, legs casually propped up on the consoles in front of her. Both eyes, tattooed and not, were busy burning holes in my skull with the intensity of their stare. "Hey," she said.

"Hey. I'm, uh, still Nev. The new loader. And you are?"

She raised both eyebrows and pursed her lips in a quick motion. "Telu. Hacker." She jerked a finger at the consoles around her in emphasis, and I noticed that they were the only thing on the ship that was thoroughly up to date. "You look awfully clean for a loader."

I nodded, shifting my travel bag from one shoulder to another, thinking of the appropriately humble thing to say.

"He's new on the planet," Arjan supplied. "Won't last."

Any humility of mine turned sour as I threw him a glance.

Telu laughed before the ship lurched, and then she swept her legs underneath her console to examine the feeds. Her fingers deftly swept through a few status screens. "Looks like we're getting close, since the captain's going straight through pretty much every flare and gravitational eddy to get us there."

I perked up, noticing another set of stairs at the other end of the room. "Should I meet her before we get down to it, then?"

"Sure." Arjan shrugged. "Dead ahead."

I wasn't sure if he was trying to discourage me with a double meaning there. Despite that, I was headed for the stairs before he was finished speaking.

"Not right now," a voice rumbled as I approached, and a heavy set of boots appeared on the steps first, followed by the rest of the speaker. My gaze traveled up . . . and up. A pale face as beaten as the rest of the *Kaitan* greeted me. A number of scars crisscrossed the craggy features, and bushy eyebrows and graying, close-cropped hair further suggested that he was a human mountain. Unlike his other crewmates, this huge man had no problem eyeing me as though I were an assassin entering the royal chambers.

"Eton, this is Nev, our new loader," Arjan piped up behind me, and I could hear the grin in his voice as he did. "Nev, Eton is our weapons tech. And muscle."

I held out my hand to Eton. "Hello, a pleasure."

I was surprised that he actually reached down and took it, but I understood why when he turned my hand to jelly in his own paw. "Introductions later. Maybe." He crossed the two tree trunks he had for arms and nodded at me. "We're about to start the run, so hustle to your station."

I was pretty sure he wasn't the one who should be giving me orders, but I plastered a friendly smile on my face instead of shaking out my pulped hand and screaming that I didn't have time for this. "Of course. I look forward to it."

━━━

Eighteen hours later, I definitely wasn't smiling.

The *Kaitan Heritage* was poised at the outskirts of a vast molecular cloud. Thanks to the projected image in the hold, intended to help me keep pace with what Arjan was doing in the skiff—the small secondary shuttle that he used to maneuver the net when it wasn't docked in the *Kaitan*—I had a front-row seat. The edges of the cloud seemed frozen in time in spite of the cosmic forces that propelled them outward. These gas streamers spread for light years, streaked with oranges, purples, and greens like the product of a painter gone mad. The fingers reached to where we hovered in the Alaxak Asteroid Sea, a stretching field of celestial rubble.

And yet the enormity of that brilliant sky crammed with stars was nothing to my first glimpse of a Shadow run. Surrounded by undulating fields of blackness, waving pinpricks of light coursed toward us in a bizarre mimicry of planetary fish migrations—a mesmerizing, swirling, diving current that invited uninitiated "fishermen" to gape unabashedly.

Which I was certainly guilty of on our first run. Now, countless runs later, I couldn't have cared less. I was frozen, depleted beyond measure. The Great Unifier himself could have reached a finger out to create a new cosmos and my response would have been to take a nap, grateful that we weren't making a run for another catch.

Captain Qole, on the other hand, had no plans for sleep. From the chatter on the comms it seemed we were raking in a catch of epic proportions, and she had brought us about for yet another run.

I had apparently arrived on the job in the midst of some intense Shadow fishing, and I didn't think asking her to stop, hear me out, and come with me, even though I couldn't tell her my full name, even *if* I guaranteed her safety and a lot of money, would go over well. Not without her trust. Which I had no idea how to earn from the cargo hold. I was having a hard enough time surviving.

The *Kaitan* floated in stillness, contemplating the endless sea of Shadow off its bow. Then it tilted, a hum reverberating through the ship as subspace engines were fueled to life, and we rocketed straight for the ten or so trillion tons of hurtling rock in the asteroid field. Shadow flashed up toward us faster than any of the debris, then parted, a thousand frantic points of light dispersing out from the ship, vanishing back into the asteroid field.

The display showed the edges of mag-couplings flickering to life as the boom on top of the ship extended out to the side. A winch unspooled the two cables—the polarized top and bottom edge of the "net" attached to Arjan's skiff—which trailed behind him as he took off.

That was when the light show started. The entire arm flared for a moment as power flowed through the cables to magnetize them, and then a web of shimmering, rippling light arced from top to bottom to create a net stretching between the skiff and the *Kaitan*.

Where the skiff went, so went the cables, Arjan's movement manipulating the size and shape of their spread. As stray Shadow began to flit past us and hit the glowing barrier that billowed like an impermeable curtain in the wind, it would explode with a myriad of colors—purple, red, yellow—and then flow like a darting stream along the mag-field net and straight toward the portal that led into the containment hold.

The *Kaitan* careened after the nearest flickers of Shadow, banking impossibly around asteroids I wasn't even capable of processing before they tore past the view of the display. The ship shuddered violently in their wake, the Shadow river strobing past in a succession so fast I knew we had completed multiple barrel rolls. The gravitational dampeners groaned and whined in the center of the ship, and several times I felt the brief disorientation of weightlessness. Somehow, Arjan was keeping pace with us in the skiff, racing parallel to the *Kaitan*.

The comms crackled to life with Qole's voice. It resonated with the timbre of someone who was steady, alert, and completely in her element. "Do your thing, Arjan."

The sharp triangle of the skiff gleamed in the gaslight of the clouds as it juked and twisted around space debris to keep up and, miraculously, keep the net out of the worst of the asteroid interference. He created a huge arc, predicting where the Shadow specks would flow next.

"Ready?" His voice came in, calm as could be, as though he hadn't just threaded the needle of death.

"Count to two, then bring it in." Qole's tone carried with it all the same emotions.

While Arjan's job was difficult, he had the more maneuverable vessel by far. What he was doing was amazing, but not unbelievable. Qole, however, was using the *Kaitan* in a way I wouldn't have thought possible. She employed every thruster on the ship to send us corkscrewing around obstacles and darting for Shadow as nimbly as a starfighter a quarter our size. In other subsystems, she would have been a celebrity, the hero of racing circuits and reality daredevil shows. Here, she was just a Shadow fishing captain. The best and from one of the oldest families Alaxak had to offer, but still.

There weren't many members of the old Shadow fishing families left alive, I'd discovered after arriving on the planet a few weeks ago. At least, not with their wits intact. I'd come to Alaxak chasing rumors of extra senses and preternatural reflexes in humans, and instead found mostly death and madness. But Qole was another matter. She was living proof that I hadn't come in vain.

For a few moments, both skiff and ship raced in parallel, nose to nose, and then Arjan veered sharply, bringing in the far edge of the net to close the circuit. Straight for the *Kaitan,* and straight into the path of a lump of space rock that had appeared between him and the ship in the blink of an eye.

A split second later, the grating roar of a mass driver echoed through the ship and the asteroid was harmless debris.

"Clear," rumbled Eton unnecessarily from his perch in the turret.

Excitement, wonder, elation, terror, wetting one's pants in abject fear—all these things are what a human might normally go through after being exposed to that experience for the first time. But this was where my job came in, and after more than a few hours on the ship, I was thoroughly numb to it all, in mind and body. The hold, though insulated to allow for human survival in deep space, was not heated for comfort. The near-freezing temperatures would have turned me into a meat icicle, if I weren't forced to hustle with all the remaining speed I had left.

"Get it processed, Nev. This flare is slowing down, so make it count!" Captain Qole yelled at me over the comm. I stumbled in semihaste, groaning inwardly at both my exhaustion and the continued delay this Shadow run was to my mission.

As Arjan funneled the Shadow into the net, artfully tucking it in, the circuit closed. It formed a containment field that kept most of the substance from escaping, but it couldn't hold such a volatile and unstable energy source for any prolonged length of time. So that was when I activated the suction scoop on the side of the hull, whisking the Shadow right into the containment hold, which was sealed off from the cargo hold

I was in. But of course *that* couldn't hold it for long either, as Arjan had told me, because of the damned poor lining.

The containers, of which there were hundreds, happened to weigh approximately half of what I did, even empty. I would heft one, jam it into the slot where it seated with the maglock, and yank the lever that would let the Shadow come blasting inside. The second it was full, I had to close the maglock and replace the canister with another. The faster I moved, the more Shadow we captured, and the less time it had to eat its way through the containment hold and blow us all to smithereens. But even that had stopped providing me with impetus for speed. Only two things kept me going: an overriding desire to be done with the job, followed by the nagging thought that I had to get out of this cargo hold before I ran out of time to convince Qole of anything.

Unless working myself to death was the only way to gain Qole's trust, in which case I was nearly there.

"Um, Telu?" Arjan's voice, slightly concerned, crackled into my awareness through the comm.

I glanced up at the display feed, and my blood turned to ice.

"Telu, there's a drone, bearing zero, zero, two. What's your status?" Qole chimed in.

Sure enough, hanging out and minding its own aggravating business directly in front of us was a mining drone thrice the size of the *Kaitan,* busy latching itself on to smaller asteroids. Five or six metal tentacles whipped out and grasped the rocks, and a beam of energy projected from the front of the dome. The asteroid split, and piece by piece the fragments were sucked into the drone's circular maw. We were headed directly for it.

That managed to wake me up a bit. I hit the comm button.

"Uh, excuse me, but drones don't take very kindly to anyone getting close to their fields."

"Thank you, newbie." The captain drop-kicked me back into place. "Please focus on your job. Everyone, we're completing the run."

I stared, somewhat slack-jawed, as we closed the distance to the drone much faster than I could fully appreciate. What I had said was an understatement—the drones were from a bygone era, but their programming was still running even though no one had tended to them in hundreds of years, and their security protocols remained as active as their mindless tasks. They would decimate anyone who drew close enough to interfere with their mining. Younger captains, and many complacent older ones, had lost their ships or their lives from drawing too near to them. Say, about as near as we were drawing now.

"Telu?" Qole's voice wasn't concerned, but it was inquiring.

"No worries, Cap," Telu's voice responded, sounding for all the world as though she were promising to sweep the floors later in the day.

I opened my mouth to yell at them all for their insanity, when the drone wobbled, rotated ninety degrees, and fired itself with savage speed at a giant asteroid in the distance.

"Suck it, Dracortes," Telu said.

Normally I would have laughed, since *suck it* and *Dracortes* weren't things one often heard in the same sentence. Instead, I gasped. Drones never left their allotted task before they were done, and that could only mean that Telu had managed to temporarily redirect the programming. Not unheard of, but usually accomplished only by carefully chosen people who had studied for years in restricted academies. To her, it was a common chore.

My thought was eclipsed by Shadow flaring inches from my face.

——

I blinked and shook my head. The world had altered around me; I was looking at the ceiling instead of the wall. It took me a moment to realize I was now on my back on the floor, ringed by several people in various stages of emotion: Telu looked relieved, Basra unmoved, and the new arrival distinctly displeased.

Captain Qole Uvgamut, my brain informed me, even as I tried to reconcile that with who I was seeing. I knew her rank, her reputation, and her voice, and yet she still wasn't what I had expected.

She was young. Much younger than I'd imagined. I'd heard she was only seventeen, but the command in her tone had made that hard to believe. A glance, from upside down and on my back, was proof enough. Her long black hair was held in a braid down her back, and she was dressed in an odd combination of warm clothing. Unlike workers in other subsystems who used synthetics, they wore local leather and furs on the *Kaitan,* because of the remoteness of Alaxak and the cost of shipping from offworld. Affordability aside, hers must have been tailored for her, because while they looked comfortable, they also hugged her figure in ways that made my eyes want to linger. Otherwise she looked about as warm and inviting as a knife. High cheekbones sharpened the curves of her oval, medium-toned face, and her dark eyes were quick to narrow.

"How in the systems did that happen? Did you let a canister overflow?" Qole didn't raise her voice, but I shrank back anyway as I sat up.

I reached out for balance as I tried to stand, but Qole evidently thought I needed help and clasped my wrist. Her hand was warm, and her grip left no doubt that it would hold until I was on my feet. In fact, she hoisted me up with enough speed to stagger me forward. I could have caught myself, but instead I stumbled against her arm. Her slight frame was unmoving, braced with excellent balance, as my fingertips pressed into her and managed to stick the nearly invisible biometric sensor onto the inside of her wrist. In spite of making myself look like a drunk, I had finally accomplished one useful thing today.

"Um . . . maybe?" I responded, stepping back. "There was a drone, and tentacles of death, and . . ."

"Yep, that's what went down," Telu supplied helpfully. "The canister overpressurized and leaked Shadow into the hold. The safety system closed the maglock when the blowback happened, but it must have been strong enough to give him a knock."

"Oh, Great Collapse." Qole grabbed her hair and scrunched it up, pulling strands out of her braid. "That's the same problem we had with the other blasted idiot. I should have known this wouldn't work out." She bent over and began to savagely stack some of the scattered containers. "Basra, comm Arjan and Eton, would you? We need to get into position for the next flare, see if there will be another run."

An idiot. That was all I was after all this—eighteen hours of backbreaking, repetitive labor. She'd dismissed me, just like that. All that to earn her respect and trust, and instead I get her contempt.

I felt myself flush with anger. I couldn't hold it in; I was too exhausted, and the pain in my skull only added more of an edge to my words. "Have you considered you wouldn't have these problems with *blasted idiots* if you directed even a fraction of the energy you spend on risking everyone's lives toward designing a better system to store Shadow more safely and efficiently?"

Qole went still. "Excuse me?"

Warning klaxons jangled in my head, all of which were firmly ignored. "You're excused. But just so we're clear, your incredibly fancy flying to gather up everyone's next paycheck won't do us any good when we're are all *dead,* from either exhaustion or a Shadow explosion." I gestured at the canister that had nearly knocked my brains out.

She fixed me with a steady gaze that shrank a portion of my anger. Well, a lot of my anger. Telu backed away a little, and Basra had magically relocated to the far side of the hold. But *in for a reentry, in for a free fall,* as the saying went. Besides, I wasn't about to back down when I knew I was right. The rough-edged captain, intriguing and impressive though she might be, wasn't about to intimidate me when I'd dealt with powers so far beyond her station it was laughable.

"I don't see anyone dead." Qole started to let heat into her words. "And since it's your ignorance of your job that led to the accident, I'm *dying* to know how you think we could do better."

"My profound and unending apologies for being momentarily concerned for the intact status of my hide, your hide, and everyone else's on this ship," I said with as much sarcasm as I could muster—which was significant, given the circumstances. "Next time, consider saving up for a proper containment hold instead of having people run ragged trying to manage a cargo that this ship was never designed to carry in the first place."

"Proper?" Qole spat out the word like something disgusting, and looked as if she would stuff it back down my throat if she could. "What the hell would you know about any of that?"

While I didn't have any working knowledge of how to

Shadow fish, I had certainly studied the industry. "Only that containment holds exist that can, I don't know, actually *contain* Shadow safely—no leaking, no degrading, no need for your crew to siphon it into different blasted containers"— I ticked off the qualities on my fingers—"and with one, your ship could carry your catch until you get to a processing station that could simply suck it out of the hold. I know that's how Shadow is shipped off-planet."

"If you actually knew what you were talking about, other than about what's *off-planet,* then you'd know how few operations can afford that type of setup here. There are maybe two ships like that on all of Alaxak."

Arjan had tried to tell me the same thing, but that didn't change the fact that this was still a stupidly dangerous, inefficient way to do things. "Well, those two are the only ships whose captains value their lives over their catch, apparently. Working like a maniac doesn't make anyone noble, it just makes them a maniac."

Qole stepped closer to me, and for a second we were face to face as she stared up at me and yet stared me down. For the first time, I noticed something other than anger in her brown eyes—something dark that flickered at the corners.

Shadow. Literally, Shadow, flickering at the edges of her whites. Great Collapse, I'd heard the stories, but I hadn't really believed it. This wasn't Shadow poisoning—this was her affinity, active in her system.

I braced myself. For what, I didn't know.

Then her eyes narrowed into normal anger, and she turned on her heel and disappeared from the hold.

I'm pretty sure we all blinked. Except for maybe Basra—I didn't get a chance to catch him in the act.

Fantastic. I'd just thoroughly alienated the one person I'd needed to befriend. In fact, I might have just gotten myself *fired* by the one person I'd needed to befriend.

I resisted the urge to rub my forehead and give away how unnerved I was. Facing an infuriated Qole had been bad enough, but the new realization trickling into my stomach was worse: As we were running for Shadow, the best I could hope for was to hear her commands over the comm as I canistered my way to a stupid death.

I ignored Basra and Telu, who were both watching me, and began hefting the fallen canisters for something to do, knowing I'd be expected to restack them anyway. *If I had a different position on the ship, if we had a moment to breathe, if we had more time planet-side . . .*

Planet-side. At first, I hadn't been able to wait to get aboard the *Kaitan.* But that was when I'd been thinking it would afford me the opportunity to get close to the captain. Other captains took time to repair, refuel, and recharge their crew in the villages. The situation would be different there, and surely, if nothing else, I'd be able to buy Qole a drink.

However, in spite of my brush with death, Qole showed no signs of quitting. She was probably even *less* inclined to stop now.

I eyed the canisters, feeling less bitter toward them. We might not need refueling at the moment, but we could easily need to address some other pressing issue.

I wouldn't dare mess with something as dangerous as Shadow, but its volatility could serve me in another way. There were panels on each canister that displayed how full it was and how intact the lining was. Very simple electronics—but it would be a serious business indeed if they suddenly displayed imminent failure.

Serious enough to head back to Alaxak.

II

QOLE

Next time, consider saving up for a proper containment hold. . . .

The sentence echoed in my mind, getting louder along with sparking surges of rage, as I made my way back up to the bridge. Nearly every word brought on a new flare that made my vision blacken at the edges.

Next time . . . "Next times" were a luxury not all of us got in the Shadow fishing business. And Telu, Arjan, and I were facing other dangers, every day, that arrogant, self-assured piece of scat didn't have a clue about.

. . . consider saving up . . . As if living day-to-day, keeping my crew well paid and well fed, and covering overhead costs that sometimes felt so huge as to crush me left me much room

to just *save up*. Not to mention I might not live long enough to save much of anything. Such a naïve offworlder.

. . . *for a proper* . . . What did that word even mean out here? It wasn't as if I could go to the blasted Containment Hold Market. He knew absolutely nothing.

No, I thought as I stopped to brace myself in the doorway of the bridge, no, Nev—if that was even his name—knew much more than nothing. He had a familiarity with ships, even *this* type of ship, which was so customized beyond its standard, outdated model as to be nearly unique. I'd hired him in a hurry without the interview that Eton had wanted to subject him to, but then, most new arrivals on Alaxak weren't eager to talk about their pasts. We'd needed a new loader after our old one left abruptly—the fifth to quit this year—and it was a position that didn't require much know-how. No one with much brainpower wanted it, anyway. And yet he was far better educated than most, especially at his age—eighteen? Twenty?

And he didn't look right. He wasn't the usual rough and ragged type that usually tried to be a loader. He was too . . . nice-looking. His teeth were very straight and white, and his light brown hair was wind-tangled but clean. His gray clothes were the right color, but also clean and mostly synthetic. He had a lump on the bridge of his nose as if he had broken it in a fight, but his pale cheeks and jaw were too defined and smooth, and his brown eyes were too rich and sparkling to have been on Alaxak for a single winter.

The guy was proud. Wealthy too, judging by his clothes, and from one of the royal planets, judging by his accent. Eton had sounded a lot like him when he'd shown up a few years ago, and Eton had served as a bodyguard on one of the royal planets, though that was about all I could get out of him on the topic of his past.

So what the blasted hell was Nev *actually* doing out here? He was probably a tourist wanting a thrill, or worse, a runaway rich boy. In either case, something stank.

I took a deep breath and let my arms slide down the door frame with my exhale. I focused on the stars through the sweeping viewport half circling my captain's chair, on the river of light made by the clouds.

I was doing everything I could. Wasn't I?

The question felt bigger in my skull, bigger than the containment hold, reflecting the expanse of space outside. I was doing what Alaxans had done for hundreds and hundreds of years before me. This could only be the right path. It felt right.

. . . For the most part. And yet one arrogant offworlder was making me doubt myself.

I wished I could ask my father. It had been his ship first, after all, and his father's before him. I missed the days of sitting up here in a spare chair, my knees pulled up to my chin against the chill, as I watched my father pilot. I'd ask him every question under the stars. It was usually just me, since Onai—the thought of my oldest brother still made me wince—would be piloting the skiff, and Arjan was usually along with him, learning how. As the youngest, I'd been riding on the bridge with my father on short Shadow runs practically before the buckles fit tight enough to hold me in my seat during takeoff. So I'd known the moment his flying began to grow more erratic, when his eyes went from only darkening in the corners during his more daring moves to turning fully black and back again.

If only he were still here. He would have been able to talk to me about everything from containment hold upgrades to suspicious strangers, and about this blackness that felt like it was eating me up from the inside out.

He would have been able to, if the very same blackness

hadn't killed him. And my mother. And Onai. And my grand-parents and all their other children. And my great-grandparents.

Ours was a legacy of pride and tradition. It was also a legacy of death and madness. This blackness was deeper and darker and more dangerous than the hidden corners of space. And it lived inside me. In my blood and bone, in the fibers of my being.

Shadow poisoning affected anyone exposed to too much of the energy for very long, but this . . . this was different. This was generations of exposure built up in our bodies, lining our cells and nerves like soot.

And it didn't only kill us. For some of us, it made us great before it did. And that scared me more than anything.

It was in moments like these that I felt very small, very young . . . and very alone. It was, I knew, the same feeling that crippled Arjan and kept him from being able to lead as captain.

And yet here I was. So I raked my hands back through my hair, threw myself down in my seat, and shook off the feeling of clinging darkness. It eventually stopped weighing on my shoulders, encroaching on the corners of my eyes.

Darkness seemed to still be pressing on the viewport, though. It was actually the middle of our day—we'd fished throughout the night and the next morning—though it was hard to tell from the blackness of space.

It was almost as peaceful as sleep. I paused for a second to watch the partial arc of the intergalactic portal float across my view. Once, it was a gateway from Alaxak to the rest of the gal-axy, and even to distant galaxies beyond, but now it was still and empty as a doorway without a house around it. Unimaginably large, the twisted girders, damaged over the centuries from meteor strikes, hovered like broken ribs. Sometimes drones would collect in front of it in an attempt to travel through it using a technology that . . . well, that nobody understood any-more. The Great Collapse was named for its loss. Eventually, the drones would revert to other programing and disperse, leaving what remained of the ruins to float alone. I found it comforting in a way—civilization had imploded, but my people had endured. Our culture had existed for thousands of years before the Great Collapse and it would exist for thousands after.

Even if I didn't make it that much longer.

My brother's voice over the comm brought me back to myself. He was using the channel that piped only into the bridge. "Great flying, little sister."

I felt my eyes tear, despite myself. Arjan had been in this with me from the beginning. We'd both watched our parents' loving gaze go dark and never change back, heard the chaotic nonsense that replaced their steady words of reason, and found them—finally—unmoving one morning over five years ago. After Onai followed my parents' dark path less than two years later at age twenty-five, it was Arjan who had eventually encouraged me to take over their operation, even with me just fourteen and him eighteen. It was looking out for him and the crew that helped me keep my self-control. Without him, I wouldn't be here, and yet I so often treated him just like any other member of the crew.

"Thanks," I said. "You too, really. Look, Arjan, when we're done with this run, let's you and me . . . go somewhere . . . different for a little while." The words tripped awkwardly out of my mouth. "You know, like, away from Gamut for a couple of days. Maybe we could camp on the beaches on the northern sea, or in the equatorial forest."

"I think it's called a 'vacation,' and I'm not surprised you don't know the word." I could hear his grin. He hadn't teased me like this for a long time. "Sounds amazing."

I grinned back, even though he couldn't see it.

"But you know," he added with a yawn, "going to sleep sounds nearly as amazing."

I was also tired. Dangerously tired, where control slipped away faster than Shadow from a net, and a laugh burst out of me. "There'll be time enough to sleep when we're dead."

My laughter hitched. That eventuality might not be too far off for either of us, if Onai was any indication. I cleared my throat and pushed the button to comm the entire crew. "Let's get back into position, everyone, in case there's another flare worth running."

Voices came back to me in sleepy assent. Unsurprisingly, I didn't hear from Nev. He was probably asleep standing up.

"Eton and Telu, eyes out for any drones or asteroids headed our way. Nev, get me a count on our remaining empty canisters—"

"Um . . . Captain?" Nev's voice was unsteady as he interrupted me—but not from tiredness. He sounded more anxious than he had at the sight of the drone.

"What?"

As if answering for him, a red light flared on the dash, followed by the piercing buzz of an alarm. Panic rose in me at the same time, until I forced it down and scanned the feeds as quickly as possible.

Someone had pressure locked the cargo hold.

"Nev!" I shouted into the comm. "What's going on?"

"A few of the canisters—the panels might be fried, because I didn't see any Shadow, but they're saying they're losing pressure."

Another pulse of fear ran through me. If he was trapped in the cargo hold with leaking canisters . . . I would not lose a crewmember this way. Even if he was new, even if I found him strange and infuriating, I could not watch his skin bubble and blacken. Even if he was lucky and only came into contact with a concentration of Shadow too weak to burn him, he would still fall into madness faster than an airship into the gravitational pull of a planet. I would no more be able to stand watching his eyes turn black than the rest of him.

And I wouldn't risk the rest of my ship. Leaking canisters could blow us all to hell. I would vent the cargo hold into space before I would let that happen, but that would of course kill Nev.

"Nev, *get out of there now.*" If he was stuck in there, maybe I could reach for the Shadow and try to direct it . . . and risk killing myself. "If you're locked in, I can manually override—"

"I'm out. I was the one who put the pressure lock on."

I let out a massive breath into the comm. "Thank the ancestors."

"Well, I didn't want to stay in there," he said with some humor. "And I didn't want anything leaking into the rest of the ship."

Maybe I'd been too hard on him. He'd not only saved himself but tried to protect the *Kaitan*. "Good work. Get away from the door and strap yourself in in the mess. Arjan, get the skiff back on board. We need to get those canisters offloaded, now." I couldn't keep the rest of my words from coming out clipped, even though I knew it was the right thing to do. "We're headed back to Alaxak."

———

The *Kaitan*'s bow parted the icy gray waves as I landed in the ocean and then taxied into Gamut's small harbor. As far as I knew, our planet was the only one where ships docked almost exclusively in water. No one had the money to build industrial landing pads, and the permafrost was too unstable otherwise. The ground couldn't take the force or heat of a ship's thrusters for long before turning into a bog.

I wished we were taking off instead. I wanted to feel caught between gravity and the plasma jets, between ice and fire, my back mashed into the seat. That tug-of-war with me at the center would mean I was moving. Here on my frozen planet, movement never came without a fight. And if what I still felt in my gut was right, this was a catch worth moving for. We should still be out there.

But no, we were headed in the opposite direction of the call I felt. The knowledge tingled on my skin, crackling along my nerves, pulsing through my bones, pounding through my entire body, a comm speaker shouting *now, now, now.*

Shadow was calling to me.

"Let's get this done quick, hey?" I was so distracted as I pulled up to the pier that I forgot to catch the local accent I often muffled for the benefit of my offworlder crew. The dockworkers outside reacted quickly to our arrival, tossing heavy lines to secure us to massive cleats while steam hissed from our hull, still hot from reentry.

From his station below me, Basra glanced up through the metal grating of the bridge floor. "I've already commed the cannery to let them know we have a situation. They're sending a containment van to get the canisters, and they'll be geared up, so we won't even have to enter the cargo hold. That shouldn't take more than an hour, and they estimated decontamination might take another two or so hours, if there is any."

I blinked. I usually couldn't get them to respond so fast or efficiently. Maybe Basra had sweet-talked them somehow. "Nice."

"The only downside is they can't offload the rest of our catch now, since they're at processing capacity for the moment."

In which case, it was doubly impressive they were coming so soon. "No problem. We can fill all the way up and deliver in a couple of days." I shrugged. "I guess that means whoever wants to can grab a nap. And we can all sleep for a few more hours after we lift off again, since we'll have to wait on the blasted drone traffic."

The cosmologists had predicted particularly heavy drone activity between us and the Alaxak Asteroid Sea over the next six hours—exactly in our flight path. The automated mining drones always got in our way, trying to blow up the ship whenever they felt I got in *their* way. Usually I maneuvered around them, but not even I would risk heading into that many. Still, we'd be back fishing sooner than I'd expected.

"What is this, *free time*? Are you getting soft?" Telu laughed from her own station. "Excuse me while I get right on the sleep. I wouldn't miss this date with my bunk for the galaxy in a glass."

"Not sleeping in your chair, for once?" I asked, attempting to return her teasing tone, even though my fingers were drumming on the dash. "What's the occasion?"

"More than thirty minutes to catch some shut-eye is an occasion. Plus"—she grinned up at me—"did you notice how fast I had that drone chasing its own tail? Any time I can stick it to the royals is cause for celebration."

She had reason to hate the royals, one royal family in particular. The Dracortes owned the mining drones. Their programming was impossible to change—not even the Dracortes knew how anymore—but temporarily rerouting them wasn't impossible for a hacker like Telu.

Not that hackers of her skill level were common. Her family was nearly as old as mine. She never seemed to be able to point the way to Shadow as well as Arjan or I could, but she definitely had the much faster reflexes gained after generations of Shadow exposure, even if she employed them in a different way. She was to drone hacking as I was to piloting, meaning she was one of the best damned hackers on all of Alaxak, and maybe beyond.

I gave her a tired smile. "Good job today," I told her. "We're fishing hard, but you're as sharp as ever."

Her eyes grew softer behind all their edges. "Thanks," she murmured.

When she stood, I added, "Set the cams outside the cargo hold to record if they detect motion." When anyone but my crew was on board, I liked to be cautious—and even among my crew, I didn't trust Nev yet.

"Already did," she replied, giving me a knowing look, one that would be more of a deterrent than cameras to thieves or saboteurs, if only they could see it. "I set an alarm too." She gave me a smirk, following fast on the heels of her death-stare, as I'd always called it. "Don't you sleep in your chair, either, hey?"

I wasn't sure if I would be sleeping, but I didn't want her to worry about me. "I won't."

Telu had only just left her station and I'd barely settled in to wait, when there was a commotion on the stairs leading up to the bridge. Eton's voice rose—no surprise, in these sorts of situations.

"I *said,* you don't get to bother the captain. That's not part of your job, as I would have explained to you in unmistakable terms if I'd been the one to hire you. No, scratch that, I just wouldn't have hired you in the first place."

28

I stood from my chair in a rush, irritation practically dragging my body upright. I knew whom he was talking to, because Eton had disapproved of my snap decision to hire Nev practically straight off the dock. I *almost* couldn't blame him: Nev was an unknown element with no fishing experience, but Arjan had found Nev and approved of him enough to recommend I give him a shot. Besides, there was no one else under such short notice—it wasn't like Gamut was a bustling hub of commerce. I expected Eton to grumble—which he had—but to second-guess me in front of Nev and the rest of the crew was a step too far.

"Well, good thing the *captain* hired me instead of you, hm?" Nev retorted, his voice far more calm than Eton's but no less loud. In spite of his being a source of plenty of irritation himself, the words made me smile. He already understood what Eton apparently still didn't.

That alone made me call out, "Eton, let him up here. It's fine."

Nev stepped lightly onto the bridge from the top of the stairs, and Eton followed with much more force, his steps ringing over the metal grating.

"Yes?" I asked Nev politely enough, ignoring Eton. I wasn't exactly thrilled to see him, but I *had* invited him up here.

Nev smiled—a nice smile with those too-white teeth. "We haven't had much time to get formally acquainted yet, Captain. I hoped we could take advantage of this unfortunate mishap with the canisters, and that you might let me apologize for losing my temper earlier. Please allow me to buy you a drink."

Eton practically choked, while I had to snap my own mouth closed. "You . . . want to buy me a drink?" I stuttered.

It was definitely the first time in my life anyone had ever offered me that. I had to fight down a hysterical laugh. Didn't he have any idea who I was? It wasn't even that I was the captain, but more *what* I was.

Nev's smile didn't lessen. "I'm pretty sure that's what I said."

Eton finally found his voice. "There's no way in blazing hell the captain is going with you."

I turned on Eton with the same incredulity, except this time my words were deadly quiet. "Are you trying to speak for me, now?"

"Qole, look at him!" He threw his hands at our new loader. "This character was apparently skulking around Gamut for days asking questions about you! He's some offworlder here for his own reasons. He doesn't know the first thing about catching Shadow."

"Like you once didn't, you mean?" The reminder made Eton snap his mouth closed and fold his arms. I crossed my own arms and stood right in front of him. The difference between our relative sizes was probably especially obvious since I came up to his shoulder, but between the two of us, I knew which one wasn't backing down. My voice stayed low, my words measured. "I think I'll have a drink with Nev. We'll be back in less than an hour."

Eton made a thunderous noise of exasperation. "Telu, do you hear this?" He looked down through the floor.

"Telu's getting some rest," I said.

"Like we all should be. Hey, Basra, Arjan! Can *you* talk some sense into Qole?"

Unfortunately, Arjan had joined Basra at his comm station down below, and the two of them were looking back up at us through the floor, watching the scene on the bridge play out. Oddly, Basra had his hand on my brother's arm. Now that I thought about it, I'd been seeing them together more and more, when we had the rare bit of downtime.

"Qole, I'm not sure that's best——" Arjan began.

Basra cleared his throat loudly, interrupting him. "This is a negotiation you can't win, so don't even bother. Let's get some sleep ourselves." He swept away from his console then, firmly guiding Arjan alongside and adding over his shoulder, "I'd advise against killing Eton, however, Captain. We need him."

Typical Basra, ever aware of the value of everything—and everyone. I didn't think he let things like *feelings* cloud his judgment. He even preferred identifying as a he, for the most part, not because he felt more like one, but because of the slight edge it gave him when haggling—something I could at least understand as a young female captain, with my every move challenged or underestimated.

Yet it raised the sudden question: What was between my brother and him? Basra had joined our crew a couple of years ago, following Arjan, Telu, and Eton, in that order, and I'd never quite figured out why. Of course we needed a trader to deal with the Shadow once we'd caught it, and he was a trader, but I'd had no idea what he was doing on Alaxak. He kept closed-mouthed about his past, much like Eton—much like anyone from off-planet, really—and so I hadn't pressed him. But as it became clearer and clearer that Basra was no ordinary trader, gender fluidity aside, I'd wondered. And now, as I glanced down at him and my brother before the door closed behind them, their hands nearly brushing as they left the crews' stations, I really wondered.

First things first. I was apparently having a drink, of all things, with our new loader, of all people. As absurd as that was, it would be worth it if it would teach Eton a valuable lesson. I was too wired to sleep, anyway . . . and maybe the tiniest bit impressed that Nev hadn't dived for his bunk first thing himself. I started away from my control console, heading for the stairs, and Nev turned to follow me.

"Qole," Eton said. He was in no mood.

I was in less of a mood as I blew past him. "*Captain* Qole. You know, Captain Uvgamut would be even better."

"Qole," he said again. "You belong on the ship." He scowled as he slid in front of me, his long, powerful legs scissoring the distance in no time. For a second, it looked like Nev edged forward in that posturing, protective way some idiot men had ... but no, he'd only shifted to lean against some lockers. "You're the *captain,* as you just reminded me."

"You mean, I'm *safer* on the ship." My scowl matched Eton's. "I think I can handle *this* guy." I gestured dismissively at Nev, and one of his eyebrows lifted.

"And so can I! At the very least let me go with you. It's my job to be your strong-arm. Let me do my job." The rumble of Eton's deep voice was louder than the scrape of his huge boots over the metal grating.

He had a point, but this wasn't a fresh argument he was raising. It just about stank with old familiarity, like a carcass washed up and rotting on the beach, and I was sick of it. Also, Nev was now watching me with appraisal in his oddly bright eyes, and for some reason I didn't want him to think I couldn't handle myself. Also, I was now blazingly furious, which had nothing really to do with either of them.

The blackness pulsed inside me, threatening the corners of my vision. Neither Eton nor Nev stepped back. Brave, I thought, or stupid, depending on how much they could see in my eyes. Shadow poisoning wasn't contagious, but most locals knew enough to not want to be near someone like me when they were angry. And you *really* didn't want to be around when they finally snapped. Some went quietly into madness, like my parents. Others didn't.

Control, I'm in control, I chanted to myself. The surges were getting worse, and I didn't seem to be getting much better at containing them. But I had to. If I didn't, I would soon be dead. Or worse: a screaming, babbling shell of my former self, too out of my mind to know I'd be better off dead.

I breathed deeply, trying to steady my anger. Even so, I took a sudden step toward Eton, making him do an agile dance to keep from knocking into me. In other circumstances, it would have been comical. As big as he was, he was quicker on his feet than anyone I'd ever seen.

He also jumped out of my way, which was the effect I'd wanted.

"Stay on the ship," I said. He opened his mouth to protest, but I added, "That's an order."

That made him clamp his mouth shut, and he turned away rather than watch Nev follow me out.

In spite of Eton's grudging compliance, my anger surged again like a solar flare. These offworlders. They were going to drive me crazy, if Shadow didn't do it first.

III

NEV

THE WIND AS I LEANED OUTSIDE THE SHIP WAS LIKE A SLAP TO THE FACE, making tears spring to my eyes. It was supposed to be early summer, but this wasn't like early summer at home. Wherever the last long rays of the sun hit, there was the vague sensation of warmth, but every shadow was a brisk reminder that if you spent the night outside without the proper gear you'd not see the morning.

A metallic clank rang out as Qole landed on the dock beneath us. Thanks to the equipment failure I had initiated on the canisters, the cargo hold was sealed off until the decon unit from the cannery gave the all clear. So instead of using the usual ramp that dropped down from there, we were exiting the ship from a small emergency airlock situated near the crew's quarters.

The fall was farther than what could be prudent for day-to-day use, but Qole didn't seem to notice. I refused to pause where she hadn't and jumped down after her, tucking my body into a roll as I landed.

Once I'd righted myself, I got my first good look at the *Kaitan* in the weak afternoon light. The ship was long and lean, in stark contrast to the bulkier freighters around it. The bridge viewport at the bow gave way to a sweeping dip on the back where the boom for the net was housed. The engine intakes on either side of the hull curved back to join in in neatly riveted plating. Like every ship I had seen here, it was an offworld design that had been customized, but the others were strewn with cabling and power couplings, and covered in poor patchwork. Despite the hull's various dents and scrapes, everything on the *Kaitan* was neatly attached and accounted for.

Qole wasn't waiting for me. Hands in her pockets, slightly hunkered against the wind, she was resolutely striding away. She might have agreed to go get a drink, but she evidently didn't see the need to walk there with me.

I sighed and started after her.

As soon as I moved, someone seized my arm with a rasping breath that sounded like air being sucked into space. A person, if he could be called that, was huddled on the icy dock in the shadow of the *Kaitan.* He was wasted, and thin, with eyes that were entirely black, sunken like coal pits above the protruding cheekbones—the eyes of the Shadow mad. Ragged scraps were all that stood between him and the brutal elements, and the only sound that came from the cracked lips was a hair-raising rattle.

I jerked my arm away instinctively, then was immediately

ashamed of myself. But what could I do? I had encountered too many of these Shadow-ravaged people, and I knew they were well beyond any form of care that would do them any real good. The Shadow-poisoned didn't come back from the brink, once madness took them. They were better off dead.

Or so I thought. Qole was suddenly there in front of me, kneeling down and pressing a heatpack into one of his hands. He turned his black eyes on her, trying to say something, but only a groan came out of his mouth.

"He's drawn to the Shadow on the ship," she murmured to me, and then spoke softly to him over his rattle. "Hold this; it'll keep you warm. I'll comm someone to take you home. I'm sorry, Gavril. You'll be out just a little longer."

I might have imagined it, but the man's face relaxed a fraction, and he hunched over the heatpack. As promised, Qole produced a comm-unit in her hand and was spitting terse instructions to someone by the time she stood and once again set off at a brisk pace toward town.

I hurried after her, struck by what I had witnessed. I had always been taught that one's time was better spent on things that would have a larger impact, but Qole had bothered to do something small when she'd had no time to spare. It wasn't exactly efficient, just . . . incredibly kind.

She cared for her broader community, and that boded well for convincing her I could help. And I could. If we finally figured out how Shadow bound to organic material when it wasn't trying to destroy it, not only could we make it available to the mass market—and have their profits skyrocket as a result—we could also make it safer for humans working in forced proximity to it.

Maybe if she knew *I* cared too, she'd appreciate that. When I caught up to her on the pockmarked gravel road, I chose my words carefully. "If Shadow profits were more exceptional, do you think that would help the situation here?"

Qole snorted derisively. "The profits *are* exceptional, just not for us. Those of us who risk our lives daily do okay; the rest scrape by. It's the people who buy it from us who are making money hand over fist. Maybe on your planet, the royals let their money trickle down to you like scat in an outhouse. But out here, we don't have any blasted royals, and so much the better."

I winced, glancing at the rusted-out hulk of a more ambitious building, snow still pooled in the deep shadows, where construction had obviously halted after funds had done the same. Money, royal or otherwise, was definitely not in surplus here. "Shadow is in high demand in some larger industrial applications." And would soon be in much higher demand, if I had any say in the matter. "Couldn't you negotiate for better prices?"

"Sure. The same way that you could argue with me for a better cut of the run. Try and see what happens."

I laughed at the truth of it, impressed with how she had so neatly expressed the problem and put me in my place. "All right then, I'll just make sure to excel at my duties and hope for the best from there."

"If you suck up any harder, I'll think we're already back out in the vacuum of space." Qole's lips twitched, her eyes still focused on our path between the buildings. I felt a glow of pleasure at that small reaction.

The rest of the walk was too short for much conversation, or maybe too cold. Alaxak was in the grip of an ice age, and Gamut was one of the most isolated communities on it. The village was mostly a small, featureless collection of buildings from the past century that had been kept in functioning condition with considerable patchwork, cannibalization of other structures, and pure creativity. The serrated edges of the cannery tower were the only defining part of the landscape that was man-made. What dominated the eye outside were distant mountains blanketed in snow and the ice that lay everywhere shadows lingered.

Soon Qole veered off the main road—if the strip of frozen dirt even warranted the name—and I followed her through a battered door that she nearly let close on me. The bar was housed in an ancient pre-fab building, and it would have been as drab and boring as those types of buildings usually were if it weren't for the interior decorating.

Reclaimed machinery, battered bits of ships, and chunks of smooth driftwood had been used to create almost every piece of furniture. An ancient heating pillar dominated the middle of the room, glowing with a distinctive purplish cast. Lurking in the back corner was a worn leather mannequin, impaled with rusty throwing knives, a crude crown cut from a cross-section of old piping perched on its head. I didn't know exactly which king it was supposed to be, but since we were in the Dracorte system, I could guess. At least it appeared no one had taken up the game in some time.

The few patrons slouched at scattered tables were even more weathered and varied. Etched, beaten by the elements like everything in Gamut, they paid me absolutely no mind. Their indifference was the most disconcerting thing, as used to attention as I had been my entire life.

The pillar glowed with purple fire, warming the entire room. The flames moved in slow motion, like oil poured into water. As soon as my eyes started to trace individual tendrils, they would snap in frenetic motion too fast to follow, then settle back into their languid dance. In their center I could spot tiny flecks of light so bright they were white, winking in and out of existence.

Shadow.

I couldn't help but shake my head. "That seems . . . safe."

Qole shrugged her shoulders, hands still in her pockets as she picked her way through the tables toward the vacant bar. "Safe is relative. If you live here, you're better off staying warm than worrying about Shadow."

I leaned up against the bar next to her and signaled to the man I presumed was the bartender that we wanted two drinks. He stared without registering, just long enough that I started to motion to him again, in case he hadn't seen me. But by then he'd turned to fetch our drinks with a disgusted sigh.

I hunkered down a bit farther, feeling no more welcome here than I had on the ship—or anywhere on Alaxak—and looked over at Qole. The corner of her lip was upturned in a marginal smile. Apparently, I was more likable when I made a fool out of myself. Being friendly, knowledgeable, assertive— all those approaches had been a lovely way to piss her off. It made almost no sense to me, but there it was.

"Thanks, Larvut," Qole said, as the man passed us our smudgy bottles. He grunted at her in return and shuffled off.

So they knew each other. She'd just wanted to see how I would handle him.

More likable or no, I wouldn't gain Qole's trust by playing the fool. I wondered how long the decon would give me, how long I could keep Qole listening. I resisted looking at my wrist feed, shoved down the panic that threatened to spike. I wanted to simply tell her why I was here, but the truth without trust would make her worse than pissed. I'd lose her forever.

"So is Shadow really your best option out here?" I tried to make my voice casual, as if I were simply curious.

Qole slid her bottle closer and looked at it for a moment before answering. "Depends on what you mean. As the best job or the best heat source?"

"Both, I suppose."

"Well, people are desperate for both out here," she said with some bite, "and it's what's available. But no, I wouldn't say it's the best *anything,* even though we use it for everything: cooking, heating, lighting." She gestured vaguely in the direction of the pillar. "I know; it's like using a nuclear reaction to boil a teapot. That's why most people here have it in their bodies."

She took a deep breath, as if fortifying herself for what she was about to say. "But it's the fishing that's the hardest on you—it's only fair that you know what you're getting yourself into. You can't take that kind of exposure without going mad and dying eventually. It's a slow death for most of us, decades until the eyes finally go black with the poison, like Gavril outside. You can escape it if you leave. But for some of us . . ." She looked away, not meeting my gaze. "It's in us already, the kids of the older Alaxan families that've been doing it so long. We have a tolerance or something that's been built up and passed down. It could probably happen to anyone, but we might be some of the first. Or the worst."

She was right. There were others from different planets, but none with an affinity so strong, at least not that had been discovered. However, I didn't want to let on how much I knew about her condition, in case she stopped talking.

"I . . . uh . . . saw your eyes flash black," I said quietly. She straightened against the counter, shooting a glance at Larvut, who'd retreated to the other end of the bar to watch a cracked news feed. I understood her reaction. Talk of Shadow poisoning made people nervous—one reason among many that it had been so hard to find someone like her. I'd pitched my voice so he wouldn't hear, but still, to put her at ease, I added, "But they changed back. So you're not poisoned, right?"

"Not exactly," she said shortly. "It affects us differently."

This was her Shadow affinity, her "tolerance," as she called it, though that didn't do justice to what I had seen. "How so?" I prodded her.

"Sometimes"—she cleared her throat and lowered her own voice—"sometimes some of us can sense Shadow."

"Is that how you pilot better than anyone I've ever seen? It must be more than that."

She glanced at me sharply, and I couldn't tell if she was surprised by the praise or by my "guess." "It's hard to explain, but I can feel everything . . . *more*. Faster. Not just Shadow. We can do some surprising things, but then sometimes we're crazy and dead before we've barely lived, so don't get too jealous, hey?"

She wasn't looking at me anymore, her eyes on the driftwood countertop, so she couldn't know that jealousy was the last thing on my mind. For a moment, everything I was working toward was eclipsed by the sobering realization that Qole could die tomorrow, and she knew it. *The immediacy of the inevitable can unravel even the strongest,* my father would say, but Qole wasn't unraveling. She was a pilot, a captain, and better at both than many I had met.

She kept studying the bar, scratching at it with a dirty fingernail. "The children of our old fishing families die younger and younger every generation, until the family eventually sputters out. It's a wonder any of us are still around." She smirked. "Still happy to be on board with me? I'm a bomb ready to blow, like anyone around here was probably happy to tell you."

I held her eyes when she looked up at me. "Like I said, I wanted the job."

She looked away again. "Why? Is Shadow really *your* best option out here?"

I smiled at the reversal and toyed with my bottle. It was devoid of a label, covered in dust. I'd been so engrossed in my conversation with Qole that I had consumed the entire beverage without noticing. In retrospect, it had tasted like fermented dishwater.

Before I could answer her, the light in the room flickered, then dimmed by half. I immediately straightened, on guard, and squinted around as I waited for my eyes to adjust.

"That's another reason to hate Shadow: it's unreliable as hell." Qole sounded as if she wasn't too bothered.

Sure enough, the pillar in the middle of the room had gone dark, and all that was left was the tiny bright speck in the center of the containment unit. Weak sunlight from the dirt-streaked window backlit the bar, and I could just make out the silhouettes of the few barflies shuffling in their chairs. I heard their sighs, too. Not all that uncommon, then.

"Great Collapse," one of the patrons cursed. "Hey, Qole, give it a jump, will you?"

"Why, Hudge, we hardly know each other," she said with such a deadpan expression that it took me a second—far longer than it should have—to realize she'd made a dirty joke. Another patron hooted.

Her apparent unconcern aside, she slid away from the bar after a sideways glance at me and slapped her hand on the cylindrical surface. Something shone under her palm, and tendrils of purple flame flared inside. A moment later, the eerie glow returned to the unit, and then the room.

An electric current ran straight down my spine. Everyone very studiously did not look at her. Not Larvut, who offered no thanks for getting his heater working again, and not even Hudge, who'd asked her to do it.

I almost couldn't blame them. It wasn't a comfortable thing to see and believe.

She hadn't been kidding when she'd compared Shadow to nuclear fusion. For most anyone else—poisoned or not, native or offworlder—touching the pillar would have burned their hand to a crisp. And she wasn't just immune to the heat; she *sparked* the Shadow.

Of course, there were rumors of people with the ability to manipulate Shadow. I'd followed such rumors here. Then again, there were many other far-fetched tales in the systems with no empirical evidence to support them. I had never imagined something so material was possible, not in my wildest dreams. Tolerance, yes. Some sort of impact on the chemical and nervous systems might follow. Direct interaction? I wasn't sure I could reconcile that with anything other than a miracle.

But I'd found her, one of the few whose old family line had survived the short generations this business tended to produce. Judging by the lack of screaming and panic from the bar's patrons, however, such instances weren't entirely unheard of, at least not where Qole was concerned. And yet, for all I'd heard about her astounding piloting and fishing skills, no one had mentioned anything like this. It seemed the people of Gamut were keeping this bit of information rather quiet. With good reason, perhaps, other than their fear of her.

People would want to take advantage of her.

People like me, I thought with a bitter taste in my mouth. Although I didn't actually want to take advantage of her. I wanted to help her, and so many others, if only I could convince her to let me.

"Qole," I said as she came back toward the bar. I paused, realizing I hadn't addressed her by her first name before, and it felt funny on my tongue. I liked it, but didn't want her to think I was being presumptuous. "Captain. That was incredible. This could change so much."

She drew up short and stared at me. "What do you mean?"

Someone like Qole, who had control over Shadow, whose biometric makeup could withstand its power—someone like her was key to unlocking Shadow as a safe energy source. Right now, outside Alaxak, its potential was largely untapped, a resource only for experimental or fringe usage. It was too dangerous to those around it. But it didn't have to remain that way.

"If . . . if people understood what you can do, it would change everything. For you, for people here, for everyone. You could be the key."

I was nearly positive she was. She just had to leave with me by tomorrow. Somehow, I had to make her understand this.

Her face didn't betray any emotion. "Oh yeah? The key to our future, right?"

"Yes!" I couldn't believe she was agreeing with me. *This might be it,* I thought, nearly sagging with relief. *She's going to understand what I have to say, and we can leave in time. In time to change everything.* "Yes. You're able to do things that would kill most people. If we could make Shadow safe like that for everyone, then everyone *here* benefits. You could use it for heat, for fuel, without it being deadly."

Qole took a step toward me, closing the gap between us with sudden ferocity. "You really think you're the first genius to have a drink and go on about that? It's 'amazing,' they say. It's 'the key' . . . right up until they see what actually happens." Her eyes were clear, but I could feel her anger radiating toward me with more heat than the pillar. "It's poison, and it kills you.

It's just a question of whether it kills you faster than everything else out here."

I held up both hands. "All I'm saying is that there's more at play here than what meets the eye. Don't you think that's worth exploring a little? Wouldn't that change the face of Alaxak?" I tried to remove all frustration from my voice, but some stubbornly clung behind. I couldn't understand why no one I talked to here seemed interested in how the future could be a better place. Was I simply unable to communicate? What was I doing wrong?

Her eyes might not have been black, but they were blazing. "We've had offworlders before, trying to *improve* things for us, as if you knew what the blasted hell you were talking about. Not as many of you as the scum who want to see what *else* they can squeeze out of us, but you're just as useless. It's so damned arrogant of you to think you have the power to actually change anything."

"But you haven't even heard what—"

"Know what's powerful enough to change the face of Alaxak?" She gestured around herself, an angry jerk that encompassed more than the bar. Her voice dropped to a hiss as she leaned even closer to me, her breath warm on my face. "*Drones.* Battleships. The money of kings, stolen from everyone else. *That's* what. And we're happy to go without, to be left alone, because no good has ever come of any of that." She leaned back and nodded toward the counter, swiping hair that had come loose from her braid out of her face. "You've had your drink."

I followed her glance. "But you haven't even touched yours," I said in one last feeble attempt to keep her from doing what she was about to do.

"I don't drink." She spun away from me and started for the door.

"Wait, Qole!" I caught her arm.

She looked at me over her shoulder, and her scowl was enough to make me let go of her. "It's *Captain Uvgamut,* and if you really are here to fish for me," she snarled, "be back on the *Kaitan* in five minutes, or I'll find the next piece of trash that blows in on the wind and hire them in your place." She strode away without another glance.

The heavy door slammed behind her, leaving only a gust of cold air where she'd been. I stared after her, at a loss.

Larvut gave me the first gap-toothed smile of his that I'd seen. "Need another drink, hey?"

What I needed was the impossible. A miracle. I needed Qole.

Before I could even consider my next move, the hidden comm in my wrist feed pulsed. My hack to the QUIN had finished transmitting, and my uncle was sending me a message back through it, and not the first one, apparently. I hadn't had much time to check while nearly getting worked and shouted to death.

Her brother is a strong candidate, but not necessary. I hope you can get data on the girl. And then: *She is the one. No matter what, bring her. Immediately. There's the usual deadline, but you may well have company if you linger.* And finally: *Why aren't you responding? Nevarian? If you don't move now, the damage could be irreparable.*

My stomach dropped. I was out of time. *Company.* Failing was the worst possible outcome for me and mine, but it would be bad for everyone, including Qole, if anyone caught up to me. How Rubion could guess this possibility from across the system was beyond me. Of course there were others who would be interested in my whereabouts, but I'd been careful to shake anyone following me.

I'd have to ask him when I saw him again. For now, I was left with a few unsavory options and a bad taste in my mouth. Because, however I managed it, Qole still had to come with me . . . as soon as possible, and whether she wanted to or not.

IV

QOLE

Telu's voice jolted me awake, piped in over the comm speaker positioned right over my bunk. "Cap, you're going to want to be here for this."

Decontamination had taken no time at all, because the containers weren't actually leaking, only malfunctioning. Since the *Kaitan* had lifted off again—with Nev on board, surprisingly enough—we'd all been napping on the border of the Alaxak Asteroid Sea, waiting for drone traffic to clear. It felt like I'd barely closed my eyes, but a glance at my infopad resting on its charger proved several hours had slunk by.

Someone else had been doing some slinking, I found, after I flew out of bed and ran to the bridge in my fur slippers, a

47

robe hastily thrown over my tank top and leather leggings. I wished I'd at least put my boots on, because as soon as I arrived and saw what was going on, I wanted to kick something.

Telu was seated in my captain's chair, typing both at control screens and on a couple of her own infopads, hastily relocated from her station. She was wearing only an undershirt and thermal bottoms, even though I could see her breath in the glow of the console. Basra leaned against the wall, looking more feminine than usual in his own fur-lined robe, sharp eyes surveying the situation. Arjan hovered above Eton, ready to assist him, both of them in equal states of speed-fueled undress.

Only Nev was fully clothed in his too-fine garb. Eton had him pinned against the ground, the muscles in his huge arms and bare shoulders bunched like massive dock ropes. Nev's cheek was mashed into the metal grating. The long bag he'd brought with him lay near my chair at Telu's feet, packed and seemingly ready to go.

Nev didn't so much smile up at me as grimace.

Telu confirmed my guess at what had happened—and worse. "He hacked the system, the bastard," she snarled, still bent over the control panel and her infopads. "A damned good hack, too. He got around the security cameras and alarms—all except one that I'd hidden extra deep in code—and tried to induce stasis oxygen levels."

"To put us to sleep," Eton grunted unnecessarily, grinding his elbow deeper between Nev's shoulder blades. Oddly, Nev didn't wince at that. Only when I looked at him again.

"If you'll let me explain—" he began.

"Oh, I see," I interrupted. "You want to explain. Like you tried to explain in the bar with *lies*. Like you were going to explain *later*, after we were unconscious and you'd robbed us blind." My words were deceptively calm. A run-up to something far worse.

"No, I don't want your Shadow, or your money—"

"So you want the ship, is it? I saw you admiring it on the dock." I crouched near his head and grabbed a handful of his hair, dragging his eyes up to meet mine. "This is *my family's* ship. You'll have to pry the controls out of my cold, dead fingers."

He met my stare with a level one of his own.

"Um," Telu said. "Actually, I don't think he wanted the ship. He'd engaged the autopilot, but on a course to intercept a passenger cruiser that took off from Alaxak ten minutes ago. It looks like he was planning on boarding the ship from the *Kaitan*. He used an encrypted channel to arrange for the pickup." She turned to look at me for the first time. "He also reserved *two* spots."

"What?" My eyes went wide as I looked down at Nev again. "Who were you planning on taking with you?" I glanced at the crew; they were all faces I trusted. None of them were about to betray me. Only *him*. "If you thought you could buy one of my crew, think again."

His lips pressed together in a firm line.

"Yeah, you *really* want to explain," I hissed.

"I'm not in the most advantageous position to do so," he said, flicking his eyes up at Eton. The brown of his irises once again seemed to flash brighter than most eyes did. "Anything I say with his elbow in my spine won't have the requisite care put into the telling. Not to mention I won't be able to finish explaining once he snaps my spine."

As if proving him right, Eton leaned into him, extracting a short, muffled groan.

"Maybe we don't want to hear what he has to say then, if it's that bad," Arjan said in a low voice.

"Or perhaps you let me up," Nev gasped. Even flattened on the ground and in obvious pain, he still had the nerve to sound like he had a say in the matter. It was a miracle Eton hadn't yet broken his jaw, because it took all *my* self-restraint not to rub his smug little face against the floor's serrated grating.

I didn't need to tell Eton not to let him up. "Someone else is in on this," I said, the thought dawning on me. "Is the second ticket on that passenger cruiser for them, hey, Nev?" Something about him being out here had seemed suspicious. He was probably the type to have henchmen with him. "You're trying to rob us with some help?"

Nev tried to shake his head, but he couldn't move with my fist still in his hair. "Trust me, I'm not working with lowlifes like that."

"Trust you," I said with disgust. "*You're* the lowlife, however you're trying to fool us. Telu, does it say if the second passenger would already be aboard the cruiser?"

Telu narrowed her eyes as she scanned the screens. "In this case, the bastard seems to be telling the truth. He cited a medical emergency as the reason for the unusual pickup, which would require appropriate transportation for someone *inert.*" She snarled the word.

Inert. Unmoving. Unconscious. Stasis oxygen levels had that effect on a human body.

I yanked Nev's head up again, craning his neck at what had to be an excruciating angle, and nearly spat in his face. "You were going to *kidnap* one of us?"

Robbery was one thing. Messing with the last of my family, my crew, was another. Arjan seemed to be thinking the same thing. His eyes were dangerous in a way I rarely saw them, one hand clenched at his side, the other around the handle of one of the knives he always wore. I hoped nothing else appeared in his or Telu's eyes. Her stare was already as ferocious as a blast from a mass driver. I couldn't see Eton's face, since he was bent over Nev, but Nev groaned again, longer this time. I couldn't blame Eton. The thought of Nev hurting Arjan, or any of my crew, made my fist tighten in his hair and panic and fury flare in my chest.

Only Basra was still silent, still observing, still unfeeling. Until he glanced at Arjan and back at Nev, and then his gaze seemed to calculate how much he could get for Nev's internal organs.

"You're off this ship," I breathed, trying to steady myself. The first hints of blackness were surfacing in the corners of my eyes. "I'm handing you over first thing. Telu, comm what's-his-name, the latest enforcement officer. Make him actually earn his paycheck for once."

"No—!" Nev tried to say, until Eton's elbow cut him off. Besides, it was too late. I could already hear Telu speaking into the comm, reporting an attempted hijacking by one of our crew.

But then Eton surprised me by leaning farther over and snarling in Nev's ear, "I agree with you . . . no law but ours. How about I just kill you?"

Eton's expression still wasn't visible, but I could hear it in his voice: murderous rage. He meant it.

Nev's strained words hitched out of his throat before I could say anything. "I really didn't want to have to do this."

And then he rammed his head back into Eton's face. It was enough to free his arms, which he used to shove his body off the ground. Torso and legs twisting, Nev then threw the much bigger man off him—and into Arjan, who lost his balance and crashed into Basra, both of them going down in a heap. Nev leapt to his feet.

I spun to face him, but Eton had already rolled up into a ready crouch, blood pouring from his nose. He grinned, teeth red, and launched himself like a plasma rocket at the younger man.

The fight was brutal and ferocious, moving too fast for anyone else to step in, though both Arjan and I hovered, looking for an opening—until Telu, who'd slipped around from the captain's chair, seized my arm and hauled me back against the wall next to Basra. Basra already seemed to know this was a fight in which he could have no impact, since he hadn't even tried to get involved.

Which probably meant Arjan shouldn't try, either. Fear caught in my chest as he moved closer. "Careful," I warned him.

Although, really, there wasn't much he could do. Like most kids growing up on Alaxak, Arjan had learned to fight, even though he had no formal training. But this . . . this was more than a fight. This was something else entirely.

A violent dance. A bloody ceremony, practiced to perfection.

Telu had wisely taken Nev's bag with her when she'd come around from the console, in case he decided to go for some sort of weapon hidden in it. But Nev hadn't even glanced at the bag once. He didn't need a weapon.

He was one.

He and Eton circled each other, stepping around the obstacles on the bridge without even glancing at them, until they met in an explosion. Their bodies collided off one another with eerie grace, like objects in zero gravity, only to return to orbit around each other. The lone debris they left behind was spatters of blood.

It was so breathtaking I even shot a glance at the glowing readout on one of the control panels—the gravity drive was definitely still functioning, though they didn't seem to be bound by it.

Nev moved his body like Arjan maneuvered the skiff. Like I piloted the *Kaitan*. It occurred to me numbly that he more than knew how to fight in the way of one who'd been trained to do something since birth. He knew how to fight like he knew how to breathe. He fought better than anyone I'd ever seen.

Maybe even better than Eton.

He ducked and dove around Eton, and as fast as Eton was, it was clear Nev was faster. One of his elbows connected with the bigger man's cheek. Eton only paused to spit out a mouthful of blood—and maybe a tooth—before driving a knee into Nev's side. But it only glanced off him, because Nev was already twisting, sweeping out his leg as he did, and nearly wiping Eton's out from under him. That stumble cost Eton, because he couldn't turn in time to fend off the fists that slammed in rapid succession into the small of his back, in the soft spot just beneath the ribs—where he'd been trying to knee Nev a moment before. By the time he turned, Nev was already gone, his fists, elbows, knees, and feet all flying from a different direction.

Nev had a bleeding gash in his brow from a blow that had narrowly missed his eye, but Eton's nose and cheek were a wreck. Bruises bloomed across his bare chest and back. I couldn't see the bruises under Nev's jacket, and there were no doubt a few, but . . .

They were both going for maximum pain, for incapacitation, and while I could barely believe it, it soon became obvious that Nev was going to be the one to bring Eton down.

I had to be ready for him when he did. The darkness encroached farther into my vision.

"Eton," I said, my voice too calm for true calm, "stop while you still can."

He glanced at me, saw my eyes, and only went in for another swing.

"Eton!" I shouted, but he wasn't stopping.

And then I saw what he was doing. He wasn't an idiot. He knew he was losing, and quickly. His twists and pivots began to take the fight farther away from me. At first I thought, in a burst of anger, that he was still trying to protect me . . . until I saw where he was headed.

He was protecting all of us.

The inevitable moment came: one of Nev's fists dropped him. Nev, because he was a fair fighter in spite of everything, didn't kick him when he was down. He instead let Eton haul himself away. Watching Eton crawl, like a broken thing, leaving drops of blood along the bridge floor, nearly made me throw myself at Nev in fury.

Instead, as soon as Eton was clear, I smashed the button for the airlock. A set of doors slid out from opposite walls and closed Nev into what was now a separate room. An antechamber. A red light above a second door—a docking hatch in the hull of the ship—began to flash. Nev looked up at the flashing light, and then at me through the windows in the barrier now separating us.

"That's right," I said. "One push of a button, and you're out in space with the rest of the trash."

"Qole," he said, his voice piped through a comm speaker. "Don't."

"You do *not* get to call me Qole," I spat. "And why the hell shouldn't I?"

"Because, whoever you think I am, whatever you think I'm doing, you're wrong."

My finger hovered over the button. "Prove it."

He started probing at his eye, as if he had something in it. An odd time to be checking for damage, I thought. And then I realized he *did* have something in it. He flicked a thin, transparent film off the tip of his finger, and then removed the same from his other eye.

Contact lenses.

He also pressed parts of his cheek and wiggled his jaw as if cracking it into a different place, squeezed the bridge of his nose and inhaled. I'd heard of disguise capabilities like this, but only rumors. The advanced drugs they required were way too expensive for anyone on Alaxak. When he dropped his hand, the lump was gone, and his jaw was subtly different, and yet the overall difference was drastic.

He'd looked handsomely out of place before, but this was just absurd. His eyes were a pale silver-gray that nearly shone, and his face was perfectly shaped, with smooth planes and edges that met in *exactly* the right places, not just some, more like it had been mat-printed from an engineer's design. In short, he was stunning, in spite of the blood trickling from one of his too-straight eyebrows.

Only years of careful selection, pure bloodlines, gave someone a face like that. And even I, who was about as far from royal as a person could get, knew what the color of his eyes meant.

"My name is Nevarian . . . Dracorte," he said.

It sounded like he'd been leaving something out. But it was enough, his name.

Ancestors. He was a Dracorte.

"Great Collapse!" Telu nearly shouted, while Arjan gaped with his jaw fully dropped. Eton was staring as much as he could through swelling eyes.

"Unifier help us," Basra murmured.

Whatever divinity it came from, I'd take all the help we could get. A member of the Dracorte family, one of the most powerful royal families in the known universe—if not *the* most—was worse than a bomb on board. He was a target for every missile in the galaxy. I thought he might have come from one of the royal planets, but I never would have guessed he was a royal himself. If I'd had even the slightest hint, I would have run as far and fast as possible.

"What . . . ?" I began, then had to begin again as I steadied myself against the wall. "What are you doing on my ship?"

His mouth quirked into an odd smile. "Looking for you."

My stomach felt like it did a full turn. "The second ticket. On the cruiser. That was . . ."

"For you, yes." His smile twisted further. "I wish you could have let me explain . . . and that you would let me explain now," he added more softly, as he saw my finger twitch closer to the button.

All I could do was shake my head. "No. No, I don't want to know. I don't want anything to do with you." I took a deep breath and steeled myself. "I want you off my ship. I want no one to ever know you were even on my ship. I want you to disappear."

Before my finger could so much as twitch again, Nev whipped out a gun, sleek and shiny with a white glow, from somewhere in the crisp folds of his jacket. So not only was he himself a weapon, he also carried them on his person. But he didn't point it at me.

He pointed it, no doubt accurately, at the junction between the hull and the first set of doors. "Tell them, Eton," he said. "They won't believe me."

"That's an XR-25 Molten-Force." Eton's shock was audible through his wet, bloody grimace on the floor. "A plasma pistol that makes most others look like toys. It's worth about half of this ship, and it has the power to blow through all of it. We'll all die."

Of course a Dracorte would be able to afford one of those ... or a dozen of them. I'd taken him for just another rich boy, but he was much, much richer than that.

"Eton, always ready to state the obvious," Telu said, but her sarcasm was only a mask for her fear.

"Now, let me out," Nev said.

I didn't move.

Basra's sharp voice cut through my hesitation. "Captain, you should open the doors."

I cast a glance at him. "But he might be bluffing."

His eyes never left Nev's face over his folded arms. "If he's not bluffing, we have to let him out, and if he is bluffing ... we have to let him out. Dracortes don't just disappear, not even their bodies." He murmured under his breath, "And something tells me this Dracorte especially won't."

Eton didn't seem to hear the last bit. "I know plenty of ways to make a body disappear in space. A few shots of the mass driver—"

"Captain," Basra said, in what was nearly a warning tone. I'd never heard anything like it from him.

My finger shifted an inch ... and hit a different button. The inner doors of the airlock, not the outer, slid open with a gasp.

Nev stepped out—if not with haste, with efficiency. *He does seem to love efficiency,* I thought with something bordering on hysteria.

It didn't feel as if I'd just released one young man into our ship. It felt like I'd released a cataclysm. Looking at him, I felt more afraid than if staring down a clogged asteroid belt I had to fly through with a sputtering engine, or at half a dozen drones, or at the darkness inside me blackening my own vision. The floor of the bridge seemed to drop out from under me, even though it remained firmly welded in place.

"Thank you, Qole," he said, as if I'd had any choice in the matter. "Now, if you'll let me finish ..."

He moved toward me, half smiling as if in entreaty. So much of it made sense now: his arrogance, his knowledge, his combat training—he could afford all of it, along with the pistol. He still didn't point the gun at me, but he kept it ready at his side.

His mistake. When he got close enough, I hit him as hard as I could in his perfect nose.

V

NEV

Ow.

Ow, ow, ow. Ow to the hours of slinging about frozen containers of volatile fuel, ow to getting knocked out, ow to Eton using me for his anger therapy, and ow to feral captains hitting me right on the soft bits of my face.

But the worst pain, and what had really left me unprepared for that punch, was the sick look on Qole's face. She was trying to present it as fury, but I could see misery there, misery from the realization at just how much her life might be changing.

If only she knew.

The lesson here being: save the sympathy for the pain you

are causing until after someone punches you in the face and the entirety of their crew comes tumbling on top of you.

Because tumble on top of me they did. As I stumbled back from Qole's punch, clutching my bleeding nose, Telu latched onto the arm that held the pistol, and Arjan launched himself straight for me.

After the match with Eton, however, this was child's play. I planted one boot firmly in Arjan's chest, let go of the pistol, and snatched it with my other hand as it dropped. I twisted my arm while rotating to pry Telu clean off, and then finished the spin facing the three of them again, this time training the gun on Qole.

There was no helping my nose, but my actions had the desired effect. They all froze.

Not that I would actually shoot her, and they might know it. I hoped that in the next few seconds they wouldn't force us to go through a repeat of what I'd had to endure with Eton. I'd been lucky there, on a number of levels. One, while I'd been busy trying to hide my skill in hand-to-hand combat since I met this crew, he'd been telegraphing his at every opportunity to make sure I kept a respectful distance. As a result, I'd been prepared for his formidable abilities. Two, Eton had definitely trained in Dracorva, and I would have been willing to hazard a guess that I knew exactly who'd taught him. I also knew that had been several years ago, because he'd used at least one technique that had fallen out of favor thanks to the development of a counter.

I didn't have to be lucky with the rest of the crew; they would have to get lucky with me. Unfortunately, that was always a possibility in a fight, so a full-on brawl would end up either with me trying to beat everyone senseless, or with them beating me dead. Neither was an attractive option.

I raised my hands, still holding the pistol but pointing it at the ceiling, and opened my mouth to yell for sanity.

The entire ship tilted sharply, and while the gravity compensator did its best to keep up, the jolt was so violent we all stumbled and went crashing.

Qole turned on me in a rage. "What was that?" she demanded. "What did you do?"

Her eyes were going black again, the discoloration creeping in around the edges, and that alarmed me more than whatever had just rocked the ship and sent off the warning klaxon with a resounding whoop.

We all paused as everyone recognized the sound at the same time. That had been the alert for a weapons systems lock, the kind of sound everyone knew but most lucky people living in the central subsystems never had to hear.

I shrugged and raised my eyebrows. "Not me. Really, not me."

Basra was giving me a strange look from his crouch on the ground, his curly-crested head cocked, as if asking, *Really?*

Then it dawned on me. "I think that was a tractor beam," I said. "We're still trapped in it, and not only that, they've targeted us." It was as good as having a gun held to our heads.

"No one has tractor beams," Eton scoffed thickly. "That would take a destroyer. And not just any destroyer, either."

Indeed. This was the "company" Rubion had warned me about, exactly what I had been trying to avoid. I pinched the bridge of my nose as hard as I could to stanch the blood and sighed, slumping farther down the wall into a sitting position. I draped my other hand, the one with the gun, over my knees. It didn't really matter if Arjan or anyone else got the upper hand now, because things had just gotten much worse for all of us.

The inter-ship comm gave a tone, and a hard voice filtered

onto the bridge, confirming what I already knew. "Attention, crew of the *Kaitan Heritage*. This is a destroyer-class vessel. We have you in our beam, a plasma rocket locked onto your bridge, and two photon turrets standing by. If we fire, you will be dead before you can scream. Allow us to board, or we will destroy you." The comm went dead.

Much, much worse.

With a percussion that reverberated throughout the bridge, the ships docked. You could dock politely, but the grating vibrations of hull on hull made it abundantly clear that our *company* wasn't being polite about it. In fact, it was positively hostile.

Telu voiced my doubts. "I think these guys might be dicks."

"Just what we need," Eton grumbled, "some more of those on board." He glowered at me from underneath the dual layer of his eyebrows and a compress that Basra had fetched for him out of an emergency medi-kit.

Qole, tense as a kite string, stared out at the ship that dominated the viewport.

Made of smooth composites with no visible seams, its hull split toward the stern into three fins that were faintly visible from our position. Big, deadly, this was a full-on destroyer that could only be afforded by one of the royal families. There weren't any identifying marks, but I knew one of them had to be pulling the strings.

Speaking of which, my family was going to be distinctly unhappy. I was most likely going to get taken hostage. At least I wouldn't be killed—just ransomed for an astronomical amount of money. It would be a huge embarrassment, but the Dracortes could afford it. Far, far worse was the fact that Qole and I would be late getting back, and *that* my family couldn't afford. I wasn't sure how I'd bear failing everyone so completely, but none of the alternatives I could conjure seemed remotely sane.

"Well, then what do they want?" Arjan demanded.

"Me, I would imagine." I gestured vaguely.

"Why? What did you do?"

"He was born wealthy," Basra replied for me. "A Dracorte by himself is too valuable an asset to pass up. If they've been following him, they know he's with us."

I found the willpower to raise one eyebrow. "Before you all say this is what happens when you have people like me onboard, I'll point out that had you just given me the chance to talk, oh, maybe twenty hours ago, or simply let me go like I suggested quite recently, then I would probably be well on my way."

"Yeah, with Qole," Eton growled.

"Quiet," Qole ordered, her voice going husky with strain, knuckles whitening as she tightened her fists. She glared at me. "Don't expect people to listen to you after you *lie* to them."

Any reply I could have mustered was cut off by the docking hatch hissing open. Masked by the noise and distraction, I hooked the strap of my bag with a foot and quickly slid it closer, setting the plasma pistol on the floor nearby to make it more noticeable. My captors would never leave a gun that valuable behind, and I wagered they'd take the bag with it, in the hopes of finding something more.

Something more was what they would definitely find, if they opened it. Having it with me would give me only a slight advantage, which I might not even get the opportunity to use, but just in case . . .

Woven body armor and military-grade plasma rifles, all

in gray, adorned the first two people on board. "Everyone on their knees with their hands in the air!" one of them barked as they ducked in, keeping their rifles trained on us and taking up positions on either side of the hatch. We all knelt obligingly. They couldn't have been more generic security personnel, and I was just about to roll my eyes when a third person entered.

It wasn't the oblong mirrored visor that masked the front of his helmet or the white rigid armor that added to the worry trickling through me. It wasn't even the quiet, relaxed way he took his position next to one of the security guards and simply clasped his hands together in front of himself, waiting. No, it was the gleaming blade strapped to his hip—a Disruption Blade. Tapered and long, with a single line of white energy gleaming in the very center, it made it clear just how serious these people were.

So much for any advantage I might have had.

"Blast it, what's a Bladeguard doing here?" Eton asked the question on my mind. They were typically found only as the bodyguards of the powerful or in elite commando teams; this really seemed like overkill. Flattering, but overkill.

"Shut your mouth." This came from the final entrant to the bridge. He sported a simple gray uniform and an annoying bristly goatee. Everything about him screamed of a child who had decided that the thrill of ordering others around was what he wanted to pursue for the rest of his life. "Now, which one of you is the captain?"

"That's me." Qole didn't hesitate, and almost stood up from where she was kneeling on the floor. "What the blazes are you doing on my ship?"

Instead of responding, he walked up to her and backhanded her across the face. Eton snarled, Arjan yelled, and Telu called him a degrading name. Basra and I were silent, watching. The man grabbed Qole's chin and forced her to look up.

Her eyes were near black. She didn't say anything, but I saw her hands flex open and shut as though grasping at something invisible.

The man was watching Qole's eyes. "Perfect," he said with a smile. "She's the one we want."

For the first time, a fear aside from failure began to gnaw at me. Why were they so interested in Qole? My family was, as far as I knew, the ones who had done the king's share of research into Shadow's potentially widespread applications. Key words being: as far as I knew. Maybe they were after more than just my ransom. Maybe they knew what I'd been after, what my uncle was after. Not only would that mean a rival family was behind this, but that our boarding party was most likely sent by one in particular, the one that stood to gain the most from stealing my family's glory and watching us sink into disgrace.

Treznor-Nirmana. If this was a move to gain political, financial, and military power on their part, then Qole and her crew were in more danger than I'd imagined. Even if they only wanted me and Qole, it meant the rest of the crews' lives were inconsequential—or even happily lost, if the Treznor-Nirmanas didn't want any witnesses.

The man turned to me, and his face flickered with worry for a second, but I had to commend him—he went back to being an idiot almost immediately. "And won't you be a pretty prize as well, *princeling.*" He turned on his heel, ignoring the rest of the room as everyone's incredulous stares found me. "Bind the two of them and bring them onboard. If any of the rest resist, kill them all."

It was an effective order. No one resisted.

I glanced at Qole as we were marched along the featureless hallways of the destroyer. She was wearing the same mag-linked restraints I was, and for the first time since she found me crushed under Eton's boot, her expression started to register something other than pure fury. The set of her jaw was softening, but her full mouth was still pressed in a firm line, either in thought or in a stern mask for our captors, I wasn't sure which. She was glaring straight ahead with a focus I admired, her eyes clearer now, and I was beginning to guess what that blackness meant for her. Rage.

A trickle of blood ran down her nose, and seeing it with her defiant expression made me realize how arrogant I'd been. I no longer even knew how kidnapping her would have been possible. She might have killed me in the attempt. A near-hysterical urge to laugh bubbled up in me, then popped with something like regret. As if Qole's life weren't dangerous enough already with its drones, asteroids, and Shadow, I'd somehow managed to introduce her to destroyers.

"For what it's worth, I'm sorry," I whispered to her, hoping our guards wouldn't notice.

"None of this would have happened if you'd been honest with me ... *Prince* Nevarian. So, you're not only royal, but a prince. How many lies can someone tell in one day, anyway? Are you trying to set a record?"

I wanted to clarify that I'd omitted more than lied, but I didn't have time for semantics. I had to tell her whichever parts of the truth that might help her crew stay alive. "This is a Treznor destroyer—"

"I know Treznor makes destroyers. I'm not as ignorant as you might think I am, *prince.*"

"No, I mean the Treznor-Nirmana family is *behind* this. They wouldn't have taken you if you weren't valuable to them. So maybe if you cooperate—"

"Shut up!" Our guards, obviously fair-minded, hit us both in the shoulder blades with the butts of their rifles.

That didn't stop Qole from scoffing loud enough for me to wince in anticipation of another blow. "As if cooperating with you people ever gets us anything but screwed!"

I didn't risk an answer. Not that I had a good one ready.

The hallway they were herding us down was remarkably different from those of the *Kaitan*. There, everything was composed of metal plate and grating that had been artfully riveted and welded together, and it was obviously a well-used vessel. Here, brilliant lights lined the ceiling on either side, and periodic viewports gave us glimpses of the molecular clouds through white paneled walls. Everything was made to look as clean and seamless as possible, like a showroom for terminally bored architects. It occurred to me that the last time I had seen something like this had been on a science vessel. Not that destroyers weren't often coldly functional, but they were usually more like military strongholds and less like hospitals. I wondered why this one would have such a sterile design, and I didn't like any of the possibilities I could think of.

The universe, sensing my discomfiture, saw fit to provide the unwelcome answer a few moments later. Using the same ID cards that had locked our restraints, the guards authorized entry to a secure door, which hissed open. We entered what was obviously a laboratory—rows of displays lined the walls, each demonstrating different applications with statistics, graphs, or models. Robotic arms wielding surgical tools and mat-printers standing ready to produce more were on sliding tables, all arranged in a semicircle around a table with restraints.

An operating table.

I felt nauseated. Qole was right: cooperating obviously wasn't a good idea. Something very, very wrong was happening here. Waiting for us were several men and women in white lab suits and the same goateed officer who had been issuing orders earlier.

"What in the systems is going on?" I demanded.

He ignored us, obviously getting a thrill out of doing so. "What is he doing here?" he asked the guards, as they tossed down the belongings they had confiscated from us—my bag among them. "We only need her right now, you idiots, not him. Lock him in a holding cell so I don't have to hear him and get her on the table."

"The hell you will!" Qole rounded on the guard nearest her and decked him in the face with her metal restraints. He went stumbling back, but more guards and the men in the white suits were on her in a flash. They lifted her bodily and carried her, kicking and swearing, to the operating table.

The goateed officer leveled a firearm directly at my face. "I'll take you where you belong then. Turn around and get walking. Don't be a hero, hm?"

"What an original suggestion." I looked at him with as much ice as I could summon through my warring emotions. "And I wouldn't dream of it."

As we walked down the perfect hallway, accompanied by two guards, I wasn't sure I *could* dream of it. What was I supposed to do? Fight a ship full of people? And then what? Pilot it victoriously, sitting on a throne of my slain enemies, toward a welcoming parade back home? Dying for a good cause was well and good, but my life was much more valuable to many people than my death. As tempting as it was to think in terms of simple heroics, I didn't have that luxury. The prudent move would be to keep my head down and go to my cell like a good boy.

The floor shuddered. The destroyer must have broken away from the *Kaitan* as violently as it had docked. But that meant the destroyer would once again be free to fire upon it if they felt like it . . .

The hallway curved around, lifting and widening, and along one wall a series of doors flanked a huge gateway. Treznor Industries was known to have a particular penchant for vessels of death, which could be used to either vaporize pirates or oppress populations. With Treznor, they'd be happy to show you how they'd addressed both contingencies within the very same model, stock configuration. And as a result, they equipped the brig with extensive holding cells, since you never knew whom you might be bringing back as a guest—note myself.

I finally felt vindicated in spending all those hours obsessing over the latest models from the shipyards, because I was a guest who had memorized the exact path from those cells to the launch bay of the onboard starfighters and could get from one to the other quite easily. Adrenaline started to weaken my limbs, and a tremor entered my hands.

My family needed me alive, but the disgrace, or worse, the weakness, my capture would show would be considerable. Escaping would be well worth it, and might actually be fairly simple if I moved quickly.

Simple, that is, if I decided to leave Qole behind.

I had scant moments before getting locked into one of those cells would make my decision for me. The Treznors obviously wanted Qole for similar reasons to my family's, but it seemed she wasn't going to survive their version of the research. And it was likely they'd blow the *Kaitan Heritage* to dust in order to hide their tracks. My escape route would be far more complex with the significant detour back to the lab, and risking my life for Qole or her crew was foolhardy in the extreme. But her life was valuable on more than one level, and in the end, my family was governed by something that most others weren't. We believed in an ideal, a greater good inherent in a brighter future for all, and in behaving to uphold that ideal.

Family, ideals, and the lives of innocents. Seemed like a fine enough reason to be foolhardy, to my mind.

The adrenaline in my limbs moved to my heart, and it began to beat faster, filling my chest. My vision sharpened. *All right, then.*

As my guards and I entered my cell, I spoke. "Ahoy, Major Bristle Chin. I think you're forgetting something."

Major Bristle Chin bristled. Even if I died right now, a part of me noted, it would be with some joy in my heart. He turned on me with a crushing comeback. "I doubt that."

I smiled. "Let me put it this way: I don't think you've thought this through. Do you know who I am? Do you even have any idea?"

"Yes, yes, you're a Dracorte whelp. You think that impresses me?"

"It should." I took one step nearer. "My family is the right hand of the Empire, and holds a primary seat in the Kings' Council. We are the single greatest law enforcer in the systems and wield technology from before the Great Collapse. Do you really believe you are *anything* compared to me? You are an insect, a bug. Nothing. Less than nothing. You couldn't measure up to me if you tried, but you won't dare try. You know as well as I that your days are numbered, Major Bristles, as numbered as hair on your scalp."

Much to my relief, he appeared utterly unfazed. He stepped

close as he mustered every reserve of height he had to stare over my chin. "Is that supposed to scare me? I was arresting princelings like you before you were born. Enjoy your cell, Dracorte, while we make your family sweat."

I smiled. "I prefer *prince* to *princeling*. Prince Nevarian Thelarus Axandar Rubion Dracorte, if you don't mind, heir to the Throne of Luvos. And you honestly think I'm here alone?"

That rocked him back a step, which was excellent, because it let me flourish the ID card I had purloined from his belt. "Why, thank you."

Terror radiated through every nerve in my body in that second, followed by a surge of lightning-hot elation. There was no turning back now.

For a heartbeat, the cell was silent as they stared at me and the ID card that I held. I waited, giving them a moment to respond as I had hoped they would, and then they all lunged at me at once. Academy muscle memory made me duck underneath the rifle butts aimed at the base of my skull, and I stepped back, breathing in time with my movements. My hands swept apart, the mag-link cuffs still attached to my wrists, and cupped the butt of each rifle as they passed by. I'd swiped the ID card through my restraints before I ever flourished it at him—I was an egotist in favor of a good show, but not a complete idiot.

I pulled back as they drove forward, and gloried in simple physics as it twisted the rifles out of their grips, wrenching their arms and sending them spinning. I tossed the rifles behind me and, just as I would on a training mat back home, shifted my feet into a wide stance as I met the onrush of the guards. I batted away a punch and ducked under the next, bringing my right fist to connect with a solar plexus. The rest was instinct, guesswork, and split-second strategy—a flurry of kicks, blocks, punches, and dodges in close quarters before I jumped back and hammered my palm down on the large red button next to the cell door.

It slid shut with a satisfying whoosh, and the petty, childish part of me felt sorry it hadn't afforded me a chance to wave at the cell's new inhabitants with all three of their ID cards, which I now possessed, or the photon rifle I'd snagged.

My body should have been screaming with exhaustion and pain. The last twenty-four hours had been brutal, and as I ran back down the hallway, I was dimly aware that earlier I had been limping from where Eton had managed to land a particularly savage kick near my knee. But now I had no limp, no pain, and no exhaustion. I felt fiery exhilaration. Unbidden, my mind conjured an image of that single trickle of blood from Qole's nose, and I knew I'd made the right decision to go back for her.

I didn't dare use the photon rifle yet, as any discharged weapon was sure to set off any number of alarms. If I was lucky, no one would know about what had just transpired in the cell for at least a few minutes. If I was fast, I could get Qole out of the laboratory, into a starfighter in the landing bay and escape. Fear gripped my heart again; this was a free fall of a plan, and it could turn to disaster at any second with just one wrong move.

I pushed it away, focused on the fire in me, on Qole, and ran faster.

When the door to the lab hissed open, I had only a second to spot the lab suits gathered around a still thankfully conscious Qole—who was also angry, frightened, and now shocked-looking—before my attention was diverted by something important I had forgotten.

They really hadn't been after me at all. Only her. There was no other reason the Bladeguard would be here, turning his featureless mask toward me as I entered, his sword sweeping from his hip into his hands in a barely visible snap.

This would have been a perfect time to use the photon rifle, if only the lab hadn't been full of equipment that I knew all too well was, out here in space, as unstable as Shadow. If I missed and hit an oxygen line at full power, we might all be dead. And yet if I took the time to fumble with the rifle settings, I'd be in meaty ribbons on the floor. Instead, I dove for where our belongings had been deposited. They were still there, off to one side, and I understood what true good fortune felt like for the first time in my life.

At some point, long ago, some clever scientist had discovered an effective energy shield against photon and plasma blasters. And then another clever scientist had discovered that the best way to compromise such a shield, which was great at stopping energy blasts and terrible at stopping mass, was a blade—a Disruption Blade. Over the centuries, certain people began to specialize in getting close enough to heavily armed soldiers to hack at them, and they turned into the elite of the elite: guardians of kings, queens, and potentates. Or into assassins. Without shields of their own, they had to be that much better at blocking and dodging, but their personal safety wasn't the priority. Wielding a Disruption Blade meant you were trained to succeed at near-suicidal missions.

I whirled up from my bag in the last split second, and metal clashed on metal. An errant spark flickered in the air as our blades grated. The white veins of light down the centers of our twin weapons made an X between us. I grinned, baring all my teeth. One family in particular was known for training the best Bladeguards in the systems.

Mine.

"I am Nevarian Dracorte. Who are *you?*"

Most Bladeguards weren't prone to flights of ego like me, so there was no response. He disengaged smoothly and lunged again, flicking his sword toward my torso and face with lethal speed. I danced back from the attack, then brought my blade in hard for his head. We met, and he swept my sword out wide and to my right, leaving my torso exposed. As he started to bring his blade back in to disembowel me, I stepped in close and delivered an uppercut right under the chin of his helmet with everything I had.

He crumpled like a discarded suit of clothes.

Oldest trick in the book, I thought. Then, *Ow,* as something hard and metallic hit me upside the head. Pain blossomed in brilliant colors across my vision. I dropped on top of the Bladeguard, twisting as I fell to bring my arms and blade up to protect myself, but another blow swept the sword out of my numbed hands. One of the lab suits stood there, face emotionless, as he lifted the storage unit he had turned into a makeshift weapon and brought it down again, hammering past my arms and into my chin. Then again.

Ow.

VI

QOLE

THE LAB TECHNICIAN HITTING NEV WAS WHAT PUSHED ME OVER THE edge.

Strange, I thought as my vision went so dark it was like I was watching the world through a black-tinted window. I'd hit Nev myself only a little while ago.

But he'd come here to help me against all odds, and when he'd started attacking, my heart felt like it was going to explode from both delirious relief and shame. Shame, because when he'd first burst in, I thought he'd sided with our captors.

I would have been horrified and furious to find that blasted Disruption Blade aboard my ship, but here I'd felt a surge of vicious joy to see it singing through the air.

... Until it had clattered on the ground after the lab technician kicked it out of his hand. Nev had brought down a Bladeguard—so legendary a warrior I'd thought them mythical—and yet all it took was one lab tech to drop *him* and begin pulverizing his face.

So fragile, these bodies, I thought, and the blackness sank a shade darker.

Except for yours. I felt so detached that the second thought almost didn't seem like mine. The cold metal of the table against my back and the stinging sterility of the air in my nose were so *present* suddenly, as sharp as the newly printed scalpel on the instrument tray next to me. And yet, at the same time, I could barely register anything, only feel it. The flood of sensation passed by me, dazing me. Shadow usually heightened my awareness, but this ... It was like facing into a blast of wind or noise so strong, I couldn't think, only act.

I acted, wrenching at one of the metal restraints that held me to the table. It groaned under the pressure.

I was in control, but not. I was sitting in the bridge of the ship that was my body, but only instinct drove me, not rational thought. This had never happened to me before. I was losing to the darkness. But I didn't care. It had risen with my rage, and I would drown them all in it.

The two lab techs who had been prepping me spun away from Nev at the noise. They must have deemed him subdued enough—or decided that I was now a higher priority—because one of them quickly approached with a syringe. The second, who had already cut off the fur-lined robe I'd been wearing with a pair of medical shears, began snipping up the center of my black tank top, as if Nev had only been a minor interruption. My leather leggings would come next, I had no doubt, and then ... what, my skin?

The darkness in my vision throbbed, like a heartbeat. The extra-awareness surged through my body like never before, and I moved.

More than moved. My arms cut through the alloy and fiber as if they were blades themselves.

The two lab techs leapt back in alarm, then immediately reversed course, diving at me with shears and syringe. I seized their plunging hands before they could reach me, and their bones crumpled in my grip like clumps of granulated snow. Ignoring their agonized screams, I bashed their heads together over the table, then pushed off them, tearing my feet out of the restraints. I rolled off the table just as the third tech, the one who had bludgeoned Nev, came at me.

Nev was still conscious somehow. After staring at me in shock—shock I should have been feeling myself—he took a hand off his bleeding face long enough to swipe at the foot of the tech and try to trip him. But I didn't need his help. I simply sidestepped the attack and shoved the tech into the wall with such force that he cracked the smooth, white surface. He fell to the floor like a broken doll.

Nev tried to say something through the blood in his mouth. I shouldn't have been able to understand him, but with my heightened senses I made out the mangled words as if he were speaking them clearly in my ear: "Other one."

I spun. There was a fourth and last tech in the corner. No, not a tech, I somehow sensed, but the one in charge of the lab—a scientist, maybe. I could tell by her stance, and my body recognized her as a greater threat than the others. She was sidling along the wall, trying to reach the alarm button. My hand seemed to move on its own, faster than I could think, catching up a fallen scalpel. The instrument left my grip just as quickly, pinning the shoulder of her lab coat to the wall.

It wouldn't have held her for long. But it was enough time for me to vault over the operating table and smash her to the wall with my bare hands. One flexed on her throat, making her eyes roll back in her head.

I had to grope for words, remember how to speak. "Tell me," I breathed. I wanted to say, *Tell me what's happening to me,* but she looked just as shocked as everyone else had, so I went to the next most important thing. "Tell me what you want with me."

I had a clue, now, since my body had just torn through a metal alloy that was probably used to build ships. But I still had to know for sure. I leaned in, my face only inches away from hers. Her expression was bordering on full panic.

My eyes probably looked pitch black to her, since I was still viewing the world through the dark pane of glass. Except now there were bright sparks in the corners, almost the reverse of what usually happened. But these sparks were brighter than the light of the normal world—something else. Something new. Something greater.

Or something worse.

As the sparks grew, shapes began to skitter around me, cracking across my hands, across the woman's face. For a moment, we both seemed to shatter . . . but then we snapped back together again.

I was starting to hallucinate. This was the beginning of the end. It didn't matter that I'd just developed some Shadow-related power that no one, to my knowledge, ever had before. Because I was also going crazy . . . which happened to everyone like me. This was the dark path that Onai, that my parents, had walked. A pulse of terror ripped through my fury, almost like a scream from inside me.

"Nev?" I said, my voice afraid, pleading, and it surprised me. I wasn't even sure what I was asking him. To make it stop? To help me?

Why would I turn to him for help? He was the one who had gotten me into this. Then again, he'd tried to get me back out of it, and he was the only one helping me right now.

Maybe he thought I was only asking for tips on how to get answers from the woman, because he burbled, "Squeezing her neck too hard."

I relaxed my grip on the woman's throat long enough to let her suck in a wheezing breath.

"You have abilities we've never seen," she rasped. "We want to understand your Shadow affinity. We need it—"

I choked her off again as I shook my head. "You ... you *want* this? This ... *affinity* ... drove my parents mad. Killed them. Killed my grandparents. Killed almost my entire family."

There was something else there, something I couldn't quite place that was stoking my anger like a plasma furnace—no, like burning Shadow. The sparks crackled in my vision.

The woman shied away, but she was still stupid enough to open her mouth and gasp, "But ... you must understand. Before now, we've only heard rumors of the heightened senses of those with Shadow affinity, but this strength is something else entirely. Your people, and others like you, have evolved an ability to use Shadow we don't yet comprehend. You *are* evolved, like super-beings. If only you knew how to use it, we—"

"If only it didn't *kill* us, you mean," I spat, interrupting. And then I understood what was making me so angry. "This is *my* life. *My* death. *My family's* tragedy. We've suffered for this for so long, and gained so little. How dare you try to just come in and take it?"

"Qole," Nev grunted from the floor. "Don't—"

"Well," I laughed, and the sound was as black as my vision. As cracked and as crazy. "Over my dead body, you will."

I'd always kept my distance, tried not to touch Shadow outside of what was already in my body. Tried to restrain myself, for my own sake, and only sense what was out there. This time, I lifted my hand—literally, there in the lab—and I reached for it like never before.

I sensed a greater pool of darkness, the way I often could when fishing: Shadow, a ways from me. It was the huge cache we had aboard the *Kaitan*. I wasn't sure how I did it, but this time, for the first time across so great a distance, I seized onto it directly. I didn't draw it toward myself, or into my body, but somehow I pulled my consciousness to *it*.

My vision exploded, fragmenting. In all of the fracturing swirls, I fell apart. I was truly outside myself, and I could hear Nev shouting at me from somewhere far away. But I was elsewhere . . . in the hold of my ship.

I was with the Shadow. I was *a part* of the Shadow.

I didn't take all of it, but I took a lot of it. And then I was racing along the vents and plumbing of *this* ship, working my way into its cracks. The ship was so smooth, but the cracks were there. I was in its veins, its blood, infecting as I went.

And then I found the ship's heart.

The massive explosion threw us all sideways. That snapped me back to my body, in the lab. That, and the alarm that went off, blaring in my ears. Red warning lights flared around the room.

I managed to stay upright and kept the woman standing with me by my grip on her neck.

"No need to go for the alarm, now," I told her.

"What happened?" Nev slurred from the floor.

"I think I blew up the ship's engine." I didn't like how far away my voice still sounded, as if I'd left it behind wherever I had gone. My words sounded insane, too. Manipulating Shadow from so far away should have been impossible, and yet I had somehow done it. But at what cost to myself?

He barked a laugh of disbelief. "This destroyer has three primary engines."

"I think I blew them all up, then."

He stared at me, realizing I was telling the truth. "Oh. Well, in that case, no need to worry about cams or anyone storming the lab. They'll be too occupied to bother with us for a while." He winced, maybe at the pain, or maybe at how muddled he sounded, and muttered, "One second."

All in all, he was taking the situation pretty calmly. Maybe he was trying to keep me calm. If I could do something like this . . . what else could I do with this power? Especially if I lost my mind?

He dragged himself to his knees and crawled over to the cabinets, holding his bleeding jaw as if it might fall off. He wrenched open a cupboard door with his other hand, then another door and another, until he pulled out a large, white box with a shiny red cross on it—a medi-kit.

The sparks were still threatening the corners of my vision, seemingly unraveling it at the edges, and maybe unraveling me. So I waited for Nev while he fumbled open the case, pulled out an injector tube, and jammed it into the side of his neck. He followed that with a tube of a different size and shape. The effects were immediate, like when he'd removed his disguise. The erupting bruises began to fade, the swelling went down, and the bleeding stopped. He gave his jaw an experimental wiggle and spat a mouthful of blood onto the floor.

"At least now I can talk," he said, wincing as he hauled

himself upright. "And hopefully move. Qole, we need to go, now."

"No," I said. I didn't quite know why, but I couldn't. I stared at the scientist, my hand still around her throat.

He scooped his blade up from the floor when he rose and kicked the still-unconscious Bladeguard's farther away from him. He might have leaned on the counter as he made his way over to me, but the tip of his sword was steady as he held it up to the woman's cheek. I stared at it. The red warning light flashed on the gleaming metal, and cracks that weren't actually there moved up the blade and into his arm—more hallucinations. At least, I assumed Nev's arm wasn't really cracking apart.

I shuddered, another scream of fear spiking from deep inside. I hoped I wasn't actually screaming. I couldn't tell what was real anymore. Maybe if insane things hadn't truly been happening around me, I could have simply assumed I'd lost my mind entirely. But no . . . I'd used my body like a weapon, seized control of a huge amount of Shadow, and directed it to do what several plasma missiles probably couldn't.

Nev glanced at me, but not for long. I distantly wondered if it was because he wanted to keep his gaze on the woman or if he couldn't meet the blackness of my eyes. A pang shot through me at the latter thought. Were they only startling, or disturbing?

What did he see when he looked at me? A scientific curiosity, like the woman saw? A monster? And why did I care?

"Qole, you can let go of her now," he said, his voice uncharacteristically soft, like when he'd been trying to stop me from sending him out the airlock. It was in stark contrast to the ear-piercing whoops of the alarm system.

"But I need to know why." My words sounded desperate, clinging to that hypothetical answer like I was trying to cling to myself. Both the answer and myself seemed to be slipping out of my grasp. "Why is she doing this to me? What does everyone want from me?"

Still, my hand fell away from her neck, and the woman gulped and gasped like I'd actually been drowning her in my rage.

Nev answered in the same soothing tone. "I'll tell you soon, I promise. But first we need to—"

"No!" I shouted, and the volume was louder than the alarms. "We're not going until I know!"

"Okay, okay," Nev said. "I'll interrogate her, but you need to focus on calming down. Here, sit on the counter."

Something brushed the skin of my arm and I jumped, the sparks leaping in my shadowy vision—but it was only Nev's free hand, scooting me behind him. My senses were so heightened that his touch drove through me like a knife, like pure terror . . . except it wasn't painful or frightening. It was electric. I fell back more than sat against the edge of the counter.

Nev didn't seem to notice as he refocused on the woman. "You're working with the Treznor-Nirmana family, aren't you?" There was no trace of anything soothing left in his voice. It was as sharp and cold as the blade he held against her throat. "Answer quickly."

She jerked a nod and coughed. The movement made her graze the edge of the sword, and even that was enough to open a superficial slice in her skin. She gasped, but Nev didn't pull back. "Yes!"

"How long have you been following my family's research into Shadow? And how closely?"

She didn't hesitate for a moment, the answer spilling out of her. "Two years and extremely closely thanks to several informants. We know of your work to bind Shadow with organic matter to make it a more stable and widely applicable fuel source. But we only recently realized why you wanted to study *humans* who have an affinity for it."

My fingers tightened so hard on the edge of the counter that the synthetic material creaked. Would Nev, or the Dracortes, have tried to do the same thing to me as the Treznors? A pit of darkness opened up inside me at the thought, and my vision blackened further.

Nev blinked. "It's a part of the same research, toward that one end, nothing more. If you think that cutting into Qole would give you the answers we're seeking, you're wrong. We would never hurt her," he said with extra vehemence, as if he weren't just telling the woman; he was telling me, too.

My hands relaxed their grip slightly. Nev hadn't wanted to hurt me. Ever. Somehow I'd already sensed that, but now I *knew.* The relief, like the touch of his hand, nearly flattened me.

"How else could we get the results we need in so little time, before you get them yourself?" the woman insisted. "It was your research into Shadow's affinity with living tissue that led the Treznors to realize the potential in *them.*" She glanced at me. "There were rumors, but no one believed them to be true until *you* went yourself, my lord—"

"Please don't waste my time with formalities after one of your underlings nearly broke my jaw," he interrupted, a sardonic note back in his tone.

"As you like, my—sir. We knew how important your mission was. The Treznors wished to make the breakthrough first."

"What *precisely* is it you want to achieve? Because I'm sure our goals aren't the same."

She swallowed, glancing at me again in fear, the red-alert lights glowing in her eyes. Whether the rest of the ship was occupied or not, Nev was probably right—we needed to be moving now. But I couldn't turn away. "Precision would take hours to explain. But, put quite simply, we want to discover what makes her work, how human beings can use Shadow, and then we want to modify it for the Treznor-Nirmanas' own use."

"You want widespread *human* application. You want super-soldiers." Nev swore. "Qole, deep breaths," he added over his shoulder, and I realized I was nearly hyperventilating.

I was also on my feet before I realized I'd moved. A massive surge of fury-driven hate had lifted me like a monstrous ocean breaker. People like the Treznors would take my twisted family inheritance and use it to kill *more* people? How could they?

Nev was trying to hold me back with his free arm, but he might as well have been shoving against the wall with all this darkness and new light swirling in my vision to lend me strength.

She wanted to see what I could do? I would happily demonstrate. On her.

I reached for the Shadow again ... and everything went completely, bottomlessly black. No tinted windowpane. Just total darkness.

———

I heard my name from far away. Heard it again.

"Qole!"

Nev was shouting my name.

"I'm here." My voice was so faint, it was a wonder he could hear me over the wailing alarms.

I opened my eyes. Nev's arms were around me to keep me

from falling. The blunt back edge of the sword pressed a cold line into my shoulder where he still gripped it in his hand, but his arms were incredibly warm. They also felt strong and stable and . . . nice.

Suddenly embarrassed, I tried to shove away from him. I blinked when I realized I was too weak. The darkness had lifted from my vision. The overhead lights had dimmed when the emergency power generators kicked on, but everything was still brighter than it had been.

The red-alert lights continued to flash, but the sparks no longer danced in my eyes and nothing was cracking apart anymore. I wasn't sure what that meant, but I didn't have time to think about it. I hadn't yet lost myself, though who knew for how long. I shoved at Nev a second time, glaring so he would get the message.

"Apologies," he said, letting go of me. "You would have—"

His arms caught me again as I almost did what I would have done before: fallen flat on my face. My legs were shaking, knees buckling, and it wasn't because of the shudders vibrating through the ship that I hadn't noticed moments earlier. I was completely exhausted. I couldn't remember a time I'd ever felt so depleted, not even after fishing for days, or even weeks straight.

Either I'd simply touched too much Shadow and tired myself out, or . . .

"Qole, are you all right?" Nev asked, a sharp tone of worry cutting into his voice. "Your eyes are better, so I thought . . ."

My eyes. *Better.* The blackness definitely disturbed him, but I couldn't really blame him, not after what I'd done.

"I . . . I can't do anything else. I'm tired. We need to go." I didn't like how frail my voice was, but, as with my legs, I couldn't force any strength into it. I was on empty.

He seemed to adjust to the news quickly. His bright silvery gaze swept the dim, red-flashing room. The woman was down on the ground and as unmoving as everyone else. Nev must have knocked her out. I didn't know how, and I didn't have the energy to care.

"I don't think you ruptured the hull with the explosion, so life support will sustain everyone on board—including those who might want to *keep* us on board. Let's take advantage of the chaos, gather what we need, and get out of here." He hesitated then. "Do you . . . um . . . want some better covering?"

He tried to avert his eyes, even as he held me upright against him.

I glanced down. I was barefoot, in my softest, thinnest pair of leather leggings that I usually wore under a pair of fur-lined pants, and my tank top was slit nearly up to my chest, exposing my stomach. I tried to pinch the gap closed with one hand, and brushed my embarrassment aside for practicality's sake. I wished my blush could have gone with it, but my cheeks were still hot as I answered, "I'm fine. Let's just go."

"We should get to a starfighter. Think you can pilot it?" He grimaced. "You look like you can barely walk, but we don't have many other options. I've trained, but my skills aren't anything like—"

"It's okay," I said. "Even if I couldn't walk, I could still fly." I took a hesitant step away from him. "And I think I can walk, too."

His hands lingered for a moment to make sure I could stand without help, then fell away from me. My skin suddenly missed their warmth. I was just cold, that was all. And tired, so tired.

Nev dove to gather his bag, sliding my fur slippers toward me. At least I had those to keep my bare feet from the chilly floor. My robe was in tatters, and I couldn't help shivering as I looked at it in its ragged pile. This ship's ambient temperature was way warmer than the *Kaitan's*, but my body didn't even have the energy to heat itself. It was like I was sick.

And dying, maybe.

"Here," Nev said. Before I could grab a scrap of my robe to use as a shawl, he shrugged off his jacket—a deep charcoal gray that looked nice with his eyes, I realized—and wrapped it around my shoulders.

I didn't even have the energy to protest as he zipped it up for me. And by then I didn't want to. The jacket was so charged with his body heat I practically melted into it. It also smelled good. *Maybe I should look into synthetic gear for the crew,* I thought sleepily, *cost be damned.*

Nev slung his bag over one shoulder, muscles cording in his bare arms, and gripped his blade in one hand and the plasma pistol in the other. The pale skin of his biceps was splotched with the remnants of bruises that the medi-kit hadn't quite healed—gifts from Eton. If I hadn't felt equally bruised inside and out, I would have felt sorrier for him.

Never mind that he'd been trying to hijack my ship when Eton had beaten him up. And here I was, trusting him to help me out of here?

Again, it wasn't like I had any other options, especially now that I'd run myself dry. Besides, he'd fought for me. He was trying to keep me alive. He didn't want to hurt me. He wanted to use me, somehow, but maybe I could use him in return. Or, if I wanted to be less utilitarian about it: he needed me, and right now I needed him.

And his jacket was *so* warm.

He cleared his throat. "I can't keep ahold of you, because I need my attention forward. But hang on to my shirt so I know you're keeping up, or if you fall."

He turned and gestured at his lower back, where his black undershirt fell to the top of his pants.

My blush threatened to flare up again. "I don't need—"

"Just humor me," he said with a touch of impatience. "Besides, you can keep an eye out behind me. In fact, take this." He forced the pistol into my half-willing hand and pulled another—yes, another plasma XR-Whatever-Force—from the front of his pants. Which meant, between us, we were now holding the worth of my ship in guns, never mind what his blade cost. Those blades were rarer than any gun, so we probably held *twice* the worth of my ship.

"But remember to hold on to me with your other hand," he said, and then waited.

Feeling like an idiot child, I snatched a handful of his warm shirt, trying to touch him as little as possible.

He jumped. "Great Collapse, your hands are cold."

I almost let go, and I felt my blush creep back up my earlobes. "I don't have to—"

"Shh, we're going," he said, moving forward and tugging me along behind him.

I was glad none of my crew could see me like this. Weak or not, dying or not, I most definitely *wouldn't* still be holding on to his blasted shirt by the time I piloted us back to the *Kaitan*.

If we even made it that far.

After Nev used an ID card he'd gotten from somewhere, the door to the lab slid open. He poked his head out into the equally dim, red-flashing hallway. It was quiet except for the screaming alarm. Only then did he move forward with me in tow. So far so good.

... Until we turned a corner and almost ran into two crew running toward what had to be the bridge, or the engine room.

Nev lunged forward, breaking my hold on him, before I or the others could blink. With a few swipes of his blade, they'd crumpled to the ground. Smart, to use his sword, even though the pistol was a far more obvious weapon. Someone might have heard the blasts. The blade was silent.

"Did you kill them?" My voice came out higher than I'd intended.

"I hit them with the hilt. They're just unconscious," he said distractedly. With equal inattention, he passed his pistol to his sword hand, grabbed my hand, and directed it back to the hem of his shirt.

I spared the energy to scowl at a spot somewhere between his shoulder blades. But I didn't say anything, because we were creeping down the hall again, in the direction the crew had come from. Nev moved quietly, far quieter than me, even though he had heavier footwear—boots to my blasted slippers. Walking stealthily was a skill I had failed to cultivate while captaining the *Kaitan*. I'd built up the opposite: stomping.

I regretted that now, especially as I stumbled into Nev's back when he stopped at a juncture. I had to steady myself with both hands, one on his waist, *under* his shirt, and the other, holding the plasma pistol, on his shoulder. He was lucky I didn't blow off his head.

I whipped my hands away as soon as I was steady. He waited, listening.

And then he flattened me against the wall, tucking both of us deep into the shadows. About five more crew ran down the hallway we'd nearly crossed, shouting about a pressure leak in a bank of valves.

They didn't stop. But I didn't even take a breath once they were gone, because Nev's arm was mashed across my chest, his elbow digging into my ribs, his other palm pressed against my hip. I felt both unbearably self-conscious and buzzingly warm, which had nothing to do with the temperature. It had been so long since I'd been touched, and never like this. I was usually too busy fishing, never mind that most people wanted to stay away from me. And even if the rare, desperate individual didn't, my brothers and Eton had been too much of a deterrent.

It didn't matter that Nev probably wasn't aware of what he was doing, and that we were running for our lives. The effect was the same. My heart took off faster than a starfighter, and blood pounded in my ears.

Well, at least I didn't have to be so embarrassed about touching *him* now.

He moved away from me, not as quickly as I had from him, slipping up to the junction to make sure the coast was clear, the red-alert lights flaring in his eyes as he glanced back and forth. When he'd apparently determined it was safe, all he whispered was "Hand."

I grabbed the back of his shirt again. This time I didn't scowl at him. I even braced my fist against his lower back, only half trying to ignore how firm he was, and fixated on the *Kaitan* in my head. *Please, Nev,* I thought, *if you get me home I swear I'll never call you a piece of scat again.*

When he was sure I was ready, we continued to slip forward. It took only a few more hallways and turns, and stepping over one more newly unconscious form, before we arrived at the airlock that led to the starfighters. A swipe of one of Nev's ID cards—where had he gotten them all?—took care of the seal on the doors.

The bay was as shadowy as everything else, with the usual

periodic sweeps of red light illuminating the looming shapes of the fighters. But the siren was quieter here, probably so anybody piloting in an emergency would be able to hear themselves think. No one seemed to be paying much attention to the small spacecraft with the much larger vessel foundering.

Or else I was wrong again. Nev cursed only loud enough for me to hear, and a voice echoed from the other side of the bay:

"Yes, they're *shooting* at us. That grubby little fishing vessel!" The revolting little man who'd hit me appeared, striding out of the shadows with someone dressed as a fighter pilot. The disgusting man was likely a vice captain, or else he would have been on the bridge right now. I wanted to leap forward and attack him, until his next words made me freeze: "Even if our ship's cannons are offline, these starfighters aren't. I want to see chunks of that heap drifting by viewports in less than ten minutes."

My ship. My crew. I realized my hand was now digging into Nev's back like a claw. He turned and touched my face, just for a second, to bring my eyes to his.

I could never in a million years have imagined a situation in which Nevarian Dracorte would have either touched my face, *or* touched my face without me punching his. But apparently this was one. He held my gaze and nodded, communicating everything he had to in that simple gesture:

It'll be okay. Wait here.

I waited. Because, for some unfathomable reason, I still trusted him.

He strolled away from the doors with the pistol at his side, swinging his deadly blade almost jauntily, as if it were a cane . . . and *whistling,* of all things.

Both men halted midstep. Their eyes were mag-coupled

to the Disruption Blade. They knew what it meant that he had one.

"Fancy meeting you here," Nev said.

The disgusting man reached for what was likely a comm at his ear. Before his hand even made it halfway, Nev's pistol was up.

"No, you know how this goes," Nev said. "That's it, drop your hand."

He strode right up to both of them, pistol pointed. He stood for a moment, as if considering them, and then cocked his head at the disgusting one.

"You *really* might want to reconsider that facial hair. And hitting other captains." He leaned forward, as if sharing a secret. "You never know when they might outrank you someday."

And then Nev backhanded him across the face. He hit him like the man had hit me, except Nev was holding the pistol and so the blow was a lot heavier.

The man only had time to let out a satisfying squeal and a dribble of blood from his mouth before the blade flashed and Nev laid them both flat like everyone else. He grinned at me over his shoulder and beckoned with his sword. Far more surprising than his inappropriate attitude to the whole situation was that I found myself grinning back at him.

I stumbled away from the wall as he lifted the microchipped key to the starfighter off the pilot, along with yet another ID card. He was building quite the collection. "Probably the only reason I'm doing this instead of just leaving him to get sucked into space"—Nev grabbed one of the disgusting man's legs and dragged him toward the airlock doors—"is so he can live with the shame of all this."

He did the same with the pilot, depositing them safely on the other side of the doorway. I was ashamed myself that I was too weak to help him, but I couldn't even attempt to offer. Nev didn't seem bothered.

Once he'd sealed the airlock again, he dusted off his hands. "Ready?"

"Ready," I said, unable to keep from grinning again, even as tired as I was. Or maybe because I was so tired. "Let's get back to the *Kaitan* and get the blasted hell out of here."

How I would explain his presence to the crew posed a greater challenge than starting up the starfighter, blowing straight through the bay doors with a pair of plasma torpedoes, and jetting for the stars through the ragged hole. Any fighters that could have followed us came tumbling out behind us, unmanned, into the vacuum of space.

VII

NEV

"You," Eton growled while stabbing a finger at me, "ought to be dead."

He sounded disappointed, rather than amazed that I wasn't. We were seated in the messroom, where the crew could eat their meals or spend some quality time stewing in awkwardness, as we currently were.

Eton had been blessedly absent before now, holed up in the turret, chipping away at the destroyer with the mass driver. Not that it had been all that necessary since, mysteriously, it hadn't even attempted to return fire or lock onto us again with its tractor beam. Maybe that was because Captain Uvgamut had so neatly and astonishingly disabled it from the inside out.

Arjan had been piloting the *Kaitan* away from the foundering destroyer, but he'd since put the ship on autopilot. And now that everyone had finished their various duties, we'd gathered here for what was shaping up to be a rousing good time.

I glanced at Qole. She looked to be at death's door— her eyes were deeply hollowed and her entire face remained shockingly pale for someone with a complexion that dark. My only consolation was that some color had finally returned to her lips.

It hurt to look at her, both in sympathy for the obvious abuse she had sustained, and because what in the *systems* had transpired in that destroyer? Shadow affinity was one thing, but what I had seen and experienced was entirely fantastical— more magic than science.

What had been perhaps even more amazing was that, in the middle of a complete rage, in the grip of some unspeakable power, she hadn't lost control. In my admittedly limited experience of Shadow in anyone other than Qole, black eyes seemed to indicate madness—obvious, nonsensical, reckless insanity. Instead, Qole had shown a restraint and quality of behavior that I knew I wouldn't have had. And she had obviously paid the price.

Here I sat, having deceived her practically since I'd met her, using tricks instead of the truth to try to achieve my goals, and I had only a few bruises to show for it.

I didn't want to think about why else it might hurt to look at her. She was sitting across the table from me, keeping her distance. I had the strong urge to close that distance, but I couldn't. She wouldn't want me to. For a moment there on the destroyer, it had been just the two of us, a polarized pair united by a common goal. But now we were back to being worlds apart. It almost made me miss the destroyer.

I wanted to share the same goal again—and preferably without the looming threat of death. I wanted to tell her the truth. All of it.

Despite looking at the end of her charge, Qole somehow managed to sit up straight when she spoke. Her voice was steady, but she wasn't meeting my eyes. "Eton, he just saved my life."

"So what? Qole, you were in danger *because of him* in the first place."

I swallowed. There was little denying he was right.

"Eton's right," Arjan helpfully confirmed. "One minute, our lives are fine, and the next you're almost dead and the *Kaitan* is shot up, thanks to him." He stood with his arms crossed, and his fury was more contained but no less potent than Eton's. "I'm glad he wasn't a total scumbag, I guess, but he's still a piece of scat."

"And did you see what he did to Eton?" Telu demanded. "He beat the snot out of him. Not what I'd say was nice-guy behavior."

"Hey." Eton scowled, an expression somehow made all the more frightening with half of his face swollen and bruised. "There's no need."

Telu shrugged. "Sorry. But I say we strip his stuff as payment, maybe rough him up so he gives us some sweet credentials to a princely bank account, hey?" Her face started to redden. She practically spat out her next words. "Then we can leave him in some scum hole and tell everyone he's there. And we can say, 'Oh hey, we were super nice, we thought he'd be okay there, we didn't *intend* to get him killed or anything.'"

"Attractive as the thought may be, you'd only be causing us a great deal more trouble," Basra said. "And he didn't call the destroyer on us—he tried to warn us about using the comms; we didn't listen."

Arjan stared at him in disbelief. "You can't be serious, Bas." He sounded almost hurt. There was tension between them disproportionate to Basra's logical comment, and I filed it away for later investigation.

"It's not that complicated," Qole said. She still wouldn't look at me. "He lied to us, and everyone got in trouble. He also saved my life, probably all our lives, when he didn't have to. We drop him off where he can get transport, he promises to never contact us again, and we're done."

I'd assumed her initial judgment would sting, but such an impersonal dismissal from her life hurt a lot more than that. I wasn't sure what I had expected from her . . . a little more credit, after what we'd been through? Acknowledgment? Acknowledgment of what? I had no idea.

Silence settled around the table as everyone considered this somewhat acceptable course of action. Acceptable, that is, to everyone but me, for whom it was profoundly wrong on multiple levels. I took a deep breath. The last twenty-four hours might have been hell, but this was going to be the hardest part.

I let out the breath. "I'm afraid you can't really do that."

"Why the hell not?" Qole asked. She only gave me a glance at that, then focused determinedly on the wall somewhere to my right.

I rubbed my jaw. The pain suppressors were making it a very disengaged servant, and I needed it in top form right now.

Basra stole my thunder. "That destroyer won't be the last one, will it?"

I nodded, grimacing. "I'm afraid that's true. That destroyer belonged to the Treznor-Nirmanas, they have a nearly infinite supply of them, and they want Qole—yes, yes, Eton, I'm getting to why they want her."

I'd beaten Eton to the punch, at least, and he paused, his

mouth open for a demanding roar. I felt a twinge of guilt at making Qole go through this, but it had to be done. *It'll be okay,* I thought, *I'll be careful.*

"Because of this." I reached out and flipped off a light. The flickering Shadow lantern on the table now covered us in its purple glow. "Shadow is difficult to harvest, but an incredible source of energy. But to most everyone else, using it in simple appliances like that"—I gestured at the lamp—"is tantamount to suicide. You've all experienced, some of you firsthand, what Shadow poisoning can do." I thought of the wasted man who had grabbed my arm at the harbor, and repressed a shudder. So different from Qole. "The rest of us use it in massive industrial power plants or space stations, or even in experimental starship prototypes, but not for mood lighting."

"That's crappy mood light," Telu said flatly.

"Good for a crappy mood, then. It's volatile, but Shadow *wants* to bind to organic matter, even as it tries to destroy it. If it achieves a binding, it stabilizes. My family has been pioneering such research, studying how to create an affinity between Shadow and algae in order to make it less dangerous and far more useful as a bio-energy source. If we succeed, this could change the systems. We're talking untold energy potential here, infinitely widespread application, and immeasurable value."

"The Treznors didn't say they wanted me for that," Qole said, eyes on her lap, now. Why wouldn't she look at me?

I grimaced. "I know. I didn't know what they were after until you did. Look, people like you, Qole, are the key to understanding how Shadow binds organically—for my family, we're after it for the algae, but the fact is, more directly, you're an example of it binding with humans. Interest in this has been a side effect of our research. But this doesn't have to be a bad thing," I added quickly. "My family can use what they find to make Shadow safer—not just as a fuel source, but also to keep it from destroying people the way it does on Alaxak. To save you, Qole, and Arjan and Telu."

"And what would you need from Qole to do this?" Arjan asked darkly.

"Our research is so close, missing only the final pieces. All we need is for her to undergo a few tests—and possibly even you, Arjan, and you, Telu—to achieve our goals."

Qole's face instantly grew hard. "Tests . . . like the Treznor-Nirmanas'?"

I held up my hands. "No! My family wouldn't do that to you. *I* wouldn't. The tests are nothing that would cause you any pain—tiny tissue and blood samples, reflex measurements, brain scans, that sort of thing. My uncle, Rubion Dracorte, is leading my family's top-secret research into this, and he assured me that no harm would come to you."

"Yeah, 'top-secret,'" Eton growled, "and 'no harm,' my ass. Did you notice the destroyer?"

A regretful sigh escaped me. "The Treznor-Nirmanas have been spying on us in an impressive capacity, which is one of several reasons why I came alone. My uncle and I couldn't trust anyone else. And, yes, their involvement makes things a good deal less safe for you, now that they know of our interest in Qole. The wisest course of action would be to come with me to Luvos, my home planet, and take shelter in the capital, Dracorva."

"So we just give the Dracortes everything they want, even though they already have everything?" Arjan sounded disgusted.

"If we can understand how this works, then no one will have any reason to go after Qole; they'll come to us instead," I said. "We can keep her safe, and she can help us understand the gift she has."

Arjan and Qole glanced at one another. "This isn't a gift," he said. "Trust me."

"But it can be. We can turn it into one."

"Why?" Qole finally met my eyes, and I shivered in a way that wasn't unpleasant in the slightest. Too bad her next question was of the less-pleasant sort. "Why does your family want this so badly?"

I took a deep breath. Only the truth from now on, I reminded myself. "To be honest, we are in serious need of something to counter the moves our enemies have been making."

"You're talking about the Treznor-Nirmana investment in Dracorte Industries," Basra murmured. "Their money gives the Dracortes the capital to pursue new opportunities, but if you can't repay them in time, they'll gain even more control of your enterprises, won't they?"

I looked at him in surprise. Most people had viewed the loan by Treznor-Nirmana as positive news and had no idea about any of the additional stipulations. Basra had a grasp on current events that belied his position. Something about him didn't add up, which, in a way, also made complete sense. Even his face defied expectations, seeming like a man's one minute, a woman's the next, and often somewhere in between. I wondered if he made his living by confusing people senseless.

"Um ... yes, and any missteps on our part will result in losing significant political power. Our family having nothing new to offer at the next Dracorte Conference and Report is something Treznor would dearly love to see. The conference is less than a week away. We're in a precarious position."

"Precarious?" Telu snorted. "Aren't you, like, the kings of the universe?"

I suppressed most of a grim smile. "Not quite. My father, Thelarus Dracorte, is the king and steward of our family and this system, which includes both my home planet and yours, and dozens of smaller subsystems and habitable planets in between. But in the scope of the galaxy, he is only one member of the Kings' Council. The Belarius family leads the council—so if you're looking for kings of the universe, they'd be the closest."

Telu, Arjan, and Qole all looked at me blankly, while both Eton's and Basra's flat looks told me not to treat them like idiots. Clearly, the offworlders were more up-to-date on galactic politics, but there wasn't much I could do to spare them the boredom. The others needed to understand.

"My family has had a long-standing alliance with Belarius ever since they invented the faster-than-light drive a couple hundred years ago, which was in turn a couple hundred years after the portals imploded in the Great Collapse. With such a technological advance, Belarius launched an empire that no family could rival, only try to join or ally with. My family had remained in possession of the drone network after everything fell apart—albeit with significantly less control over the drones than we'd had previously—and so with our raw materials and Belarius's new transport capabilities, we were a logical partnership. And it stayed logical . . . until recently."

"Oh, are you *slightly* less filthy rich than before or something?" Telu sneered.

"In a word, yes. But more importantly, we're less useful to Belarius. Our drones, as you know, keep mining no matter what we try to tell them and are still digging up raw material that was long ago rendered obsolete. They're bringing in fewer and fewer resources of value to us, and we can't reprogram them. Meanwhile, over the last hundred years or so, the Treznors have developed a manufacturing empire. They now make the best military-grade ships in the systems—like that destroyer we all just became intimately familiar with. They also joined forces a few years ago with the Nirmana family through a marriage alliance, practically doubling their wealth and political clout. They stand to replace the Dracortes as the right hand of the Belarius family empire . . . unless we do something to maintain Belarius's interest in us, and thus our preeminence."

"And Shadow is your best bet," Qole murmured. It wasn't a question.

I nodded, almost wishing it weren't true, that I didn't have to put her through this. But then, if we didn't find a way to make it safer for everyone, not only would my family suffer . . . but Qole would, too.

"You still haven't given us much of a reason to believe you," Arjan said, "other than you helping Qole on the destroyer— but, like I said, we were doing just fine until you came along. Why in the systems should we trust you, or even give a single ice-shaving about what happens to you or your rotten family?"

I put both of my hands on the table, willing the truth, the strength of my conviction, into my words. "Because my family *isn't* rotten. I know that no one on Alaxak has any love for the royal families. But this isn't about the wealthy, or the powerful; it's about all of us. The systems are in political upheaval, the kind that hasn't been seen since the Great Collapse. There is one, only one"—I held up a finger—"family with a charter that mandates the greater good, not family prosperity. There is only one family that maintains the precepts of the Unifier and believes that our existence is only here to improve the existence of others."

There was silence in the messroom for a moment, and only the languid flame of the Shadow moved. Then Telu started laughing.

"Oh man, that is such a load of scat. Do you even hear

yourself? *Unifier,* that's great. I just . . . I don't even know where to start, hey?" She wiped a mock tear from her eye.

Frustration flashed through me that my speech had gone over so poorly. "I didn't take you for a Scientist," I snapped. In some systems, people worshipped science, especially the science that had been lost in the Great Collapse, nearly as devoutly as others worshipped the Great Unifier.

Telu barked a laugh. "I'm not. No one on Alaxak cares about any of it—Unifier, Science, you name it. We've been here since before the Great Collapse. Nothing changes, you all just think it does. We have our family"—she looked around the crew—"and that's all that matters."

I glanced at Qole, who wasn't giving much away. What in the systems was she thinking? "Well then, you should at least be interested in the very tangible results I can offer. Because things will change, after this. With Shadow as a widely usable resource, Alaxak will experience wealth like it never has—my father would make sure of it. Treznor wouldn't grant you the same favor, and they *will* pursue my family's research if we don't, in whichever way they see fit. With us in charge, your people will be looked out for, and they'll prosper. And in the meantime, I'll repair your ship, keep Qole safe, and help you learn how to survive your Shadow affinity. I promise."

"I've heard enough." Eton stood up and moved to the galley. Out of a drawer, he pulled a device with a dozen different kinds of wire attached to four different rotating arms. I watched in bemusement as he quickly assembled them around a bowl and began to feed dried, dark fruit from a bag into a receptacle at the top. He flipped a switch on the device, and it began to whip the fruit into a fine paste over a sheet of parchment paper he placed under the wires. "You make beautiful promises, speeches about the future ahead of you. But the minute something goes wrong, you'll scramble and crush anyone in your way to protect your own hides."

"Is he … cooking?" I looked at the others, who hadn't even been paying attention.

"Eton?" Qole glanced at where he was now waving a plasmic heater of some unknown variety over the paste. "Yeah, he's the ship cook. Why?"

"I … ah." I opened my mouth and shut it. Eton, the chef? Words would probably not suffice.

"I still don't see why you didn't just tell me all this in the first place instead of trying to abduct me." Qole's gaze was back on her folded hands, and her saying it as calmly as she did twisted my gut.

"I wanted to, I did." *I tried,* I wanted to say, but I didn't think that would help. I leaned forward over the table, as if that would help my sincerity reach her. "That's why I got on board this ship, so I could have a chance to earn your trust, convince you, but I ran out of time. My transport was departing and …" I hesitated. "As a prince and heir, I was only granted a limited amount of time for this venture, and even that was difficult to arrange." That was putting it lightly. "And I have to be back to Dracorva in time for the Dracorte Conference and Report, whether or not I bring back any good news. This is one of my family's last chances to prove to the galaxy that we're not a dying star … one of our last opportunities to devote our resources to research that could save you and your people, along with us."

Qole's face was as expressionless as Basra's.

Frustration flashed through me again. "Look, I have a strict deadline. If I'd told you all this in the bar in Gamut, would you have *remotely* entertained my request? Without knowing me in the slightest, or trusting me at all?"

She finally looked at me, her dark brown gaze locking onto mine with the force of a mag-coupling.

"We still don't trust you," Arjan muttered.

Qole ignored him, and she didn't break her stare. Then she shifted, blinked, and let out the breath she'd been holding. "No, I wouldn't have," she admitted.

I'd been holding my own breath, and felt nearly dizzied by her sudden concession. Maybe I was getting through to her.

But she only fell silent afterward, and Arjan shook his head. "Even if you weren't a maniac, it's the peak of the fishing season."

"I'll cover your losses on fishing and compensate you well beyond. I know this goes against a lot of what you believe, but things are changing." I turned back to Qole, appealing to her directly again. "The systems are changing, and your way of life will change too. You can change it for the better."

She remained silent but drummed her fingers on her armrest. I hoped that was a sign that she was at least thinking about it.

Something crashed in the galley, and I twitched in my seat. It wasn't my fault that any sudden moves from Eton made me jumpy. A platter had slipped from his fingers as he deposited the layer of frothed fruit on top of something cakelike, and now he was picking up the pieces angrily. "Qole, you can't seriously be considering this royal. Can you not see how dangerous he is? Can't all of you?"

"I *am* dangerous," I responded evenly. "But the alternative for you, this ship, my family, and Alaxak is much more dangerous."

"She's not thinking about it," Arjan said. "She's just thinking about the best way to get rid of him."

Telu leveled a stare at me, one that made me nervous

with its intensity. But then she said, "Nev *does* make a certain amount of sense. And we're going to need money for repairs after the hits we took from that blasted destroyer."

Still, Qole was silent.

"A vote," Arjan said suddenly. "We can put it to a vote."

"All in favor of watching me beat him senseless?" suggested Eton.

"All in favor of dropping our friend here off somewhere and going back to a normal life?" Arjan amended generously.

Arjan and Eton raised their hands. Shockingly enough, they were the only two.

"All in favor of going with him and believing his lies and becoming a lab rat?" Eton snarled.

Telu snorted. "Well, when you put it like *that*. How about all in favor of listening to the nice prince with guns and money who probably doesn't want to kill us but has enemies who probably could?" She raised her hand.

I felt a disproportionate sense of satisfaction; I had won over a member of Qole's crew who had been adamantly against me only moments before.

Arjan looked at Basra. "Bas?"

Basra shook his head. "Neutral."

"Surprising," Telu said. Arjan looked visibly disappointed.

"It's not a vote." Qole spoke, finally, and stood up. She looked around the room at each of them. "You don't get to decide what I do, and you don't get to decide what I do with my ship."

"Fine." Eton let out an exasperated breath. "Captain, what are we going to do?"

"What I'm going to do is go with Nev."

Such relief washed over me that I almost sagged in my chair. I had to remind myself to focus on what she said next.

"I'll give each of you the option to stay if you want, but decide now. If you come with me, you remain on the *Kaitan,* and you listen to me. And that includes you," she said, meeting my eyes again. "Promise me that you'll follow my orders, that you will protect this crew and my ship, and that you'll compensate us for any losses we incur."

I nodded, taking my time—no, relishing her clear and steady gaze. "I promise, Captain Qole Uvgamut. You have my word."

"Good. We'll find out what it's worth. Does anyone want to leave?"

Everyone else was silent.

"Good," she repeated. "Telu, set a course for Luvos and get to sleep. Eton, make some dinner, and wake me up when it's ready. Everyone else, to your quarters. You need to get some rest as well."

Eton nodded. "Do you want something heavier with sauces, or something refreshing?"

"I want dinner, Eton. Pick something."

"Aargh." He threw his hands in the air, and then set to sharpening a knife by hand, running a flint along the considerable edge. He was as precise in that as he was in a fight, and as my gaze lingered on him, his eyes rose and latched on to mine. I opted to leave. Sleep sounded incredibly nice . . . but first I wanted to talk to Qole privately. To thank her.

As I exited the mess room and headed down the hall, I heard Telu's voice behind me. "Hey, Nev, hold up."

I turned around, unable to help my smile. At least I had one other ally on the ship. "What can I do for you?"

Telu walked up and lowered her voice. "You know I'm a hacker, right?"

I nodded. "Yes, I've noticed. Impressive work, I might add."

"You bet I'm good. I had that destroyer compromised and their weapons offline and they never even knew it happened."

I blinked. So it hadn't only been Qole who'd disarmed the destroyer, even though she'd disemboweled it. "That is good. I . . . That's impressive. And that was the fastest drone rerouting I've ever seen someone pull off."

Telu drew nearer. I could see the intensity of both eyes, even through the sweep of her dark hair. "Yeah. So when I say I'm going to hack something, you know that it's going to happen, hey?"

I nodded. "That seems like a reasonable statement to make."

"It is. So is this." She stood on her tiptoes and whispered in my ear. "If you ever hurt Qole, I will hack you to pieces. Real small ones."

Then she was gone.

―――

My encounter with Telu hadn't exactly instilled me with the confidence I would've preferred to have to approach Qole alone in her quarters, but there wasn't anything else for it.

The messroom was on the second-to-highest level of the ship, with only the bridge above it. This same floor housed Telu's and Basra's stations, which Qole overlooked through the grating at her feet. But she wasn't up on the bridge now, with the ship on autopilot. Below this level were the living quarters and a few maintenance rooms, above only the cargo and containment holds and the engine rooms. I took a metal staircase down.

Her quarters were the biggest, farthest back down the hall. The riveted door was cracked open, so I hoped that meant visitors were still welcome. I knocked.

"Hey?" Qole responded, her voice tired.

Her room was as functional as the ship, equipped with a bed, a plate-metal desk, a trunk, and a few shelves. The only decorations were some faded, ancient-looking photographs—I didn't even know those existed outside of museums anymore—and a few other obviously old trinkets: bits of braided leather, a string of blue stone beads, and a dented tin mug, together with the photographs. It looked almost like a crude, cobbled-together shrine, flanked as it was by two dim Shadow lanterns. A curious mix of dusty past and dangerous present. A single painted picture also hung on the wall. It was an abstract of a Shadow run, all blacks, purples, and whites.

I pushed the heavy door farther open to see her sliding down the fur-lined robe she'd borrowed from Telu, baring her tawny, toned arms and the ruined black tank top she'd been wearing since we'd left the destroyer. Her black hair was freed from the constraints of her braid, hanging long and wavy and wild down her back.

Great Collapse. "Oh—uh, I can go," I said hurriedly. I took a step back into the door frame, ready to close the door and run.

"What do you want?" she snapped.

What was wrong with me? I was no stranger to a little skin. I'd spoken not only to captains, but generals, kings, and even a few women without much clothing—some of them captains and generals themselves—alone in their quarters at night. There shouldn't be anything to this. And yet I found myself dallying in her doorway like a nervous cadet, stubbing my toe while I was at it.

"I'm sorry," she said right after. She rubbed her eyes with one hand, holding her robe closed with the other. "I'm just tired."

"No apologies necessary." I paused. "May I please have your permission to come in?"

She smirked at what had to be my formal tone and gave a hilariously incorrect, exaggerated curtsy before plopping herself down on her bed. The bed was a good size, mounded in soft-looking furs. "I can't believe anyone actually takes the time to talk like that. Don't you have better things to do?"

"Oh, it can get far more elaborate." I bowed my most formal court bow, which was so ridiculously out of place she burst out laughing. The sound was just as incongruous in this room, high and lovely as it echoed off the cold alloy walls. "My lady, if it pleases you, might I request the honor of your presence for a few brief moments of pleasant conversation?"

"Lady?" She snorted, a sound that nearly, but not quite, ruined all memory of her laughter. "Only if you promise it'll be *pleasant*." Her eyes still glinted with unguarded mirth as she said, "Otherwise I might have to throw you out on your royal posterior." She laughed again and suddenly looked as young as she was. Systems, she was only seventeen. I kept forgetting, and remembering made me flush. "Posterior—that's the right word, isn't it?"

"Yes," I said, blinking in surprise. "You know, your vocabulary is actually quite excellent for ... erm ..."

Her smile dropped from her face as if I'd shot it down with plasma missiles.

"No, I mean, you're brilliant. It's just that, without formal training, I wouldn't expect ... you know." I found myself fumbling my words—practically unheard of—on top of flushing. "Anyway." I cleared my throat. "Who painted that picture?"

Inwardly, I cringed at my obvious and awkward change of topic.

"Arjan," she said, her voice as clipped as return gunfire.

"He paints?"

"Yes. Well, he did, when he had more time."

"The photographs . . . are they of your family?"

Her face went still. "One of my parents, one of my grand-father."

"Is this all . . . um . . . some sort of shrine?" I asked, pointing at the collection on her desk.

"Piece of the past," she said shortly. "From my ancestors."

"So, like ancestor worship?"

Her lips twisted in distaste. "I wouldn't call it worship. We don't believe in anything like the Great Unifier, some all-powerful presence who has it all figured out, sitting up in some perfect place watching us all screw up. We only believe in experience. In the people who came before us. They watch us, but not . . . not like that."

"Ah," I said inarticulately, trying to understand but not wanting to offend her by asking any more indelicate questions. I desperately wanted to go back to just hearing her laugh. "So you *are* like Scientists on this ship."

She only stared in response to my poor attempt at a joke.

I hurried to explain, not wanting her to think I was fur-ther insulting her intelligence by referencing things she might not know. "Their version of a deity is Ismar Ravinye, the head scientist who gave his life trying to keep the universal portals from collapsing four hundred years ago. Not the best person to divinize, in my opinion, given that he failed catastrophically and civilization imploded . . . but talk about the ultimate form of experience to have."

I was babbling, and failing in an equally catastrophic fash-ion to Ismar Ravinye. This conversation was becoming my own Great Collapse.

Qole finally sighed, saving me from my self-induced verbal torture. "Nev, what are you doing here?"

"I just wanted to thank you. You know, for agreeing to come with me."

"I'm not exactly doing it for *you*."

"I know," I said quickly. "Of course not."

"I'm doing it for me, and Arjan, and Telu . . . and Alaxak. And you'd better deliver on your promise to help us, and I don't just mean financially."

"I know," I said, her tone worrying me. It was rapidly sliding into something distinctly dark. "I will. I promised then and I promise now. We'll figure out your Shadow affinity . . . together."

Qole's laugh was suddenly bitter. "We've heard something like that before."

"This time, it's true," I said, with the utmost sincerity.

"How can you be so sure? What do you really know about anything?" She met my eyes, but now with only sparks of anger. "You know why my people are on Alaxak, Nev?"

I straightened, blinking, trying to remember as much as I could, to prove to her that I understood whatever she might want me to. "Before the Great Collapse, portals enabled people to settle on planets spread across the galaxy, and they developed, or strengthened, their own cultures—"

"No. No, I don't want you to spew up a general history lesson from one of your princely tutors or whatever. Why are *my* people on *Alaxak*?"

Her anger was as fierce as Shadow, flickering and then burning suddenly white hot. She had so many triggers, and I seemed to set off every one. "Um . . ."

"That's right, you don't know. And you know why you don't know? We weren't deemed important from the beginning. That's how we got our planet, because no one else wanted it, and no one would give us anything else—"

A small measure of frustration entered my own voice. "The Galactic Union didn't really *dole* out planets to different groups before the Great Collapse. It was a lot more complicated than——"

"Are you listening to me, or am I listening to you?"

I clamped my mouth shut. If she wanted me to be silent, then I would be silent.

"Thanks," she said, brusquely. "Anyway, we carved something for ourselves out of that icy wasteland. It was brutal and rough and small, but it was *ours*. We Shadow fished, poisoning ourselves because we had nothing else. And do you know what happened then?"

I winced, because I knew where this was headed. "I can guess."

"No, you *know*," she said, her dark eyes boring into me. "The Dracortes sent their mining drones to Alaxak. They gutted our planet of precious metals and minerals that we could have used someday——"

"Your people sold the rights to those resources to——"

Her shout cut me off. "We didn't know the worth!" Fury rose like toxic steam from one of those mines. "And since the galaxy was happy to leave us toiling ourselves to death in our frozen corner, no one bothered to tell us. We didn't have the technology to know the extent or value of those deposits . . . or the damage they would cause." She took a deep breath, as if trying to calm herself. She didn't sound much calmer afterward. "Those drones *ravaged* Alaxak, Nev. And do you know what? They're still doing it, hundreds of years later! Still mining underground for *nothing,* hollowing out the planet, and even sifting through our asteroid belt, blowing up any fishing vessels they decide have interfered with them."

"You know we would reprogram them if we could," I said quietly, maybe in the hopes that if I softened my voice, hers would follow.

"I know, I know, poor Dracortes, confounded by the Great Collapse," she said with a sneer. "As if that excuses you for everything your family did before that, for the people you were ... or for what's still happening, for the people you still are. You're still profiting from the drones."

"But we're not *still* trying to extract minerals from Alaxak—it's by and large mined out. It's programming gone wrong, a worthless endeavor."

"My planet is *not* worthless," she practically spat. "My people are *not* worthless."

"I didn't say that!" Frustration rose higher within me before I could quash it. I took a deep breath of my own. "There's always been the value of Shadow as a high-risk energy source, a niche market to be sure, but now ... there's what your people can do with it."

"Right. Now that our Shadow affinity is more than just a crazy rumor from a crazy planet, suddenly everyone in the systems is interested in us when they never bothered before. Now my people are worth something, because we're something you can use. But I've always known our worth. This is my history." She slapped the furs underneath her, kicking up some dust. "My people. My family. *Kaitan* means family, in our nearly dead tongue, if you didn't know that. My grandfather named the ship the *Kaitan Heritage*. I never even knew him." She gestured at the pictures on the desk. Her gaze followed, and the heat faded from her eyes. "He died young."

The anger also seeped out of her voice as she finished, leaving her looking deflated. She had to be exhausted. I'd come to thank her, but all I'd done was remind her she should be furious with me and make her miserable. For systems' sake. And I actually claimed to be skilled in diplomacy?

Maybe she was right. Maybe I knew nothing.

"Qole," I said, feeling an inadequacy I was entirely unaccustomed to. "I want to help you."

She sighed, preferring to look at the riveted wall rather than at me. "Wrong. You want to help your family."

"I want both," I insisted. "They're not mutually exclusive."

"I don't think there could be two more opposite families with different needs than yours and mine."

"My family may have wealth and power, but they believe in the greater good. I promise you that."

"Greater good." She scoffed, ignoring me. "I mean, I try to imagine what growing up must have been like for you. Did you eat off crystal platters for every meal, command servants to carry you around your palace, spend every day lying in the warm sunlight with maids fanning you?"

I felt my face harden. I was tired, I had nearly been killed at least twice today, and everyone seemed to forget that in favor of their own hard times. If I didn't know anything about her and her family, she didn't know anything about me and mine.

"As a matter of fact, our platters *are* starlesian crystal," I said, trying to keep my voice from adopting its own crystalline edge without succeeding. "But turbolifts took me around the citadel, not servants. I've spent every waking moment practically from the day I was born in grueling training. My father didn't allow for much leisure time, let alone lying about."

She stood bolt upright. "Oh, am I supposed to feel sorry for you? Poor you, because your father, *the blasted king of the system,* was hard on you. Guess what? I don't *have* a father, or a mother, or an older brother, because most of my family is dead, hey?"

She'd said as much on the destroyer, but I hadn't had time to process it. I still couldn't grasp it, couldn't understand what that would be like. Which was probably why I heard myself snap, "*I* didn't kill them. I know you'd like to blame me and my family for everything that has befallen you, but you can't put all your troubles at the feet of others. Some you have to bear yourself."

For a second, Qole looked as if she would slap me. She didn't, miraculously.

I groaned. My anger was doing nothing for my case, and I tried to force it down with yet another deep breath. "That was callous. Forgive me. I understand why you're mad at me, I really do. We're hugely different, but that doesn't mean we can't find common ground. Or at least I'd like to think that."

She only stared at me like I was insane. Maybe understanding each other *was* impossible. Maybe our worlds were just too far apart—literally and figuratively.

But then something gave way inside her, and her shoulders slumped. "All I have is Arjan . . . and Telu, Eton, and Basra." Her voice cracked, but she pressed the heels of her palms into her eyes before tears could show. She spoke from behind her wrists, set like a barricade against me. "And now you come and put them all at risk."

"True, but what's the greater risk?" I asked tiredly. "Me or Shadow? I thought we had that conversation."

"We have. You're right." She dropped her hands but turned away at the same time, before I could see her face. "That's the only reason I haven't put you out the airlock."

It was obvious that *this* conversation was now over, as well, and that I had been as good as dismissed. I ducked out without saying anything and closed the door as quietly as possible behind me. It felt as if I'd lost a sparring match, failed a vital test, and disappointed someone whose opinion I valued, all without knowing quite how.

———

By and large, the *Kaitan* was utilitarian. But the crew's quarters had two modifications from your typical freighter that were surprisingly comfortable. The floors were covered in slatted wood that had been worn and polished to a shine over time by many feet. I wasn't sure if they were made from the driftwood on Alaxak or from one of the forests closer to the equator that had so far managed to survive the ice age, but the result was that they were much warmer than the bare metal would have been. Second, each bed, not only Qole's, had an abundance of furs that were heavy, deliciously warm, and liable to make you enter an impenetrable sleep after a solid day of mayhem and victories that felt like failures. When I reached the room that had been assigned to me, I shucked off everything but my underwear, crawled under the furs, and did exactly that.

I woke up to a choke hold. If I hadn't been partially shaken awake by arms sweeping up under my shoulders, I would have been unconscious in seconds. As it was, my sleep-addled brain somehow managed to remember basic training: shoulders up, chin down with everything you have. Both fighting back and panicking, my brain informed me, were excellent options.

I split the difference. I thrashed my body to the side, placed both feet on the wall, and heaved as hard as I could. It took every ounce of strength I had to move the mountain that was hanging on to me, so it didn't take much guessing to know who had come back for a rematch.

We went crashing to the floor in a pile of furs, the hold still tight on my neck. I dug my hands under the elbow wrapped around my neck and pushed up, trying to relieve the pressure while my feet scrabbled for purchase on the too-smooth floor.

"Eton," I gurgled, "I don't think . . . I'm . . . dinner."

"No, but I'm also the garbage man," Eton rasped in my ear, with far too much delight. "So we're taking you out."

We? Qole would never have agreed . . . would she have?

Arjan appeared in the periphery of my swimming vision, holding what looked like a large sack. "Is he still awake?"

Ah, we. I was as relieved as I could be, given the dire circumstances.

"Not for long," Eton replied, and tightened his massive biceps further. It felt like gravity was altering around my throat.

In our scrabbling, we'd started to move around the floor, closer to the bunk. I snatched the wastebasket by the foot of the bed with my left hand and dunked it over Eton's head. He swore and flinched in surprise. That lessened the pressure just enough. I heaved again, this time driving my shoulders over his and toward the ground. Now I was no longer being choked, just hugged to death.

I gasped. "Gentlemen, I really don't think this is the best idea." But they seemed uninterested in any alternatives I might have to offer. Arjan had industriously slipped the bag over my feet while I was dealing with Eton, and now he had a tight hold on both.

"Forget about knocking him out," Arjan said. "I closed the other door in the hallway. No one will hear us taking him to the airlock."

My eyes widened. *Airlock. For the Unifier's sake, not again.* "The hell you won't! Help! *Help!*"

I hoped my shouting might deter them from their mission,

but no such luck. They were entirely unfazed as they bodily lifted me and carried me out of my quarters like baggage.

"Have you lost your minds?" I hissed. "What in the systems is possessing you? How is this going to help anything? Do you even know what happens if you open an airlock while traveling faster than light?"

"What we're doing," said Eton, "is making damn sure you don't end up killing the captain."

"I'm sorry," Arjan said resolutely. "But Eton is right. You're dangerous, and you already almost got us all killed once. Now you want to experiment on my sister? Whether she sees it or not, you need to go."

I thrashed and kicked, but the bag around my legs and Arjan's tight grip limited my options significantly. And Eton's strength, in any other situation, would have been commendable. I had no idea where he was finding the energy to do this after our fight earlier. It felt like two metal bands were around my bare arms and chest, wound so tightly that I was growing dizzy from lack of breath. I didn't even have a shirt as a buffer; I'd gone without since the furs were so warm.

Glorious. Escape from a destroyer full of enemies only to be killed by my erstwhile allies while I was half naked. I gave up the struggle for a moment and thought of something to say that might throw them off.

"So, Eton," I panted. "Tell me. Why did you leave Dracorva?"

"Shut up." Eton's voice was a warning growl.

Arjan looked over his shoulder. "What is he talking about?"

"Nothing, except that your friend here was obviously trained in the Academy. Master Devrak Hansen teach you that choke hold? 'Make a knife with your hand, put it behind the head.' Still echoes in your mind, doesn't it?"

"Shut up." Eton's voice lowered.

"What were you, commando? Did you get kicked out, or did you just desert because you couldn't control your anger? Kill someone?"

"I *said*—" Eton let go and punched me in the stomach faster than I had anticipated. His fist drove me to the floor like a battering ram, knocking my head on the cold metal and the breath from my lungs. *"Shut. UP."*

I wheezed, stars swimming in my vision. I had to fight back, but my energy had pretty much dried up. This was it. The end.

"Oh, damn." Arjan stopped where he crouched, no longer hoisting the bag farther up my torso.

Groggily, I craned my head to see what he was staring at.

Qole was standing there, dressed in a tank top and pants almost identical to the ones that had been destroyed earlier. In some part of my abused skull, I thought they showed skin in all the right places. It was nice. And I was delirious.

She looked uncomprehending, shocked at the scene in front of her, and then her eyes started to fill with black. She didn't even ask what they were doing.

"Let him go," she said.

That sobered me right up. "Qole, it's okay."

Eton grabbed hold of the bag and yanked it up to my shoulders, and then he savagely drew the drawstring tight.

"It will be," he said. "Qole, you just don't understand how much danger you are in. It's my job to protect you, and I refuse to fail at my job." He grabbed my shoulders and nodded to Arjan. Arjan hesitated and then obviously steeled himself. He grabbed my feet and picked me up.

"Eton's right," he said. "This outsider is offering us riches for what we have, and you know as well as I do that always ends the same way for us on Alaxak."

"Let him go," Qole repeated and stepped closer. The air crackled around us and my skin crawled.

This wasn't good. They hadn't seen Qole fully in action like she had been on the destroyer, and none of us needed a repeat of that on the *Kaitan*. I still didn't know how completely in control she really was when she . . . when she *what?* Seized Shadow? Became possessed by it? Was just exceptionally awesome at being really mad?

"Qole," I said as calmly as I could. "It's really okay. Let's just talk this out, shall we? Maybe put me in a holding cell? Huh, guys? Compromise? Vote?"

Everyone ignored me. Arjan stood in front of his sister. "You know I'm right, Qole," he said. "Please, let's not destroy everything we have."

Qole didn't move. "You've just stooped to the same level you accused him of being on—acting behind my back, trying to control me, *harming one of my crew*. Now for the last time, let him go. Or so help me, by our ancestors, you both will never set foot on this ship again."

"Enough of this nonsense." Eton threw me across both shoulders like an overlarge, lumpy scarf and walked straight up to Qole. "You simply aren't old enough to understand what you're dealing with here." He put a hand on her arm and pushed her aside.

Or tried to. Qole stayed rooted in the spot, completely against the laws of physics, given her and Eton's relative mass. She looked up at him, grabbed my legs, and hauled me off his shoulders and onto the ground next to her as though I were made of straw.

Eton shook his head and headed for me, only to have Qole dig her palm into his chest and shove him staggering backward several feet. He stared at her in disbelief, as Arjan grabbed her arm and twisted it down. "Qole, *calm down.*"

I could have told him that was the wrong way to go about it. She let him bring her arm down, then grabbed one of his pant legs and heaved up, sending him into a surprise somersault onto the floor. He lay there, gaping at her, as Eton moved in and attempted to simply pick her up. Maybe he thought he could carry both of us out on his shoulders.

She moved faster than he did, ducking out of his grasp and stepping aside, with fluidity befitting a level of training she didn't have. He ignored her, diving for me, and that was when her eyes went completely black.

Her arm snaked out and she grabbed his shoulder, pulling him back. As Arjan came up behind her and attempted to put her into a hug, she punched Eton so hard he landed sprawling on the floor next to me. He groaned and didn't get back up, which meant he was approaching what I felt like.

"Qole, listen to me—" Arjan began.

She didn't. She whipped her arm up over her shoulder and smacked him in the face. He staggered backward, then fell into a sitting position.

She whirled around and knelt near him, grabbing his shirt and pulling him close. "No, brother, you listen to me. I may be young. I may not know what I'm doing. But those are not choices you get to make for me. Not now, not ever. I don't make your choices, and you don't make mine. Do you want off this ship? Then get off. I would never stop you. But do not pay lip service to me and my life one minute, and then decide I don't have the right to take the risks *you* wouldn't. Risks that, if not taken, would have us both working in the cannery in Gamut for scat to eat."

She looked back at me, where I had finally staggered to my feet.

"Qole, it's okay, I—" I started, but she cut me off.

"You, shut up." I did. She turned back to Arjan. "I expect outsiders to try to control us. But you're my brother, and you would make a slave out of me by taking away my choices." She stood. "How could you?"

Arjan looked up at her, blood running from a cracked lip, and his eyes welled up with tears.

For once, I couldn't think of anything to say.

"Now," Qole said, her eyes blacker than ever. "What am I going to do with all of you?"

VIII

I SHOULD HAVE FELT SATISFIED AT HOW EASY IT WAS TO REACH DOWN and seize the collars of both Arjan's and Eton's jackets as if they were unruly children and not men who were twice the size of me—or three times the size, in Eton's case.

Instead, under the cold anger that encrusted my emotions like the darkness coating my vision, I felt a tremor of fear, as if I were standing on the surface of a frozen lake that had just shuddered beneath my feet.

I couldn't keep this up. Using Shadow this much would kill me faster than being outside without a coat in an Alaxak winter. I'd only gotten a few more hours of sleep since using it on the destroyer, and I'd nearly died then, I was almost sure of it. I wasn't doing nearly as much this time, not reaching beyond what already dwelled inside my body, but I could still feel the toll it was already taking on me.

I was also nearly as sick from the betrayal. I had to do something with these two quickly, either before my strength ran out or before I used that strength to throw them out into space.

Out into space . . . That gave me an idea. Probably the same one they'd had for Nev.

Nev braced himself as if he thought I was about to grab him too, but he didn't try to run. He looked too exhausted to move, and just stood there, shirtless and panting, over the bag they'd tried to put him in. But I only passed him in the hallway, dragging Eton and Arjan behind me as if they were now the sacks of garbage or laundry headed off the ship.

For once, Nev hadn't done anything.

Arjan didn't struggle, probably out of shame, and neither did Eton, probably because he was still dazed from the less-than-gentle tap I had given him. Actually, I'd tried to be gentle so I wouldn't kill him. The blow had still gotten the message across, apparently.

Hefting them up two flights of stairs to the bridge was nearly as easy as dragging them down the hall, except for maneuverability. I didn't take as much care as I could have to keep from bashing limbs or heads against the metal railings.

"Qole, where are you . . . You're not crazy, are you?" It was Arjan, fear in his voice, but I didn't care if he was afraid. In fact, so much the better.

"Not yet," I said through gritted teeth. "Now shut up."

Groaning, Eton reached up to try to grab my hand at his collar, but I shook him off as I crested the last set of stairs and hauled them onto the bridge. Halfway across the room, I hurled them the rest of the way. They landed and tumbled with a clatter over the metal grating of the floor . . . right onto the solid paneling of the airlock's base.

I mashed the button, sealing them in with a whooshing hiss.

"Qole!" Arjan shouted, pressing his hands against the windows of the inner doors. His cry tore at me, but I ignored it. Even Eton mustered the strength to roll to his feet and pound once in frustration.

I pushed the button that silenced their end of the comm. But they could still hear me, for now.

"I never thought you would pull something like this," I snarled. "I told you that you would both be off this ship if you didn't listen."

There was something heartbroken in both of their eyes at that moment. Arjan had the humility to look like he deserved everything I was doing to him, but Eton stared at me like I'd gutted him.

But I was the one *they'd* gutted.

My anger went out of me like Shadow from an open maglock. I sagged against the wall and blinked as my vision brightened. It was still dim on the bridge with the lights at their night setting, but less dim now. I also blinked tears from my eyes that I quickly wiped away with my forearm.

"I can't believe either of you," I said, growling through the quaver in my voice. "Consider this your holding cell. Until further notice, you are off the *Kaitan,* as soon as I can get you off. Make yourselves comfortable in there."

I silenced my end of the comm too, and turned away from them.

. . . And I nearly jumped to find Nev leaning against the wall in the shadows behind me. It wasn't a relaxed pose, more

of a depleted one, but he still managed to slide out of it grace-
fully.

"Sorry, I wasn't trying to eavesdrop," he said, his voice low.
"I just wanted to make sure . . ."

I glared at him with all the anger I could muster, which
wasn't much. "That I wasn't going to kill them? Of course I
wouldn't. But if you're going to try to tell me what I should or
shouldn't do too, there's still room in there." I tossed my head
over my shoulder at the airlock.

Nev didn't say anything, and I glanced behind me.

Arjan pivoted away from the windows so he didn't have
to meet my eyes, while Eton was trying to kill Nev with his
stare alone, by the looks of it. I'd silenced all sound between us
and them, but there was more than one way to communicate.
I pushed another button and the clear glass panes tinted until
they were too dark to see through.

I looked out the sweeping viewport ringing my command
station, at the strange, warped streaks of light like frozen reflec-
tions of stars on a rippling black ocean. I'd never been this far
from home. The *Kaitan* had, no doubt, since it had made the
journey to Alaxak in the first place, but it hadn't gone much
farther than the planet's asteroid sea in decades. We'd left that
boundary behind nearly as soon as Telu had programmed a
course for Luvos and I'd engaged the dormant Belarius Drive
however many hours ago.

"Needless to say, thank you for saving my life." Nev's voice
moved, coming alongside me, perhaps so he could take in the
view as well. "Airlock's getting more use than it has probably
had in a while. As sociable as you all are, I can't imagine you
dock much in space."

Even his jibe was weary, but the corner of my mouth still
twitched. His ability to dredge up a sense of humor at inap-

propriate times might have come from his carefree upbringing, but I somehow still appreciated it. Sometimes, I even wished I had the same ability.

"When it's company like yours . . ." I trailed off as I noticed the blood dripping from his scraped elbow, the raised gouges crisscrossing his already bruised arms and chest—though the bruises were significantly lighter than they should have been, thanks to whatever he'd jammed into his neck on the destroyer—and the oozing cut from who-knew-what, maybe the zipper of Eton's jacket, swiping down the length of his back. Even the gash on his brow from his first fight with Eton had reopened. "Nev."

"Hm?"

"You're a wreck."

He glanced down at himself. "So I am." Then he winced at even *that* movement and rubbed his throat.

"Here." I was moving before I thought about what I was doing, on autopilot. I opened one of the many lockers set into the wall and pulled out the ship's medi-kit, which was also getting a lot more use lately.

"You don't have to—" Nev began.

"Sit," I ordered.

He perched on a bench in only synthetic thermal bottoms, his feet bare on what had to be freezing metal grating, shirtless and bleeding, head hanging.

Maybe one of the bonuses of strong-arming half of my crew into an airlock was that the rest took me more seriously . . . if Nev could even begin to count as crew. Despite looking like anyone who'd had the scat beaten out of them several times in a row, he was a royal. Not only that, a blasted prince. And not only *that,* but in line to rule as heir to the entire Dracorte family empire.

"We don't have anything too advanced here," I said, suddenly self-conscious about the battered case I held. "I'm sure you'll tell me that next time I should consider saving up for a *proper* medi-kit, but—"

He held up a hand and accidentally—or not—brushed my forearm with his fingers. He wasn't looking up, or trying to move with much precision, almost like he was drunk. He must have really been tired. About as tired as me. "My apologies. I was being an ass."

The words warmed my belly like a gulp of something hot to drink. I could also probably admit that I'd been an ass too, earlier. Everyone had been using Nev as a punching bag—the leather dummy in Gamut's bar came to mind, which was actually supposed to be Nev's father, the Dracorte king—but I didn't have to, as well. Not *everything* was his fault.

But I couldn't find the words to apologize like he had. I sat next to him, sifting through the contents of the kit.

"This is going to sting," I said. "Here, turn."

He shifted his back to me. "I'm not too worried."

I hesitated before touching him, unsure, suddenly, if I was even allowed. Were there rules against touching princes? But since when had I cared what I was or wasn't allowed to do?

He didn't flinch or make a noise when I started in on the long cut down his back with a swab soaked in acidlike disinfectant. Still, I moved quickly, cleaning the wound as best as I could without causing him too much pain.

I stuck bandages over it afterward, then said, "Elbow."

Without arguing, he gingerly rested his head against the wall, keeping his back off it, closed his eyes, and curled his arm up to give me the best angle at his elbow. I tried to ignore the fact that the arm was nicely muscled as I leaned forward to swab and bandage the bleeding scrape. Looking at the rest of him as little as possible—it felt too sneaky, somehow, with his eyes closed—I finished the job in silence.

But I didn't feel like stopping there, and Nev didn't move. I could almost think he was asleep, if I didn't know firsthand how much this disinfectant burned. I set his arm down for him and began cleaning the reopened gash on his once-perfect brow—though, for all his injuries, his face still looked pretty damned *near* perfect.

He could have reached the gouges on his chest himself, but he'd likely mess up his elbow dressing in the process. Besides, his eyes were still closed. With only a brief hesitation, I doused another swab in disinfectant, leaned over him so that I hardly touched him, and dabbed at the worst of the wounds there.

When I risked a glance at his face again, his eyes were open. He watched me in a still way, almost holding his breath, as if *he* didn't want to startle *me*. I went back to work, trying not to feel the weight of his silvery stare.

"Thank you," he murmured, when I finished.

"That would be all I'd need, for you to come down with an infection." It wasn't exactly what I wanted to say, but it was the easiest thing. I still didn't look up at him. With all the idiotic, whirling nervousness I'd had in my stomach since he'd touched me on the destroyer, what if Shadow appeared in my eyes? I'd been avoiding his gaze for half the previous day for that reason. I busied myself packing up the medi-kit.

"Well, then thanks for sparing yourself an inconvenience and letting me benefit as a pleasant side effect." He was still resting against the wall in a posture that looked like every part of him must hurt.

I paused on a small bottle. It wouldn't work as fast or as effectively as one of those injector tubes, but it would deaden the pain a bit. "Open your mouth," I said, unscrewing the lid.

"Qole, I don't want to deplete your entire kit—"

"Then buy me another one and open up." By now, there was no point in denying he had a million times the resources I had. No point other than pride, but I was feeling less proud and more off-balance and tingly, at the moment.

He sighed. I thought he might accept the bottle from me as I raised it toward him, but he apparently took me literally and tilted his head back, lips parted. I smiled to see the incongruity of a prince and wielder of a Disruption Blade opening his mouth for medicine, waiting like a child. As I tipped the contents into his mouth, my breath caught when I tried to push down the laughter that rose inside me. I ended up sloshing a few drops on his face.

He choked and grabbed my hand in reflex. "That tastes terrible."

"Sorry, my prince," I said, with as much sarcasm as I could dredge up. I pulled my hand out of his without quite ripping it away and packed up the rest of the medi-kit.

He winced, but apparently not from pain. "I really can't abide the sound of you calling me that, for some reason." He relaxed, as much as he seemed to be able to, into the wall again. "Maybe I'm just tired," he added, with a hint of a sardonic smile, "and I won't mind hearing it after I get some sleep."

My lips curled, in spite of themselves. What an arrogant brat. He was funny about it, but he was still an arrogant brat. Just moments before I'd been furious and filled with Shadow, and now here I was laughing with a systems-be-damned Dracorte. "Well, you won't hear it again, so don't get used to it."

"I won't. You are my captain, after all. Captain."

"Don't even pretend to—" I began with a scowl.

"I'm not." He met my eyes in all seriousness. "I'm on your

ship, and I've promised to follow your orders. I'll respect you as my captain."

The tingling increased to a full-body buzz. My blood sang, my heart pounded. Nev, a blasted prince, was acknowledging me as his captain when my own crew barely could. And he meant it. Sometimes he said things just because they seemed like the right thing to say, but I could tell when he *felt* them.

I held his eyes finally, wanting to say something without quite knowing what, but then whatever last bit of energy I had drained out of me. I slumped against the wall next to him, my bare shoulder brushing his for a second before I tipped slightly away. "At least someone does." I snorted. "*You,* of all people."

"You shouldn't snort. It's a rather unbecoming noise," he said, yawning. ". . . Captain."

Unbecoming. I grew up on a frontier world of dust and ice. I didn't even know what that word meant. To prove the point, I snorted again, but I couldn't help the smile that kept tugging at my lips.

"Seriously, though," he said. I thought he might be talking about snorting until he said, "I think Arjan and Eton are good people. They've got your back, and now that they've been reminded you're in charge . . . you might want to give them a second chance. Although, don't tell them I said that." He glanced toward the airlock, where Eton and Arjan were still hidden from view. And here was the man they'd tried to kill, suggesting I go easy on them. Nevarian Dracorte, for all his faults—like being a Dracorte—was an oddly decent person. Or maybe *I* was just tired, thinking that. And I was, so, so tired. I closed my eyes and let the feeling wash over me.

"Tell me about them."

"Hm?" I said, blinking at the sound of Nev's voice next

to me. I'd almost dozed off sitting up, and suddenly realized I was leaning into him, my whole side pressing into his more and more. I wasn't sure if it was ruder to stay like that or pull away, but the warmth was comforting on the cold bridge, so I decided not to move, tingling all the more.

"Tell me about the crew. They're my crew too, now, after all."

"Well, you've met Eton and Arjan," I said dryly. I plucked at a stray thread on the inner seam of my leather leggings. Somehow I'd once again found myself alone in his presence without wearing too much. At least this time he was equally, if not more, undressed. His synthetic thermal bottoms still made my leather pair look rough-cut and shabby. "What do you want to know?"

"Meeting someone is hardly knowing them."

I wondered if he wanted to know me beyond meeting me—beyond knowing *what* I was, whatever that was. Beyond my Shadow affinity, at least. How much of me was just a science experiment to him?

"Where are Eton and Basra from?" he continued. It didn't quite sound like what he wanted to ask, his voice careful for some reason. Maybe he didn't want me to think he was prying, and he was easing me into this, coaxing me into talking.

I was tempted to scoff again. "Of course you'd ask the question I know the least about. Outsiders who end up on Alaxak don't always like to talk about how they got there." I shot him a pointed look for emphasis. "I know Eton is from one of the royal planets, maybe yours, and he was some type of bodyguard. Maybe for a family, but he never said which, and I didn't ask him. Basra I know even less about. He's incredibly skilled for how young he is."

Nev was smiling beneath half-closed eyes. "Basra must be

around twenty-five or so? Hard to tell for sure, and young, no doubt, but I'm sitting next to a seventeen-year-old who just so happens to be the best Shadow fishing captain on Alaxak."

Flustered, I asked the first stupid thing to come to mind. "How do you know how old I am?"

He tilted his head to raise one eyebrow that as good as said, *Come on, what do you take me for?* "I believe I've demonstrated that I know how to ask questions. In fact, I'm demonstrating it now."

Of course he's aware of my age, my skill, I reminded myself a little bitterly. The fact that I'd come so far so young and was even still alive was probably how he'd determined I could be of the most use to him.

But his eyes weren't the least bit insincere or beguiling as he asked, "Well, if you don't know where they're from, how did Eton and Basra come to join your crew?"

"I met them both a little over three years ago after . . . after I was just getting started fishing." I'd almost said, *After most of my family died,* but I didn't want him to think all I did was dwell on it. Usually, I didn't; I *couldn't*—I was too busy. "Eton first. He came out of nowhere. Someone was hassling me on the dock for I don't even remember what. I was an easy target; I was only fourteen, never mind that I had my own ship. Or maybe it was because I had my own ship. Anyway, before I knew it, Eton hauled this guy away from me and flattened him. I needed a strong-arm and weapons tech, and so I asked him a couple of questions: did he know how to shoot a mass driver, and if so, did he want a job?"

"Did you offer him the chef's position then or after?"

I grinned. "He just sort of fell into it, since he was the only one onboard who knew anything about cooking. At that point, it was only me, Arjan, and Telu—a bunch of kids, really, even if Arjan was eighteen then. But you wouldn't make fun of Eton if you'd tasted more of his food. The guy wields kitchen gadgets like he wields his guns . . . and has an equally large collection of both."

Nev shared my grin. "And Basra?" he asked.

"Basra found me too, soon after. I'd seen this strange, hooded figure around Gamut for a week or so, and it always seemed to be watching me—watching everything, really. And then one day, this person approached me while we were unloading a huge catch of Shadow, pulled down the hood, and there was Basra. Perfect timing, since I was struggling to find a stable market that would offer a decent price. He told me that, for a percentage, he could make me deals I couldn't imagine for my Shadow, and he wasn't kidding." I frowned. "Seems like he could be making way more money somewhere else. I'm not sure why he stays. He's the best there is."

I wondered what was going on between him and Arjan again, but I didn't have long before Nev interrupted my thoughts.

"Like I said, you're also the best at what you do. It's pretty obvious once one meets you. Basra must have been looking for you, like I was."

I bent forward and put my head in my hands. My hair was loose, falling in a long, tangled curtain on either side of my face, all the easier to hide my blush or anything else he might see in my eyes, unpredictable tears or something darker. "If I'm the best, then why does everything always seem to fall apart around me?"

My family, my ship, my crew, my life . . .

"I don't think you realize how much you're holding together, and what few resources you use to do it." Something definitely rose up inside me then, but not tears or Shadow. It was a hot pressure, coiling around my rib cage and pinching my lungs too tight. It felt horrible, and good, to hear him acknowledge that. I rubbed at my eyes just in case, and he hesitated. "I'm sorry, Qole, if I've crossed a line. What about Telu. How did she join you?"

I pulled my hands away from my face, but kept leaning on my knees, unable to look at Nev just yet. "I've known her . . . and her family . . . practically since she was born. We grew up together. She's a year younger than me." I held my palms up, looking at the lines there, reflecting on everything Telu and I had been through, ups and downs alike.

Nev straightened slightly at that. "She's only sixteen? Wow. The girl is . . . formidable . . . for someone so young." He barked a laugh. "Terrifying, actually."

I tucked my hair behind my ear to look at him. "There's a good reason she's that way."

He sobered. "No doubt. Are her parents . . . ?"

"Both are alive, actually," I said, and he blinked. "But they're not exactly . . . present."

He waited for me to explain.

I took a deep breath. "Both of them have a Shadow affinity, but only enough for them to go a little crazy and not die outright. Her father had a ship and was a decent fisherman, until he decided to drink all the time to ward off the hallucinations. Drink and take out his fear and frustration on Telu and her mom. For the longest time, Telu just buried herself in a virtual world. That—and her Shadow affinity—is why she's such a good hacker. Her mom was too out of it to do anything to stop her father, but Telu eventually tried. Law enforcement didn't listen."

Nev grimaced. "Why not?"

Now it was my turn to bark a laugh, a bitter one. "They

don't care. We have one officer in Gamut, and they change all the time. Beyond making sure we're not burning the place down or messing with the drones—your drones," I added sourly, "they couldn't care less what happens to us, or whether a father beats his wife and daughter senseless every so often. So, Telu, she . . . uh . . ."

"She what?" Nev asked, his voice softening.

I cleared my throat. "She asked for my help. I took her dad's ship when he was passed out drunk, and I . . . I shot down a drone." I looked at him, daring him to get offended.

He looked amazed, instead. "You shot down a *drone* with a fishing vessel? By yourself?" I nodded. "What kind of vessel was it?"

I shook my head, laughing in exasperation. "What does that have to do with anything? You and your ships. I don't know, it was like all the fishing ships in Gamut, some kind of mishmash."

He laughed at himself. "Fair enough." His face quickly moved from boyish curiosity to seriousness, his smile sliding away as his eyebrows dropped. "But . . . how did you survive? Even if you managed to shoot one down, drones swarm when one is attacked . . ." He trailed off, thinking of the implications. I sobered, too, suddenly and irrationally angry at him again. Whole communities had been wiped out because of that drone function.

I exhaled slowly. "Telu hacked the alert signal," I said, "to keep it from calling the others."

"The authorities would have to know it had been sabotaged."

I pulled my lips back into a humorless smile. "I know. Exactly."

"You . . . ," Nev said, stunned. "You pinned it on her father."

Even now, I felt a grim satisfaction over what I had done. I leaned back into the wall, feeling the cold surface press into my shoulders. "The authorities paid attention to him *then*. He was too drunk and crazy to even know whether he'd done it, and they didn't look into it all that deeply. Hauled him off-world to some prison. He hasn't bothered Telu or her mom since. They confiscated his ship, of course, so now Telu works with me to support her mother. She viewed it as a fair trade."

Nev was looking at me as if seeing me for the first time. I didn't know if it was good or bad. "I see," he said.

I felt defensive without even knowing if I should be. I opened my mouth, but he spoke over me.

"I see, even more now, why you're the best captain on Alaxak at seventeen. It makes perfect sense." Before I could sputter anything, he said, "But the one I don't quite understand is Arjan. He's four years older than you, twenty-one now, right? Did he not want to captain?"

I swallowed and glanced at the airlock doors, even though I couldn't see inside. "No," I said shortly.

Nev was silent for a moment, and then his voice prodded me gently in the dimness. "Why not?"

"He's . . . scared. Scared of this." I held my hands out in front of me again, not to look at the lines in my skin this time, but as if to see what dwelled *underneath*. "You've seen how he pilots the skiff. He has this too—the skill, the darkness. But he watched it kill my parents. And then our oldest brother, Onai, only two years later, just after he'd turned twenty-five. Arjan wants to hide from it, and not lose himself or anyone else. Captaining would have required him to take responsibility for a crew, and to face his fears every day. He still faces them in the skiff, but it's different. Less pressure. Less of a chance to snap." I swallowed. "And he's the only one at risk if he does."

Nev was quiet for a moment, and when his voice came again, it was practically a whisper. "Are you scared?"

My hands started shaking and I clasped them together. I hadn't cried in years, and yet again today I felt that sting in my eyes. Maybe it was just bone-deep exhaustion. Or maybe nobody had ever before asked me if I was afraid. It was sort of taken for granted on Alaxak. We all had to face it, so why talk about it?

What he asked next was even more shattering. "Why do you put yourself through this, then, day after day?"

"I don't have a choice," I said, my voice small.

"No choice . . ." His smile was bitter when I glanced over at him through my hair, trying to surreptitiously wipe my eyes. "Now that, I can understand all too well." I wanted to ask him what he meant, but then he continued, "But what do *you* want, Qole? If you could choose?"

I opened my mouth, closed it, and shrugged helplessly. "I don't even know what that means. I want to live long enough to do what would have made my parents proud. To do right by my ancestors. And that's what I'm trying to do now."

"Let's assume you're at rights with your ancestors." Before I could get irritated with him for casually brushing them aside, he said, "And I *know* your parents would be proud of you." He had no way of knowing that, actually, but the words still made my throat too tight to speak. "And let's say you don't need to work, to Shadow fish, for the purposes of this exercise. So what would you want to do with yourself? First thing that comes to mind?"

Honestly, I'd never really thought about it. That was a luxury, as much as dwelling on my parents' deaths, that I didn't really have. But this was in a hypothetical universe. I could try to use my imagination . . . though I'd have to dust it off first.

I swallowed. "Um . . . let me think. I would . . ." I closed my eyes, tried to put myself somewhere other than the *Kaitan.* Where would that even be?

I felt a breeze. A *warm* breeze, on my face. And maybe the sun. I smelled flowers.

My voice came out hesitantly. "I would want . . . to be in a field. With grass. And sunlight. Lying on my back and looking at the sky . . . doing nothing. Nothing but laughing."

I almost felt the imaginary touch of a hand on mine. *Laughing with someone.*

As soon as I said it, I expected him to laugh *at* me. It was such a stupidly unsophisticated, selfish desire for me to have, when he was trying to change the systems for the greater good, and all that. I should want to do something much more amazing, especially if money were no object in this hypothetical universe. My eyes fluttered open and I glanced at him.

He wasn't laughing. He looked sadder than I'd ever seen him. I must be so pathetic he felt *bad* for me.

I scrubbed my face and cleared my throat. "Okay, enough imagining things in imaginary worlds. Especially since my imagination is rusty." Before he could try to claim that it wasn't, I said, "Besides, *you* said you have no choice in what you do, either. Why? Tell me about your life, Nev."

Not only was I happy for a change in subject, I was also genuinely curious.

He flinched. "I'm not sure if you want to hear about that."

He was probably remembering my reaction in my quarters, the last time he'd tried. "Really, tell me. I'm . . . I'm sorry about earlier." *Finally,* I could say it. "I was tired and stressed and angry, but I shouldn't have taken it out on you."

"I . . ." He looked mildly surprised. "Apology accepted. What would you like to know?"

"Tell me about your family—they're a good place to start.

I'm probably going to meet them, after all." At the thought, my stomach tipped a little on the perfectly level bench.

"Okay." Nev took a deep breath. "My father . . . he's the most duty-driven man I've ever known. He lives for Dracorva first. He expects a great deal from me, but he gives me the tools I need to excel. He's a good man, and I . . . well, I would be happy to think I'll become half the ruler he is." He sighed as if he was somehow failing. After pausing for a moment, lost in thought, he smiled. "And Mother, she's as duty driven as my father, and yet, just as any moral fiber I have comes from him, any sense of decency I have comes from her." He chuckled. "To you coming from me, that probably doesn't speak well of her. But she's a good person."

Maybe he believed it, but it might also be a lie he'd been fed his entire life as a royal, and he didn't know how else to see his parents.

As if he knew what I was thinking, Nev nearly groaned. "I'm sorry. I'm talking like we're at a dinner, or an event, or . . ." He looked away, as if embarrassed. In front of *me.* "The truth of the matter is, I don't think we are anything like what you understand as family. We don't spend our days and hours together, we don't share hopes and fears. We see one another at set times, by appointments and it's all"—he moved his fingers in a funny motion—"all a pantomime. A sort of play. Sometimes I love it, but I think what I love best is when I *accidentally* spend time with one of them and we talk about something that doesn't matter at all."

I supposed I could understand that. Those were my favorite times with Arjan, when we weren't focused only on fishing. "Do you have any brothers or sisters?"

"Two, a sister a year younger, and a brother nine years my junior. Both have strong personalities—if quite different from each other—that sometimes chafe against the strict mold we're all forced into as our parents' children."

"What kind of mold? You mentioned training, I think, before I went off on you in my quarters." I smiled feebly and nudged his shoulder in an attempt at another apology. "Training in what?"

At my playful gesture, he smiled back crookedly, sleepily. It was a smile to get the wearer anything they wanted, and I briefly wondered if he'd trained at *that*. He tried to lean back against the wall before he remembered his injuries. The change in direction brought his arm back into contact with mine, and he left it there. "Oh, training in everything. History, as you've already noticed, but also governance, debate, finance, politics, war tactics, hand-to-hand combat, fencing, piloting, astronomy, poetry . . . the list goes on."

"Wow." A whole galaxy of knowledge lay between our worlds, not just an actual galaxy. I only managed a second word. *"Poetry?"*

A giggle burst out of me, in spite of myself.

Nev's odd silver eyes seemed to light up at the sound, which made me swallow it self-consciously. Great Collapse, when was the last time I'd actually *giggled*? "Like I said, no choice. I'm no good at composing, but I can recite the Eminents with the best of them."

I didn't even know who or what "the Eminents" were supposed to be. *Eminent,* apparently. "Poetry sounds really rough," I said, softening my sarcasm with a smile.

He shrugged, giving me another crooked smile. "Oh, I don't mind a lot of what I've had to learn, honestly. I just spend more time with tutors and trainers than I do my parents or siblings—to say nothing of my friends, such that they are, since no one outside my family is allowed too near me for very long.

The sciences have been my escape, actually, simply because they have nothing to do with ruling."

Loneliness was audible in his voice, a surprising amount, and my stomach rang hollowly in response. "If you royals have time for poetry, for ancestors' sake, then your parents should spend some of that time with you." *They're lucky enough to still have you, and you them,* I wanted to say.

"My father is very ... traditional," Nev replied hesitantly, as if a lot was being said in the space of that one word. "He doesn't really see me as his child anymore, like a common parent would. I'm the heir. I don't really belong to him, but to our system."

I frowned, trying to ignore the sting of *common*. "Royal or not, you're still his son."

Nev shook his head. "You don't quite understand."

"Because I'm common?" I asked, failing to keep the bite out of my voice now. "Explain it to me, then."

He looked at me warily, as if he knew he was on thin ice. His jaw hardened, but not in anger—more in determination— and he nodded. "All right. When I was officially named heir at age eight, I had to undergo a trial known as my Rendering." His lips twisted. "Its meaning is manyfold: it rendered me into an heir, my parents rendered me in service unto our people, and the burden of our people was rendered upon me."

"Burden?" Something in the way he said it made it sound literal as well as figurative.

He paused, staring off into space as if seeing something else. "There was an audience. I had to stand in front of witnesses, including my parents, while my shoulders were weighted down with heavy sacks. I couldn't cry or ask for help, and my parents had to watch without pity—proof they had given me up as their child for the greater good of our people."

144

I blinked. "How long did you have to stand there?"

"All night," Nev said quietly.

It was his closed expression that disturbed me more than anything. Like he was living it again, bearing such a load without faltering. "There's no way a kid could stand like that for hours," I insisted, as if I could somehow make it so this hadn't happened to him. "Your muscles would have cramped; you would have fallen."

He nodded. "Indeed. I did."

"What happened when you did?" I almost didn't want to know.

"I would be beaten with batons until I stood up again."

My breath caught as if I'd dropped into icy water. These were *royals,* the people who thought they were better and more sophisticated than everyone else. It was the most barbaric tradition I'd ever heard of. "But you were eight!" I sputtered. "And your parents just watched?"

"Without lifting a hand to help me or comfort me," Nev said. "I mean, they couldn't, that was the point. But while I could tell my mother was trying not to cry, my father stared right at me the entire time without flinching. It was my duty, my rightful burden, in his eyes."

"That's the stupidest thing that's ever glued on wings and tried to fly." I couldn't help the words—and that was the least of what I wanted to say. Picturing the boy version of Nev, trying to make his parents proud like I always tried, but with them *right there,* standing in front of him, cruel and unyielding in their judgment . . . it almost seemed better to not have parents.

Rather than get offended, Nev laughed. But the weight that had settled onto his shoulders with the story didn't lift. "I know how it must sound to you, but it *is* my duty. I've been training all my life, never mind that I don't have much of one, or even much opportunity to put my training to use. *That's* what bothers me more than anything. I'm supposed to be everything for my people—shield, sword, link to our illustrious past—but so often a ruler just . . . sits. My parents are crafting me into the perfect instrument, which, upon completion, is put on a shelf." He acted out the motion with tired arms. "Or, in this case, a throne."

I changed the subject, bringing us back into safer territory. "So if you were doing all that, how in the name of the ancestors did you find the time to come dig around in the ice and dirt of Alaxak? We must be the farthest planet in the system from Luvos."

"You are, by far." Nev scrubbed a hand through his hair and then winced when it tugged on his split brow. "And how I managed it is a good question. Probably through some combination of my uncle's support, family tradition, and pure obstinacy, on my part. I took advantage of something called my Flight—yes, another trial, the second after the Rendering, once the heir comes of age. It's a solo undertaking for the purpose of advancing the family's prestige. It could involve anything from discovering an old ruin or a lost bit of history in some dusty archive to besting infamous pirates like my father did."

At least this Dracorte family tradition sounded better than beating a child in front of an audience. "And you chose Alaxak." I snorted, half on purpose to get the look that I got from him—that spark of light, the sharpness, instead of the dull heaviness in his eyes whenever he mentioned his father. "You must not have checked the weather report before scheduling your trip."

Nev maintained his wry look. "I wasn't coming for the weather. I needed to *do* something, something real, without trainers, instructors, bodyguards, or even my family hovering over me. My uncle's research has always fascinated me, especially once I realized how much it could benefit us. He supported my bid to come here, since I was one of the few he could trust wouldn't leak our plan to another family. My father wanted to send someone more experienced, in spite of that risk." He rested his forearms on his thighs and leaned toward me. "But I found you. You, your crew, this ship . . . this has been more real than I ever could have imagined."

Now the light in his eyes was so . . . earnest. It was almost like all *this,* somehow, was what he would want to be doing more than anything else.

I was surprised by how good it felt, to have him think of my life as worthwhile, and maybe not just because of any Shadow affinity, but because he *saw* me.

He didn't look away. "We can help each other, Qole, trust me. This isn't just about my family. I want your planet to thrive as well as ours. I want Arjan to stop being afraid. I want him, Telu, and you to live beyond twenty-five. I want you to have whatever it is *you* want when you close your eyes and let yourself dream. I want this as much as I've ever wanted anything for myself."

There was no stopping the sting in my eyes this time. My hope for all that was so tentative and desperate I didn't want to acknowledge it for fear of losing it.

Trust him. "I don't think I could actually put you out an airlock," I blurted. *Ancestors, so much for social graces.* I stumbled on, anyway. "I only thought about it for a second before you pulled that plasma X-Force-Thing on me, but I don't think I could have done it. I'm sorry that Eton and Arjan actually tried."

Nev gaped at me. *"I don't think I could actually put you out an airlock?"* He burst out laughing. "That might be the sweetest, most genuine thing anyone has ever said to me."

My face grew hotter than an engine block. He was definitely making fun of me, but I deserved it for saying yet another idiotic, unsophisticated thing. I scoffed and leaned away from him, about to stand. I had to sleep before I babbled anything else I'd regret.

But the second I moved, his hand caught mine.

"Wait, I'm serious," he said. "Don't go."

His touch, warm and solid, drove through me as it had on the destroyer, a solar flare bursting through his skin and radiating through my whole body. Something inside me rose to meet it, a mix of emotions so strong that I didn't know how to fight it off. I was drowning in them, tumbling like I was caught in an ocean storm: excitement, confusion, guilt, fear, and finally *wanting,* a want so potent, I almost reached for his face with my other hand.

But then the darkness flickered and swirled across my vision, like smoke and sparks. Since Nev was staring intently at *my* face, he saw it.

His eyes widened and he suddenly dropped my hand. "I'm sorry," he said, startled. "I shouldn't have ... I don't think I should ..."

All other feelings were devoured by a cavernous shame, hollowing my insides. The darkness was already gone, but the damage was done.

I was too different. I *was* disturbing.

"I'm sorry," Nev started, half-standing. "I didn't mean to ..."

I was sure he hadn't meant to, but he couldn't help it.

I spun around and left the bridge so fast I was nearly running. I didn't look back.

IX

MY EXTENSIVE TUTORING INCLUDED AN OVERVIEW OF THE NOTABLE DIsasters in the history files. To pick a few:

Systems Date 0: The Great Collapse—the portals that provided instantaneous travel to different systems and galaxies inexplicably implode. Civilization as it was known ends.

Systems Date 216: Belarius the First commissions the first test of his star drive design for faster-than-light travel. It, the ship, and the hundreds onboard are never seen again, but some postulate that it will be responsible for the singularity that ends existence.

Systems Date 345: An attempt to do a solo spacewalk between Thalius IV and Sonmara results in a collision with an unaware spacecraft, which in turn leads to a chain reaction that burns the atmosphere of the Sonmara moon to an uninhabitable crisp.
Systems Date 416: Prince Nevarian Dracorte attempts to cook.

That last one wasn't recorded yet, but looking at whatever I had doled out on various platters in the common room, I felt certain that it would be. I had been trying to re-create the same baked fruit paste that Eton had whipped together in moments the night before, but the congealing slabs in front of me looked more like primitive ancestors of that food. Which had then been fossilized. And then melted under the thrusters of a ship.

I had gone to bed unsure I'd be able to fall asleep again. Attempts on my life involving the airlock and Qole transforming into a super-being were becoming routine, and yet our conversation had been anything but. I still wasn't quite sure what had happened during the course of it . . . and especially not at the end.

I leaned over the infopad in the galley, trying to concentrate on the recipe and find out where I had gone wrong. "After the consistency probe reads point-four-five, disperse two tumbler-widths of Tantion spice and resume with the plasmic dehydrator. . . ."

My mind wasn't on it at all. I had grown up being taught the fine art of conversation and had only a tiny subsection of family and teachers with whom I could rely on for mentally and emotionally stimulating interactions. But last night—well, four hours ago—I had experienced an impromptu conversation that had been simultaneously fascinating, challenging, and . . . and what? Exciting, I supposed. Maybe it was because we were both so tired and our guards down, but I hadn't connected with another human being so genuinely in years. Or maybe ever.

And then I messed it up just like this free fall of a meal. I turned the infopad off in frustration. I wasn't sure how, but I'd made Qole angry enough to nearly black out again. Had it been taking her hand? I hadn't meant to grab it; it had just been automatic.

More and more of my interactions with Qole were just coming naturally. When I gave up trying to preempt her responses, quit planning out my own words and actions as if I were in a diplomatic conference or a war game simulation, then everything with her ceased being an actual battle. Touching her had felt like something completely new. I hadn't wanted to stop. And yet . . .

I wasn't sure how it had felt to her, but it obviously wasn't good. So when I woke up, the first thing I had done—outside of getting out of bed very stiffly—was try to find her and see if we could continue the conversation now that we were both in a different frame of mind.

I'd found her on the bridge with Basra, and it didn't take any training in social graces to see that she hadn't wanted to talk to me. She'd informed me that as a next-to-useless member of the crew who was part of the reason the chef was locked up, I could take over cooking duties and provide everyone with a hot meal.

I surveyed the meal I had created. It was undeniably hot, yes. I tried to remember if she had specified that it had to be edible as well.

Basra coughed discreetly at my elbow, materializing out

of nowhere in the disquieting manner that he had. "Feeling finished?"

I sighed and ran another eye over my creation. "In the words of my great-great-grandfather, I have yet to begin fighting."

Basra also eyed it. "Have you ever heard the saying, 'Only a royal would rage against a dying star'?" He changed the topic without preamble. "The *Kaitan* hasn't used its Belarius Drive in years, so we're almost out of antimatter. We need to stop and refuel, and it's a good chance for me to unload the Shadow catch we have in the hold before it degrades the canisters any further. The captain wants you to come with me."

"She does?" I busied myself scanning the infopad to cover my confusion. I wasn't sure why she'd be sending me off the ship with Basra. Of what use would I be? "Where?"

"We never unloaded the Shadow at the cannery, so we need to find someone who can buy *and* process Shadow canisters," Basra explained. "That limits our options somewhat. Fortunately, we're within a few parsecs of Nirmana. I can easily find a purchaser there."

"Is that wise?" I looked up from the infopad sharply. "That would require ducking out of the Dracorte system, and we just saw that the Treznor-Nirmana family is not what could be described as friendly. We also have the deadline of the conference that we're already cutting too close for comfort. Besides, I'll cover the value of the Shadow."

"Perhaps the captain feels that hedging her bets financially is a wise idea," Basra replied, "and the Shadow market is about to spike, so it's an opportune time to sell. Regardless, you can't manufacture fuel, we need repairs, and it's easier to be lost in a crowd than as a single ship at a remote station. This is one of the busiest trading ports in the galaxy. We'll be in and out."

I tapped my fingers on the table. He wasn't wrong on any

of those counts, but I felt safer knowing we were within the boundaries of what was considered my family's dominion, even if our control over it had grown a little more ... lax around the edges.

Something else nagged at my attention. "Wait, how do you know the Shadow market is about to spike?" That was news to me, and my family essentially dominated the Shadow market.

"I keep myself well informed," Basra said shortly.

He did spend half the day sequestered by himself at his comm station. But still . . .

"So do I, and I have access to the most priority-level feeds in the system." I hesitated, wondering how I should broach the question, especially since his face had gone blanker than usual. I went for the direct approach, hoping to catch him off balance. "What in the Unifier's good name are you doing on this ship, Basra? Shouldn't you, I don't know, be running a major corporation somewhere more important?"

He shrugged his slightly slouched shoulders, unflappable. "I don't suppose you'll accept my usual answer?"

"If it's acceptable to morons, then no." I smiled thinly. "I'm not a moron."

"I gathered. I also know that if I choose to ignore the question, you'll pry into my business in an irritating fashion." He sighed as if already irritated. "Maybe—I'm saying nothing for certain—this isn't my only means of employment. And perhaps this other position requires me to lay low."

He probably traded for very powerful people, in addition to trading for Qole on the side. He just used the *Kaitan* as his base of operations.

I dropped my voice. "None of this outside business you *might* do could jeopardize Qole's or the crew's safety, correct? Merely curious."

Basra smiled, but it didn't reach eyes that had become as cold as knives. I'd crossed a line. "I'm not going to dignify that with a response. Suffice it to say, I cover my trail better than anyone you will ever meet in your life . . . certainly far better than you, Your Highness." His face smoothed. "Now, will you be joining me on Nirmana?"

I wasn't going to gain another step in this line of inquiry, and I was somewhat satisfied, anyway. For now. "All right," I said agreeably. "When do we arrive?"

"Shortly after we eat your meal, I imagine." Basra glanced again at the dish, upon which a lingering bubble burst. He turned and left.

"No need to be so excited," I called after him.

"What did you *do*?" Eton stared, aghast, at the food I slipped through to him via a smaller airlock that would have normally been for transferring tools to anyone working in zero-g.

I pursed my lips thoughtfully. "You know, I'm not entirely sure where it all went wrong. Does the applicator normally make it bubble so much? I think that's where things started going downhill."

Eton grimaced. "You touched the applicator? Please tell me you cleaned it. If the fumes from this harden . . ." He took a dainty bite with the tips of his teeth, an entirely incongruous sight on the giant man. "Yech. Ick. Ugh, you followed the instructions, didn't you?"

"What do you mean? You're not supposed to?"

"Of course not, you idiot."

I blew out an exasperated breath. "You *did* train at the Academy, didn't you? It's nothing but reading old combat manuals and then having Devrak tell you to ignore them."

I couldn't help myself. I was on a roll after Basra, and this was an especially convenient time to prod Eton since there were shatterproof windows and doors separating me from his fists. Something about him jostled my memory, and I wanted to see if I could find out what it was.

His face turned to stone behind the window, and he glanced down at Arjan, where he lay curled on the floor of the airlock, presumably sleeping. "You don't know anything about me, you royal waste of space."

I lowered my voice. "I *do* know you're from Dracorva, or at least spent a fair amount of time in the Academy studying under Devrak. He's head of my family's security now, did you know that?"

"Good for him, whoever he is," Eton said tightly. He wasn't as good at lying as he was at navigating incomprehensible recipes, nor as good at schooling his own face as he was at punching people in theirs. There was a curious mix of respect and grimness in his eyes at the mention of Devrak's name.

I made my tone thoughtful. "Yes, but security is a tough business. Never know who you can trust."

Eton spoke through gritted teeth. "Oh, I know exactly who I can trust. And it's not royals." He shot me a molten glare. "You're far more of a danger to everyone on this ship than I could ever be."

At least he didn't respond to my insinuation with threats of death or dismemberment. And, most importantly, he was telling the truth this time—his past wouldn't be a problem. As with Basra, it was enough to satisfy my curiosity for the moment.

"It's all just a misunderstanding, I guess. So is this recipe, apparently," I added in a more normal tone. "If you could give me a clue as to where I went wrong . . ."

Eton looked torn for a moment, but the temptation was too great. He cleared his throat. "Sure, sure . . ." He suddenly leaned toward the glass and dropped his voice again. "But if you tell Qole any of this, I'll repeat a few things about your family that will never let her look at you in the same way again." He leaned back, smiling in satisfaction, and said, "Tantios cookbook, right?"

I nodded, feeling vaguely unsettled. My family wasn't perfect, of course, but they were principled, upheld the law, and always tried to live up to our ideals. What could he mean? Nothing, no doubt. He was just trying to use leverage he didn't have against what I *did* have. It was leverage that he'd given me, because he'd practically admitted in his own words that I was right about where he was from, and that he didn't want anyone else to know.

"You can't follow any of the directions in the Tantios cookbooks; their measurements are all . . ." Eton stopped midsentence, his face growing sober as he looked over my shoulder.

Qole was there, looking calm and serious. "No, you're supposed to follow instructions. Or, how about orders? What do you say, Eton?"

He didn't answer at first, but Arjan, instantly awoken by the sound of her voice, popped up beside him. "Qole, I'm so sorry. Look—"

"Save it. We're about to land on Nirmana to fuel up and get some repairs done, and I need both of you to make yourselves useful. You get one more chance to stay on the ship, if you want it. Which means no arguing, no fighting, and nothing but nodding your head and saying *yes, Captain* and *no, Captain.*"

Arjan nodded. "Got it. Yes, Captain."

"And you, Eton?"

The man took a deep breath. "Yes, Captain, I understand."

Qole hit the big red button next to the airlock door and it hissed open. I flinched.

"Well, great." She put her hands on her hips. "All I have to do to get you two thick skulls to listen is throw you around and put you in a cell, I guess. Now that we're a crew again, all of you shake hands."

I grimaced. Eton's handshaking hurt, and would likely *especially* hurt now. Not so great timing on our chat, after all. "Must we? I feel very at peace with everyone already." Qole gave me a look, and I reached out. "Okay, okay."

Eton hesitated, glanced at Qole, and then took it. To my surprise, he didn't crush it. But he did hold on to it for a moment longer than necessary and look me in the eyes. I understood as clearly as though he had spoken: one sign of ill intent on my part, and he'd happily try to kill me again, whatever the consequences.

Arjan shook my hand, but I couldn't tell what he was thinking. The entire experience seemed to have hit him the hardest; Qole and this ship were nearly all that he cared about in life. I doubted she'd ever threatened to take it away from him before.

Qole nodded, satisfied. "Good. Remember, I don't need to work with people who can't voice opinions, but there's a difference between sharing your thoughts and not following orders. I know you don't trust him, but if you're going to be on this ship, it's me you have to trust. Now, you"—she pointed at me—"are going with Basra to sell our Shadow and make sure he doesn't get mugged in the process. I want those canisters out of my hold. You two"—she jerked a thumb over her shoulder—"get cleaned up and ready to get the *Kaitan* fueled and shipshape. We don't have much time, and we have to make this quick."

A series of suggestions and considerations rang out briefly, until Qole raised both eyebrows and crossed her arms. I shut my mouth along with the rest.

———

A few hours later I was wearing the same disguise I had used on Alaxak, and Basra and I were on our way. The landing bay the harbormaster had assigned us was at the top of a roughly eight-hundred-foot tower composed almost entirely of docking bays and a web of walkways all in dangerous proximity.

"Do you think Qole is just trying to get me away from Eton?" I asked Basra as we descended one of the gangplanks leading from where the *Kaitan* had landed. She had reverted to one hundred percent captain mode, all signs of the personable girl I'd talked to the night before gone. I couldn't deny that I found that interesting in its own right, but I couldn't stop thinking about our conversation.

Why had I taken her hand and ruined everything?

"Maybe. Or maybe she knows that making these transactions carries its own set of risks." Basra's reply was entirely unsatisfactory. Then again, the only one I would have properly appreciated would have been, *Absolutely, Nev, because you inspire such terror in him. And also, there is no way she's trying to avoid you, in case you were wondering. Here, have a refreshing beverage.*

Instead, he glanced at me again, and then to the bag I carried slung over my shoulder. "Do you think it's wise to carry your blade with you? If someone saw it, they would recognize it and ask uncomfortable questions."

I shook my head. "Once you earn a Disruption Blade, you try to keep it with you at all times, and I've been failing enough at that. Besides, I think I've shown I can keep it secret.

Why in the systems are we walking on these instead of taking a turbolift?" I asked, changing the topic.

Basra was leading me down the gangplanks that connected to an increasingly complex series of catwalks. Low fencing and solid plate flooring gave way to woven rope and grating; it would have been dizzying at this height, but the city below felt too abstract to register. It was a precarious and crowded system as we danced around groups of workers carrying equipment and supplies or just loitering on corners and talking.

"Most of the harbors on the outskirts of the city are old and cheap, which also makes them the most crowded. The turbolifts are only used at certain points of the day to transport heavy cargo in order to prevent them from breaking down. Either that," Basra amended, "or they are already broken down. If you don't mind attracting attention you can bribe your way on, but I think we can manage."

I glanced around at the hive of activity. Other towers, their edges like jagged combs from all the docking bays, were constantly disgorging a wide variety of smaller freight ships. "Do you know this all from a previous life? The *Kaitan* couldn't possibly have gotten this far before now."

"I grew up here," Basra said, ushering me through a doorway that looked identical to the others. "Tell me, how did a prince of the Dracorte family, the heir no less, manage to land in the outskirts of the system by himself without an army of bodyguards?"

I paused, not due to an unwillingness to talk, but because of the vista that had just opened up in front of us. My view from the landing pad had been obscured by the *Kaitan* before Basra had whisked us on our way, but now I had an unobstructed perspective of Ranta, the largest city on Nirmana.

I had been to Ranta before. The Nirmana family, renowned

for their skill at all things financial—stock markets, banking systems, secure transaction concepts—had spent a measure of their immeasurable wealth making Ranta one of the most beautiful cities in all the systems . . . along with outright buying the planet itself and renaming it after their family. Nestled in a rain forest at the foothills of mountains that had remained largely untouched by drones, the city was a wonder of architecture, learning, and art. In my studies, I had visited their Econom Academy on multiple occasions to listen to lectures or participate in debates.

In all my visits, I had never seen the outer city.

Ranta itself was surrounded by a thick wall of carefully tended gardens. But just outside those gardens lived everyone else who wasn't wealthy enough to dwell in the city proper. While Ranta was white and gleaming, the outer city was dull red from rust and the way the light caught a dusty haze. Industrial pipes belched fire and smoke, and jagged apartment blocks rose impossibly high out of an endless sea of tiny housing. It looked as though a giant child had tipped a bag of toy houses out into a pile on the floor, kicked them around, and left.

In the Nirmana culture, economic worth was the ultimate value, and they supposedly believed that even the poorest citizens could become wealthy through hard work. But looking out over the rabble in front of me, I doubted every one of these people had been given the same opportunity as the royal progeny with whom I had studied.

However the Nirmanas chose to govern their own planet should have been none of my business, but lately it was becoming mine. It was still the biggest news in recent history that the Nirmanas, the most economically powerful family, had entered into a marriage alliance with the Treznors, the most militarily powerful family. Now Treznor-Nirmana was one of the most powerful royal families in the systems, and they were obviously angling to place themselves higher on the list, at my family's expense—and perhaps to more than just the detriment of my family. Who knew what would happen to citizens in the Dracorte system if the two most morally bankrupt families took our place near the top of the food chain? It depressed me to see all the poverty in Ranta, and frightened me to think of what the Treznor-Nirmanas might do with more power in places like Alaxak.

It also made me all the more determined to keep that from happening.

"So this is home to you?" I asked.

Basra shook his head. "No, I was born here. You didn't answer my question." He motioned to me and we headed down another set of ramps that descended toward ground level. "How did you get to Alaxak alone?"

Taking all this in, I'd entirely forgotten he'd asked. "Right, my apologies. Qole asked as well, and the answer to both of you is: not easily. Not everyone in my family sees the potential in Alaxak that I do. It isn't the only planet near sources of Shadow. We couldn't get results from emissaries we sent, and no one seemed eager to return since it was across the system. Instead of leaving it alone, or hiring mercenaries who would do a less ... delicate ... job, I volunteered under the terms of my Dracorte Flight."

He cocked his head at me. "But why?"

"For all the reasons I gave everyone on the ship." I shrugged. "And perhaps because it took me so very far from home. What about you? What made you leave here?"

"Circumstances," Basra said vaguely, which irritated me after I'd given him such an honest answer. But there wasn't time to press him. We had reached ground level and had arrived at what was evidently the singular turbolift servicing our tower. A skinny man in a dirty blue uniform, cradling an infopad, sat on a rickety office chair next to the turbolift doors. He looked entirely uninterested in us, his infopad, the turbolift, or anything else, for that matter. In contrast, the other character by the doors seemed too interested in everything. Short, squat, and with a blond buzz cut, he was dressed in a dirty old suit that had fit him once long ago. His small, deep-set eyes were bright and clever, and I didn't like how he scanned me up and down at all.

"Whaddya want?" the man in the blue uniform drawled. "Have a shipment?"

"Yes, thank you." Basra ignored the other seedy gentleman, and I pretended to study the surrounding skyline while keeping an eye on everyone. "We'll be lowering twenty-one pallets a little later this afternoon. What times does the lift run?"

"Every two hours. What's the weight and content of your goods?"

"Six-five thousand four hundred units, Shadow."

I didn't know how often Shadow made its way through here, but the uniformed man didn't even blink. "Very good. You're on the list, and the lift will stop at your landing pad first. Thanks."

The other gentleman more than made up for his disinterest. "Shadow, is it? That's quite a cargo, especially right now." He pointed at a dusty feed of the planet's financial station.

We all paused to listen as an overly powdered announcer quoted the current headlines:

Hersius Kartolus has begun purchasing a vast amount of commodities from Dracorte Industries, particularly Shadow. This bold

move has driven the price sky-high in a play that analysts are calling
both daring and foolish. . . .

"See?" the blond buzz cut said.

Indeed. I managed not to shoot Basra an incredulous look.
Not only had he gotten the jump on financial news regarding
my own family but also news originating from Hersius Kartolus, one of the wealthiest and most secretive people in the galaxy . . . and a *significant* investor in my family's business, second
only to us ourselves and Treznor-Nirmana. No one saw the
elusive fellow often, though I recalled meeting a white-haired,
wiry gentleman at a banquet long ago.

Could Basra *possibly* be working for Hersius on the side?
That would explain why he had to lay low, but . . . Basra was
good, but that would be bordering on utter financial genius.

Blond buzz cut looked us over for the twentieth time.
"Where are you coming from?"

"Just traded with some fishermen from Alaxak." Basra
smiled politely. "Now, if you'll excuse us."

We headed off down the street, and I could feel the man's
eyes on my back.

"Why did you mention Shadow?" I hissed. "Or Alaxak?
They'll be dying of curiosity."

"Shadow isn't as uncommon here as you think, and avoid-
ance breeds curiosity," Basra explained. "They can trace the
ship number as being registered in Alaxak regardless, since
Qole does things legally. Hiding its origin would be inviting
scrutiny."

I was uncomfortably reminded of how vulnerable our position was here. The sooner we were gone, the better.

———

Basra led me with the complete assurance of familiarity. We wound our way through narrow streets that overwhelmed me with life. If I had been thinking smugly on the failed economic policies that had led to the outer city forming, I hadn't been prepared for the sheer excitement and variety that was thrust at us at every step. Merchants hawked their wares, street performers hawked their acts, people hawked themselves, and children tugged at us, alternately attempting to beg or to sharpen their pickpocketing skills.

My thoughts were interrupted by Basra ducking into a small door with a sign that simply said *Exotic Matters—material and theoretical, available here.*

After a brief conversation with the young, dead-eyed man behind the counter, we were escorted to a back office. It was empty except for slatted windows, a temperature control unit that kept it so cold fog was forming on the windows, and a corpulent woman sitting on an office chair that looked like it was just about ready to surrender.

"Basra, Basra, Basra, you beautiful creature, you. I never thought I'd see you again when I'd heard you left."

"Mother Orr, the pleasure is mutual," Basra murmured, pulling up another rickety chair and settling down in it. I remained standing, arms crossed. The entire situation was disquieting. I couldn't imagine conducting business of any importance in an office that would have looked abandoned if it weren't inhabited by someone who seemed merely unable to leave. On top of that, even in the chill air, I was still sweating profusely, as the city's temperature had sunk into me. I was entirely overdressed.

"Hm, feeling more masculine today, are we, lassie? Looks good on you. And who is this?" "Mother Orr" eyed me. Her expression seemed devoid of interest, but her scrutiny was thorough. "Very tasty. Is he yours?" She chortled to herself.

Basra ignored almost all of what she said, which I was realizing was one of his strengths. "I recently made an advantageous trade for a shipment of Shadow from a captain who was eager to divest. Because you were always my favorite, I thought of you first."

"Favorite? You had favorites?" She snorted. "Let me tell you something, my lass, when I processed the first years at Number One's recruitment complex, I wasn't anyone's favorite. *Oh no, big ol' mean Mother Orr, am I right? Just stomping around giving us hell. Boo-hoo, we're all indentured servants.* Well"—she threw her hands up to encompass him—"just look at you now. Peddling Shadow and cavorting with hot, young, lithe ... men." She looked me up and down again and grinned. "Let me tell you, sonny, you could make me ... ahem, *yourself* a pretty penny."

It was possible a corner of my eyelid twitched from a profound desire to raise my eyebrows. Everyone in the systems knew of the Big Two—ancient towers in Ranta that trained accountants from childhood. Parents indentured their children, who then had to purchase their freedom at exorbitant rates. Only if you were good with finances did you get out. *Very* good. And the Number One tower provided only the best training to the most skilled ... who consequently had a much higher sum to work off. The thought of a young Basra in such an environment, contending with this creature who was looking at me like a piece of meat at the market, made me even more uncomfortable.

But Number One was definitely the type of place to spit out a financial genius. One that would drop right into the eagerly waiting hands of rabid recruiters. Maybe Hersius Kartolus *had* somehow snatched up Basra.

"True, it's not just my fondness that brought me to you," Basra responded, ignoring roughly half of what she'd said this time. "My previous buyer and I had a disagreement, and I've found myself wanting to sell to another party. I'm in something of a hurry, so I was willing to go to someone who I knew wouldn't give me as high a price."

"Oh? What price was this 'other buyer' offering you?" Mother Orr narrowed her eyes. "Does this 'other buyer' have a name, or did you just invent them?"

"I'd rather not name the sum," he said, inclining his head, "as they would want me to be discreet. Suffice it to say, I'm aware that you possess fewer means and greater shrewdness."

"Fewer means?" She glared. "Let me tell you, lassie, going up the ranks as quickly as you did gave you an attitude I'm not sure I approve of." She yanked open a drawer, withdrew a dirty rag, and wiped her sweating brow. Then she used that to wipe down the condensation on her infopad, which she held up to her face closely, finger hovering over the screen. "But you're damned right you'll profit less from me. Fair but harsh, that's my motto. You'll get what you deserve. I'm still looking out for my students, you know."

Basra steepled his fingers. "I'll take fifty percent over market price."

She guffawed. "You will, will you? How about I give you fifty percent *off* the market price?"

"No. I'm not interested in losing my shirt, although I'm willing to lose some. Don't forget, I'm delivering this to you with no third party—you would normally need to buy from a wholesaler. You would be paying market price plus ten percent no matter what you do."

"Fine, then that's what I'll give you," she retorted.

He remained silent, eyes fixed on her. She looked from him to me and back again. I stared at both of them, fascinated;

I had the strange feeling they were conducting a mental argument with one another, both understanding what the other would say next.

"All right. I'll give you fifteen percent," she said.

Basra sighed and held out his hand, palm up. "Agreed, but you pick it up from our landing pad."

Mother Orr slapped his open hand. "It's a deal. If the Shadow market weren't on the rise right now, I'd have just kicked you out on the street."

He smiled. "I know. A pleasure, as always."

"Mmm-hmm. You can bring in arm candy anytime you like, Basra. Oh, and the person you purchased this from—were they from that ice planet? Alaxak?"

"They were," he said. "Why?"

"There's a bounty for any of the crazies from that planet, if they've got Shadow poisoning. Any of them, but especially this particular one." She held up her infopad.

My heart went still in my chest, and I fought to keep any expression from my face. Fortunately, she was focused on Basra, who of course displayed nothing whatsoever.

If only the infopad had been as blank. It glowed with a computationally generated image of Qole.

———

"So, that's bad," I muttered as we exited the building. "The ransom isn't through any official channels, nor is it likely traceable to Treznor-Nirmana, but still, I thought they would have kept quieter about their interest in her in order to avoid revealing their hand too soon. This is escalating much more quickly than I'd anticipated."

"It seems to be getting worse," Basra responded in a low voice. "Keep walking down the street and point out something interesting to me, bearing twenty-two five."

I scanned the street to my northeast and pretended to point to a sign advertising a house of ill repute. What could I say, it was all that was available. As I did, I noticed the blond buzz cut from the corner of my eye, bobbing along slightly behind us on the opposite street.

I was roasting in the humidity of the streets, but I still shivered. For him to follow us like that, in this crowd, meant he was probably a bounty hunter, and a good one. And he'd managed to identify our ship as a possible match. There was a reason we'd slipped in among hundreds and docked at the highest point on the most distant, congested tower.

Basra pretended to laugh. "When that vehicle passes," he said with exaggerated amusement, "follow me down the alley to the right."

He must have been thinking what I was. If we could lose the fellow, then perhaps we could make it back to the ship and escape before any other bounty hunters knew to swarm. A large cargo vessel, rusting and paint peeling, rumbled down the street toward us. I was glad of the size and racket, which would obscure us from our follower.

The second it began to pass us, Basra sprinted for the end of the alley, with me right behind him. He took a series of turns I never could have remembered, and then stopped in the middle of an intersection, scanning up and down the street. I couldn't see anything other than garbage and a passed-out vagrant, but they seemed to serve as sufficient markers, as we took off pell-mell again. The next thing I knew, we were climbing a rickety ladder up the side of a deserted and crumbling building. Some rungs had rusted out altogether, but we made it to the top.

"Oh boy, now what?" I wheezed. At least he was breathing somewhat heavily as well.

He pointed toward the docking bays in the distance. "We can head over the rooftops back to the ship." His other hand activated the comm on his ear, which, now that I noticed, was far nicer than anything the rest of the crew sported. "*Kaitan*, Basra."

"Basra, Qole. Find a buyer?"

"Yes, but we've attracted attention. We're taking a different route back, and might be delayed. Tell Eton to be on the lookout for company."

There was a pause on the other end, but then Qole's voice came back, calm and steady. "Affirmative. Stay safe, and let us know if you need any assistance. We'll be ready for takeoff when you get here."

Basra turned to me. "Follow me, and do exactly as I do."

I tried my best, while Basra scrambled across boards, climbed old ladders, jumped between adjacent shacks, and scaled walls with cleverly chiseled footholds. He either had supreme faith in my abilities or didn't care what happened to me.

It took a while, but it finally began to dawn on me, as we picked our way through the sunset-drenched rooftops, that I was viewing yet a third ecosystem of the city. Here, things were quieter, and anyone we met left us to ourselves, as we did to them. These were the pathways of the people who had to stay out of sight and out of mind, people with no power. Basra was ignored, but anytime someone caught sight of me they shrank out of sight as quickly as possible. I had known my traveling clothes were a bit too sharp for rustic communities, but here I apparently reeked of wealth. It was a level of disparity I was not used to.

And Basra must have come from it, to know it and fit

in so well. Maybe his parents had indentured him to the Big Two because they couldn't afford the extra mouth to feed. Or maybe Basra didn't have parents, and he'd indentured himself.

In any case, Basra, in spite of his unique appearance, knew how to blend in and lay low. Though perhaps he now stayed for other reasons, this was no doubt why he had chosen Alaxak and the *Kaitan* at the start, especially if he was secretly working for someone powerful. It was the last place somebody would think to look for anyone or anything of significance.

Well, until now.

Basra bribed the turbolift operators for our final ascent, something I was grateful for. Speed was more important than stealth at this point. We arrived at the landing pad without incident—outside of my general anxiety and profuse sweating. Eton met us, face grim, with a snub-nosed and very polished photon gun cradled in one hand. It wasn't anything like the XR-25 Molten-Force, but it was well taken care of and would still do the job of punching a sizzling hole through someone's chest.

"It took you long enough," he said. "Come on, get yourselves onboard."

"Shadow?" Basra asked.

"Payment received and cargo unloaded," Qole informed us, walking down the ramp. "Just waiting on you. It's been quiet up here, no chatter or snoopers, so let's leave while the leaving is good."

Eton swore, spying over the side of the landing pad with a set of vision-amps. "There's a fellow in a suit leading six goons into the turbolift on ground level. Are those your friends?"

I peered down. It was too far down to see anything but indistinct shapes, but I was sure I spotted a tiny blond head disappearing into the building beneath us. "If there's a blond crew cut, yes."

Eton nodded and raised an arm to usher Basra and me up the *Kaitan*'s ramp, but I ducked under, turning away.

Eton swore. "What are you doing? We've got a minute tops before they're up here. Get on the damn ship!" He barked at me again when he saw me run for the turbolift doors. "The controls up here don't even work!"

I didn't answer. Instead, I reached into my bag and felt the familiar shape of the sheath that contained my blade. My thumb easily found the release point, and the case popped open, feeding the sword into my hand.

Disruption Blades weren't just called that because they cut through energy shields. Any sword would be one, otherwise. They were Disruption Blades, because when you activated a switch in the hilt, they would output an energy field that could destroy shields, communication waves, or anything electronic in close contact with the weapon.

A flip of my thumb, and blue light shot up the middle of my blade as I ran toward the turbolift door. The light blinked more rapidly as the lift drew nearer, and I drove the point of the sword into the turbolift controls. Sparks arced in a miniature lightning storm, scoring the metal around it and leaving the smell of burned ozone. The lights above the door dimmed, brightened, and then went out.

I yanked out my blade and ran back to the ship, past a stunned Eton, snagging my bag as I went. It felt good to be useful again.

X

QOLE

I WAS TOO FOCUSED ON TAKING OFF AND TOO DEAFENED BY THE ROAR of the engines as we left the planet's atmosphere to notice him coming up behind me. But then I felt the pressure of a hand on the back of my captain's chair. I wasn't sure if I knew it was him, or hoped it was, or dreaded it. A quick glance through the floor's metal grating to the level below told me it wasn't Telu or Basra—they were both at their stations. And Arjan and Eton were still too shamefaced to approach me with anything less than an emergency.

I missed the days of my uncomplicated crew family. Nev was something else. He was too complicated. I felt good around him, and I hated myself around him. It burned, practically, the two pulls. Like liftoff, the tug-of-war between gravity and the thrusters, with me squashed in between, with his stupid smile and his damned eyes.

And then, when I'd let myself get too close to him, *my* eyes had made everything worse.

Without giving him the chance to speak first, I said, "Please go inform Telu of how we should approach Luvos so she can set our precise coordinates once I activate the Belarius Drive."

"I already did," he said. "Qole—"

"I don't have time for any—"

"I know. And by all means, lay on the speed until we reach a safe range to engage the drive. But we've got some time yet. You need to see this, and I wanted it to be me who showed you."

Nev leaned over my shoulder before I could object, coming uncomfortably close to touching me as he tapped at an infopad plugged into its stand on the dash. He was no longer wearing his jacket, just a fitted black undershirt. That wouldn't last once the chill of space set in. Good thing, too. I tried to lean back, tried to quiet my pulse, tried hard to hate the muscles in his forearms. Instead, I found myself noticing that he smelled of sweat from Ranta's heat, and something else, something indefinably *him*.

I did hate knowing how he smelled. Probably because I liked how he smelled.

All my anger and embarrassment was replaced by shock, though, when my face appeared on the infopad screen. "Why . . . ?" I swallowed. "Why is there a very large sum of money listed under my picture?" It wasn't a picture, but a three-dimensional composite, likely from the video footage they'd recorded of me on the destroyer.

. . . A destroyer belonging to the Treznor-Nirmana family,

who were, according to Basra, now richer than the Dracortes. The family that wanted to surpass the Dracortes in every way. The family whose planet we'd just left.

I knew the answer to my own question before I'd finished asking it.

The sum listed under my picture wasn't enough to buy a moon or anything, but several ships at least. Gamut's villagers—hell, my own *kin*—would probably turn me over for that much money. Not Arjan, so maybe it was good he was the only kin I had left.

Nev seemed to understand this, because he said, in his softer tone, "I'm sorry." That was why he was apologetic—not for something as stupid as recoiling at the sight of my Shadow-clouded eyes, like I'd been hoping. "I just want you to know that my family isn't behind this. They only wish to protect you—"

"And their interests," I added, but my voice was empty of any anger. I was too stunned to even remind him that the Dracortes were the reason I was in this situation in the first place. Their attention was what had drawn everyone else's.

"And those," he conceded. "Which is why they wouldn't want to broadcast your unique importance to every last system like this. As unfortunate as it may be, my family citadel in Dracorva is truly the only place in the galaxy you'll be safe now. I wouldn't even trust your safety to anywhere else on Luvos."

His words wrapped around me like his arms couldn't. I'd been captain of the *Kaitan* since I was fourteen. Taking care of our little crew for so long. And every single one of them had my back, but this was the first time I'd been powerless to protect them myself. Even if he only wanted our safety for *his* family's sake, I held still in that embrace for a moment, until he spoke again.

"I just wanted to emphasize this," he continued, "in case this caused any second thou—"

The rest of what he'd been about to say was drowned out by the now-familiar whoop of the weapons lock alarm.

"Blast it all," Nev finished.

I'd already launched bolt upright, scanning the feeds. "One ship locked on . . . not a destroyer, at least, but a trade vessel of some kind—"

"A weaponized Orbit freighter, retrofitted for privateering," he said, peering over my shoulder. "Obvious bounty hunters."

"And two more following."

"Posting a ransom through discreet channels is one thing, but at least Treznor-Nirmana isn't moving more openly, yet." He was trying to sound reassuring.

"A Treznor destroyer is taking off from the planet now, too," Basra added from below, several comms held to his ears at once. "How's that for open?"

Nev and I exchanged grim glances. Unlike the smaller ships, the destroyer would be able to employ its tractor beam to keep us from escaping.

Arjan burst onto the bridge. This constituted enough of an emergency, I supposed, to risk my presence. "Eton's already headed for the turret," he said.

"It won't be enough," I muttered. "They're better equipped than we are, and gaining on us. We might be able to reach a safe distance to engage the Belarius Drive ahead of the destroyer, but not these three. They'll catch us and disable us."

It seemed inevitable. We couldn't outrun them, and we couldn't activate the drive right now; we were too close to a planetary body, and we'd risk tearing holes in space-time where they shouldn't be torn. Or, as far as I understood it, we'd die, and maybe take a lot of people with us.

Nev grimaced. "They'll want to secure their bounty before anyone working for the Treznor-Nirmanas gets here. You're going full speed," he said, with only the hint of a question. At least he didn't take me for a total idiot. "How long until we're at the distance we can engage?"

"Five minutes."

"We won't make it," Arjan said. It had only taken him the barest glimpse at the screens over my *other* shoulder to come to such an accurate conclusion—proof that it was by his choice alone that I sat in this chair instead of him.

For half a second, I almost wished he were in my place. Then I realized how cruel that was as the terror filled me like freezing water, seizing up my lungs. There was no way Arjan could take this, not when I barely could.

Or so I thought until he straightened, glanced through the floor at Basra, and said, "Qole, I need to do something, and you have to let me." It wasn't a request, more a statement of fact.

"Do what?" I asked.

He faced Nev and his jaw flexed with tension. "You promise that you will cover any damages to this ship?"

"Presuming we survive capture, torture, and possible explosive dismemberment, then yes," Nev said, summoning his dry humor from somewhere, even at a time like this. I had to hold in a hysterical laugh.

"Good. I have an idea . . . but I'm going to need our net." Before I could ask what in the systems he was going to do with it, he clapped Nev on the shoulder. "If I don't make it back for whatever reason, I just . . . Please, take care of my sister."

And then he was off the bridge before I could argue. Nev looked oddly winded, as if Arjan had punched him in the stomach instead.

Basra called after Arjan without getting a response, and there was something in his voice I'd never heard before, though I'd heard it in all of ours at one time or another.

It sounded a little like fear.

———

The glinting triangle of the skiff jetted out of its small docking bay in the upper midships of the *Kaitan* a minute later. The cables of the mag-field net whipped out behind it, unspooling along the boom. I wasn't entirely sure what Arjan was planning, but I had a hunch.

I commed him. "Arjan, don't tell me you're going to do what I think—"

"Be ready to cut loose on your end of the net as soon as I say."

"Those ships aren't Shadow, Arjan! They're a lot more solid—"

"And therefore *way* easier to catch," he said with a hint of a smirk in his voice.

"It's too dangerous!"

"Less dangerous than a Shadow run, probably." He paused. "And far less dangerous than doing nothing."

"Shadow doesn't shoot plasma rockets," Nev said behind me.

As if triggered by his ominous words, a flare went up from the closest ship, leaving a bright arc of white across the blackness.

Telu's voice hissed both from below me and through the comm speaker. "Sorry, Cap, I was trying to get their weapons offline, but they're locked down tight, and they have hackers of their own. They're trying to get on the comm channel we have open to Arjan, and it's all I can do to keep them out and it open."

Eton's voice piped through the comm at nearly a shout. "Should I respond? The mass driver won't be much against their energy weapons, but I have another little something I could always go get ..."

He had a "little something" on board that would be more effective against ships than the mass driver? What the hell was Eton hoarding on the *Kaitan*? I almost didn't want to know.

Before I could ask, Arjan said, "Hold." The skiff flew in a glinting streak straight for the three ships, their plasma rocket heading out to meet him. "I'll draw their fire."

"Arjan, are you kidding me? If they don't blow you up first, that destroyer will be right behind them!"

"Just trust me."

I didn't have many other options, especially now that Arjan was out in the skiff and I couldn't activate the drive and leave him behind. Not that we would make it far enough to engage it in the first place with the other two ships entering firing range.

Just before the first plasma rocket hit Arjan head-on, the skiff barrel-rolled in an insane blur. The rocket missed, glanced off the twisted cables behind him, and exploded harmlessly off to one side. Arjan leveled out, but only for a half second. He dove under the ships, already rolling back the other way, both to dodge the lightning storm of fire now raining down on him and to straighten out the cables. He managed to keep track of all his turns and soar up and around the ships in a dizzying arc.

Arjan's voice came calmly over the comm, even though his brain should have been scrambled from all that spinning. "Brace yourselves."

Trust, I thought, then threw our extra stabilizing thrusters on full blast.

"Engage the mag-field."

I hit the button, and the dark space between the net's cables crackled to glowing, radiant life.

We all felt it the moment the net caught the ships' undersides. The *Kaitan* lurched and shuddered. If the skiff's arc had been violent before, now Arjan was like a missile on the end of a string as he wrapped the net around our pursuers. The meteor shower of actual missiles cutting the sky behind him could no longer come close to catching up to him. The problem was, with the cables winding around the ships and losing length, Arjan was flinging himself directly into them.

"Arjan!" I cried.

"Cut loose in three, two, one . . . *now!*"

I smashed that button. The cables popped free of the *Kaitan,* rippling outward from the broken tension. It gave him enough slack to close the loop, encircling the bounty hunters' ships in a golden magnetic field. He even cinched it tighter, crunching them closer together.

Just before he would have careened into them, Arjan cut the cables loose on his end and shot off into space.

Two of the ships began firing at each other to get free, and the other was caught between them. Their thrusters burned into each other's hulls. One of them would probably explode before too long, but I didn't want to stick around for the show.

The sleek destroyer, huge and pale as a moon, was rising behind them.

I turned off the stabilizers and, as much as I didn't want to, I eased off the throttle too, just for a moment. "Arjan, get back to the ship, now!"

"Already there," he said a second later.

The vibration of the opening bay doors hummed against my feet. I barely waited for them to close before I slammed the forward thrusters into full throttle. My back smashed into the seat, and Nev would have gone rolling if he hadn't seized onto my chair.

"Hold on," I said unnecessarily. "We have thirty seconds before I can engage the drive."

Eton, Basra, and Telu all swore simultaneously.

"What?" But it only took a moment's glance at my feeds to know.

A white, crackling ring of energy was rippling out from the destroyer. As it hit the three ships jumbled together, all their lights went dead and the net went haywire, arcing and sparking like a magnetic storm. Because that was exactly what it was.

It was an electromagnetic pulse, bigger and faster than any I'd ever seen. Not that I'd seen that many. In any case, it was tumbling and crashing toward our ship like a tidal wave on the ocean or an avalanche down a mountain—much, *much* faster than we were moving.

"That will disable us," Nev said, his voice breathless. "We're out of range of the tractor beam, but this is even worse. I can't believe they're using *that* on us. Go, go!"

"I'm going as fast as I can!" I practically shouted in his face.

"Don't you have a turbo you can engage, or something?"

"This isn't a damned racing ship! The only form of blasted *turbo* we have is called a Belarius Drive, and I'm going to engage it in—"

Telu shrieked, "Stop-fighting-and-engage-it-then-because-it's-almost-on-us!"

She was right. The wave had nearly overtaken the *Kaitan*, lapping at the glowing jets of our thrusters. This was a safe enough distance. Any safer, and we would be done.

Undeniably abusing my equipment, I hammered on the button.

For a moment, everything seemed to freeze. I thought maybe the pulse had caught us, and the *Kaitan* was dead in the water. But it was only that I wasn't yet used to activating the drive.

One second, there were stars, fixed in space, and the next they were bleeding by the viewport like drops of liquid light. After a few more seconds, we might as well have been on the other side of the galaxy from the destroyer, we were so far away. Finding us would have been like trying to pinpoint a twinkle in the night sky.

I collapsed into my chair. Nev flopped over the back of it. For a little while, I didn't care that our heads were only inches apart as we breathed.

"Well," Nev said, practically in my ear. "That was fun."

I couldn't help it; a laugh tore out of me. We met each other's eyes in surprise—Great Collapse, the silver-gray was so *bright* this close—but before I could say anything, Arjan and Eton burst onto the bridge, followed by Telu and Basra. I was barely on my feet before Arjan threw himself at me, almost toppling me with his hug. Before Basra could object, Arjan snatched his coat and dragged him into his arms too, going so far as to plant a kiss on his shocked face.

For a second, the three of us froze, even Arjan, but the kiss was lost in the chaos when Telu, as small as she was, somehow wrapped herself around all of us—including Eton, who nearly crushed my ribs with one of his own hugs. And then we were laughing and shouting and jumping up and down.

At first, Nev stood off to the side, but then Telu seized his wrist and yanked him between the two of us. We both stiffened for a second, but then his silver gaze locked onto mine again, and both of his arms enveloped me, and behind me, Arjan. In the tangle of limbs, Nev's hip pressed against mine, and one of his hands found the small of my back. I closed my eyes as everyone whooped and jostled, and let their euphoria wash over me. My family. And Nev.

I'd sworn I'd never touch him again, but, well, that was before we'd all almost been, in his wry words, captured, tortured, and maybe explosively dismembered.

Another laugh flew out of me, and I tossed an arm around his shoulder, the other still around Arjan.

This. This was what I would do anything to protect. This was why I was risking everything to go to Dracorva. And if the man standing next to me, a certain Nevarian Dracorte, had something to do with it, in more ways than one . . . so be it.

———

Several days of smooth, faster-than-light flying later, the Belarius Drive deactivated itself at the coordinates Nev had supplied, and I got my first view of Luvos. It took my breath away. Bright greens and blues twined the surface of the planet—sparkling oceans and lush landmasses—and even from here I could see the lines of white and gray, fractaling out like frost in discernible but complex patterns.

"Cities," Nev said next to me, his eyes alight with the excitement of being home. Unfathomably *massive* cities, he meant, but ones that looked incredibly organized and beautiful even from space. He pointed. "There's Dracorva . . ."

And then we saw the line of destroyers. They took my breath away too, if not in the same way. It didn't help that they were all of Treznor make. The Dracortes couldn't help it,

I supposed, since they were resource barons, not war-machine-manufacturing barons. Treznor made the best, and of course the Dracortes would have the best.

It still wasn't a pleasant sight.

"Quite the welcome wagon," Telu said, sounding nervous. I couldn't blame her. "I knew they'd be expecting us, Nev, but what exactly did you tell them?"

Nev had commed home and let them know he would be arriving with me on the *Kaitan,* isolating himself for a couple of hours to talk to his father and uncle. I was amazed the ship's QUIN still functioned—I hadn't exactly been talking to anyone across the system recently, and I doubted my father ever had. It was eerie to hear the smooth voice of the AI program help direct Nev's comm, or maybe it was just strange to know a vessel so well and to have never heard it speak. Nev hadn't used it before because he said he'd needed to keep a low profile—*hah*—and to do all this on his own because of the Dracorte Flight thing, which sounded absurd ... though, as a Shadow fishing captain, I wasn't one to scoff at crazy family traditions.

I nonetheless hadn't been able to resist raising an eyebrow. "So, let me get this straight. I'm like some prize you're bringing back to your family to prove your manhood?"

It was my first time seeing Nev blush. Then he'd lapsed into "formal" speak. "Not at all. Forming diplomatic relations with you as a representative of your planet and hopefully advancing our ability to use Shadow is the accomplishment with which I will present my family and complete my Flight. And it's not about manhood—I'm already of age, for systems' sake—but about becoming a functioning member of the family and proving I'm ready to ... um, inherit."

"Well, whatever," I'd said, not wanting to interrogate him

further if it was an awkward topic. "It still would have been nice to have some of your family's destroyers helping us out."

I hadn't been sure of that even as I'd said it—how in the systems could I want *more* destroyers in my life?—and I was definitely reconsidering now. Maybe it would have been better if he hadn't alerted his family ahead of time . . . if we had just slipped in instead.

Because now the destroyers were hovering around us, flanking us in a flight pattern that I couldn't help but read as threatening rather than protective.

Nev seemed to agree, because he pushed the inter-ship comm button without asking my permission. "This is Prince Nevarian Thelarus Axandar Rubion Dracorte." I blinked at his full name, at the raw power in his voice. I imagined we all did, even though I couldn't see everyone, especially not over in the destroyers. "That isn't an offensive formation I'm detecting, is it? Because I find offensive formations rather . . . offensive."

A cool but slightly strained female voice came back. "No, my prince. This is on my king's orders. We were to first confirm your biometric signal, which we have, and now we're to escort the *Kaitan Heritage* directly to a holding bay in Containment Block Three—"

Nev's eyes narrowed. "Did my father say I couldn't countermand his order with a direct one of my own?"

"No, my prince."

"Then take us directly to my family's private docking bay in the citadel. Immediately." His tone left no room for argument whatsoever.

The woman didn't argue.

The destroyers still escorted us through Luvos's atmosphere as if we had no choice in the matter. Not even a closer view of the planet's intriguing surface could shake my uneasiness.

In fact, it increased it. My hand clenched the controls in a fist. What were we doing here? Nev belonged here, of course, but not me.

Nev touched my shoulder, and I almost jumped. "It will be all right, I promise. Nothing bad is going to happen to you here. You're safe."

His voice was reassuring, but even his words put me less at ease. It was for an absurd reason, but part of me still thought he shouldn't have had to repeat himself so much. I swallowed and refocused on flying, tailing a lead starfighter to our destination.

Dracorva itself, though, rising out of a green, forested plain, did take my mind off just about everything else for a moment. I'd never seen a city so beautiful.

White spires stretched into the blue beyond like a forest of pale winter trees, or endless inverted icicles. And then I got closer and realized I didn't really have the means to describe them. The towers weren't natural or haphazard. Intricate patterns carved and decorated their entire lengths, and elegant skyways arched between them. *Like lace,* came the thought, though I'd seen the material only a few times outside of an infopad. Even the glittering river that ran through the towers was too symmetrical, with bridges cascading over its width. Or maybe there was something in nature so beautiful: a snowflake perched on the tip of my finger before it melted, standing like a miniature palace of ice. But this city wasn't nearly so impermanent or, of course, miniature. From this altitude, the white swept as far as my eye could see, and it looked as if it had stood, and *would* stand, forever.

So *this* was the capital city of the people who had hollowed out my planet? For a split second, I wouldn't have minded watching it all burn.

"Home." Nev breathed the word next to me, his hands on

the dash as he stared out the viewport. I joltingly remembered that this was his city too. I couldn't imagine calling such a place a home, but he turned to me and said, "You're going to love it."

"Tell me some of your favorite things about it," I said in a choked voice. Maybe if I saw it through his eyes, it would look less intimidating, less outrageous. He could be my bridge to this place. Preferable a bridge less frilly and impractical than the one I'd just flown over.

He smiled almost wistfully. "The architecture. It expresses the traditions and values that have likewise stood for centuries, especially in our palaces, temples, academies . . . our bridges."

My grip on the controls only tightened.

He glanced at me, as if realizing that I certainly didn't see any of our "architecture," such that it was on Alaxak, that way. "We also value nature for its inherent value to society, unlike others who might only see it for how they can profit from it. Parts of Luvos are protected, untouched. Those are some of my favorite places on the planet."

Funny, coming from the family that owned the mining drones. And our nature on Alaxak usually tried to kill us while we tried to scrape a living from it. Not that I didn't value it for its sort of savage beauty, but still, my hands squeezed the throttle as if they wanted to strangle something.

His eyes grew distant. "Most of all, I love the joy, the laughter. People here have hope, express it, and work toward it for others."

Having hope was probably pretty easy when you were filthy rich. The sight of Dracorva made it even harder to cling to my hope that these people could somehow save the ragged remains of both my family and my planet. Nevertheless, that hope was the only thing that kept me flying forward.

My doubts weren't alleviated in the slightest by the time

we approached a denser cluster of spires that stood taller and grander than any other. They rose from the side of a mountain at the far edge of the city, the first in a range that stretched into the distance. I didn't need to be a genius to guess that this was the Dracorte citadel.

Which meant it was even more Nev's home than the city, as if it were a blasted house like any other.

"And we even made it in time for the conference tomorrow." He sighed in evident relief.

The conference, with many people in attendance. So many, so rich, and so important . . . so many people who would want to use me.

"What am I doing here?" I asked before I could stop myself. "This isn't . . ." I realized I was breathing faster and faster. "This isn't me."

He looked at me in mild alarm, which vanished under a confident expression that unrolled across his face like a royal carpet. "You'll be treated like family, I promise."

"But . . ." I wasn't sure I wanted to be, if it meant a place like this would be my home too, if only temporarily. I didn't say that, because I didn't want to spit at his offer.

Not saying it didn't change the fact that people weren't—or at least, *I* wasn't—supposed to live like this. Not when most of the people on other planets in the systems lived the way they did, in the dust and ice and mud.

But there was no going back now. I highly doubted the destroyers would let me turn around, especially not with their prince still on board. And maybe not even without him.

Do it for Arjan, for Telu, for Alaxak . . .

We docked alongside one of the towers, in a bay that was more of a warren of bays on different levels. It sheltered more jets and ships than I'd ever seen together in one place, and in every sleek shape, size, and color. And this was just his family's private collection. I distantly, half deliriously, wondered how many of them were Nev's.

Inhaling deeply, I tried to get my breathing under control while I set us down. I was beginning to feel light-headed.

"Qole?" Nev asked, lowering his voice to the gentle tone someone would use to coax an animal out of its burrow. I realized I'd squeezed my eyes shut as soon as we'd landed. I kept them closed as he continued. "Can you drop the ramp? There's a contingent waiting, and I—we—need to go meet them."

A contingent? "Can I just stay here a second?" I asked through a clenched jaw.

He half laughed, cutting off when he realized I was serious.

Someone took my hand, sliding it away from the controls and placing it firmly in their own. My eyes snapped open, and I stared at Nev's hand in mine.

He was holding my hand. And he wasn't letting it go. It made me no less light-headed—if anything, my heart pounded even faster—but at least I was less scared of a stupid citadel and any contingents it might throw at me. Nev had fought for me before, and he wasn't abandoning me now, even though I didn't feel good enough to set foot in his home—either worthy enough or like it was *right*.

"Come on," he said, and gave me a gentle tug.

I let him pull me out of my chair. His hand stayed around mine as we wound down the stairs from the bridge. When I passed by the others, I tried to pull away, but Nev held on tighter. Maybe he was trying to say he was sorry for dropping my hand before. Or maybe he thought I would try to run. In any case, Eton looked like he'd swallowed a sour rock, but Arjan smiled faintly at me as he stood next to Basra, who was as expressionless as usual. It occurred to me that I'd hardly seen or heard from Basra since leaving Nirmana. He'd said he'd been "buying things," and I wondered if that was his way of alleviating stress about what was coming.

Telu was flat-out grinning. "Did you see that view? Can we come with you?" she asked excitedly.

Dazed, it took me longer than it should have to gather myself enough to say, "Maybe you should stay on the ship. Eton, stand guard. Basra, monitor any comms, and Telu—"

"Arjan and Telu should join us, at least, as fellow representatives of Alaxak," Nev said. It was more a declaration than a suggestion, and a brief flash of anger cleared my head even more.

"Telu stays." I rode over them when both he and she opened their mouths to object. "No, I trust you, Nev, but no. Tell no one that Telu is a native of Alaxak until we know more about the kind of attention we'll receive." It was too late for me and Arjan, since Nev had already told his family about us—and especially since I had a bounty on my head—but at least I could protect Telu's privacy a little longer. "Can you give a command, or whatever, that my crew can stay on the ship and should be left alone?" I waited until he nodded before turning to Telu. "I want you to keep out of sight as much as possible. Only Arjan and I will go until we know more about what we're getting into."

She grumbled, but retreated to her station. Arjan exchanged a look with Basra—and gave him a smile that was less showy than a kiss, but that still lit up my brother's eyes in a way I'd rarely seen. Basra, in actuality, was working wonders on him, whatever Arjan might have been doing to him in return.

"Ready when you are," Arjan said.

I nearly wondered if he was speaking to me or Basra. The latter was looking at Arjan like a particularly perplexing set of accounting figures.

Nev assumed he was talking to me. "Then let's go." He strode down the ship's ramp as if he owned the massive bay we were entering. As heir, I supposed he practically did. The waiting group of soldiers—Bladeguards, all ten of them—certainly treated him like he did.

But they looked at me, and at our linked hands, as if they weren't sure I should even be here, let alone touching their prince.

Everything I was afraid of.

"Welcome home, Your Highness. Might I advise against such proximity to the . . . Alaxan," the head guard said, clearly searching for a suitable word as we approached, "until we know whether she is safe."

At first I was horrified, ashamed . . . and then I was furious. As if those who had stolen everything from my planet thought they had any right to say what I could even *touch* from theirs.

At least, this time, Nev was furious too. He dropped my hand, but not in any sort of chastised fashion. In fact, as soon as he turned his ferocious silver-gray eyes on them, it was the whole group of Bladeguards that looked thoroughly chastised, if not cowed. His now-freed hand twitched at his side as if he wanted to move for his own blade strapped to his back.

"Never, and I mean *never*, speak about Captain Qole Uvgamut in that tone again. She is our guest, to be accorded every honor befitting a diplomatic envoy. You will hereafter address her as Captain, and never question my actions with regard to her."

His words lent me some pride, even though the fact that

he had to give it to me stung. My back straightened, and my shoulders squared. I glared at the guards.

"Yes, my prince. I beg your pardon." The head guard bowed to him, and then, shockingly, to me. "My apologies, Captain."

"It's fine." Angry or not, my voice still sounded so tiny, so out of place in the cavernous space. I was used to it filling the *Kaitan,* the comms.

On the other hand, I'd never seen Nev like this, and yet he was undoubtedly in his element. He was *Prince Nevarian* here. That, followed by a bunch of other names, ending with *Dracorte.*

"And this is her brother, Arjan Uvgamut," he said, "also to be accorded due respect."

Arjan nodded nervously and they all nodded back. The head guard even said in a careful tone, "Sir." I was pretty sure Arjan had never been called that in his life.

"Now," Nev—the prince—commanded, "escort us to my father."

XI

QOLE, ARJAN, AND I STRODE ACROSS THE LANDING BAY WITH THE Bladeguards flanking us. My hands burned with the effort of staying clenched, of keeping my outrage under control. These were my visitors, and I wouldn't tolerate their mistreatment.

I glanced at Qole and Arjan as we made our way to a series of turbolifts at the end of the landing bay. Arjan seemed to have retreated inside himself, but his eyes were taking in every detail around us. He was wary, but fascinated. Qole, in contrast, wore the same expression she had when the Treznor destroyer had boarded the *Kaitan*. There was a bubbling fury underneath the mask of her features, which she was keeping contained as she focused on the task at hand. She had a job to do, whether or not it was unpleasant.

With such a bad start at pleasant, I had my work cut out for me.

When I'd spoken to my father over the QUIN, he'd assured me that Qole would be received properly. Perhaps our definitions of *proper* differed, though our perspectives on something so basic had never varied that much before. What else might have changed, since I'd been gone?

Being surrounded by familiar walls and faces filled me with elation and relief, but a new sense of unease tainted it all. I supposed, if I strained, I could see why my father had ordered out the guard. I had been at risk on this voyage, and Qole was an unknown element, possibly dangerous, and of unfamiliar standing. But I would soon correct that perspective. My father would know Qole as the astonishing person she was, worthy of the utmost respect. Even from princes and kings.

Our arrival at a single turbolift set apart from the others stopped our procession and my thoughts short. Optic filigree with the family crest pulsed softly above the doorway, the only indication that this might lead anywhere different from the other lifts we had passed.

The Bladeguards flanked the official entrance to my family's private quarters. As I approached, the doors silently slid apart. Attuned to my biometric signal, they would open only for a member of the royal family. There were other ways to the family quarters, but this was the fastest.

"Thank you." I nodded to them as I entered the turbolift, and turned, clasping my hands behind me. "That will be all."

Qole and Arjan entered behind me, arranging themselves somewhat awkwardly to one side of the circular space. The Bladeguards at the entrance saluted and stepped back, and the turbolift doors slid to a close. Someone not born with people listening to them wouldn't have noticed the beat of hesitation after the dismissal. I did.

Anger nipped at the heels of my unease again, but I brushed aside the feelings sternly. It was uncommon for anyone, let alone strangers from offworld—one of whom was known to possess unusual powers, at that—to be so summarily invited into the depths of the family chambers. The guards were on edge because the king clearly was. As with any other rare occasion that my father and I were at odds, all I would have to do was demonstrate that my judgment was sound in how I was proceeding—pass another test—and all would be well.

I raised an eyebrow at the two Uvgamut siblings standing so close together and grinned. "Feel free to spread out. There's plenty of space."

"I wasn't sure how many guards you might need to ride a turbolift," Qole replied, her fury giving way to familiar irritation as she sidestepped away from Arjan.

There you go, I thought, *just make her annoyed at you and she'll forget to be angry about everything else. What a strategist you are, Nev.*

"With people I trust and respect? None." I gestured upward with my open palm, and the lift began to rise slowly, before accelerating with stomach-dropping speed. "Pardon the lift. It has a ways to go, and some people find the velocity unsettling."

Arjan actually laughed. "Let us know if it hits escape velocity."

Of course. They had practically grown up violently leaving the atmosphere of their planet. I felt foolish, and distracted them by moving my palm again, this time sweeping it sideways. The walls of the turbolift became transparent, the entire cityscape revealed before us.

The arches of the tower surrounded us on each side, acting as both supports and a frame for the city below. The lift was perfectly positioned, drawing the eye to different landmarks in rapid succession as it rose. There was the Temple of the Great Unifier, its crystalwork dissolving into the river. There was the Luvos Intersystem Starport, its myriad landing pads and docking bays sweeping out to disappearing points that made the ships look as though they were dispersing like pollen from the stamen of a blossom. Then the residential district, the foliage of the trees and the width of the streets sweeping in patterns that stood in stark contrast to the outer city we had seen in Ranta.

"This view is one of my favorite things," I said to no one in particular. "Function and beauty are celebrated at the same time. It demonstrates everything we believe in: practical idealism, working toward the benefit of all."

Qole stepped forward, and I was acutely conscious of her standing next to me. This was who I was, bared before her. What did she think of it?

Her brown eyes took in the city below us. "Where I come from, nothing about this is simple. Or practical."

Apparently, not much.

"Your bodyguards sure didn't seem happy to see us," Arjan observed. "What are they so jumpy about?"

"It's their job to be jumpy," I said. "Don't worry, my family is going to be delighted to see you." Which was probably not entirely true, since I was breaching protocol. But I knew my family, and they would treat these people, who were risking a great deal for a good cause—*our* cause—with the respect they deserved.

Not that he had asked about my family. I might have been reassuring myself a little.

———

At the top of the tower, the turbolift walls went dark again, and the doors slid open to reveal an antechamber. Tall double doors stood opposite the lift. Two smaller doors led off to each side. Waiting for us was a man of medium height whose blue and silver officer's uniform fit his well-built frame perfectly. His black goatee and sideburns were streaked with gray, standing out against his dark skin, but his bearing and movements spoke of nothing but vitality.

"My lord." He bowed deeply. "It is a pleasure to see you home again."

"Master Devrak." I smiled and bowed in return, if not as deeply. Custom was custom, although my respect for my teacher and our head of security was limitless. "It's wonderful to see you as well." I straightened and gestured to Qole and Arjan. "These are my guests."

Devrak nodded and reached out a hand. "Captain Qole Uvgamut. I am Devrak Hansen. Thank you for returning our prince safely to us."

We were all caught a little off guard, although I ought not to have been. Gravity was the only force in the systems as dependable as Devrak at doing its job. Or maybe Basra.

"Uh, no problem," Qole replied and shook his hand. "We're all glad to be in one piece."

"I've heard snatches." Devrak solemnly turned to Arjan to shake his hand. "Arjan Uvgamut, thank you for your services as well. It is a pleasure to meet people from Alaxak, which I have heard so much about."

"Really?" Arjan said, surprised. "That's weird. I mean …" He trailed off. "Um, thanks."

Devrak spread his hands. "My prince, I need to scan all of you before you enter the royal quarters. You are fresh from offworld, and we have to make sure that everything is safe for His Majesty."

"Of course," I said.

Devrak produced a small rod that had a long loop on one end. It beeped and whistled at me, and he smiled. "You are wearing quite the arsenal. Shall I take it for you or are you comfortable with its weight?"

"If you would, Devrak, I would appreciate it." I shed my overcoat and unstrapped the holsters holding my plasma pistols and sword while he scanned Arjan. To my surprise, I did miss the weight a little when I passed the bundle to Devrak; the past week had made me associate being armed with a certain level of security.

When he passed the scanner over Qole, the light on it flickered and died. Devrak frowned and examined it. "It seems to have broken."

Qole shifted uncomfortably.

"Well," I said, "it didn't make any noise, did it?"

Devrak glanced up at me, amused. "I suppose not. Thank you for letting me do my job. Now, go reunite with your family. Please pay my respects to them."

Before I could stride to the double doors and fling them wide, one of the side doors burst open instead. "Nephew!"

I blinked. Rubion stood before me, his sleek dark hair and deep blue lab coat as meticulously in place as ever, except he was perhaps breathing harder than usual. "Uncle?" I said. "I wasn't expecting you here. At least, not *outside* the royal quarters."

He tossed his head at the double doors in a smooth, dismissive jerk. "I thought you would be arriving elsewhere, and besides, you know I haven't the time or the stomach for banal family gossip." He turned to Qole with an eager light in his Dracorte silver eyes. "And I thought our special guest might feel the same."

My eyes narrowed a fraction before I quickly smoothed my expression. I wanted to be in total control in front of my uncle, not to mention Father—especially since it was Father's fault we had nearly arrived in the containment block, not Rubion's. But we'd already made it this far; I wasn't about to get derailed now from giving Qole a welcome with at least marginal fanfare.

"Uncle, our *guests* have come a very long way, and proper introductions are in order before we get down to business. Speaking of which, Qole, this is my uncle on my father's side, Rubion Dracorte II, and Uncle, this is Captain Qole Uvgamut and her brother, Arjan Uvgamut, of Alaxak."

My uncle swept up Qole's hand and brushed his lips lightly over her knuckles in a graceful gesture before she could respond. "Pleased. I've heard much about you. And you, of course, Arjan." He held out his hand to Arjan. "Both your data sets were the most promising I've ever seen."

Arjan's smile turned puzzled.

"Right, apologies," I said hurriedly. "I placed biometric sensors on both of you when we first met. I forgot to tell you."

Both Qole's and Arjan's looks could have killed me.

My uncle saved me from falling over myself in further apology—or Devrak from having to intervene in my self-defense—when he said, "Honestly, I was absolutely astonished when I saw the results. I've never seen an individual, let alone two, with a greater concentration of Shadow working in their systems. And you're both so functional. I can't wait to see—"

I lightly cleared my throat. "After they meet Mother and Father, yes. No doubt everyone will be excited." I didn't want Qole and Arjan feeling any more like lab animals than they already might.

"Of course, of course." Rubion's enthusiasm lessened to such a small extent that only I could have noticed. Still, he wasn't yet excusing himself, and his eyes kept returning to Qole. "It was ever so worthwhile to send you to that desolate rock in spite of the Treznor-Nirmana threat."

My polite cough turned into a choking sputter.

But Devrak's response dwarfed mine. *"What?"* He even took a step closer to Rubion, coming the barest fraction between us. He didn't raise his voice one iota, but it cut through the air with enough heat to make me cringe inside. I had heard it several times on the training fields, seen it send elite soldiers cowering. "You knew they would be following?"

"Of course. We have spies in our midst, yes?" Rubion responded blithely. "What spy could resist following a prince off on some lone, lengthy, secretive mission? It couldn't be helped, and the gain was greater than the risk. And at least my nephew could be trusted not to spill our secrets if caught . . . or to approach Treznor-Nirmana in the first place with secrets to sell."

I wasn't sure if Devrak caught it, but there was an implication that anyone outside the family couldn't be trusted . . . perhaps even our own head of security.

But Devrak had implications—rather, outright accusations—of his own. "You *deliberately* sent our prince into danger?" he demanded.

"Oh, calm down, Devrak. I wasn't putting him in real danger. It's all just posturing on the part of Treznor-Nirmana. At worst, we would have had to pay his ransom. The true threat was to our interests. And they're the family's interests, not just mine ... especially if we want these threats to remain mere posturing."

No doubt Qole and Arjan were fuming over the very real danger *they* and the rest of the crew had been put in, but before they could speak up, Devrak continued.

"Nevarian is *heir to the Throne of Luvos!*" His countenance was thunderous. I'd never seen him so angry with a member of my family; I'd rarely seen him so angry at all. Apparently, his duty to look out for my safety far superseded any need to respect my uncle's station. "He is more valuable to the family than any of your experiments, political games, or publicity stunts!"

"No doubt," Rubion said, unfazed. "But what is the point of the Dracorte Flight if not for our heir to learn how to handle the real world on one's own while still bringing honor to the family?"

"How would the prince getting taken hostage and ransomed bring any honor to the Dracorte name?" Devrak's voice grew softer ... and the heat leached out, leaving pure ice. "I would honor it more than that, and I'm not even a Dracorte myself."

"Devrak." I put a calming hand on his shoulder. "You are very much a part of this family, if not in name. I appreciate your consideration, but my uncle is correct with regard to the terms of the Dracorte Flight, which I argued very strenuously to undergo. Whatever his concern for my personal safety, it was my test, and I made it through unscathed. Mostly."

Arjan shifted next to me, his discomfort more obvious. Right, the airlock. I'd definitely be keeping that tidbit to myself for his sake.

My uncle's charming smile returned as he clapped my arm. "Not only that, but you surpassed our wildest expectations and brought us this young lady and her brother."

"Who very much risked their lives to be here, and whom Father would very much like to meet," I said, shrugging off Rubion's hand and sidling past him. It was rude, but my uncle had been far ruder. His all-consuming interest in his work didn't often leave room for social niceties. "If you'll excuse me, Uncle. We'll continue this discussion later."

Without registering the slight, Rubion took a step back, his eyes sliding from me back to Qole and Arjan, as if he didn't want to let them go quite yet. "Yes, of course. Later. But let's not forget the point of their journey, no?"

Before I could assure him that I wouldn't, he'd already nodded in farewell and exited through the door he'd come through.

Finally. Because no matter what my uncle claimed, his tests could wait for a few short moments, just so I could have *this* moment. Here, with my family. With Qole.

Not allowing for further delay, I threw open the double doors and strode inside. "Great Collapse," muttered Qole, stopping short next to me.

A sinking feeling took me as I pictured the scene through her eyes.

The walls of the great room curved and arched without any sharp edges from top to bottom, where they flared to meld seamlessly with the glass that wrapped one entire side. Every beautiful piece of furniture was arranged with purpose, to create areas of conversation and flow. Here one might practice music, there one might attempt to paint the staggering view of the sunset. Blue synthetics edged with silver accented the white leather harvested from the southern woodlands of Luvos. Some protested that the source was now endangered, but these pieces were ancient, and of course that much more valuable.

I thought of the *Kaitan,* with its riveted alloy walls, dim lights, and wooden floors. The largest space on the ship was the scum-streaked hold, and it was far smaller than the room we had just entered.

I had always thought everything here was a testament to understated art in a living space, the way my teachers in design had taught me. Now, with Qole's voice echoing in my ears, I compared it to the home I had known for the past week, and it looked as though a supernova had indiscriminately splattered wealth and riches to every rounded corner. There was no way she would ever feel comfortable here.

There was a moment of silence as we surveyed the great room, and its inhabitants—my most immediate family, who'd obviously gathered for our arrival—stared back from their various couches. There were only four of them, without any attendants, but somehow their presence was all the greater for it.

Then the silence was broken by a gleeful shriek, and ten-year-old Marsius, terror of the citadel, burst from his chair. My brother hurtled toward me and wrapped his arms around my waist. "Nev! You're back! From Alaxak! With friends! And gifts, right?"

I laughed and staggered backward, peeling him off. "Thank you for your brilliant observations. Yes, I'm back with friends . . . although if I'd known you were going to smash into me like a meteor, I might have thought twice."

He turned his attention to Qole and Arjan. "I'm Marsius Dracorte III," he said. "I'm number three because the name wasn't mine first. Only the oldest brother and sister, like Nev and Solara, get new names, but that's okay, I don't care—"

"Marsius, calm down," Father chided. He stood from his seat and strode forward. Marsius quieted. Son or not, when Thelarus Dracorte gave an order, you obeyed.

I tried to see him the way Qole might. Tall, with a straight back that carried the dark suit he wore with absolute comfort. His trimmed beard hid the angles of his jaw that I knew were so similar to mine. Age had set his silver-gray eyes slightly deeper than mine, however, and his body was thicker, if still enormously muscular. His voice made one think of warmth and foundation. It was evident in every detail that the man was born to rule, and I was always certain that if my father had not inherited a crown, the universe would have spontaneously created one for him to wear.

I bowed my head. "Father."

"Son, welcome back. We are overjoyed to see you returned safely."

My head still inclined, I felt my brow furrow. I knew when Father was overjoyed, and if this was it, then Eton was overjoyed to see me every day. Had I so overstepped my bounds in redirecting our arrival, undermining his authority? Nothing worse than embarrassment could result from that, but then, Father hated being embarrassed almost more than anything.

So be it. Even if I could have reversed time, I wouldn't have done anything differently.

I straightened. "And I am overjoyed to return to you, with my auspicious guests. Father, this is Captain Qole Uvgamut, of the *Kaitan Heritage.* She and her brother, Arjan Uvgamut, are the best Shadow harvesters on Alaxak, and have agreed to help us understand its binding effect on organic matter."

Father favored them with a smile. "Indeed, this is most fortunate news. You are both welcome in Dracorva."

"Qole and Arjan," I continued, as was proper, "may I present you to Thelarus Axandar Rubion Marsius Dracorte, King and Steward of the Dracorte Family Empire."

"It's an honor to meet you, sir . . . sire." Qole extended her hand to him, and I winced. She couldn't have known that the only proper way to greet a king was with a bow or curtsy. I should have thought to warn her.

But Father was nothing if not decorous. He hesitated only a moment before taking her hand and shaking it in return.

"My dear, it's not customary to shake hands with the king." My mother, Ysandrei, descended upon us, indulgent concern creasing her beautiful face. She was arrayed more opulently than Father, in a deep blue gown that hugged her just enough to show a figure more youthful than she had any right having. Mother would never show too much skin, but as she never tired of telling us, she believed one should take pride in one's appearance.

She didn't fail to notice the look on Qole's face after I introduced her as the queen. "Don't be distressed, of course," she said. "I know navigating these social straits is difficult. Nevertheless, Thelarus, is it safe for you to be touching her? I hear Shadow poisoning is very common on Alaxak." She smiled in apology at Qole. "No offense intended, my dear. My life's purpose is to think of every detail."

A mixture of emotions warred across Qole's face—confusion, embarrassment, anger—before she swallowed them. "It's . . . I'm not catching, if that's what you mean."

"Isn't catching Shadow exactly what you do?" Inviting and musical, the voice treated the words with bored amusement. The owner hadn't bothered getting up, but I didn't find that surprising. My sister, Solara, reclined on a couch with an info-pad, finger slowly moving through whatever she was reading. She had few passions outside the latest palace gossip and interpersonal news. Politics, science, and history were not her calling, and I rarely found that our interests aligned. Her golden gown perfectly matched the sunlight that glinted in her blond hair as she glanced up—no coincidence, I was sure.

"Qole and Arjan, meet Solara Dracorte, my sister," I said, trying to keep the irritation out of my voice.

If Marsius couldn't help but listen to Father's order, he also couldn't help but forget it as curiosity seized him again. "Oh yes, Shadow! You fish for it! How do you do that? Do you have a rod? Or nets? Is it true you do it on the edge of a molecular cloud? Do you have your own ship?"

Neither Qole nor Arjan could repress a smile, and some of the tension went out of their shoulders. I could have given Marsius all the presents in the world.

Arjan knelt in front of him. "We *are* on the edge of the molecular cloud. You start with a mag-field net, see, because . . ."

I left the two of them to discuss the particulars of Shadow fishing, moving deeper into the room with Qole to find a seat. The king and queen followed almost warily. I touched Qole on the arm to indicate a chair that she could take, and she started, betraying a nervousness I hadn't known was *so* acute.

I couldn't blame her; as eager as I had been, I now saw that I couldn't have thrust her into a more foreign experience.

I turned to the king before I took a seat. "Father, do you know why the Air Guard tried to escort the *Kaitan* to a containment block?" I asked as if it were no great concern. "They said it was on your order."

I knew why, of course, but I wanted to hear him justify it. I wanted Qole to hear it.

He narrowed his eyes slightly. "It was. I was advised that following rigorous safety protocol in light of the attacks on you was advisable, and I gave the go-ahead."

Qole considered this, then gave a brief nod, even though Father wasn't directly addressing her. Good. At least she saw the logic behind the decision too, even if it was nonetheless ill-mannered.

I considered my next words carefully. Now I had to put both my family and Qole at ease, and it dawned on me that my strategies for each might be at odds with one another. These were two different worlds I was trying to bridge. In one, you could simply walk up to someone's door, knock, and talk. In the other, there were protocols—often good ones, for good reasons like security, efficiency, and order—but sometimes they hindered direct communication.

While these worlds might be different, I didn't believe they were mutually exclusive. I couldn't. I needed each to see the other the way I did.

"Father, I hope you understand why we didn't land at the containment block. It wasn't a fitting welcome for Captain Qole"—I was careful to emphasize her rank—"particularly after she saved my life. Probably more than once."

Mother looked at Qole with sudden, newfound amazement that was almost indecent, as far as her usual standards . . . and with appreciation, I was pleased to see.

The king raised his eyebrows, then inclined his head in gracious acknowledgment. "Then our gratitude is unending."

The queen collected herself enough to incline her head as well, holding it as long as decorum allowed for a great gift. "All of Luvos is grateful to you. And I, as a mother, am in your debt."

Qole looked baffled, rather than mollified. Unable to find the words to respond, she stuttered for a second, then blushed furiously.

I suppressed a wince. If this was supposed to make her feel

better, I'd likely failed. I opened my mouth to prompt her and she, anticipating me, shot me a venomous look that said *Shut up, I can speak for myself,* as clearly as a blaring comm speaker.

Finally rallying, she said, "Thank you, Your Majesties, but we were all in danger and just doing what we could to survive." She hesitated, but only for a moment. "I'm happy to be here. It's been . . . quite the trip."

I tried not to smile. Couching unpleasantness in euphemism—Qole was figuring out the game already.

The king nodded. "We've become aware. Apparently, there is a significant price on your head, Captain Qole. It would seem the Treznor-Nirmana family is exceedingly interested in what you might have to offer them. But you needn't worry; they can't reach you here."

"Yes, they were interested," Qole said with some heat. "They were so interested they tried to cut me open."

So much for euphemism.

"That's very disturbing." Father frowned. "Tell me, did they say what they hoped to accomplish with that?"

I grimaced inwardly. In spite of her bluntness, I didn't think this was a topic Qole really wanted to revisit. "What does that matter?" I asked, stepping in. "They are unscrupulous lunatics, willing to take shortcuts in their research at the expense of someone's life. What matters is that with Qole's help we can unlock the key—"

"Oh, systems, what kind of horrid conversation is this?"

There is a maxim in royal circles: for every social situation, the most socially uncomfortable thing that *can* happen *will* happen—hence, as the popular wisdom went, one must avoid anything that could lead to awkwardness. Such as conversations that were interesting enough to warrant staying awake.

But given that maxim, putting Qole in the same room as

Ket was, without a doubt, the worst social misstep I could have made in my life to date.

To be fair, I hadn't known Ketrana would be here, nor had I seen her lounging in the shade on a recliner as we entered, or else I might have aborted this attempt at an introduction altogether. My family, I could handle. My mother mostly confined herself to worrying about etiquette and impropriety, Marsius was always so good natured that one suspected drugs, and Solara was, just, well, Solara. She gossiped and went to parties.

But Ketrana ... She looked the picture of a fine-blooded princess. Her tiny frame was perfectly proportioned to distract, and her regal neck led to fine features: lips designed for pouting, cheeks that dimpled just so, and a nose that had the perfect curve.

But the dimples of every smile were calculated perfectly, and the nose was held in a way that indicated not playfulness, but distaste. The first time I had ever met her, I'd been as taken as any red-blooded adolescent would be, especially since she'd worn a gown as alluring as the one clinging to her now. Since then, I'd realized there was a fine line between vapid and malicious. It was a line she played fast and loose.

Now there was no hope for this to be anything but a painfully awkward experience for Qole.

"Are you the Alaxan? I can't believe they let you up here. This must be the thrill of a lifetime!" Ketrana stepped around the back of my couch and fixed Qole with a disbelieving stare. It was true that Qole's fur-trimmed leather jacket and knee-high boots merely served to accentuate her ragged dark hair and the stark contrast of her features to those of Ket. Where Ket was fine as a perfect piece of miniature artwork, Qole was as healthy and wild as the nature that might have inspired that artwork. "From Alaxak to the royal chambers," she continued, "it's like something out of a reality vid."

"Ket," I said with some force, "Captain Qole is my guest. And she's seen sights that do not make a royal common room much of a thrill."

I hesitated then, even though I well knew that etiquette demanded a *proper* introduction. I wasn't sure why I was having trouble saying the next few words. Maybe because I didn't know how Qole would take them. Would she be indifferent? Or confused, since they no doubt did things contrarily on Alaxak? Angry, because I hadn't yet had the chance to explain?

Part of me almost wanted her to be angry, for my own reasons that weren't fully realized. But then I knew that because of etiquette and protocol, I couldn't tell her why she shouldn't be. Not here, alongside Ket. Not until we were alone again . . . whenever that would be.

"Qole." I finally turned to her, having waited long enough for Mother to give me a look. "This is Ketrana Dracorte, my second cousin . . . and my betrothed."

For a brief moment, I could have sworn blackness flickered at the edge of Qole's eyes. "I . . . see. I keep learning new things here. Congratulations must be in order, hey?"

She was definitely angry. Furious, by the looks of her, though it wouldn't be obvious to anyone else.

I, on the other hand, didn't know if it was a thrill of alarm or excitement that I felt.

"Oh, *hey,* that's adorable." Solara materialized over my other shoulder, smiling. "You are a dear, Captain. Please don't mind Ket, we simply haven't met anyone such as you before. You can't imagine how stimulating we find it. Isn't that right, Ket?"

Ket laughed, her eyes as cold as ice. "Stimulating. I didn't mean to be rude, I'm sure. It's a pleasure to meet you, Qole."

She sat down daintily at the edge of the couch next to me. "Aren't you happy to see me, Nevarian?"

She batted her eyelashes, and I heroically controlled my gag impulse. Typically, I had no trouble with Ket. Marriage for royals was about bloodlines, politics, and tradition. We were bred for specific traits and, as we were frequently reminded from birth, genetics did not care about passion. I'd always recognized that as part of my duty and had felt I could do much worse than Ket. She was certainly beautiful, and while her disposition was egregious, I could largely ignore her. Except now I was somehow finding that impossible. It was as though every fake thing about her, every inauthentic motion, was coming into sharp relief.

"Oh, you two lovebirds don't need to talk." Solara leaned over me and batted Ket's arm. "You'll have plenty of time for that later, don't you think? No, we should take this opportunity to learn about our new guest. Tell me, Qole, what do Alaxans do for fun?"

I breathed silent thanks to Solara. I didn't know why she'd felt compelled to come to my rescue, but as patronizing as she was being to Qole, it was a thousand times better than what might have resulted from Ket.

"Well, um . . ." Qole was off to another uninspiring start, but then her voice picked up strength and speed. "We don't have a lot of downtime, but when we do, a lot of families in my village like to gather. We each bring a meal, and eat it together as one big feast."

The corners of her lips had the beginnings of a smile, her eyes a glint of remembered pleasure. It wasn't a look I saw on her face often, so I committed it to *my* memory.

"*Each* household brings a meal?" Solara asked, incredulous. "No one hosts?"

"No, that's sort of the point." Qole's face was already closing off, her tone flattening. "It's a shared thing, called a potluck."

"I get it!" Ket nearly shrieked. "The luck of the draw—or the pot! You never know what you'll get, right? Unifier's name, how could you just trust all these family's cooks like that?"

"Um, we don't have cooks. We cook. Ourselves." Qole must have anticipated what sort of response she would get from that because she went on quickly. "Anyway, *I* like it. It's fun."

Ket swooped back in—for the kill. "Well, there must be *something* else you do for more amusement. Oh, oh, let me guess, this will be a blast." She pursed her lips as if deep in thought. "For those quaint fur clothes of yours, do you hunt and skin the animals yourself? I've heard that locals of the outer planets like to do that. I've seen vids of people up to their elbows in blood—some even drink it steaming! Do you do the same?"

Great Collapse.

"Do I *drink blood*?" Qole opened her mouth, then closed it. I hoped she was too shocked to get infuriated.

Mother tried to salvage the moment, to her credit. "Or what about other cultural traditions, dear? Do you have any festivals?"

Qole's face went still. Festivals? *Alaxak?*

But then she surprised me by saying, very calmly, "Sort of." Her face was beyond still. A mask. "Once a year we gather on the tundra and light off Shadow flares for each person who has died in the past year. Every year we launch dozens, in a village that has only hundreds living in it. The flares are supposed to carry their souls up through atmosphere, to the molecular cloud where we catch our Shadow. It's Shadow that kills us, so that's where we go, when we die."

211

Utter silence had descended over the room. Everyone was staring at her. Even Marsius and Arjan had halted their animated conversation at a table to look over.

If Shadow was where Qole's people ended up in death, Qole was where polite, inane conversation went to die.

Solara, oddly, looked impressed.

As for me . . . it wasn't at all funny and would have been the most inappropriate thing I could have done as far as either my family *or* Qole was concerned, but for a moment I wanted to laugh hysterically.

Mother cleared her throat first, followed by a chorus of the sounds. "Well, isn't that fascinating? I'm sure we would love to hear about Alaxak all afternoon, but preparations really must be getting underway for tonight's celebration."

I knew what would happen now. Everyone would scatter, and soon I would be so tied up in an evening of protocol that I wouldn't be able to move, let alone talk to Qole.

I turned to Father. "We must discuss a few things."

He nodded. "Agreed. However, there will be time later. Right now, we must arrange for accommodations for our no-doubt exhausted guests. Food, baths. And you, Nevarian, must prepare for the ball tonight, and for tomorrow's events."

I nodded. "I know. And so should Qole. We must make sure that she is properly introduced."

"What?" Qole stared at me, shocked out of any last vestige of propriety. "Are you mad? I'm not going to any ball."

The king frowned. "Indeed, I'm not sure what the purpose would be."

"She would no doubt be terribly uncomfortable," Mother chimed in. "It's probably best that she get her strength back."

"What would she even wear?" Ket giggled.

I felt myself flush slightly. "It makes *sense* because tomorrow is the Dracorte Conference and Report. Qole and I both risked much to get here in time for that, and for the major yearly accomplishments that will be celebrated in advance, tonight."

"Like our betrothal," Ket said with satisfaction.

"Yes, yes. And like the fact that we have an official representative from Alaxak who will be the key to unlocking Shadow's widespread energy potential, an arrangement in which I've played an instrumental part. This was the point, Father. If we don't impress everyone tonight and give them a reason to have faith in the Dracorte heir, then you know that the rumor networks will start churning."

Father hesitated. "I know Rubion was anxious to begin his study—the very basis for any confidence we might have on display tonight."

"He's not going to finish his study tonight, and, anyway, Qole's appearance will do much more for us than some Shadow-saturated algae, with all the rumors no doubt flying around about her. Her bounty put her in the spotlight. She's wanted, and we have her."

The words brought even more warmth to my cheeks, but I tried to disregard it.

King Thelarus stroked his beard thoughtfully. "Perhaps. A delay for just this evening might be permissible."

"No. No, no, no," Qole said. "Ketrana's right. Her Royal Majesty is right. You're both *so* right, and Nev is wrong." She stood in a rush and dusted herself off. "This was an honor. An honor and a pleasure. But I'm the last person who wants ... who you want at a ball."

Solara sprang up beside her, grabbing her arm. "Oh, please reconsider, Qole. It will be ever so much fun, I promise. And Nev is right, it will make such a splash. The networks will be raving about the great things the Dracorte family will accomplish with someone like you to help us. What do you say, Father?" She turned to Father and pouted at him. "Do let's invite our guests to the ball."

With Solara's help, it seemed that I might yet get everyone—my family included—to accept Qole as a proper envoy of her planet and not something I'd tracked in on my boots. "Qole hasn't received the best welcome on Luvos," I added pointedly. "It's time to set that right, and to show the world what we are made of and what the future holds for us."

The king nodded slowly. "I suppose. Solara, prepare the captain for the ball. Ysandrei, please find a manservant to help Arjan with preparations as well." He raised his eyebrow at her.

A perfect smile fell into place on the queen's face, one that I knew masked disagreement. "Of course. Arjan, Marsius, do let's get you both decent and more comfortable for the party."

Marsius looked up from the table where he'd brought Arjan drawing materials to illustrate how a Shadow run worked. "What? Party? Party! Oh, Arjan, we'll have so much fun."

A few minutes later, only Father and I remained in the great room. The chandeliers had been dimmed, and we stood side by side looking at the view of the city through the glass balcony. The sun was beginning to set, and a million lights flickered to life, some running like rivers and others twinkling like stars. Bright streaks traced the contours of the Starport as ships departed and arrived.

Maybe this wasn't so bad after all.

It seemed like Solara, at least, had taken to Qole. Marsius was fast friends with Arjan, and Ket . . . well. It hadn't served me to contemplate her too much before this point, and now I felt like I had a major incentive to do so even less.

"Congratulations on completing your Flight," Father said quietly. "I had my doubts about the whole plan, but you and Rubion persisted ... and you were right to persist," he added, making me blink. Father rarely admitted to being wrong, mostly because he typically wasn't. "What you're going to accomplish for this family, for this system, is worth being proud of."

The words warmed me, but I shook my head. "I'm beginning to realize, Father, that the people who deserve thanks are the ones who trust us to do the right thing. Qole went through a great deal to be here, and that was after I tried to force her to come."

He nodded. "Our responsibility is toward our subjects, and we cannot forget that. But don't let your fascination with one person upset your responsibility to everyone, Nevarian."

I stared out the windows, trying to understand what he meant. Or rather, understand *all* of what he meant. Thelarus Dracorte never spoke of anything without multiple levels of intent, and I had grown up to be better than most at discerning his words.

Except this time, I wasn't sure I liked what I was reading. "I've remained focused on nothing but the mission, Father. Every action I've taken has been to further our goal of improving the lives of everyone. When we announce that we can make Shadow a safe source of energy, show that we have an example to work from, everything will change. But I'm also happy that, in the process, I'm learning more about our subjects and what they need."

Father nodded, and we remained silent another moment. I always enjoyed our conversations here, viewing the city. They had grown less frequent as I grew older, but they always gave me the same sense of connection to him and to our purpose.

"That's commendable, Nev," he finally said. "Remember, however, that if you seek the best for people, you cannot afford to care for them too much. Your mind must remain clear to the realities."

I stared him directly in the eyes. Even now, no longer a child, I felt a little audacious for doing it. "I promised Qole her safety, and I would do anything to keep that promise."

"Of course," he said, in a firm tone, using the words more as a *but* than an agreement. "I'm not talking about her safety."

He meant that I should keep my distance. That I was above her.

"That may be a lesson I don't know how to learn," I admitted, without breaking my gaze.

The king looked back at me with calm expectation. Suddenly I was eight again, at my Rendering, standing with weights on my shoulders and trying not to fall. "You will find, son, that life will teach it to you. Your only job is to be prepared for the lesson." He turned. "It's time; you should get ready."

He left me alone then, and my eyes wandered up to the fading orange sky. Somewhere out there, one of those points of light was the Alaxak subsystem. Somewhere there were asteroid belts, and gravitational currents, and molecular clouds with rivers of Shadow.

I was supposed to be happy here; I had everything I wanted. So I wondered why I had felt more at home yesterday, on the *Kaitan Heritage*.

I pushed it from my mind. It was indeed time.

XII

QOLE

IF IT WERE POSSIBLE TO DIE OF MORTIFICATION, I WAS PRETTY SURE I
would be dead. And if that mortification was a weapon, then
the Dracortes were wielding it. Or, at this very moment, five
lady's maids were, in the form of the soaps, scrub brushes, and
hair combs they used to attack me. But it had been an unending assault from all corners ever since I'd stepped off the
Kaitan.

I sat in a scooping silver basin filled to the brim with more
scalding water than I'd ever seen outside the few hot springs
on Alaxak. The water was also infused with more perfume oils
than I could hope to use in a lifetime, never mind at one time.

The head lady's maid, Ollava, leaned over my head and

sniffed me, of all things. She eyed the dozen or so perfume bottles sitting by the side of the tub. "More spice, less floral. We need something sturdier to counteract the fur and leather still clinging to her."

There was nothing still clinging to me, in fact. I was stark naked in the tub, in spite of my huge audience. They were all women, but still, no one had seen me naked since my mother, and she'd left off dressing and bathing me by the time I was five, well before she'd died. My loud protests that I could take care of this myself went entirely ignored. They hadn't even let me undress myself. Instead, they'd stripped off my blasted clothes for me and practically shoved me in the bath, where they'd given me a cursory once-over with scrub brushes. *Everywhere.*

My clothes were already being removed from where they'd been discarded in a pile, so there was no chance I could snatch them back to cover myself. The maid picking them up held them away from herself with such horror, it was as if she thought they would come alive and bite her.

"Who would wear a hideous thing like that?" the maid tittered to another in the corner, not quite quietly enough. Or maybe Shadow was enhancing my hearing in this extreme state of mortification.

"What do you expect? I hear she drinks animal blood."

"Did you know she *touched* the king? With hands like those!"

If my face wasn't already burning from the water and the scrubbing, it would be from their words. I wasn't even sure *how* I could feel more humiliated than I already did.

Ollava sniffed for about the hundredth time, this time in the direction of my clothes. "To the incinerator with those," she told the maid.

"No—!" A bucket of water cut off my shout, dumped over

my head by another maid. It only stoked my anger instead of dampening it. Sputtering, I said, "Could this water be any hotter? And if you burn my clothes, I'll . . ."

I didn't quite know what I would do, and threatening people was probably yet another uncivilized show of my "rustic upbringing." Solara had already pointed out several of those, never mind that stripping, sniffing, scrubbing, and then stewing someone to death seemed pretty uncivilized to me.

She was an unfortunate addition to my audience. Her golden hair and creamy skin weren't in need of washing, only styling and painting, respectively, so she sat at a curving desk of polished dark wood that was nearly as big as the command center of the *Kaitan,* ringed in lights, mirrors, and a few other maids. Fitting, since she was the pilot of this whole disastrous venture. And yet she looked more like a queen than a captain.

Solara Dracorte was gorgeous in a way I'd never seen. Even Ketrana Dracorte paled in comparison, and *she* was so lovely she'd made my teeth grind. But Ket reminded me of an iceraker, a type of fish that swam in Alaxak's cold seas. Its eyes were huge and shiny to reflect the light from the pack ice above and draw attention to itself, and then when unwary prey got near enough, retractable jaws shot out to claim its life—falsely beautiful until you got too close and saw what lay within.

Nev's sister, on the other hand, possessed a beauty so powerful, it almost hurt to look at it, like the glinting edge of a Disruption Blade, or a blazing star. I had no idea what she and I were even doing in the same room.

This was my room, technically—or rooms, since it was a sprawling suite in silvers, dark browns, and deep purples meant to complement my coloring, or so Solara had said. I'd choked when I realized she was serious. Apparently, the Dracortes had enough massive suites to pick one that best matched my hair

219

or eyes or whatever, as if it were a blasted shirt. But equally apparently, I didn't have the right to keep anyone out of it, and Solara had insisted on helping me get ready. So her maids had dutifully trekked her chests of cosmetics, soaps, and oils over here, where they were now piling her golden hair on top of her head in elegant, twisting loops and dabbing at her face with all sorts of creams. She'd said I would be next.

Lucky me.

She laughed now, her voice like a golden bell. "Why would you want to keep those scraps?"

"Those *scraps* keep me warm in deep space," I said through gritted teeth, as two maids took to scrubbing my hair. Pointing out the usefulness of my clothes didn't make me, or my scalp, feel any better.

After my braid had come undone, the tangled black waves had fallen nearly to my waist, so there was a lot to scrub . . . and to wrench at with torturous combs. I should have brushed it more often, if only to avoid this, though my hair wasn't exactly a top priority during the peak of the fishing season. Here, I was getting the impression that things like hair and complementary colors were the utmost priorities. I hugged my bare chest and slouched deeper into the water in spite of the burn, both to hide from Solara's piercing metallic stare and to shy away from the pain at my scalp.

"After this party," I reminded her, "I have to go back to deep space. You know, to *work*."

"Our dearest Nev no doubt promised you whatever you might want, so the least we can do is clothe you," Solara said with an insinuating tone I didn't like at all. I liked the mention of Nev even less. In the middle of such humiliation, the last thing I needed was to think about him. "Our tailors can provide you with the finest synthetic thermal gear in the galaxy."

"I don't want the finest in the galaxy, I want *mine*." I sounded like a stubborn child, but I couldn't help myself.

"Hm, how ... sentimental," Solara said, then glanced at the maid who still held my clothes pinched in the tips of her fingers and as far away from her liveried uniform as possible. "Have her attire cleaned and mended to the best of your ability." Her already bright eyes lit with inspiration. "And why don't you add a thin synthetic layer inside for extra warmth? There! A mix of rustic and modern, new and old—the best of both worlds, yes?"

I felt like remarking that her world was no older or newer than mine, but I bit my tongue. Besides, she was trying to be nice. She was just failing at it miserably.

Before the maid could leave, she added, "Oh, and add a nice ruff of melori fur at the collar."

I had no idea what melori fur was, but it was most likely as expensive and opulent as anything else a Dracorte would want to use as decoration.

"No!" I said, and my sharpness made both the maid and Solara blink. I tried to lower my voice. "No ... Your Highness ... thank you, but—"

"Are you quite sure?" Solara interrupted, her voice nearly as sharp as mine had been, before a smile melted away the edges. She evidently didn't like being told no. "The bright white should offset the darkness of your face—"

"Is there something wrong with my face?" I was beginning to wonder, with how hard the maids were scrubbing my arms. I'd heard of certain systems where people valued either darker or lighter skin, and the Dracortes were all nearly as white as fresh snow. "That's not dirt, hey."

"Did you hear her accent, *hey*?" The maids tittered again, and for a second I *hated* them so powerfully, it shocked even me.

221

These were the people I was trying to help? These were the people who stood for justice and decency in the galaxy? They were supposed to have welcomed me like one of their own. If this was how they treated family, or even those who happened to share the same system with them, then maybe I should let them fall.

The only reason I didn't was that they would take what was left of my family down with them. I was still clinging to wild hope, to Nev's promises that almost sounded too good to be true, that Arjan, Telu, and I could live longer than another handful of years if I cooperated. That we could maybe, someday, have families of our own.

Hold on, you can get through this. You've been through worse.

Maybe.

"Oh my, do you think us so backward as to care about something like skin color? *Us?*" Solara asked incredulously, really meaning *me*—as if someone as backward as me could even presume to think them on the same plane as myself. "Haven't you met Devrak, our head of family security? And there's not darker skin in the galaxy outside of the Belarius family, whom I'm sure even you've heard of. They're a royal line as noble, if not quite as old, as ours." She sighed. "Their prince and heir, Heathran, is *quite* to my taste. You see, Dracortes can appreciate the beauty in all colors, whether of fabric or skin ... just with their proper accompaniments."

We were back to complementary colors.

I'd been through more near-death experiences than I could count, and yet I'd rather have been facing a thick asteroid belt, a difficult drone, or hell, a Treznor destroyer than this. To them, I was being a rustic idiot, but I was really only trying to maintain a fingergrip of control over the situation ... and myself. And not just over my appearance. My anger was spiking, my shame deepening, and nothing I said or did—or *tried* to do—had any effect. I didn't doubt that I was a better pilot than anyone in this room, maybe even the whole blasted citadel, and yet I didn't know how to navigate this situation. I wanted to duck under the surface of the bath. Instead, a maid dropped another bucket of water over my head.

"There," Ollava said after another sniff at my hair. "That should do it. Now, help her out, girls."

Before I could object, the maids who'd been scrubbing my arms now used them to haul me upright, leaving me bare and red and steaming for all the systems to see. Not for the first time, I wished I could flee into the walk-in closet—which was much bigger than my captain's quarters on the *Kaitan* and yet the smallest room in this suite—and maybe barricade the door.

But my humiliation was far from over. In fact, it was just beginning.

Solara lifted her infopad from among the iceberg sea of cosmetics jars on the desk, and held it up toward me for a few seconds. When she laid it flat again and pushed a button, a hologram of me appeared over the top. At least I didn't have to watch a bright, fully detailed image of my nude body spin around in the air for very long before various fabrics and colors covered it.

"These are all my dresses. You are a bit sturdier than me, but a mod can be done in a hurry, don't fret," she said, never mind that I hadn't been "fretting" about anything other than standing naked in front of everyone like a piece of meat at the market. I almost wished I could disappear entirely. A maid finally took pity on me and wrapped me in a soft, white robe.

"Hm, that one might work, if we shorten it. Or not. That one's too bland. Too bright. No, no." Solara was muttering, swiping away the options she didn't like, which seemed to be most of them, in spite of the fact that they were all hers. I could hardly get a good look before they were gone.

"Aha!" she finally cried, but she waved the image away before I even caught a glimpse of it. "Just the thing to catch our dear Nev's eye."

"What?" I stumbled as one of the maids directed me to a chair in front of the wide, curving desk and mirrors, my skin definitely burning in a way that had nothing to do with hot water now. "Why would you want to do that? Isn't he . . . ?"

I couldn't even say the blasted word. But why had I been so surprised? How could I have thought . . . what *had* I even been thinking?

I still wished Nev would stride through the silver double doors, swinging his Disruption Blade, and get me the blasted hell out of here like he had on the destroyer. That desire was second only to how much I wished I never had to see him again. On the *Kaitan,* he'd told me so much about himself, his family, his hopes and ideals, and yet failed to mention his *fiancée.* I'd trusted him to not mislead me, and yet he had.

Idiot, idiot.

I heaped the insults on. As if everyone else in the room weren't doing a fine enough job.

"Betrothed," Solara supplied. "Yes, of course, but it's no fun if he simply *dotes* upon her. And I've seen how he looks at you. You do have a certain rustic charm."

I hoped the heat of my skin wouldn't combust the chair. *Rustic charm,* like I was a damned trinket from offworld, not the deftest flyer this side of the galaxy had ever seen. That, along with *complementary colors,* were two phrases I never wanted to hear again.

Nor did I want to hear that Nev had been looking at me like that. A day ago, it might have sent a thrill blasting through me as hot and powerful as a ship's thruster. But not now. Because if it was true, despite him being betrothed, then that was a problem. For me, for him, for Ket, for the whole royal family. So why in the systems would Solara try to fuel the flames? Maybe she secretly hated Ket, who, I had to admit, was pretty deserving of hate.

"B-but . . . ," I stuttered eventually. Solara was watching me with an intensity I found uncomfortable—as uncomfortable as everything else, rather. "But if this is the event where they officially announce their betrothal, why would you want to make waves tonight, of all nights?

"Oh, it's just a game we royals play—all in good fun. You wouldn't understand." Before I could simmer over that—or wish I could evaporate—she went on. "Besides, my brother could never be so dull as to focus his attentions on one person, anyway."

At my astonished look, her laugh rang out again.

"Oh, you poor dear. You think he's been waiting for Ket? Maybe that's how it is on your planet, but I assure you, that's not how it's done around here. He'd never be so indiscreet as to muddy the bloodlines, if you catch my drift," she said with sly enthusiasm. "But I have no doubt he dabbles wherever he wants. He could have anyone in the systems, after all. I *know* he's been with a Xiaolan girl—not the heiress, Daiyen, but one of her cousins—and a Nirmana girl or two while he was studying at their Econom Academy. Oh, and then there was that *friend* of Ket's, but maybe that was before their unofficial betrothal . . ." She began ticking them off her fingers as the list went on.

I tried to figure out what this feeling was, and then I realized it was like my guts were falling out through the bottom of the chair. I wasn't sure why I was shocked. I should have known. Nev was a blasted prince, gorgeous and wealthy beyond imagining. Of course he would have been with other women. Dozens, by all accounts. Unlike me, he hadn't grown up on a backworld ship surrounded by only family and friends so close they were like family, nor with blackness in his eyes to frighten everyone else off.

Suddenly, I felt just as naïve and quaint as they'd been saying all day.

Solara reached over and patted my cheek, snapping my eyes up to hers. I'd never wanted to bite someone so badly before. Talk about uncivilized.

"Don't look so forlorn! It's a party." She grinned at me, her own eyes flashing—so much like Nev's, but so different. "And you'll be dressed to kill."

I didn't like the sound of that. At least not when she said it, though I might not have minded killing Nev at the moment. Perhaps with my bare hands, while cursing him for bringing me here, for making me a part of the "games royals play."

After decreeing that her hair and makeup were done—the maids had dabbed her lips in the vividest red—Solara leapt up from her chair and began directing the maids in how to do mine. Before I knew it, my dark eyes were glittering with a charcoal shadow that swept above and to the sides. More shadows emphasized my cheekbones, and the deepest purplish-red stained my lips. Solara was ecstatic, exclaiming how "exotic" I looked. I thought I looked nothing like myself.

I reached up to touch my face as I stared in the mirror, but Ollava smacked my hand away. "Not until I set it." She looked to Solara for final approval, then waved a glowing wand over my face, where I felt a strange warming, then firming sensation.

I prodded at my lips with a finger after that, and the color didn't budge.

"Now for her hair," Solara declared. She could have been directing ships into battle with how seriously she coordinated the placement of my endless, unruly waves. After enough concoctions were sprayed on them and more glowing wands waved and thrust like swords, they soon fell in something like a braid, though only in the loosest sense of the word. My hair more resembled a black waterfall, twining and cascading over one shoulder. In the various flowing twists, Solara instructed the maids to weave in strands of glittering white jewels, which were likely worth more than my ship. It was a waterfall sparkling in the starlight.

Unlike my face, I couldn't help admiring it. But then, with a fierce heat in my chest, I decided that I would much rather have the *Kaitan* than a few strings of sparkly rocks. The Dracortes would not change *that* while simply fixing my hair. They could never make me value my ship any less, or take it from me in any way.

My dark eyes looked deadly in the mirror before I quickly smoothed my face. Still, I tried to hold on to the image of the *Kaitan* like an energy shield to deflect whatever else was coming at me.

"Done!" Solara decreed. "Your dress mod should be done as well, by now. I'll retreat to my quarters to get into my own gown—with only four of you," she added, as the maids rushed to attend her. "Ollava, you make sure Qole is properly looked after. We wouldn't want her foiling everything we worked so hard to achieve, would we?"

"No, my princess." Ollava said it like she meant it, and shot me a warning look. I fired a glare right back at her before I could stop myself.

Deep breaths . . .

I had no choice but to surrender myself to five eager pairs

of hands as Solara swept out of the room. I honestly believed they would have tackled me if I'd tried to run from them. These maids were destroyers, ushering me into a dress like the fleet had escorted the *Kaitan* into Dracorva. Both parties threatened an equally aggressive response if I didn't comply.

One pair of hands even covered my eyes, blinding me, and I heard Ollava's shocked voice say, "Silly girl! Don't you know it's bad luck to see the dress before you're wearing it?"

No, I'd had no idea, as a matter of fact. And I didn't think this evening could get much worse, bad luck or not, but I closed my eyes, clenched my jaw, and let their hands have their way with me. And yet . . . without sight, being dressed was sensual rather than intrusive. Soft material slithered over and then hugged the skin of my chest and waist, falling over my hips like water to swirl around my legs. Nothing needed to be loosened or tightened, like it always did when I had my leather gear fitted to me on Alaxak.

My shame suddenly widened, deepened, darkened, like I was falling into a pit. Black fury caught me. How could I like even a small part of this? The dress held me flawlessly, no doubt thanks to the accurate image that Solara had generated of my body. They were treating me like a doll, a pet, and I was letting them. A maid lifted my feet, one at a time, and slid them onto a slope steep enough to nearly topple me. Firm ties lashed around my ankles, keeping me bound where I tottered. A hobbled creature, ready for display.

The hands soon guided me a few steps, and then Ollava told me to open my eyes.

When I did, I couldn't help it. I gaped at myself.

If I had barely recognized my own face under makeup, I had no idea who this woman was, standing in front of me in the mirrors. She was dark, dangerous, tempting, so much like the whisper of Shadow in my mind.

And that was exactly what I was supposed to be. The glittering-sky darkness of my hair curled into the shimmering black swath of fabric that wrapped in a spiral across my chest and around my waist. Only a panel of sheer, nearly invisible material filled the gaps. The disparate pieces joined around my hips—almost baring too much, but not quite—before falling in luxurious dark folds. In between those folds, the material changed from black to near-glowing purple, before fading to blinding white. When I swished my skirts, or even shifted, really, I looked like dancing Shadow. If I actually moved a step, two high slits parted up my thighs, revealing the black straps of heels winding up my calves.

"Great Collapse," I said. I had to admit I painted quite the picture, never mind that they'd only dressed me up like Shadow in order to parade me around. I was now both the strange, rustic girl *and* the exotic resource that they were using to save their royal necks.

"Our Solara knows what she's doing, she does," Ollava said proudly.

The princess herself came bursting through the doors as if the suite were for her own personal use, not mine. I gaped at her too.

If I was Shadow, Solara was blood. The red of her gown matched her lips and practically dripped down her chest, plunging almost to her navel between her breasts. It was non-existent in back, only pooling at the waistline to fall in slippery lines to the floor. She was stunning.

I was even more shocked to realize she was staring at me in nearly the same way.

"Hm," she said, with almost scientific reserve. "You look even better than I predicted." Then she smiled, her face lighting like a supernova. "Come. The party is waiting for us. And, since neither of us is beholden to anyone this evening ... yet ... then I will be your date." She gave a mock, flourishing bow, as if she were a man.

Solara Dracorte looped my arm through hers and dragged me out the door.

———

The ball was in the Dracorte citadel, but the palace was big enough and the ballroom far enough away that it felt like a walk across a city. Especially in the heels that were destroying my feet. I was dressed to kill, indeed; dressed to kill myself. It was appropriate then, I thought bitterly, that I was dressed like Shadow.

We weren't alone for long as we took several turbolifts and then wove our way through a hallway that was so grand, the white arches overhead vanished into both darkness and twinkling lights that looked like stars. Several of those lights, through some clever manipulation, rained down like meteors, illuminating the guests' faces.

Even the hallway was a storm of colors, perfumes, voices, and liquid-smooth or gem-encrusted fabrics brushing against my bare arms. The sensations and the sheer number of people threatened to overwhelm me; I had never in my life even seen so many people, let alone such opulence. It was too much, and I began to panic, my breath hitching. But Solara didn't give me the chance to stop and pull myself together, threading through the crowd as smoothly and fearlessly as Arjan piloting the skiff through an asteroid field, or Nev wielding a blade, while I lurched and bounced around behind her like a maimed ship getting towed at full power in another's wake. She was a born socialite, dodging greetings, questions, and even blatant advances from obvious suitors without pause, but always with a clever word or two. She only said I was her "special surprise guest" when anyone asked about me.

"Where is Arjan?" I asked as it occurred to me. I also wondered how the others were doing on the ship, but I was more worried about him. If the rest of the crew had followed my orders, then at the worst they'd be bored. My brother was out here, in all this.

Solara swiped a shimmering glass of something and passed it to me. "You'll see. Drink to calm your nerves."

Without much else to distract me, I downed the liquid in a gulp. My eyes and throat burned. Before I could even look for somewhere to set the glass, an unobtrusive server freed it from my hand.

I turned, startled by the unexpected motion, and almost groped a young woman standing nearby, deep in conversation with a much older man.

"I would be most delighted," the man said to her, "if you would share a bit of insight as to the recent market upheaval. Your opinion is clearly more valuable than anyone else's in this place." He scoffed at our surroundings as if they were shabby.

I was about to scoff at his overblown flirtation, an advance as heavy-handed and swaggering as the one Solara was currently fending off on the other side of me, when something about the woman snagged my attention.

Her hair was shaved on either side of her ears, a center column frozen in a curling bronze wave, like an ocean roller, and her dress was a glittering midnight sheath, exposing sharp shoulders and collarbones. Her skin was sleek and coppery, shimmering nearly as much as her dress. That sly smile, coming from dark lips was what gave her away.

Basra. Almost certainly a woman at this moment, too. I almost shouted her name. So much for this member of my crew, at least, passing the night in boredom on the ship.

Basra met my eyes and held a painted fingertip to her lips—no doubt to keep me from identifying her.

I was too addled to do anything but nod dumbly.

And then Solara slipped her arm through mine and tugged me away into the crowd. Just like that, it was as if I'd only hallucinated Basra looking more stunning in a dress than most of the royal women at this party. *Ancestors.* I hoped at least Eton and Telu were both still safely on board.

What the blasted hell was Basra doing? Perhaps she was only trying to have a ritzy evening out with Arjan. But no, she wouldn't have disobeyed my direct order to stay on the ship just for that. She had to be up to something else entirely. She could have turned or ducked away and I never would have been the wiser, so I suspected she wanted me to see her. I trusted her judgment, in that case . . . but I still would have liked to know what was going on.

And *how* in the systems could that man think my Shadow trader's financial opinion was one of the most valuable in the galaxy? Basra should have been so outmatched here that any market advice of hers would have been laughable.

I didn't have the time, or the ability, to investigate. Golden doors loomed nearly as tall as the indistinct ceiling at the end of the hallway, and the crowd made way for us. For Solara, rather, with me in tow behind her.

What am I doing here? The thought was like a gasp. This was crazy. Basra fit in better than I did. I belonged here like Solara belonged on Alaxak, working behind the counter with Larvut in Gamut's only bar.

I was tempted to turn around in spite of Solara's arm riveted to my own, but the ballroom stopped me short. Music rose in waves of stringed instruments over a deep undercurrent of synthetic bass that throbbed through my heels into the soles of my feet. Sleek, glistening masses of people swirled and pulsed to the sound, as colorful as the molecular clouds where I fished for Shadow. The room itself felt as endless as the black space around those clouds.

But I couldn't take in much of the scene before my eyes followed gaps in the crowd, like paths leading me, to a grand dais. All around the sweeping, tiered platform hung swaths of translucent material lit from within by holograms that made the cloth look like an actual nebula, billowing in unreal, entwining patterns. Underneath this imaginary sky stood Nevarian Dracorte.

Nev's light brown hair was more neatly combed than I'd ever seen it, falling effortlessly along the sides of his ridiculously perfect face. But it wasn't his face that made the air leave my lungs and my stomach plummet as if I were crash-landing. It was what was behind the face: the ironic arch of his brow, the challenging spark in his eyes, and the laugh on his lips. It was *him*.

A strange mix of both relief and longing hit me like a tidal wave. It suddenly didn't matter that I was furious with him. He was the one familiar thing in the whole ballroom. My eyes clung to the sight of him as if he were an island and I was drowning. I desperately wanted him to take my hand again, to guide me through this without letting go, without letting me lose myself.

I hardly noticed the woman *actually* by his side, holding his hand: Ket, in a swooping gown of white and silver. That was how intensely I was staring. How crazy I was. Nev was a prince, heir to a throne, betrothed to a sharp ice-fish of a princess, and I was a rough, ragged fishing captain from a forgotten corner of the galaxy. We were beyond polar opposites . . . but I couldn't tear my eyes away.

He looked more royal than ever before, every inch a prince, and I wasn't sure if I loved it or hated it. His suit glinted in shades of black, and his vest gleamed the darkest blue. His tie shone bright silver to match his eyes, eyes that were scanning the crowd.

They rested for a moment on a woman in a daring red gown, and I realized, with a start, that it was Solara. She had slipped away, leaving me standing alone. I didn't know how long I'd been staring like an idiot at Nev, but it was enough that she was now on the other side of the vast room. His gaze slid away from her and up to the ceiling, as if searching for something up there, then dropped back down . . . and found me.

Our eyes met, and now the entire room faded away: all sounds, colors, and faces. Everyone's but his.

XIII

Over and over, I had to push Qole from my mind.

Even Ket, stunning as always in a silver dress cut just low enough and just high enough to encourage the eye to carry on, merely made me wonder what Qole was going to be wearing tonight. I hoped she would forgive me for whatever Solara had done to her. For that matter, I hoped she would forgive me for bringing her here. I had been so stupidly, selfishly naïve and excited to show off Luvos and Dracorva to her, I had completely failed to see how out of place she'd be, how surprised she'd be by my family. By Ket.

"If I could just get her alone" seemed to have been my motto when I'd started on Alaxak, and it still was, even now that I was back on Luvos. *Perhaps we should just stick to ships where people want to kill me,* I thought bitterly, smiling at Ket in the same instant. My face must have gone through a brief spasm before it found the right shape.

"Ket, you look ravishing, as expected."

She smiled just enough to show her dimples and coyly turned her head, as it just so happened, in the direction of the media. "Why, thank you, my prince."

"You are famously welcome." I scanned the ballroom from the dais, hoping to either spot Qole or at least mentally fortify myself for the next conversation.

Conceived and built centuries ago, the room echoed many older design elements of the Dracorte family. Sweeping birds with silver-tipped wings were carved into the domed white walls, fading into darker blues as they rose, until they turned a pitch black that made the ceiling invisible. There, glowing faintly, were lights representing the Dracorte system. I craned my neck attempting to spot it, and sure enough, on the far edge of the cavernous ballroom flared the dot of light that represented Alaxak. Ket squeezed my arm, bringing my attention to the man approaching us.

It takes nerve for you to show up here, I thought. Dressed in the black and symbol-bedecked uniforms his family preferred, and possessing scrupulously shaved and lotioned cheeks, the man was burned into my memory from dozens of inter-system war games held at the Academy.

"Lord Khala Treznor-Nirmana." Even those born well before the marriage alliance had changed their surnames, as if to make it so the families had never been separate. I waited to bow until he finally did. I matched his with one almost as deep, except a shade shallower. Was that a slight, on my part? Observers wouldn't know, but they might wonder.

"Prince Nevarian Dracorte. It is such a relief to see that you have returned from your travels in such good health."

I raised an eyebrow. "Space travel can indeed be treacherous, but I was fortunate. I found only some trivial annoyances on an otherwise fruitful trip."

The lord smiled thinly and bowed to Ket, extending his hand, in which she placed hers.

She curtsied perfectly, to the exact right degree. "My lord, your presence here on Luvos is an honor. Are we fortunate enough to have King Treznor-Nirmana with us as well?"

I had to hand it to Ket, she had picked up my cues of displeasure with the man perfectly. And she could be so very, very mean. She had just reminded Khala that while he was the closest living male relative to the current leader of the Treznor-Nirmana family, King Makar, he wasn't a prince. It wasn't even known if he was an heir or not, since Makar Treznor-Nirmana was the very definition of eccentric and had made no announcements. Khala was simply the best the family could do for a representative from their systems, and it was a bit of an embarrassment. Still, this arrangement would have had at least Makar's tacit approval, and while everyone knew he was crazy, I also knew he was an unquestionable genius. That meant Khala was here for a reason.

He was too experienced to let such things show, but I had spent enough time staring at his shiny face across the table to recognize the pinched quality around his lips as annoyance. "Sadly, he had pressing business and could not attend."

His counterinsult wasn't subtle enough for Ket, since she practically sniffed in disdain.

I suddenly felt tired of every sentence being a duel of its own. I thought of Qole, and of honest conversations. I scanned the room again.

"Prince Nevarian, you look like a caged rimueng," a female voice said nearby, laced with amusement.

For once, I didn't feel a surge of annoyance and smiled when I turned. "Princess Daiyen. You've come far. And I'm sure I don't know what you mean, unless rimuengs cage themselves with the people they are most honored to join."

Daiyen Xiaolan, the eldest daughter of Queen Shanyi Xiaolan of planet Genlai, was dressed in a green sheath that started just above her knees and ended at the top of her throat, leaving her arms bare. It was made of hundreds of interlocking pieces reminiscent of leaves, and they clung to her like a second skin. She was as small as Ket, but her body had the lean muscle of a dancer or gymnast. Although she was by far my favorite of the royal offspring at these events, I had very little contact with her and didn't know how she occupied the majority of her time. In fact, it was kept enough of a secret that the media rumored she pursued untraditional hobbies for a Xiaolan heiress, such as piloting and combat. As much as that further warmed my heart toward her, I suspected it was a master ploy by her mother to build her mystique. The Xiaolans' style and quality was the envy of everyone, but they also controlled their image with an iron fist.

Her laugh was proper, but sincere. She dipped her knees in a curtsy that, considering her dress, defied the laws of physics and came off elegant. "Let us say that is the case. We are all glad to be in this cage, and to see you and Princess Ketrana so happy together."

It was nothing but a pleasantry, but I barely fought off the urge to shift in discomfort.

Lord Khala all but scoffed. "I hope you don't plan to distract us with your happiness because there isn't much to announce tomorrow."

I smiled. "We have prepared quite the distraction, especially since our good friends the Treznor-Nirmanas could use a little less attention on losing another border station so unexpectedly." My mother had taught me at an early age to always scan the most recent news feeds before any social events for ammunition, and it was one of my favorite tools. I had spotted this bit of information on the feed mere moments before leaving for the ball. Confusion flitted over Lord Khala's face, and I continued before he could interrupt. "We have some advances in Shadow I think you will be very interested in."

After all, I didn't see the harm in a small teaser of tomorrow's events.

Daiyen frowned. "I hope you've found a way to reduce its volatility. We would love to use Shadow in our engines, or even more widely in our system, but it's easy to see how it could have caused the Great Collapse. My mother isn't a fan."

"Oh, come now, that's superstition." I chuckled. "We have no evidence that Shadow collapsed the portals. We don't even know what *ran* them. Fear only breeds misunderstanding, and I think we're past that now."

Khala spread his hands. "Are we? We don't know, do we? That story got its start somehow."

Ket, either avoiding a scene or simply bored, went for more essential conversation. "Tell me, Princess Daiyen, did you arrive here with someone?"

"I did," Daiyen said dryly, taking a sip of her drink. "But he became engrossed in his own conversation." She leveled a cool look across the ballroom, and I followed her gaze from the dais to where Solara was holding resplendent court. She laughed gaily and slapped the chest of the current subject of her attentions. I blinked. Most people didn't do the party equivalent of an elbow dig to Heathran Belarius. It wasn't that he was heir to the most powerful family in the systems, the one we theoretically had an alliance with, so much as he had the humor of a frozen moon. He was tall, broad shouldered, and dark skinned, and possessed the strong features that made so many swoon over Belarius men, but I didn't think I had ever seen a smile grace his face. That is, until now. I glanced at Daiyen, but she had turned back to Ket, and I couldn't read anything in her expression.

The portion of my mind that typically enjoyed these games considered the implications there. Treznor-Nirmana had been trying to intimidate Belarius into distancing themselves from us, and I wondered if Xiaolan was making a move into what they perceived as a power vacuum. Leave it to Solara to thwart that little play at the party level—but not even that held my attention for long.

For once, I didn't feel as though my heart was in the social "niceties," duty or not. Ket ended up handling the brunt of the well-wishers, and soon, I was glancing from face to face with only one anticipation.

The strings started, bittersweet, and the bass hummed through the floor. I looked up from the dais toward to Alaxak again. When I looked down, I saw her.

She stood at the far edge of the ballroom, at the north entrance, and the crowd melted around her, keeping their distance. I could guess why. The Qole I had come to know was competent, keenly intelligent, and completely grounded. She stomped on the grating of her ship, she commanded mountains of men, she stood with a wide stance as if she expected a punch, and she would throw her own to protect her crew. Her greatest dream was to lie in a sunny meadow and watch the clouds. She was as rough as the planet she came from, and as surprising.

The Qole that I was looking at now was as mesmerizing and striking as the space in which she fished. Her hair rolled down in glittering coils like black smoke and stars. The dark swaths of her dress wrapped around her body, softening it to all arcs and curves, but nothing about her suggested that she was a safe plaything. If the other Qole was dangerous like a meteor, this Qole was dangerous like Shadow, an unknown element to the people around her, and they stayed well away, casting sideways glances.

Our eyes met. Hers were free of anger or intention, unguarded, taking me in. Like open windows, they invited me to see this other side of her that I hadn't yet met.

I had to talk to her.

Even possessed of a certain madness, I knew I couldn't simply abandon Ket and stroll over to Qole for some light evening chitchat. There would be attention on Qole before long, but we wanted the attention to be related to her diplomatic relationship with my family and her upcoming contributions to science. We distinctly did not want it from the tabloids.

Which meant I had to stop being a moody, disengaged princeling and put my skills to good use.

"Ket, my beautiful mirage," I murmured, "I'll be right back. I see the *Royal Times* photographer and I've been meaning to ask him about engagement photos."

Ketrana craned her neck to where the man was in busy conversation with a duchess. "Oh, Nevarian," she whispered excitedly. "He's considered simply the best for arranging candid moments."

I smiled. "I'll arrange a fortuitous moment with him right now."

To make it to the photographer, I distracted a potentate who was complaining about the erratic behavior of our drones by introducing her to a member of the clergy who had a theory regarding divine intervention and the relevance to drone activities, snatched a glass from a passing waiter in time to hand it to someone opening their mouth to speak to me, and pretended to not see an uncle once removed attempting to get my attention a few feet away. I arrived at the photographer's shoulder, and his wife's simultaneously alarmed and delighted expression caused him to turn and half choke on his drink.

"Your Highness! What a pleasure to see you on this auspicious day."

I smiled and nodded. "Indeed, made all the happier thanks to your presence. I'm an eternal fan of your work. My betrothed, Ketrana, would love nothing more than to speak to you about where you found those touchingly beautiful models to represent disadvantaged youth in your social awareness piece."

"The . . . Princess Ketrana? I would be honored, thrilled, pleased, I . . ." The photographer finished surreptitiously brushing crumbs from his waistcoat and ran out of words.

"She's right over there." I pointed. "You would do me a great favor if you could find it in your heart to have a brief conversation with her. In the meantime, I would be happy to entertain your wife with part of this dance."

Three startled partner changes in half as many minutes later, I was standing in front of Qole.

"My lady captain." I bowed. "Custom dictates that we continue this dance together."

She started as if alarmed by my presence. I supposed I had essentially materialized out of the crowd, but it didn't entirely explain the delicate flush to her cheeks that sprung up under her sharp-edged makeup.

"That's the third terrible idea you've had today," Qole retorted with her customary bluntness. I found it especially re-freshing after the past hour. "I dance about as well as a rock. Or about as well as I fit in here."

"Some rocks do dance, as you should know after expend-ing extensive time in asteroid fields, and you're right, you don't fit in here," I said. "You're much too beautiful for these people."

She started again as if I'd insulted her instead of compli-mented her.

Beautiful. I'd never called her that before. I hadn't even truly thought it, but what else could I have said? Anything other than that would have felt false. She was, in this moment, utterly beautiful to me. Now that I came to think of it, maybe she always had been and I just hadn't realized.

"Here," I continued, reaching out to her. "You can't come to a ball and not dance. And I promise you, I am the best teacher you will find here."

Qole hesitated, but I was playing dirty—you can't exactly deny a prince who is standing in the middle of a ballroom with his hand outstretched.

I watched her own hand rise and rest in mine. The warmth of her touch radiated down my arm and through my entire body. I stepped closer, placing my other hand at the small of her back, and then we were off.

Part of me expected to simply float off in a cloud of dy-namic dancing, the sort of synchronicity that planets and stars experienced. Instead, we reaffirmed that Qole was not in the habit of exaggerating or lying. She tripped in her heels, and I almost stumbled in turn as her feet got caught between mine.

"See," she hissed. "I implode at this."

I grinned. "You made me cook, I make you dance. The universe is in balance."

A hint of a smile played in her dangerous eyes. "The

universe has a ways to go, since I doubt I could be as bad as your cooking even if I face-planted this second."

I nodded agreeably. "You speak the truth. However, as luck would have it, my skill at dancing is inversely proportional to my skill at cooking. Just stop fighting me."

Qole stiffened even more at the suggestion, but then, miraculously, she relaxed, and I swept her in a simple pattern of half circles across the dance floor. The skirt of her gown looked like burning Shadow licking around both of our legs before I pulled her closer again—closer than before. The material covering her back where my hand was pressed was so thin, I could feel the heat of her body against my palm. I had to fight not to stare down at her, but, rather than awkwardness, I almost felt giddy. I loved to dance.

A single string left the ensemble to climb higher and higher. The bass began to beat faster with it, and every dancer on the floor responded. My feet remembered every step from hundreds of hours of practice, and I remembered my mother's advice—I was there to provide the focus, the structure, for my partner. I was the frame, and Qole was the painting.

We circled, and in perfect tandem with the couples around us I placed both hands on Qole's waist and lifted her for a full spin. Her hands instinctively found my shoulders, fingers tightening into me as her dress fluttered, revealing the smooth length of her leg.

Hundreds of couples spun through the air with us, movement and color blurring overhead, blending and fading into the points of light and darkness above us. When Qole dropped down, her body slid along mine. I felt like I was leaving the atmosphere.

We were together, finally. Now I'd have a few moments of peaceful conversation with her that no one could overhear, nestled in the dance floor like this, where everyone was only paying attention to their partners.

I leaned close to her ear to be discreet and caught the scent of her. There was spice there, leathers, metal. I should have apologized. I should have told her what to expect in the next few days. Instead something else seized control of my brain and words I hadn't even begun to consider saying came out:

"It's really good to see you."

The calm on Qole's face flickered, and I thought perhaps I had upset her somehow. Again.

But then she finally said, "I'm . . . glad. Too." She challenged me with her gaze to make a joke about it. I couldn't have if I'd tried, since I was far too busy being ridiculously pleased.

"Look, I'm sorry my family was so awkward with you," I said. "In truth, they aren't accustomed to dealing with outsiders any more than people on Alaxak are."

"But Alaxans *have* reasons to hate outsiders, particularly the Dracortes—not the other way around," Qole remarked without looking up at me, her lowered eyelids as dark as when her gaze was Shadow-filled. Her fingers tightened a fraction in mine. "Congratulations on your upcoming wedding, by the way."

I grimaced. Qole, being Qole, was not beating around the bush. I hadn't intentionally neglected to mention my betrothal, but the truth was that Qole made me wish Ket didn't exist. "Congratulations aren't exactly in order. The marriage is a political convenience. Every member of the royal family is paired with whoever is viewed as the best mate. We don't have any say in the matter."

It was what I'd been wanting to tell her all evening, and I felt like she had to understand.

"Sounds . . . romantic," she replied. "So, what, would you prefer condolences?"

We circled with a group of dancers, moving in rhythm to the strings and with the bodies around us. As the bass crashed into a long, low reverb, we all dipped our partners, and I supported Qole's weight in the crook of my arm. She resisted at first, tensing, but then she melted into me. Her waist against my arm, the movement of her body, felt as though it were feeding some part of me that was ravenous. I wrenched my eyes up to hers, and we lifted back into position.

I changed my mind—all evening I *had* been wanting to talk to Qole, but now all I wanted was this. To be with her, holding her, moving to the music.

And definitely not discussing my impending marriage.

"Not condolences either, no." I sought for a better way to explain. "While it is a part of our lives, it's a formality."

"Maybe that's why you forgot to mention it."

"I didn't mention it because it doesn't matter. Ket doesn't mean anything to me; it's simply that her bloodline, parenting, and genetics will work best with mine. Besides, pairings like this don't really change the outside relationships of many people."

Qole's eyes narrowed, but her voice was neutral when she spoke. "What do you mean?"

"I mean that many royals are in love and have relationships with others, even of lower classes, despite their official marriage. It's not advertised, but it's a well-known and accepted fact of life."

"It's sure not an accepted fact of life anywhere I've been." Her tone was no longer neutral, it was distinctly cold. "I don't know who would agree to come second—or third?—to that . . ." She swallowed whatever she was about to say in a bitter mouthful. "Although, right, what would I know? I haven't even been many places. But at least where I'm from we still have our pride, despite how much has been taken from us."

"Qole . . ."

Her brief silence was just as frosty. "But you don't mind if someone's poor, hey?"

This was treacherous ground. Her accent always meant trouble. It came out stronger only when she was distracted or furious, and she definitely wasn't distracted. From me, at any rate. She was so focused on our argument that she was actually dancing rather well.

"No, I—" I didn't get far.

"Then all those lucky girls will be *so* grateful for your interest." Sarcasm wasn't like her, but it seemed like she'd been practicing.

"No, I don't want that," I insisted.

"Oh, just the royal classes then, because everyone else's genes are so far beneath you?"

"No, I didn't mean that, either!" Once again, language was utterly failing me with Qole. "I mean that I can still have whatever relationship I want. Systems, *no,* I mean . . ."

I want you. But I couldn't say it. Not when she was glaring at me like she wanted to kill me. At the same time, her eyes were growing more distant. It was like she was slipping away from me, and I didn't know how to stop it.

"Since you can supposedly have whatever—whomever— you might want," she bit out, "then you shouldn't *have* to marry the ice-raker, hey?"

Ice-raker? Whatever that was, I gathered whom she meant. Frustration bubbled up within me. "Of course I have to." I jerked my head to encompass the people, the party. "Isn't it obvious?"

Qole stopped, and I almost bumped into her. "Not to me."

"Then I must be doing a very poor job explaining, because it's not like you're making this any harder than it has to be," I hissed with sarcasm to equal hers. "It's just an aspect of royal life you obviously can't understand."

Her eyes flashed alarmingly black for an instant, and it wasn't a trick of the light. "Of course I could never understand. I'm a simple, rustic idiot, after all." Her tone was raw and harsh. "It's for the best—my genetics are a bad match for just about anyone, anyway."

"Qole . . ." She'd never looked down on her family or her history before. For a rare moment, I was at a loss for words. What had happened? Where did I go from here? All I knew was that I somehow had to hold on to her, not let her go.

The music chose that inopportune moment to fade to a lingering end, and Qole pulled away to bow curtly. She should have curtsied, but I wasn't about to correct her.

Someone snickered, though, and I remembered we weren't alone. We were surrounded, in fact.

"Your *Highness,* thank you for the dance." She turned and attempted to walk away into the crowd.

Unfortunately for her, the crowd parted, letting her pass, and I realized that everyone around us was staring. Which meant the entire ballroom was staring. We were officially no longer being either surreptitious or unnoticed in our interaction.

"Oh, systems. Don't pay it any attention, Ketrana. My brother always did like to play in the mud, and I suppose he hasn't grown out of it."

Solara's voice, as pleasant as always, rang like the last clear note of the music across the ballroom from where she was standing next to Ket. Snide laughter followed it. A white-hot blade of fury sliced through me. Qole stumbled, almost flying into a group of people who backed away from her. Clutching at the skirt of her dress, she disappeared through the doors without another glance.

I strode after her, appearances be damned. I would make this right, and if it caused some gossip, so be it. I wasn't going to let Qole suffer another major embarrassment in my home by my hand—or Solara's.

"Ladies and gentlemen." The deep tones of Father's voice carried through the sound system and across the ballroom. "Please gather for the dance of the betrothed, as we celebrate the upcoming marriage of my eldest son, Prince Nevarian Thelarus Axandar Rubion Dracorte, to Princess Ketrana Akensia Sirine Gwenara Dracorte."

My steps faltered, then died. I could dodge decorum on many things, but not this. I couldn't flout my father's wishes publicly. I had a duty. It almost felt heavier than I could shoulder, yet I couldn't set it down.

Somehow, this seemed worse than all the dangers Qole and I had survived together. I had to abandon her to whatever she was feeling and dance with a fiancée I could not stand, never mind how *I* felt about any of it. How I felt about Qole.

I turned and walked back to the royal dais.

XIV

QOLE

FOR A BLINDING MINUTE, I HATED EVERYTHING ABOUT NEVARIAN Dracorte and his arrogant, revolting royal family. I wished they would all get sucked into a black hole so I would never have to see them again. A black hole, I thought with a bitter laugh that came out like a sob, had to be powerful enough to take care of even a Dracorte.

Without seeing, and walking as fast as I could in my blasted heels, I brushed by people in suits and gowns and even more ridiculous outfits I didn't know the names for—some that were barely there—before I turned a corner and found myself in dimmer, less populated hallways of white stone shot with silver. Dark blue carpets ran the stretching lengths, and ornate

250

alloy wall sconces emitted faint, frosty glows. I only paused long enough to wipe my eyes—*idiot tears from an idiot captain over an idiot prince*—before I continued moving, my arms hugging my half-revealed stomach through the whispery, twisting fabrics of my dress. The citadel was more than warm enough, but all the mocking eyes on me had raised my flesh like a chill. Made me feel naked.

How did Nev stand it? So many people watching him all the time ... *No,* I told myself firmly, *you are not going to feel sorry for him.* Besides, he seemed to thrive under all the attention. I, on the other hand, withered and shrank, seeming to lose more of myself every minute.

... I had to get out of here.

I turned another corner so quickly that my ankle buckled in one of my heels and pitched me against the nearest wall ... and almost into a white statue that looked suspiciously like Nev. No one was around to raise a too-sleek eyebrow at the biting curse that ricocheted around the high, narrower hall. For once, I was alone.

Sagging against the cool, smooth stone, I slid down until I hit the floor, not caring an atom's worth that this was an inappropriate way for me to be sitting in this gown ... or to be sitting at all. I cared so little, in fact, that I twitched aside the black, purple, and white folds of the skirt, baring nearly the length of my legs, to get at the buckles of my damned heels.

Once the shoes were free of my feet—or vice versa—and dangling in one hand by their long straps, I stood, shoved away from the statue of maybe-Nev, and set off down the hall again. Part of me wanted to drop the heels, but then another absurd part of me thought Solara might want them back, never mind that she probably had five hundred pairs. And that they might not even be in her size.

I crushed what felt like light-years of soft blue carpet under my bare feet. I wasn't sure where I was going. All I knew was that I wanted to head in the opposite direction of any invasive, mocking pairs of eyes, or any member of the Dracorte family. And if my march took me in the direction of my ship, and off this systems-damned planet, so much the better.

...Did I really mean that? In spite of Nev's and my agreement, if that was all it had been, was I willing to abandon this place? Maybe, now that I'd seen the type of people who wanted to benefit from studying me. I'd almost believed, for a little while, that they were different from how they seemed. Nev had believed in his family's goodness, rightness, after all ...

But he obviously believed a lot of scat that no one but a reeking royal would swallow about the *greater good,* when all royals really cared about was themselves. Nev seemed blinded by the dazzle that he'd been raised with, and I almost couldn't blame him. With all these vibrant colors, these masking perfumes, these luxurious textures and vast indoor palaces, I couldn't even get my bearings. The ground underneath me still felt off-kilter, in spite of my feet being out of the heels.

No, I wouldn't leave yet. But at the very least, I wanted to talk to my crew to regain some perspective. Even Eton's belligerent arguments would be reassuring right now. The *Kaitan* was where I needed to be, a home away from home. There wasn't any more Shadow on board, so I couldn't sense that to find them, but somehow I'd reach my ship eventually.

Whipping around another corner, I skidded to a halt, as did my thoughts.

Standing in the shadows in front of me were twelve armored guards. For a second, we stared at each other. And then my eyes shot around. This hallway was a lot darker. The carpet had vanished, leaving only chilly stone under my toes. No perfumes scented the air, and the dim lighting was even colder. There were no other people within sight or even my hearing range.

"Excuse me, Miss Uvgamut," one of them began. He was the one with the Disruption Blade. The others had an array of guns. He sounded perfectly polite, but that made no difference. "May I ask where you're going in such a hurry?"

"My ship," I breathed. "I wasn't welcome there, at the ball. I just want to go home." *I want to see my friends and wrap myself in my furs,* I almost added, but seeing my small form reflected in his polished armor made me not want to sound any more vulnerable than I already was. I straightened my back, trying to stand taller.

His eyebrows rose. "Miss Uvgamut, I'm very sorry. That's not possible."

Worry arced through me like a static charge. My voice hardened. "Why not?"

His hand dropped and he spread his fingers wide at the soldiers behind him—a signal to them to fan out and start circling around me, I realized, when they started to do so. "Miss, would you come with us, please?" But he said it in a voice that didn't sound at all like a request.

All my internal alarms started screaming at once. This felt very, very wrong. But now, my confusion vaporized. I was no longer off-balance. My breath quickened, my muscles tensed, and my weight shifted to the balls of my feet. My body was telling me exactly what to do.

It was telling me to run.

I spun in place, and I ran. I heard the Bladeguard swear and issue a soft command; before I made it ten steps and heard their boots pounding on the ground behind me, I knew I wouldn't make it. They were faster than I was, especially with the damned gown tangling around my legs.

"Sub her!"

I didn't know what that meant, and I didn't want to find out. I halted, gripped the long straps of my shoes in either hand, and pivoted in the same breath.

One of the heels whipped the first guard in the face, probably destroying his cheek in the process, while the other one crushed the second guard's hand and sent his pistol spinning away. My vision began to darken.

"Get her before her eyes go!"

One of them tackled me. His sizable mass brought me to the cold, hard ground. My dress tore, but the damage to my body was worse. My breath left me in a rush, my ribs creaked, and my shoulder screamed.

Scream. I opened my mouth and let out a shriek that practically vibrated the walls. The guard who'd tackled me clapped a hand over my mouth, mashing my lip against my tooth. I tasted the metallic flavor of blood.

I jerked my head, and my teeth sank into his hand with all the strength in my jaws. I tasted *his* blood then, even through his glove.

He shouted a curse. His other hand ripped free from underneath my weight and cuffed me over the head. My temple bounced against the ground, and stars flashed in my vision, brightening the rapidly encroaching darkness. They weren't the subtly twinkling stars of the still sky, or the liquid streaks of an engaged Belarius Drive. These were violent stars, bursting and popping like high-speed supernovas. Only then did my teeth let go of him.

Somebody seized a handful of my hair, breaking some of

the jeweled strands braided into it. A tinkling rain of gems on the hard floor accompanied the sting of an injection in my neck.

The stars burst all over my body then, tingling, weighting my limbs with their impossible gravity. I couldn't move. I could barely protest as two guards lifted me up by my arms and began dragging me down the hallway, away from the direction of the ball or any help. Into the darkness.

But the darkness was barely in my eyes anymore. I tried to reach for the Shadow beckoning at the edges of my vision, and I couldn't. Whatever they'd given me kept me from it, just like it kept me from lifting my head.

My eyes rolled back under heavy lids, and a different sort of darkness claimed me.

———

I opened my eyes only a few more times before we arrived, enough to know that I had no idea where I was, and that they'd carried me, silently, for a long way. Long enough for me to wonder at the inefficiency of not using a chair or bed equipped with hover jets, or even old-fashioned wheels. But maybe they didn't want to draw more attention to themselves than one limp body could already bring. All the turbolifts we took, dropping us deeper into the depths of the citadel, seemed to be for private use only.

After we passed through a pair of thick, alloy doors—any opulence in the décor long since abandoned—I realized, with a sickening lurch, that the room almost looked familiar, even in my blurred, murky vision.

It was white, lined in counters, cupboards, and shiny equipment. The closest object that I could make out in the center of the room was a long table, outfitted with straps and blinding spotlights. An operating table, nearly identical to the one on the Treznor-Nirmana destroyer. Other tables were beyond it, but I had trouble focusing that far.

I couldn't fight nearly as much as the last time, however, as they hefted me, gown and all, onto the table. The bindings bit into my arms and legs as they positioned and tightened straps, but I was unable to even tug against them, let alone break them.

The guards blurred into the background. Maybe some of them had left, but I couldn't tell. Time passed, but how much I wasn't sure. Maybe only a half hour. Maybe hours. Voices faded in and out, and my shoulder blades grew sore and cold from the metal surface of the table.

Eventually, I heard a voice that caught my drifting attention. It was vaguely familiar, and angry, unlike any of the other voices. "What were you thinking? She isn't supposed to be here."

"Apologies, my lord," the Bladeguard replied in his polite, steady tone, "but she was attempting to return to her ship to leave. She resisted, and we had to act fast. This was the only place we could take her where she wouldn't be seen in this condition."

"Did *she* see?"

"Her eyes have been open intermittently."

There was a sigh. "The damage is already done, thanks to you, but perhaps we can control it. If this sets us back, there will be repercussions."

"Yes, my lord. Should we move her?"

"This is the most secure place at the moment. We don't want anyone else getting their hands on her." The voice was only irritated now, the anger under control. "We'll move her elsewhere when all our guests have departed. Stand by, for now."

Someone else came into focus then, leaning over me: a man with close-cropped dark hair, a clean face, and a dark blue lab coat over a sleek black suit. Other than the lab coat, he could have just come from the ball. His silver-gray eyes reminded me of scalpels. They were already cutting into me.

"It's a pleasure to see you again, Captain Qole Uvgamut," Rubion Dracorte said in a too-smooth voice. "I apologize for your treatment. I didn't mean for this to happen. You and I were supposed to meet for testing tomorrow, and those tests wouldn't have involved any of . . . this." He glanced down at my restraints with a regretful expression. Still, his eyes were curious, eager. "Your guards panicked. Really, I regret it, and I hope you'll let me make amends."

His eyes didn't linger on me as he said this but glanced somewhere above.

A strangled, terrified laugh escaped me. "Amends? Should have thought of that before you strapped me down." I sounded drunk, but I couldn't make my words any clearer.

"This doesn't have to be uncomfortable." Again, Rubion glanced over the top of me. I tried to turn my head in that direction, but, at his nod, bright lights blinded me. All I could see was him, looming over me on a background of glaring white.

I flinched and squinted, my fear spiking. My heart felt like it was trying to leap out of my chest and run, like I couldn't. "This isn't comfortable."

"We'll find you better accommodations soon. In the meantime, how about we get rid of these?"

To my surprise, my arms and legs suddenly came free, and

a pair of hands found my bare shoulders, helping me to sit up. For a second, I was so relieved I almost didn't care that they were Rubion's.

I didn't trust my legs to stand. I perched unsteadily at the edge of the table, bracing myself to hold my body upright. The lights were behind me now, and Rubion looked a little less threatening without the glare surrounding him.

He rested a hand on my arm. "There's no need to be afraid. Like I said, this was all unintentional."

I shrugged off his hand and tossed my head at the ringing lights, the lab. A wave of dizziness swept over me at the sudden movement, so I squeezed my eyes closed and said through a clenched jaw, "What's with the setup, then? You *accidentally* have a place like this? Looks pretty intentional to me."

"This lab is used for our research, yes, but you were never meant to be here. As for the lights, I prefer to meet your eyes while we talk." He tapped my chin to get me to look at him again, smiling apologetically. "I'm sure you understand."

He wanted to make sure he didn't see any Shadow there. He wanted me defenseless. "Oh, so you want to *talk* before the knives come out. How civil."

"My aim is not to hurt you, I promise."

"Right." I let out another choked laugh. "You're just like the other royals. You Dracortes like to pretend you're not, but you're the same as everyone else."

"No, we're far beyond everyone else," Rubion said, pulling away only to lean next to me against the edge of the table. I wished I could scoot away. "Our research has far surpassed the Treznor-Nirmanas'."

I hadn't meant the research, exactly. He must have been deliberately misinterpreting me. Either that, or he was crazy.

"They still imagine it's possible to beat us," he continued, "but we've simply been feeding their spies false information, with just enough truth to keep them occupied. Unbeknownst to them, we've had the formula to bind Shadow as a more stable, organic form of fuel for some time now. The grand reveal tomorrow will be real, of course, but serves double duty as prelude to something else."

I shook my head, my thoughts stumbling to keep up. "If you already have what you need . . . why do you need me?"

He smiled in a genuine way that I found more frightening than his eyes. "Don't you know? You have a Shadow affinity like nothing anyone has ever seen. You have abilities that could be far more valuable than anything to do with fuel."

I leaned away from him even at the risk of toppling over. "That's exactly what the Treznor-Nirmanas thought." It didn't matter that Rubion had let me up from the table and wasn't exactly coming at me with knives; I wasn't close to reassured.

"They think that because we thought of it first. Again, we're much farther in our research than they've guessed. Of course, we've already been testing others with milder affinities," he clarified, as if I'd asked, "from other nigh-uninhabitable planets near smaller Shadow harvesting areas. They've taken us far, but not as far as we need. Either the levels of Shadow in their systems were too low, or they were mad already, rendering them less optimal subjects. But your family line has undergone more generations of Shadow exposure than anyone else's we've yet found, and you're still alive for our tests to analyze—for a while yet, we hope. Your kin go mad and die early, yes?" He paused, as if actually waiting for an answer. When my mouth only dropped open and nothing came out, he continued. "All the more reason for haste. We hope to learn as much from you as we can."

"But . . . I don't understand." I shook my head again, trying to clear the fog still in my brain, the blinding light, the rising panic. It didn't work. "Even if you want to study me for something other than fuel, there was no reason to bring me here before the conference. For the ball."

"The timing is distinctly beneficial, though not crucial for our experimentation as I led Nevarian to believe. It's more for . . . how shall I say . . . the presentation. Our adaptation of Shadow into a mass-market energy source is already enough to keep our family afloat and to satisfy our investors and the public when announced tomorrow. But we needed an edge, a deathblow to our competition. The Treznor-Nirmanas *needed* to comprehend what we were doing so that they, and everyone else, understood our triumph. We let slip enough for them to grasp your importance, once Nevarian found you."

Rubion was the reason the destroyer had come after us. He hadn't only put his nephew in danger, he'd orchestrated the danger.

He rubbed his chin almost ruefully. "We let slip too much because they acted faster than anticipated, and it nearly cost us *you*. But, no matter, what's done is done, and our victory will be all the more triumphant for it. Tomorrow, amid the celebration of our revolutionary new fuel, I'll plant the news in a few choice ears that we'll shortly have the capability to engineer superhumans. Now that they know we have you, and have even seen you with us, on shining display"—he tugged at the skirt of my gown almost playfully—"they'll have no doubt. It was brilliant to bring you to the ball, actually. Nevarian has been so useful in this and many other things. Thelarus didn't believe he was up to the task, but with a bit of misdirection, my nephew can be quite capable. I would thank him, but . . ." He shrugged that graceful, nonchalant Dracorte shrug. "It's just a pity he couldn't have *kept* you at the ball."

"Nev . . . Nev doesn't know about any of this?" I knew the

answer even as I asked. Of course he didn't. There was no way. He was a Dracorte, and at times he might be naïve, arrogant, and blind . . . but he wasn't this.

"Prince Nevarian has no idea what is happening at the moment, and it's for the best. He had to believe he was accomplishing something noble, rather than something great . . . a fault in him that Thelarus regrets, since it requires the heir to be kept in the dark for some tasks that require harsher methods. But my nephew is young; he's still learning. Someday, he'll understand these efforts were necessary."

A bitter taste rose in my mouth. The king had let me take his hand, thanked me for coming to help his family and for saving his son's life . . . and then he'd commanded the guards to stop me if I tried to leave and told Rubion to use me as he saw fit, wiping away any illusion of choice I might have had.

The thought of Marsius doing these types of things for Nev someday made my stomach turn. Or maybe it was the way Nev's uncle was still looking at me.

But Nev and Marsius were still good, I knew it—not that it made me feel better. That made it worse. Because somewhere along the line, when kids like Marsius became men like Rubion—or when Nev became king like Thelarus—the Dracortes learned how to be monsters. They didn't even need powers like mine to do it.

Those Dracortes were the strange, disturbing, inhuman creatures. Not me.

"But you needn't fear this," Rubion continued. "You will be part of something important. I don't mean the conference, or even my family's forthcoming successes. Something *greater.*" He brushed the scattered strands of hair back from my face, peering into my eyes as though seeing the Shadow deep inside me. "Something you couldn't possibly imagine."

"If I can't understand, why bother explaining then?" I demanded, my back straightening as I tried to summon some anger—maybe even actual Shadow. But my voice came out high, and only tears were in my eyes. "Why not just cut me open now and get it over with?"

He waved his hand. "There will be none of that. I want us to be friends. You and I are going to do something together that no one else has dreamed. Of course, being a very special young woman at a critical time that means that, while I'm sure everyone would prefer to take more care with you, there are things we must learn quickly. But luckily"—his smile was almost regretful again—"we now have others more suitable for our . . . baser . . . experiments. Experiments you will never have to witness or undergo, so you never have to worry."

I missed most of what he said after *we now have others.*

Others. My breath, my blood, all thought in my brain screamed to a halt. My entire life teetered in that moment, on that one word.

"I hoped if I explained, told you the truth—because unlike Nevarian, you appreciate the truth, don't you, delivered without garnish?—I hoped you would understand. You'll be kept safe, even comfortable after this unfortunate mishap, and become part of something more important than even my family's well-being, or anyone's."

I wasn't really listening to him. "Where's Arjan?"

Arjan. He was supposed to be at the ball, but I hadn't seen him—only Basra, who had probably been looking for him too, along with whatever else she might have been doing. She'd had *very* good reason to disobey my command to stay on the ship, if that was the case.

Rubion paused, lips pursed as if disappointed in my response, and began to say something reassuring in that smooth tone. But his hesitation was enough.

"Where is my brother?" I lunged forward on the table, half sliding off, and seized the lapels of his lab coat. The darkness shivered on the edges of my vision, as if trying to creep farther into my eyes.

I just needed more . . .

Rubion recoiled as if I were an unfortunate mess that was coming too close to getting on his shoes, while other hands seized my shoulders and pulled me back.

"If you'll excuse me." He slid the lab coat from his shoulders and straightened the cuffs of his suit. "I hate royal functions, but I hate unnecessary emotional outbursts more. I must say my formal farewells this evening anyway, for appearance's sake. I'll return once you're calmer and more willing to listen to reason." He pivoted away as I was forced back down onto the table, my restraints snapped into place once again. I tried to fight, but I was so dizzy and weak I mostly just cursed and yelled. "Keep the light on her, and try to keep her awake. Monitor her eyes along with how much suppressant you're giving her. If they turn more than twenty percent, increase the dosage. Put her out, if necessary."

In the blinding glare, I didn't see him leave. But I heard the heavy hiss of a door opening and closing.

So, Nev's uncle *had* just come from the ball, and now he was going back like nothing was happening here. Like he didn't have me strapped to a table, like he didn't have Arjan . . . somewhere.

Where was Arjan? The light . . . It wasn't only for them to see me better. It was to keep me from seeing the room. Not whatever, but maybe *whoever* might be in it.

I needed the darkness inside me *now,* in more ways than one. I gritted my teeth against the sobs trying to escape and took a deep, shuddering breath.

"Please," I whispered. *Please, please, please.* I mouthed the word silently as I strained as hard as I'd ever reached for anything in my life. None of the guards who were no doubt in the room would actually see me reaching, since my struggle was entirely on the inside. Maybe they would think I was praying.

The blackness at the corners of my vision pulsed, once. I closed my eyes before anyone could notice. But even behind my lids, the light grew darker. Dark enough to see, I hoped, when I opened them again.

A hand fell on my shoulder. "Miss, please try to stay awake."

I almost didn't want to, but I turned my head in the direction Rubion had been looking earlier in our conversation, dropped my cheek against the cold metal table, and opened my eyes. My vision focused through the dark veil . . . and my lungs became a void. I couldn't breathe. I couldn't speak. My chest was collapsing.

A guard let out a shout, but I barely heard him.

Arjan was laid out on a table on the far side of the room. He had only a towel draped across his hips, the rest of his body exposed, aside from where the straps held him down. Wires, tubes, and needles plunged into every part of him or clamped onto the ends of his fingers. Along one arm and hand, patches of skin had been burned or cut away, like earth being tested for minerals to mine. A clear film coated any open wounds to keep out infection, but it didn't hide what they'd done, leaving the tissue exposed as if under glass. And even from this distance, I could see that one of his eye sockets was rimmed in synthetic lining—empty, where an eye had been.

For a moment, only one thought pulsed with every beat of my heart: *Arjan, Arjan, Arjan.*

The void in my lungs shrank, shrank, shrank . . . and then exploded.

I wasn't sure when I started screaming, or if it was even originating from my mouth or from what felt like the gaping hole in my chest. But then I could feel it ripping through my throat. My hand strained for Arjan against the straps.

A half-dozen guards were already holding me down, and someone in a lab coat was readying a syringe.

I couldn't free myself. But I did encounter blackness like never before. Blackness that entirely swallowed my vision, and then turned to the brightest, purest white.

XV

NEV

KEEPING A SMILE IN PLACE WHILE RETURNING TO THE ROYAL DAIS WAS one of the hardest things I'd had to do in my life. It took everything I'd ever learned about controlling my facial features and body language. As I made my way through the crowd, part of me didn't care if I managed to fool the hundreds of onlookers into thinking Prince Nevarian was as lively as ever. And yet I had to care. Saving face for myself might not matter, but if I embarrassed my family here, now, with all the systems watching, the result would be catastrophic.

I heard people talking, and the Unifier Bishop spread his hands in blessing, but it was in the background. My mouth formed a smile and my hand took Ket's, but all I could think about was Qole, somewhere in the palace, angry and despising everything about me.

The music began again, a choir lending our first dance as a betrothed couple an almost reverential air.

Ket tilted her chin up and didn't smile as we began to dance, alone on the giant ballroom floor. One of her hands rested in mine, the other on my arm, which I held out in the rigid posture customary for the slow walks and cross changes of the form.

If Ket remained this emotionless and unengaged, it would almost be worse than not having the dance at all. I tore my mind away from Qole and set it on the task at hand.

"Ketrana, you dance as lovely as you look." Before the sentence was out, I knew it was a pathetic attempt.

She didn't respond, except to arch her neck away from me even more. My dance with Qole must have been more attention-grabbing than I had realized. That, and Solara's snide commentary couldn't have helped.

I briefly toyed with ordering her to look happy, but if that made her angrier it could seriously backfire. I couldn't fight with her on the dance floor; I had to make her smile.

Everything I'd been learning about how to make Qole smile simply didn't apply here. Any sense of the absurd, any self-recognition, and most especially any honesty would have the exact wrong effect.

Which probably meant I would just have to act the opposite.

"This is one of the most important moments of my life," I told her. If I hadn't felt such revulsion, I would have laughed hysterically.

No reaction.

"The honor you grant me is supreme. I thank you, truly,

from the bottom of my heart." *I want nothing to do with this; I want nothing to do with this.*

Evidently, Ket was vain enough to believe she was honoring me, since she relaxed a little into the dance for the first time. Her tiny frame felt so different from Qole's that I remained silent for a moment, trying to process it.

It was progress, but not enough, and we were running out of time. I knew what she wanted to hear. I knew the lie that would kill anything real.

I tasted bile in my mouth as I opened it. "I'm glad to be finally dancing with someone who knows what they are doing. I was just trying to be polite, but that poor, rustic girl was so bad it was embarrassing."

But the dance was so much better.

I couldn't bring myself to say anything directly against Qole's character, but even so, it felt like I had betrayed her yet again. First each member of my family had mistreated her, and now I was joining in, behind her back.

Ket giggled and tossed her hair. "Oh, I know." Her hand lightly caressed my arm. "There's nobody quite like me."

Mission accomplished. I felt misery settle into my bones.

———

When the song finally ended, applause erupted, cheers rang out, and everyone felt like they weren't uptight, backstabbing poseurs. Except, notably, me.

People crowded back on the dance floor as another song began, but I moved to escort Ket back to the dais to greet my family. Solara intercepted us. I narrowed my eyes, trying to decide if a public altercation with my sister was worth it.

Given how publicly she had demeaned Qole, it was an attractive option.

"My darling, gorgeous Ket!" Solara cried. "You were a vision. Would you mind terribly if I tore my brother away from you for just a moment? I've asked the musicians for 'Flight of the Dracortes,' and I doubt anyone else here is up to speed. Besides, it's tradition. Unless you're *afraid,* brother." She grinned at me, tugging on the lapel of my suit.

"Flight of the Dracortes" was as dynamic a piece as it was a difficult dance. Most participants never attempted the proper steps, and instead used a simpler variant that had been developed over the years. Customarily, a Dracorte performed it after officially completing the trial of their Dracorte Flight, as a further sign that they had proven themselves.

"Afraid? What would I be afraid of? *Your* skills?" I brushed her hand off my lapel. "But honestly, I haven't the time for this, Solara."

"Prince Nevarian and Princess Solara shall now dance 'Flight of the Dracortes' in a brother-sister dance," an entirely too-breathless announcer nearly squealed. Sure enough, the beginning solo notes began to lilt, filling the air with electricity.

Great Collapse, is there no end to the hoops I have to jump through? I grabbed her hand, all but snarling. "Very well, then, I'll show you what I'm capable of."

Solara smiled. "That's what the dance is for, my brother."

Some dances were difficult not because they were fast, but because they were slow. The measured pace of the movements was critical, and flaws could arise in the steps, hand gestures, and fluidity that were not nearly as visible in high-energy dancing. "Flight of the Dracortes," at one time, had been this kind of dance. It had become faster and faster over the centuries, until it now encompassed the worst of both worlds. Requiring dizzying speed and complete accuracy, it would have been hellish if it weren't a joy to learn.

I had mastered it at a young age. Every hook, every heel pull, every step I had learned with the same precision as fencing or sparring—which was exactly what Solara and I were doing.

Without faltering, she matched me step for step. She responded to my lead with complete assurance. She wasn't backing down, and that served only to make me angrier. I raised her hand and spun her into me, then framed her as she went through a staccato burst of footwork to the beat that infiltrated the piano and strings.

"Have you no shame?" I seethed through my smile. "How could you treat our *guest* that way? She's lost enough as it is, and her cooperation is crucial to our research."

Solara finished in a free spin, two steps away, as all music except for the rumble of the bass line faded away. She smiled, an expression that didn't match her serious tone as she murmured so only I could hear, "Father commanded me to make Qole leave."

The music resumed. We moved without touching, in perfect sync with head and hands, a motion that rolled down our bodies to our feet. With a snap and a step, we were back together.

"What?" I covered myself with a laugh that to my ears sounded ridiculously hollow.

"I don't know, but Nev, it seemed really strange. He was very clear." Solara's expression didn't waver; it remained happy and carefree, even as I felt like I'd been gutted.

What was going on? Why would Father order Solara to do such a thing? For a split second, a terrifying thought flitted through my head, but I dismissed it immediately. My family would never . . .

My foot faltered a step. I recovered almost instantly, but had we been judged in this dance, Solara would have won. And yet, as the song ended to thunderous applause from the audience, I couldn't have cared less who'd won or lost. I bowed to my sister, my thoughts already racing ahead. I needed to find Father; I needed answers.

But the king was nowhere in sight.

———

"Marsius! Have you seen Father?"

Marsius evidently knew of the same secret passageway out of the ballroom that I did, for which I had to give him credit—I had been at least two years older when I'd discovered that one of the curtained alcoves accessed a hallway leading to other parts of the palace.

He looked up and blinked from the deep concentration he had been bestowing on approximately half a cake. "No. How did you find me? Hey, do you want to play Assassins and Kings?"

I smiled hollowly. "Not right now, I'm afraid. I have something I must take care of. Soon, all right?" Guilt nagged at me, and I called over my shoulder as I passed, "I'm sorry that I haven't spent much time with you lately."

"It's okay." Marsius shrugged and went back to devouring his cake. "I had a great time with Arjan. He knew some really fun games. And he showed me some tricks with knives!"

That stopped me short. "Marsius, do you know where Arjan is?" Perhaps Qole was with him.

Marsius looked up at me and rolled his eyes. "How could

I? He's not here. But he got invited to the party so that's probably where he is." He shook his head in a very adult manner.
"I don't like this kind of party all that much."

I hadn't seen Arjan anywhere at the ball, but then, I had
been entirely focused on Qole. I hoped he was at least having
a better evening than she, and that Father hadn't given any
particular orders to embarrass him as well.

What in the systems was the matter with my family? It was
time they started living up to the standards we'd long been
spouting in our rhetoric and using to judge others. It was time
I had a serious discussion with the king.

The delay it took to find Father in his private office had
distilled my confusion, guilt, and misery into a towering rage.
The room was as elegant and functional as he was, with a
great semicircle of a desk, tall-backed leather chairs, and most
importantly, network access to anything he might need. He
stood at his desk rather than sat, still wearing his gray suit and
no doubt expecting to return to the ball shortly. Disappearing
to deal with a matter of urgency was not unusual for him, but
right now, I didn't care what it might be.

"Where is Qole?"

Father looked up from the series of images projected
along one wall of the study. Everything from news feeds to
security cameras was playing within the dizzying array before him. I had always been impressed with how he seemed
able to parse all the information in seconds. For a moment,
I felt reassured to see him standing there, the straight lines
of his posture always making me think of the strength and
confidence I had relied on so many times over the years. But
then that was supplanted by the anger that had been building
all evening.

"Hello, Nev. I see you decided to leave your ball." There was a touch of disapproval in his voice.

"Never mind the ball," I snapped. "Where. Is. Qole? No one knows, not security, nor even Devrak. I've looked in her room and checked in with her ship. She's vanished, and you and the rest of the family are directly responsible for driving her off." I was starting to hit critical mass. "Do you know how dangerous it could be for her? This place is practically crawling with Treznor lackeys."

"Fortunately, I can assure you that she won't be appropriated by them. And it's safe to say that the rest of the family has had nothing to do with her disappearance . . . nor Devrak. Not even he is privy to this." Father sighed and flicked a finger at one of the security feeds. It dimmed and vanished. Before it did, I caught a glimpse of an unadorned hallway. It was one of a hundred like it, and could have been anywhere.

Questions piled on top of one another, and it was almost impossible to pick one out of the mix. "What—what do you mean?"

"The Alaxan had to be taken for examination and testing. Something came up, and we could no longer wait."

I gaped. "Testing? Tonight? Why didn't you tell me?"

Father considered me. "You're so focused on her that you won't even ask *what* came up? But I'll indulge you. It's quite obvious you are smitten with her, and so I didn't tell you because your reaction wouldn't have been any more constructive then than it is now. I didn't want to distress you—you need to at least look the part of the triumphant Dracorte heir for our guests, if you're not going to behave like it. Which is perhaps more reason for us to move forward with the Alaxan tonight. The earlier you are separated, the better."

Smitten? A little voice in my head questioned such an un-ceremonious term, whether or not it was apt. And how could it have been so obvious to him when I wasn't even entirely sure? Right now, all I felt was sickening worry.

"Father . . ." I paused before asking the question that had formed first, but I had been most afraid to ask. "You're not hurting her, right?"

"Not so far as I'm aware, but I've had more important things to do than memorize the specifics of what is to come for her. Does it matter?"

"Yes, it matters!" I almost yelled. I collected myself while he stared at me as if I were Marsius throwing a tantrum. "Is she comfortable? Did she consent to being there?"

"With this new turn of events, not likely. And no."

I struggled to pick just one emotion to feel out of every one crashing into me. "What new turn of events?" I finally asked.

"She tried to leave, and we couldn't allow that."

The bottom dropped out of my stomach. She'd stormed away, not just to leave the ball . . . but to leave Luvos. Because of me. And now she was being held against her will—not by me, but *I* was the reason she was here in the first place.

It was all because of me. Not that I couldn't be enraged at those who had helped.

"You drove her off!" Father's eyes narrowed, but I didn't let him interject. "And Uncle is fine with this? He knew all along that there was a possibility he might forcibly study whomever I brought back?"

"Since he was far less surprised than I that you brought anyone back at all, then I'd guess yes, of course he knew. I'm not sure what purpose this mental exercise is serving, Nevarian."

Rubion. My uncle was far more insidious than I'd ever imagined, and he'd taken full advantage of my naïveté. But I would have to deal with him later. "How can you be so calm about this? This is . . . horrible. This is the exact way the Treznor-Nirmanas would behave." I felt the same disgust that I had that day on their destroyer, except now I stood in Father's office and felt it for him.

For us.

"No, it's not," Father replied sharply. "They were ready to kill her on the spot for convenience. We are running tests, and nothing unnecessary will be done. This is a critical part of the research, I'm afraid—research that you were eager to have us conduct."

"*No,* I was *not,*" I snarled at him, stepping closer, angrier than I'd ever dared to be with him. "Not like this. I was taught that people should be treated with respect and dignity. I was told that we should honor our word. I told *her* that we were different from the rest of the scum in the galaxy."

The king remained impassive. "I was afraid you would feel this way. Nevarian, at some point you will have to learn that being a leader is a question of sacrifices. I would rather not hurt anybody. I would rather live in peace and harmony with our neighbors. But there are times and situations where that is simply impossible, and the more dire the times, the more dire the choices that need to be made in order to protect all that we hold dear."

"Our times are so dire that we need to conduct experiments on unwilling subjects we kidnap?" I laughed bitterly. "Then aren't we the ones creating the dire times? What happened to the teachings of the Unifier, that we only exist to serve others?" I had heard these mantras so many times over the years, they were part of the fabric of who I was. Anger grabbed a hold of my tone again. "Our right to rule is based on *helping* people, not hurting them!"

For the first time, something sparked in Father's eyes, and his voice became hard. "Do you take me for one of your Academy fellows to fall to such amateur debating tactics? Your reasoning skills disappoint me, my son. Morality is not a zero-sum game. The same choices in different situations can be good or ill—it is intent and results that matter, or else we are all nothing but murderers and thieves. My intent, as you so helpfully noted, is to follow the commandments of the Unifier, to not fail the mandate of the Dracorte family, and to be a beacon of hope to the galaxy. Tell me, Nevarian, how much of a beacon do you think we would be under the boot of another family?"

I didn't back down, staring back at him defiantly. "Unless you mean Belarius, I'm certain it's the other royal families who are more likely to be under our boot. And yes, thank you, I am aware that we are in dangerous times. But unless you can tell me that everything is about to come crashing down, your actions tonight are categorically wrong."

"Well then, allow me to enlighten you to just how dire the situation is." Father's voice became harder yet, and he snapped to the room, "Systems analysis, previous quarter."

The images on the wall faded out, and then one large display appeared. Bar charts and graphs surrounded a large map of the explored galaxy. Father stabbed a finger at the wispy blue lines in between the systems. "You see those, Nev? Those represent the drone networks. Dracorte Industries hasn't had a major success in synthetics or alloys in years. Newer products on the markets from competing families haven't supplanted ours yet, but they are better, frankly, and we are losing market share hand over foot. Right now, the only business that is steady is our mining ventures, thanks to the drone network."

He swiped across one portion of the screen, and a line graph showing a precipitous drop appeared. "But the yields from those are diminishing rapidly, not to mention that it seems some drones are finally starting to malfunction now, after centuries without maintenance. None of that is anything, however, compared to the fact that our enemies have been poisoning the ear of Belarius the Elder. The other families are pushing to share in the fruits of the mining operations, claiming it is only reasonable since the drones mine in their systems."

I stepped back. "But that would never happen. Belarius won't let them; that's always been the agreement. They gave us the drive, we gave them access to the drone security functions and any resources they wanted."

"Nevarian, you are not listening. That's the agreement now, but if we fall out of favor with the Belarius family, then why wouldn't they support something else that benefits them? All they'd have to do is stand aside while another family simply seizes the mining yields from the network in their system. We are one disgrace away from that happening. Xiaolan is courting an alliance with them, trying to encroach on our favor. And Treznor-Nirmana has us exactly where they want us with their investment in our operations." He paused and rubbed his brow, worry lines creasing it.

I felt like clutching my own head. I had thought myself well informed of the political forces affecting our family. None of these facts were new, but I hadn't fully grasped the severity of them, the full scope—I doubted anyone had, other than Father and his closest advisors. A future without mining or material production would mean that, really, truly, all we had left to pin our hopes on was . . . Shadow.

Qole.

It was either that, or to continue allowing the Treznor-Nirmanas to invest in us to stay afloat. They would own us in short order. "We just need to pay the investment back in time," I said without conviction.

"Do you know how aggressive the timeline on our repayment is? If we can't generate enough revenue, their terms are punishing. Our holdings will become theirs. The markets are unstable already; all it would take for our investors to lose faith in us would be to fail to impress the systems in the next few days, or worse yet, disgrace ourselves. Which I will *not* allow you to do." He took a step toward me, and a new anger crept into his voice—not the anger of a father, but of a king. He'd directed this at me very rarely, and only after a massive personal failure.

"I still don't see how you can justify coercing Qole," I said, though my own voice sounded weaker. "You could have given her a choice."

"I am not sorry for the choices *I* have made. If you think I'm going to let the fate of our family, of the system, ride on the selfishness of a single girl and boy with adolescent feelings for each other, you do not yet understand the role of a king."

The anger burned in Father's steel-gray eyes now, and he turned off the image on the wall with a grip of his fist. "For you, I *am* sorry. I failed you—failed to teach you soon enough that difficult decisions are not those made in comfortable moral exercises. The choice a leader must make isn't whether to hurt someone, but whom to hurt, and how much." I stared at him in shock, but he didn't seem to notice, or care. "We are going to hurt the Alaxan as little as possible and help billions of people stay safe and prosperous in the process . . . a trade I would make over and over as long as I live, and one that I hope you someday possess the fortitude to make as well."

I found myself with my back to the door. I hadn't even noticed his advance until I had nowhere to run.

"Now, your fascination with the Alaxan has gotten quite out of hand," he said finally. "Go to your quarters, talk to no one, and stay there until I tell you otherwise. That is an order."

I opened the door and stood in it for a moment, shaken. I wasn't sure how to respond, but there was only one thing that kept coming to mind.

"Her name," I said quietly, "is Qole."

XVI

AT FIRST, THE LIGHT WAS SO BLINDING I COULDN'T SEE WHAT WAS happening. But I'd reached . . . and found what I was looking for. There, lying in wait in a massive containment center even deeper in the citadel than where I was trapped in the laboratory, was more Shadow than I could have ever fit into the *Kaitan's* hold. Only one of many such caches. They must have been storing it for a purpose.

But now it was mine. Deep or not, it hadn't been too far for me to touch. To seize, even, and drag toward me. It had all happened so fast: darkness as deep as a void, followed by the brightest white from the core of a star.

I still couldn't see. I only felt the strange intensity somewhere between hot and cold—yet somehow an extreme, all-consuming sensation.

And then I heard the screams.

Sight returned to me with sound, and I blinked to find the room crawling in liquid black flame. It flowed in seductive waves, like fire in zero gravity. Burning white glowed within the center, giving the blackness a purplish cast.

Like my dress was my first delirious thought.

Except when this flame touched flesh, it didn't flutter around it like a party trick. It devoured it.

The screams rose from the half-dozen or so guards lining the table I was on. Some of them tried to run, but the flames leapt at them the fastest, unwinding like a sinuous predator to bring them down. Their blackened bodies fell to ash before they hit the ground. But even those who didn't run and simply shielded their faces died like that, frozen in dark silhouettes lit by fire. And then they crumbled like pillars of sand.

A few guards discharged their weapons, but the bright bursts of white plasma were no match for the flames. The fire swallowed the blasts, absorbing the energy, and then swallowed whoever was shooting.

It took me a few seconds to realize I was the one responsible for this, that this was what I'd reached for and brought back with me. This was the force I was controlling, if not entirely consciously. And that was about how long it took for the Bladeguard to come to the same conclusion. In a flash, his Disruption Blade was gleaming white in his hand, and then he charged me where I was strapped to the table, sword raised over his head.

I had time for a single thought: *Help.*

The burning Shadow reacted not as if I'd forced it to, but

as if it were responding to me. It moved between me and the Bladeguard faster than I could blink. Maybe it was my imagination, but for a moment it looked like it parried the blow—and rendered the blade into molten goop—with flame that had a point and an edge, almost in the shape of a blade itself. But then the fire dissipated, as did the Bladeguard in a shower of ash.

The room was suddenly empty. Everything was blackened and sizzling. The doors to the lab were mangled strips of dripping metal, opening onto an equally charred and silent hallway. The way out was open, if only I could get to it. And there wasn't even anyone to witness. Anything that had once been a comm or a video camera was now a melted lump of synthetic material like all the others coating the flaking walls and warped countertops. Still, someone, or several someones, would no doubt be here soon to investigate why their feeds had gone dead.

My head whipped over to Arjan. The flames hadn't touched him—the damage to his body had still been done by human hands only. My own dress was stuck to my legs in places, scorched to nothing in others, from when actual burning Shadow must have replaced the mimicry, but I wasn't badly burned. I was, however, still bound to the table.

Breaking my restraints should have been easy in comparison to what I'd just done. But when I lifted my head and tried to leverage my arm against one of them, dizziness crashed over me like a breaking wave. The weight of the entire citadel suddenly seemed to press down on my body, and the back of my skull hit the metal table with a thump.

The ceiling shivered above my face, and I thought for a second it might actually be about to give way, until the cracks that rippled along it began to glow. The eerie fissures fractured the air in my vision as much as the ceiling. They ran down the walls, along the floor, and up onto the table. When my hands and arms started splitting apart, I knew I was hallucinating.

The hallucinations didn't stop there, though. My skin began peeling away like the ceiling and floor, exposing tissue and bone. I saw my ribs, and then my beating heart before it, too, dissolved.

I tried to breathe, but I wasn't sure I could without lungs. *Stop, stop, stop.* At some point, I started screaming the word.

Arjan groaned.

Arjan. I had to move. I had to get him out of here. But time was cracking like the room, like my body. I had no idea how long I'd been here, watching it happen. Maybe only seconds, but the seconds felt like hours. And I still couldn't break the restraints.

I tried to talk to him, but my voice only erupted in screams. The noise was disturbing him; I could tell from the grimace on his ravaged face, though not from the emptiness of his eye socket. That told me nothing.

. . . Other than that I had to kill whoever had done this to him. The blackened, crumbled ruins of bodies on the ground weren't enough. They would never be enough. My screams turned to cries of rage, and I reached for Arjan again.

Like last time, I didn't actually reach *him* in the attempt. Or maybe I did.

The breaking room vanished, and Arjan along with it. All I could see was a strange, glinting outline of him, a framework. It was as if his veins were all that was left of him, lit like glowing wires. The lights were racing around his circulatory system, moving almost too fast to trace.

I tried anyway; I followed them to where the light grew brightest, somewhere inside Arjan. And then I could hear him.

Qole . . . ?

Arjan?

Help. Help me. Hurts. It hurts.

I'm trying, Arjan, I'm trying to help you, but—

It hurts. IT HURTS HURTS HURTS HURTS—

Arjan's pain reverberated through me like a shock wave. I recoiled somehow, flying away from it. This wasn't helping him . . . and I couldn't stand hearing him and being unable to help.

But I had to do something. I reached out again, my mind stretching like an arm, a hand, fingers . . . stretching to a point where I thought it might break.

And then I was on the *Kaitan,* moving along the familiar metal panels and wiring, the pieces of a ship I knew as well as my own body. It was almost like trying to sense Shadow, but this time, my entire consciousness headed out with the pinging signal, seeking . . . There was another glimmering framework of a person there—only one, and one I recognized. Maybe there were others actually present, but she was the only one I could *see* like this.

It was Shadow; I was seeing the Shadow in her body, like I had in Arjan's.

Telu?

The sparkling shape that was Telu jumped as if I'd sneaked up behind her and shouted in her ear.

Qole? Captain, where are you? Her voice hummed through me, louder than Arjan's had. Perhaps she was speaking with her mouth as well as her mind.

I'm . . . I'm trapped, and I need help. Shadow is helping me, but not enough. Arjan, they've . . . I didn't know how to describe what they'd done, it was so horrible. *I can't . . .* My own voice grew weaker.

WHERE ARE YOU?

Down, deep . . . find . . . Nev . . . Nev was the only one, in this place, with the power to help us. In spite of everything, I knew he would. *You can trust . . . help . . .*

It was too much. I couldn't keep hold of her, no matter how hard I tried. My grip on the connection slipped, something broke, and then I was torn from her as if someone were dragging me back, or as if I'd been sucked out of the airlock. Both Telu and the *Kaitan* flew away from me, and I was thrown into a blackness like space, except there were no stars.

Part of me still felt my back on the table in the lab, but the rest of me, the conscious, thinking part that mattered, was fading. And then I couldn't feel anything. My mind dissolved in the darkness, and all my thoughts and memories and anger and fear broke apart as if they'd been torched with Shadow.

My mind was gone. Myself, gone. I drifted on a midnight ocean, utterly lost and uncaring.

It was there, within the slowly undulating, black waves, that the stars finally came out. They appeared gradually, on the edges of my diluted consciousness. They looked at first like only sparkles of starlight on the nonexistent water, but then the points of light sharpened and flared to life.

I floated through them, or maybe they floated through whatever was left of me. They began to gather in strange ways, as if outlining something. And then I realized they were outlining my body. They highlighted the shapes of fingers, and suddenly I had hands again. The stars moved up my arms, rebuilding them as they went. They ran down my sides like glittering rain, and I could feel my ribs and lungs again.

My mind was still mostly gone, and so my first thoughts—

were they *my* thoughts?—were more like feelings than clearly defined words:

Need. Open.

That felt right, in some distant part of my brain that could still register these things, if only barely. *Open. Out.*

Not out. Open. Embrace.

For a moment, the light was beautiful, warm on my arms, and the thought of embracing it didn't seem half bad. And then enough of my mind came together to remember that I didn't want to embrace anything.

I wanted to destroy.

The lights flickered and shimmered away from me, as if shying from my touch.

But the lights were helping me. They could help me do ... something. What I needed to do. *Out. Destroy.*

No.

Before they could shiver away from me again, I lashed out with my newly formed hand and seized them. The light exploded, obliterating the darkness. Black turned to white.

There was a ringing in my ears, and suddenly my body was no longer floating. It was heavy, held down against something, but I didn't know what. I wrenched against the resistance and finally broke free of whatever it was. I couldn't remember or see. It didn't matter, because then my feet were moving.

It was like I'd been staring into the sun for hours. My light-infused eyes could barely make out shadows. I squinted and staggered, feeling my way along a wall. I had no idea where I was, or where I was going. *Who* I was. The walls turned sharp and cut my hands, but I didn't stop. I had to keep going.

Out.

That was the only thing I knew. I had to get out. I wasn't

sure how long I stumbled, crashing into things and half falling until I scrabbled my way up from the cold ground. My feet were bare, my legs mostly bare and battered, my hands wet with blood. Finally, my weak knees buckled and I crumpled to what felt like a stone floor.

XVII

NEV

For one brief, shameful moment I considered staying in my quarters as Father had ordered me to.

It would mean I could deny that anything bad was happening. It would mean I could trust my parents to take care of me and everyone else in the way to which I had been accustomed, that the right decisions would be made, and that even if the wrong ones were accidentally made, I would not be responsible for them. It would mean my family would prosper, and our lives would proceed the way that Father intended.

Staying in my quarters would mean abandoning Qole in the horrible situation I had put her in. Refusing to take responsibility for what I had done to her. Forgetting about her.

And that was impossible.

If my thoughts were defiant, my actions, by all appearances, followed orders precisely. I returned to my suite as quickly as possible, without talking to anyone. I considered asking someone for help, but I couldn't imagine there was anyone in the palace, perhaps on the planet, who would disobey their king. Even if Devrak, the one to whom I would most likely turn, wasn't a part of this, he wouldn't work against Father. It was unthinkable.

So what was I thinking? I wasn't sure what I could do, exactly. There was no clear plan in my head as I stripped out of my party clothes and donned the dark gray protective training gear I had used in the Academy. It would allow me to move quietly and stay unnoticed if necessary, which would help me in the only course of action I was sure I wanted to take—finding Qole as quickly as possible.

From the dock on my desk, I snatched an infopad and comm, which I had been sorely missing. It was tradition for guests of the ball to leave behind any device that would be considered a distraction, and although many people broke the rules, I did not.

After all, I believed in the rules. Our rules were there to serve all.

My comm had a single flashing message. It was from So-lara, and it was short.

Atrium, be quick.

I didn't know precisely why Solara couldn't simply comm me with whatever she had to say, but maybe she was worried the lines were monitored. Considering the need for stealth in my family's citadel felt strange, but I was coming to the realization that nothing was as it had been before. I was in uncharted space in my own home.

At the exit to my suite, I hesitated, glancing at the wall where a thoughtful servant had placed my Disruption Blade in the dock that served as a display case and charger. Its twin rested beside it, both of them glinting under a halo of decorative light. Two swords were typically seen as the height of impracticality in combat, the province of mass media entertainment only. But a very select few Bladeguards were trained in another rare form of combat that incorporated dual weapons to fight multiple opponents. I almost never traveled with both, and I didn't see how I could possibly need the second one now, but I'd been taught to be prepared for the unexpected.

I took both of my Disruption Blades with me.

The night sky seemed impossibly bright and close in the sweeping space of the Atrium. The craters of the two moons stood out in sharp relief, the stars glittering like the gems that had been in Qole's hair. With a cunningly crafted roof that was completely clear and curved to magnify the sky, the Atrium was lit only by moonlight. It was deathly still, and the night-blooming flowers, with their faint luminescence, gave off a dreamlike air.

Or in this case, a nightmarish cast. It was hard to believe that I was here to meet my sister in secret, and that my father was holding Qole against her will and doing . . . I wasn't sure what. But Father had been talking a lot about needing to make sacrifices, and my gut roiled to think of how far he might be willing to take that with Qole.

"Nev." Solara's quiet voice carried across the open space, and I felt uncustomary relief. Solara and I had never been inimical, but we had never been close, either. From age ten onward, our training had taken very different paths.

She appeared out of the shadows of the gardens, the red of her dress in vivid contrast against the moons and the snow-capped mountains looming above us. Those mountains were the original seat of Dracorte power, where the first rich veins on Luvos had been mined. Family memory didn't even stretch that far back. We'd been able to deduce as much because drones had stopped going through the motions of mining it. That only happened if someone gave them an order to stop, something no one had known how to do since the Great Collapse. Reroute temporarily, yes. Stop, no.

As a result, the mountain was a warren of abandoned tunnels, most of which had been sealed. Some, like the ones at the end of the Atrium, were open for a short ways to act as a grotto for the plants that required caves. It was a beautiful place, and a strange one to be meeting. I couldn't remember the last time Solara and I had actually spent time alone together, and now, apparently, we were both willing to subvert the will of our family whose greatness was in evidence all around us.

Perhaps we weren't as different as I had always assumed.

"I can't believe this," I said by way of greeting. I scraped a hand over my face. "Father must have wanted you to drive Qole out of the ballroom so they could apprehend her and feel justified in doing whatever they wanted afterward. I just—" I was carrying on, everything inside me boiling over, but I froze as something occurred to me. "Have you seen Arjan?"

"Father said he sent him back to the ship so he wouldn't interfere," Solara said. There was no one around, but she spoke in a hushed tone regardless, far more collected than I was.

My sigh of relief was short and constrained. "At least there's that. But Qole—"

"I think I know where they're holding her," she interrupted without preamble.

"How? I can't find anything on her!"

Solara's lips quirked in a slight smile, red lipstick looking almost black in the moonlight. "A member of the guard." Who was infatuated with her, no doubt. "There's a security lockdown on one of the lower levels . . . right underneath us, conveniently enough." She tapped her heel on the floor.

I glanced down at the smooth, reflective stone. "Really? I thought there was only an abandoned hangar down there."

My own *home* was big enough for me to be unclear on details like that. Much clearer in my mind was the look of disgust that Qole would have for me, if she knew such a thing.

Qole. The ache in my chest doubled, if that were possible, as did my need to find her.

"Well, it's not abandoned now. Security and emergency personnel are both flocking there, and parts of the palace are being closed to visitors."

Once, I wouldn't have thought that one person could merit such a reaction, but that had been before I met Qole. If she tapped into her Shadow affinity, she would be more than dangerous enough to inspire panic.

Part of me felt sorry for anyone who would cross her path, but . . . if she was dangerous, security might decide she would serve my family better dead than alive. My heart started beating faster. "Then I'm going down there. I can't let them hurt her, Solara." I paused, considering my sister. "Don't tell anyone where I've gone. You won't, right?"

Solara shook her head. "I'll even go with you. I know a way down to the hangar from here. That's why I had you meet me here."

For an absurd moment, all I felt was brotherly aggravation. "I've spent years crawling around this citadel, and now you're giving me the tour. How is that even possible?"

She turned, the red of her gown making her easy to follow as she slipped into the darker parts of the garden. "You sought adventure, I sought privacy."

Privacy for what? I wondered how many hearts she had broken in these gardens at night. Right now, I was glad of it.

"They'll try to stop us," I warned her.

She laughed. "We're royals, Nev. We can do whatever we want."

That's the problem, I thought.

———

A few minutes later, an ancient service turbolift had deposited us in a dusty utility room. All I had to do was peer out a door to see the old hangar stretching out in front of us.

It was chaos. Security guards were flooding in from the main entrance, even as others rushed out. Lights bobbed around on the heads of medical responders who were pushing a screaming man on a repulsor-sled. His arm and face were almost entirely gone, burned to nothingness. I shuddered. I was pretty sure Qole couldn't have done that. Or could she have?

"If security is running around like that, I doubt they know where she is," Solara whispered alongside me.

The thought gave me hope. What if Qole had tapped into her abilities and escaped?

That would mean I just had to find her before a hundred armed guards did. Shadow or no, they would gun her down if she really had caused all this.

"Agreed," I murmured. "And that means we need to get through here to look for her. If *I* barely know all these old passages, she's sure to be disoriented." I scanned the hangar again, taking in the deserted equipment, the corroded doors that had once accepted ships now lost to time. Old ventilation shafts and power cables were everywhere, hanging from the ceiling and snaking across the floor. The design was old, belonging to a more practical and urgent age.

"There." I pointed to a small door directly opposite us across the yawning space.

My sister narrowed her eyes. "If we can make it that far without being seen. And how can you be sure she went that way?"

"There are four ways out of here. We're in one, and the other two are crawling with guards. What choice do we have?" I unsheathed one of my Disruption Blades from my back. "We can't cross the hangar with this many people in here, or someone will report us. On my signal, take twenty paces in a straight line as fast as you can. And you might want to remove your heels."

Solara looked annoyed. "I was just dancing in them, brother dear; I can manage a run. What's your plan? What signal?"

"You'll see." I slipped out into the open.

I wasn't being dramatic. I had to make my exit at that moment, because a palace security guard had just walked by. He'd obviously been assigned a perimeter patrol because his commanding officer wanted to look as if he was accomplishing things, even though no one had any idea what to do.

Normally I would have helped bring order to the situation; instead, I was about to do the opposite. I put that unsettling thought out of my head as I shadowed the guard, walking in perfect, silent pace with him. No one paid attention to the motion already in their periphery, and the guard was unsuspecting. I rotated my blade and raised it high, point down. Blue light flowed down the white band of energy in the middle at the flip of the switch.

As I stepped over a power coupling strung across the floor, I drove the point of my blade into it with all my strength. Electricity arced out from my sword into the air, sparks trailing behind.

The entire hangar went dark. The old electrical system couldn't handle the load on the circuit, and somewhere a breaker had blown. I'd guessed something like this would happen, but I didn't have time to congratulate myself on being right. I tapped the hilt of my Disruption Blade to snuff its light.

I turned on the spot and ran at a measured pace through the blackness, counting my steps. If I'd calculated wrong, Solara and I would be separated or, worse, I might run into the wrong person and risk discovery. But my hand connected with what was unmistakably her shoulder, and I gave a silent sigh of relief.

Holding tight to each other, we ran pell-mell through the cavernous darkness. Helmet lights and plasma torches flared to life, giving their owners some measure of sight. But if we were spotted, we were just another bit of indistinct movement along with everyone else.

The next minute, we tumbled into the room on the other side of the hangar.

Solara shook her head, gasping. "I lost one of my favorite shoes."

"Sacrifice noted, Sol." I instinctively called her by the childhood nickname I hadn't used in years. But then I realized something. "If the security finds your shoe, won't they know you were down here?"

Solara looked unconcerned. "They can know I was here, just not why. I'll imply that I was using this abandoned place for more *clandestine* affairs."

That was good enough for me. I looked around. "I think this is the way to a control room. Look"—I pointed—"there's an old lift." I jumped onto the platform that was mounted on a single pole—technology that belonged in a museum rather than in the Dracorte citadel. "Come on."

Solara climbed on with me, after pulling off her other shoe and tossing it over her shoulder. I kicked the pedal that activated the lift and, with a hiss, it propelled us upward. The room we arrived in was covered in dust, and strange buttons and levers punctuated the consoles along the walls.

I started to smile as my eyes found an exit, but it died on my lips. "Did you hear that?"

"Hear what?" Solara asked.

It had been faint, but I knew without a doubt that I'd heard it. There it was again.

A moan . . . Qole.

Fear and relief clawed at me so strongly that our next dash through the hallways became a frantic blur. Qole was alive. She was likely hurt by the sounds of it, but alive.

We finally found her curled up at the corner of a hallway, eyes closed. Her skin was ashen, and there were bruises and blood on her arms and legs. *Cuffs,* I thought grimly. Her hair was wild and disheveled, as though she had just survived a windstorm, and her dress was in such tatters that it could barely have been considered decent. In any other circumstances, I would have had a hard time not staring like an idiot, but right now I couldn't take my eyes off her for a vastly different reason. All I felt was a deep, burning rage.

Solara sighed nearby. She'd managed to keep up with me in her bare feet. "Shame. That was an exquisite dress."

Qole shuddered. My chest constricted, my rage vanishing in an instant. I dropped to my knees beside her and scooped her into my arms without thinking. Her skin was cold to the touch, and I fumbled for the pulse in her wrist. It was weak and erratic.

The words were out of my mouth before I could contain them. "Qole, I'm here. I'm with you. Are you hurt? What happened?"

I didn't expect her to be able to answer, but her voice came, hoarse and cracking. "It . . . burned them. I . . . broke apart."

That was hardly reassuring. It didn't matter; I just had to get her out of here. "Can you move? Can you stand?"

"I talked to . . . I talked. I could see."

"She's not making sense." I glanced up at Solara in despair. As far as I could tell, Qole was physically whole, but she didn't sound or *feel* right. It was like she was crumbling from the inside out, and I was deathly afraid that moving would finish her off in some way I couldn't understand. I could only imagine that drawing Shadow had caused this, but the last time she'd done so, she had remained coherent after she'd blacked out. A cold thought settled into my mind: Both of her parents had gone insane and died. Maybe the same was happening to her.

"Forgot . . . I need to . . ." Qole groaned and shivered. I clutched her closer to me, trying to will away her cold and pain, feeling utterly helpless.

"Well, she's not going to get very far like this." Solara seemed unaffected by her predicament, but at least she was being practical. "Did you have a plan for what to do when you found her?"

I brushed away a few strands of hair from Qole's face. "I was going to get her to her ship so she could get as far away from here as possible." *And from me.*

Solara gave her a critical once-over. "I don't think she's in any condition to walk, much less pilot a ship. And if you comm anyone to come get her, palace security will hear all of it."

As if on cue, the comm in my ear beeped. My wrist feed couldn't identify who it was.

I opened the channel hesitantly. "Um, yes?"

The voice in my ear was loud, worried, and very welcome. "Before you let me know this isn't safe, I've been running phishing attacks all night on the contacts I stole from your wrist feed. I'm all over the comms now, but anyone watching will just think it's your idiot friends calling you."

"Telu!" I said, relief flooding me. "You're exactly who—"

She cut me off. "What the blasted hell is going on? Basra has been gone all night, and now we've got soldiers outside the ship, and I just had the weirdest free fall of a thing with Qole that—"

I winced at the volume. "Telu, there's no time. Are you sure this line is encrypted? All the palace encryption protocols have backdoors."

"I know, genius, that's why I made my own."

"But you can't use a third-party encryption algorithm on the palace comms . . . ," I started, confused.

"You can if you keep the signature the same," Telu snapped. "Look, are you in a hurry or do you want to conference about your crappy security?"

I hesitated, collecting myself. "Right, listen. I can't explain now, but we need to get Qole off-planet immediately. Everyone will try to stop you, and you can't let them. Do you hear me? She's in a bad way. If Arjan can fly the ship, I'll give you a location where you can meet us. If Basra doesn't make it back in time, I'll look out for him. He'll be fine, but Qole won't be."

"Nev, Arjan isn't on the ship."

Her words hit me like a kick to the stomach. "What?"

"He hasn't come back since he left with you and Qole! Should I be worried? I thought he was with you. Basra is the one I don't—"

"Can you fly the ship?" I cut her off, my tone ruthless, my face going still. It had to be this way. Qole might never forgive me for leaving her brother behind right now, but this was my only chance to get her out of here. Father had evidently lied to Solara about where he was, so I would have to find Arjan after Qole was safe.

Telu's brusque voice turned hesitant. "Um ... damn ... yeah, I can fly, probably, with the autopilot system and a little creativity, but only in a pinch."

"This is a pinch, Telu, the absolute worst."

"What about Arjan?"

"I can't carry Qole and look for him at the same time. I'll have to come back for him later. Just meet us at the Atrium, on the north side of the citadel. You can't miss it. You'll have to punch a hole in the roof, but it's glass and you can set the entire ship down." I paused, trying wrap my mind around the things I was saying. This was my home, my family, and I was trying to plan a special op against them. What did that make me? A traitor? Never mind that I was trying to uphold the values we supposedly stood for. "And Telu? Don't take off until I comm you. You're going to have a small window of opportunity before the Air Guard tries to bring you down."

"Don't bother. I can get a fix on your comm every time you click the channel open. Just hit it every once in a while and I'll see where you are."

"Understood. Keep an eye out, and we'll see you soon. Be careful."

"Just get her out. And then you'd better get Arjan out too." Telu's voice was as much encouragement as warning, and the line went dead.

I gathered Qole into my arms. "All right, Qole, listen. I failed you, I know that." I was failing her even worse by leaving her brother behind for the moment, but I couldn't think about that, not right now. "And I know you're hurt and tired. But I'm going to carry you until you can walk. Just promise me you're not going to let this beat you. You are going to pilot the *Kaitan* again. You and your crew are going home."

Her eyes were shut, and she didn't respond, but her breathing grew steadier. I hadn't known my own eyes were wet until I looked up at Solara. My sister was watching me with her head cocked, a curious expression on her face, as if she'd never quite seen me before.

I blinked and stood with Qole in my arms. "Keep an eye out for anyone behind us." I took a deep breath. "Let's get the captain to her ship."

We wound our way through corridors I had not frequented since childhood, abandoned and dimly lit with an ever-present, wan white light. A palace such as the Dracorte citadel required a vast infrastructure to support life within it, too vast for the security cams to cover at all times. As children, both Solara and I had learned just how to avoid detection. We stuck to maintenance routes and corridors that connected storage areas to kitchens and kitchens to servants' quarters.

Twice we almost stumbled into patrols searching for Qole, and both times I carefully deposited her with Solara and then went ahead to direct them to different parts of the palace. After the second time, my comm beeped.

"Um, Nev, I'm monitoring the situation, and all the guards have just been ordered to detain you on sight. One of them reported seeing you, and the order came down soon after that. Guess you're supposedly drunk and out of your mind on drugs or some such."

"Acknowledged, Telu, thank you. Just be ready to pick Qole up." If I hadn't been distracted, I would have been impressed, for the second time that day, by the degree to which Telu had been able to infiltrate the palace network.

"Check . . . and, uh, Basra just showed up in the cargo hold in a dress. This sounds crazy, but I think he snuck on board without anyone noticing. I'll get an update and get back to you." She closed the line.

At least Basra was back, but I'd honestly had bigger things to worry about . . . and still did.

I glanced at Solara, breathing heavily, my legs unsteady from the strain. Lifting Qole in a dance had been effortless—carrying her nearly limp form across the length of the citadel was another matter entirely. "We don't have much farther to go."

Solara had a thoughtful look in her eyes. "No, I suppose not. Let's hope that no one is waiting for us there."

Footsteps echoed in the hallways behind us, along with the unmistakable sound of comms stuttering and people barking orders.

I swore breathlessly. "They must be doubling back to try to find me. Come on, we have to run."

Solara grabbed my arm and gave me a pitying look. "Nev, you're not going to be able to outrun them while carrying her. I'll stay and distract them. It will buy you enough time to make it there."

I shook my head. "Solara, no one knows you're part of my madness. I can take Father's wrath, but there's no need for you to—" I stopped as she put a finger over my lips.

"Shhh, brother mine. A few palace guards are child's play. I'll tell them I just saw you—in a different direction—and then I came to get them. Get your poor captain to her ship."

I nodded. "Thank you, Solara."

She laughed, an incongruous sound in the moment. "I'll make you pay, don't worry." Then she was gone.

I didn't pause to hear how she stopped them; I picked up my pace.

My muscles were screaming with fatigue, and my lungs felt ready to burst. No matter how light the person, no matter how you went about it, carrying a body for a prolonged period was simply an untenable position. Misery washed over me in waves, adding to my burden. Evidently the game was up: Father knew I was working against him, and soon everyone else would as well. And not only did I have to get Qole out, I then had to do everything in my power to get Arjan back to her. There would be severe consequences. My life was about to drastically change.

But I had to make a stand. They had to see how wrong their actions were. My family couldn't be so blind. Even Solara had proved she wasn't, and I couldn't bring myself to believe everyone else I had trusted would be hell-bent on ruining the life of the woman I . . .

It was right there, in that dim service corridor, in the dead hours of the morning, that I finally admitted it. I was too exhausted to carry any pretenses with myself any longer. Qole was more than a responsibility, and if she was just a friend, well . . . hers was the most profound friendship I had ever experienced, and I wanted it to be something even deeper. Something more.

And now I would have to send her away. Not only that, I was sending her without her brother, because there was absolutely no way, once the *Kaitan* was off with Qole, that they'd be able to come back to get Arjan. There was only the tiniest of chances I'd be able to get him out myself. Would she ever forgive me?

I pushed it out of my mind. *Just get her there, Nev. One foot. Another foot. That's all it takes.*

That was when I heard other footsteps ahead of me. I froze. Solara must not have succeeded in fooling everyone, because this was the last place I had expected to see another search party.

My comm beeped at almost exactly the same moment, but Telu would have to wait.

Seven guards, all of them armed, rounded the corner and stared at me. I stared back at them.

And then I bobbed my head. "I'll be right with you, but could you wait for a moment while I duck into this door here?"

They blinked at me in confusion, and I took the opportunity to do just that.

It was an empty banquet room, one that had been used to host parties just off the Atrium before it had fallen out of vogue. Rather than use the Disruption Blade, I locked the door with a swipe of my finger over the biometric scanner. They could override it, but it would take them a few minutes to get in touch with the right people.

I looked around wildly, perhaps with the hope that I would spot some sort of plan.

Qole opened her eyes. They were groggy, but they were open. In spite of everything, relief surged through me.

"Nev . . . where are we?"

"In a bad spot. Hold on." I set her as gently and quickly as possible on the floor. I touched my comm. "Telu."

"Why aren't you there yet and why haven't you answered?" Telu nearly shouted. "Basra is freaking out and says that Arjan is in serious trouble—"

"Listen, Telu," I interrupted, taking a ragged breath. "I don't think I'm going to make it. Qole is in a room not far from the Atrium, and we're trapped. I can draw them off. I'll give her my comm so you can send Eton for her, and I'll make sure that—"

The door exploded into the room, reminding me that one didn't always need an override to gain an entrance.

Guards began to pour in, some armed with photon rifles, some with stun batons. They formed a semicircle around me, weapons brandished.

"I'll call you back," I told Telu. "I have a party." I clicked the comm off and straightened to my full height.

"My prince," one of them began. "You are not yourself. Please come with us for your own safety and protection. The Alaxan is dangerous—she has murdered several guards."

What am I supposed to do? I screamed at myself. Fight them? There were too many to knock out. Kill them, then? My own men?

They hadn't asked a question, so I didn't give a response. I didn't have an answer for myself either. All I knew was that they weren't going to take Qole. Maybe, just maybe, I could keep them busy long enough for her to come to her senses and escape on her own. I settled into a defensive position and reached for my Disruption Blades.

As soon as they recognized my stance, the guards broke formation and ran at me, electricity crackling up and down their batons.

That was the precise moment the wall opposite the door exploded.

One second, it had been behind us, as solid as could be. The next, it was a gaping hole, revealing the breathtaking mountains outside and, impossibly, the *Kaitan* listing like a drunken insect. However Telu was piloting it, it wasn't very well.

And yet her limited abilities were enough to direct the open cargo ramp toward us … from which Eton launched himself like a meteor, framed by the early-morning rays of the sun.

A muscular giant of a meteor. The ship bucked in the turbulence, and he used that as a springboard to fly across twenty feet of open air, crashing like a missile into the guards rushing for me. They scattered in all directions like shrapnel. The only one still standing nearby swiped at Eton with a baton. The hit landed, and thousands of volts of electricity sparked up the rod into his body.

He shrugged it off as if it tickled. With a growl, he latched onto the hapless man with both hands and lifted him bodily over his head. As half of the guards paused to stare, slack-jawed, he threw him directly into the other half, who were bringing their photon rifles to bear. They went down in a pile of flailing arms and legs. He roared, his voice incoherent with rage.

"Eton!" I shouted in warning, as one of the downed guards leapt to his feet, leaving his stun baton where it lay and pulling out a knife instead.

It was too fast for Eton to turn, but not too fast for me. As the man threw himself at Eton's back, I propelled myself into the fastest spin kick I could muster. My foot connected solidly, and the guard collapsed in a heap, clutching his chest.

Eton and I fell upon the group together then, driven by a similar anger. Eton's moves were brutal and somehow beautiful. He darted out of harm's way with a dancer's grace, blocked, and then countered with the force of a mass driver. I was already acquainted with how nimble he was, but to watch him put that to use against multiple opponents was nothing short of awe-inspiring.

Not that I had much opportunity to watch. I had my own crowd to control. I let them come at me, inviting their blows, and hammered their batons with my Disruption Blades. As the batons' charges winked out from the interference, I stepped in with elbows and fists to knock the guards staggering. I got lucky with two, dropping them to the floor in a daze, but this was temporary at best. The electronics in some of the batons fried and stayed dead, but others fired back to life. If I tried to incapacitate this many with the hilts or flats of my blades, it would get ugly.

"Get her to the ship!" I yelled at Eton.

He spun to snatch Qole up off the ground as though she weighed nothing. "Where's Arjan?" he yelled back at me. "Basra searched all night!"

Please forgive me, Qole.

"I don't know. I'm going to figure it out, but you need to get out of here before the Air Guard arrives!"

Eton was no doubt fond of Arjan, but if there was anything I could trust, it was that he would protect Qole at any cost. Even if Arjan was the cost. I didn't stop to watch if he'd take my advice. I turned back to the guards still on their feet after Eton's assault. Four. Too many.

"Stand down," I ordered. "It's not worth it. You can tell my father you didn't want to hit my royal face," I added bitterly.

I recognized one of the guards I had sent away earlier in the hallways, a kid barely old enough to wear the uniform.

"I'm sorry, my prince, but your father is the king, not you," he replied, and three others dove for me, batons in hand.

We met in a staccato burst of swords-upon-sticks. Electricity arced between us as the batons died after engaging with my blades. I worked in a furious defensive pattern, parrying the batons again and again, until I trapped one between my swords. I kicked one guard in the face, sending him staggering into another, and then with a twist of my wrists I wrenched the baton into the third guard. It flickered just as he tried to knock it away, and he dropped to the ground, twitching.

Three down. But the kid was no longer in sight.

I whipped around. Qole was lying on the *Kaitan*'s ramp, where Eton was grappling with the young guard. The kid fell back, pulling out his blaster and leveling it with trembling hands. Eton shrugged and, faster than the eye could follow, pulled out a subcompact and blew his head off.

I froze in midsprint, staring as his body crumpled and rolled, falling onto the Atrium floor. I didn't have any emotion outside of horror—simple, irreversible horror.

I wasn't given any time to process it. "Where's Arjan?" Basra yelled, appearing at the top of the ramp and sounding nearly frantic, while Eton scooped up Qole again. "We can't leave him!"

I looked over my shoulder. "I don't *know!*" More guards were pouring in to reinforce the last few. I shook my head, then reached for my comm as I closed the remaining distance between us. "Telu, you have to take off now, now, *now.* Head north!" I sheathed my blades the second before I shoved Eton, sending him farther up the ramp with Qole in his arms.

I was only planning to make sure they were safely aboard before going back to find Arjan and face the consequences with my father, try to convince him and Rubion to return to reason and decency, but one of Eton's hands closed around my wrist. At first I thought it might have been his military training to leave no one behind, but then I saw his face.

"What are you doing?" I yelled at him.

He gave me a grim smile and shouted over the roar of the engines. "Making sure you don't get away with this. They have Arjan, we have you."

The next moment, we were a hundred feet over the citadel, then a thousand, and then we were skimming over mountaintops, heading far away from my home.

XVIII

COLLECTING MY WITS FELT LIKE GATHERING FALLEN SNOW BACK INTO clouds. And in fact, by the time I succeeded in fully returning to my own mind, snow was billowing outside the main viewport of the *Kaitan,* backed by a heavy sky that turned the daylight gray.

For a disorienting moment, I thought we were back on Alaxak. But the harsh details of my surroundings made me realize I wasn't hallucinating, wherever we were. I lay on a cold bench on the bridge with fur blankets piled over me and the remnants of the Shadow-inspired gown still stuck to my chest and shoulders. I gazed at mountains outside that were defined, sharp, and unrecognizable. Not home.

Then I saw Nev and Telu both in front of the control console, Telu in the captain's chair and Nev bent next to her, like they'd piloted through a team effort, which struck me as indefinably surreal. Why were they piloting? Snippets of the previous evening came back to me in blasts, as if from a photon rifle. I was pretty sure that I'd seen more than a few of those firing last night, and that the shots had been aimed at me. I'd been captured, but I'd somehow gotten out, and Nev and Telu had helped me.

The others were nowhere to be seen. If I'd had to guess, I would have put Eton up in the mass-driver turret, Basra down at his station monitoring comms, and Arjan . . . Arjan should have been piloting in my place, not Telu.

"Arjan!" I sat bolt upright, knocking the furs away. Every part of my body ached, but that didn't stop me.

Telu spun, and Nev was kneeling at my side in an instant. He grabbed my hand and ran his thumb over the back of it.

"It's okay, you're safe . . . -ish." He cast a glance toward the viewport.

"Where?"

He knew me well enough to be specific and began rattling off coordinates, which I admittedly didn't understand. "We're in the northernmost quadrant of Luvos, just off the pole," he added. "You've been out for hours. The terrain is inhospitable and scrambled by drone interference, and we flew in low enough that Telu could hide our signal. We've escaped the reach of the Air Guard. The drones shouldn't bother us, though some of them are moving more than they should be, deactivated though they supposedly are."

I didn't care about drones. "Where's Arjan?"

A grimace like I'd stabbed him flashed across his face. "I don't know, we had to leave him—Qole!"

I was up before he could stop me. My muscles cried out in protest, but my memories of Arjan came back to me with far more agony.

"You left him?"

But it hadn't just been him. I'd left him too. We all had.

"I'm so sorry," Nev said. "I was going to go back to find him, but—"

His apologies and explanations faded to the background as the image of my brother's eye socket sprang to the front of my mind. *We left him, we left him. . . .* The pain was so strong that I could barely gasp for breath. My head felt light, and I couldn't get enough air. *We left him.* A high buzzing rang in my ears as I tried to suck more air in. *We left him.*

"You're hyperventilating, Qole."

But we left him. Arjan had been tortured, then abandoned. For so long I'd tried to protect him from his fears, but now I'd left him in the worst of nightmares. *Arjan, Arjan, forgive me, we left you, please forgive me.* And then, when I finally caught a breath, the pressure in my chest, neck, face, released in a wrenching sob. It ripped through me. I felt shredded. Like I'd never be whole again.

Nev seized my arm, trying to pull me back down to the bench.

And with that, I snapped back into myself. I looked at his hand, then at him. "Let me go."

He did, luckily, so I didn't have to make him. If Nev had gotten me out, he'd also helped leave Arjan. He was the reason we'd come to Luvos, after all. For a split second, I felt like tearing him apart with my bare hands, but the devastation on his face stopped me.

I straightened my spine, wiping my tears on the back of my

hand. "Telu, get everyone on deck," I said. "And please get me some *real* blasted clothes."

Telu shot Nev a glance, and he nodded. He moved back over to the console to keep track of the data feeds while she slipped away from the bridge. She soon returned with a folded stack of leathers and thermals.

"I'll be back with Eton and Basra," she said, and ducked back out.

I looked at the clothes on the bench and then at Nev's back. There was nothing else for it, and I was beyond caring. He stayed facing away while I clawed off the remnants of the ragged dress. Afterward, I yanked on a pair of leather leggings and a tank top, followed by a fur-lined jacket and boots. It wasn't cold enough for more, though I almost wished it were. I craved the protective layers.

Nev seemed to know when I was done changing, because he glanced back at me. "Qole, I didn't know about Arjan until—"

"Save it," I snapped.

We were spared from having to say anything else by the arrival of the rest of the crew. Maybe Nev wanted to speak more, but I didn't, not to him. Telu, followed by Eton and Basra, filed onto the bridge.

They all looked at me with an intensity I'd never seen, each in their own way. Telu seemed like she wanted to both cry and scream along with me. Eton stared as if I were bleeding out in front of him, and he didn't know how to save me. Basra . . . on the surface, Basra seemed indifferent, back to a more neutral appearance with his usual androgynous attire. But in his eyes, I caught a flash of the same depthless rage that burned in my own core.

In that instant, I knew none of them would disagree with what I was about to say. "We have to go back for Arjan."

"Tell us something we don't know," Telu said.

"I'll tell you something *I* don't know." I sat down harder on the bench than I meant to. Whatever way my anger empowered me, my body was still exhausted. "And that's how we're supposed to go about it."

"I know how," Eton said, as blunt as a boot. "We ransom the little prince to get him back."

Everyone looked up at that, even me.

Nev sighed. "That won't work. I wish it would, but it won't."

Eton rounded on him like a gun ready to fire. "Of course you would say that."

"No," Nev snarled, suddenly angrier than he'd ever been at any of us. "I *would* have gone back to try to find Arjan and get him out no matter what, but instead—"

"And you expect me just to believe that?" Eton shouted back.

Nev got right in his face, his words blistering. "I just betrayed my family, fought *my own men* at your side and watched them die for you, for Qole, for this crew. You damned well should believe it."

Eton opened his mouth to respond, but nothing came out. Not even he could argue with that.

"Which is why"—Nev scrubbed his hands through his hair and took a step back, as if restraining himself—"my father would likely not make the trade. I'm a traitor, so now Arjan is probably worth more to him than I am. With Qole's escape, Arjan is the key to my family's survival."

"No," I said, and he blinked at me. "Arjan is the key to their triumph, not survival. Your uncle told me he already *has* the formula to make Shadow into a widely usable fuel. He wants us for the same reason as the Treznor-Nirmanas, as far as I could gather. Our abilities."

"I can't believe this." Nev's hands turned to fists in his hair, which he dragged over his face, covering his eyes. Almost like he couldn't look at us. "I trusted them. . . ."

"Regret your family and your idiotic gullibility on your own time," Basra said. He didn't spit the words, but somehow his flat tone was worse. "For now, this is about how you can repay *us,* repay Arjan."

I thought Nev might get angry at that, but instead he took a deep breath and dropped his hands. "As I was saying, my father would likely refuse to deal with you, simply to teach me a lesson if nothing else. He's fond of those, and I've just failed him more thoroughly than he probably thought possible. Even if he agreed"—he swallowed, as if whatever he was about to say was less pleasant than admitting his father was a ruthless piece of scat who wouldn't bargain for his own son's life—"then I'm guessing he wouldn't play fair. He views the family's success to be nearly as crucial as the family's survival. He wouldn't give up Arjan, and at the same time, he would try to get Qole back or kill as many of you as possible, even at risk to me. If we try a trade like that, we lose all element of surprise. We walk right into a trap of his own design, and my father is very, very good at such things."

"Is he?" Basra sounded unconcerned. Then, surprisingly, he said, "Nev is right."

"Next plan," I said. A mostly numb part of me didn't mind leaving that one behind.

"Full-scale assault?" Eton suggested without missing a beat. Oddly, he didn't sound too disappointed, either. Maybe Nev had made an impression on him in a way that his fists hadn't.

Telu cracked her knuckles, then flexed them as if to type over an infopad. "In more ways than one. I have other ways of hacking them to pieces."

Basra smiled coldly. "We have three ways, actually."

"Right, all this sounds lovely, but perhaps we should take a moment to consider." Nev didn't quail when everyone shot him glares as powerful as energy blasts. "First of all, our full-scale assault will be nothing against the armies of an entire *planet*. We need to plan. This area is covered in drones that have blaring signals to hide us, and that would respond to a direct threat. We'd be difficult to attack here. The Air Guard didn't shoot us down in the first place only because my father likely commanded them not to—"

"Are thanks in order, then?" Basra asked, his tone like a slap to the face.

"No," Nev said, as patient as could be. "I mean to say they might be more inclined *to* shoot us down now that my father's had time to mull my betrayal. And since we're no doubt being hunted by every ship in planetary security, it might be wise to lay low while we can."

To be fair, I did take a moment to consider his words. I met his eyes. "I'm sorry, but I can't wait. I saw him, Nev. It was worse than . . . It was the worst. Who knows what they could be doing to him, even since we left? I just . . . can't." I shook my head, trying to dispel the memory of Arjan's pain so I could focus, and then I cleared my throat. "So, I have to say this. If any of you want to debark, I will let you off without question, with as many provisions as you might need. Not that it would be completely safe here, but—"

Telu snorted loud enough for everyone. "*Whatever.* Like any of us would give up on Arjan like that. He's as good as our brother too, and he'd return for any of us. Now let's stop wasting time and come up with a plan."

I could have hugged her . . . and surprised myself when I actually did. I stood and threw my arms around her before realizing it. "Thank you," I breathed into her shoulder.

She gave me a tearful smile, one that was also as sharp as a knife. I appreciated her edge like never before. We needed it.

We also needed Basra, I realized, as soon as he spoke up.

"I have something that might help, a way to hit the Dracortes where it will hurt them the most—their finances. I've actually been working on it for over a week in case things went sour here on Luvos," he added, almost as an afterthought. "However, it necessitates my going back in. If I'd known things would fall out like this, I would have just stayed in the citadel. I'd tried and failed to comm Arjan, and went in to make sure he was all right. I was only able to get a few things in place while looking for him. A pity I got back to the ship before you could leave me, Telu." He shrugged slightly curved shoulders, and for a moment he looked incredibly *un*threatening. "So we'd better not count on it. We should still try to save Arjan as if it were entirely a suicide mission."

"Okay," I said, feeling too grim to be amazed that he could talk about giving his life for my brother so easily. His determination to get Arjan back was second only to mine, it seemed. But then wasn't everyone else saying the same thing, in their own way? "Then we'll come up with the suicidal part."

Planning began in earnest then. Whether or not we were walking into a trap, returning to Dracorva *was* practically suicide. The discussion occupied most of my attention, but it didn't escape my notice when Nev stepped off the bridge. I left Telu, already hammering at different infopads, and Eton and Basra, debating the merits of different aerial approaches to the city, to follow him.

———

Nev, as it turned out, was no longer on the ship. I tracked him into the hold and found the hatch open to the white expanse of a blizzard, his footprints curving off into the snow.

Something like pain—as if it were possible for me to feel any more—spiked through me at the thought of Nev abandoning us. Maybe he'd decided he'd rather not risk his life going back for Arjan after all. I pulled my fur jacket tighter around me as I stepped outside.

He stood near the hatch, his arms braced above his head against the hull, as if he were holding the ship up instead of leaning against it. Even if it was warmer than Alaxak, he had to be cold in his thin synthetic jacket and pants.

I almost didn't want to disturb him. Maybe it was the look on his face, more somber than I'd ever seen it. I took a breath with relief that he was still here, and then immediately found myself angry; I hated him for bringing us here, I hated him for leaving Arjan, and I hated him for walking away and making me worry when we had more important things to be doing.

We didn't have time for this. My brother didn't have time.

"What are you doing?" I asked, my breath billowing and my boots crunching through the snow as I made my way over to him. "We still need you on the bridge. You're the one who would know of any weaknesses in the structure where they're holding Arjan. Stop wasting time."

It came out harsher than I'd meant, but what could I do?

Nev didn't respond immediately. He only stared out over the landscape, his usually bright eyes as clouded as the sky.

When he finally spoke, he sounded far away. "I'm sorry. I know I should be helping. Somehow, I just . . . I feel as useless as those drones, right now. The purpose that I had, my values—it all came from my family. And now it's gone. Worse, it was all an illusion to begin with."

I stepped closer to view the scene from his angle. The *Kaitan* was nestled deep in an icy, mountain ravine, and massive shapes lurked around us behind a veil of snow—drones, several times the size of the ship. But they weren't moving much, or paying us any attention. These were the drones the Dracortes had deactivated before the Great Collapse, back when they'd finished excavating mines like the ancient one that supposedly still riddled the slopes around the citadel. The Dracortes had been able to keep the drones from ruining their own planet, of course, just not most everyone else's. And yet, here were the giant metal monsters hundreds of years later, lying in wait for an activation code that could make them tear through whatever stood in their way.

What would Nev do without his driving purpose?

As if we were both thinking the same thing, he murmured, "And even though I'm furious at the hypocrisy of my family, I just keep thinking of Marsius's hugs. Even Solara's indomitable will to get the latest and best gossip. Father, when he would give me an approving nod. Mother, always putting her hand on my shoulder whenever she came up behind me to let me know she was there."

It hit me, what I was asking him to do. I was asking him to attack his family, turn on his home and country, and betray everything he had been born and raised to believe. In his position, I wasn't sure how I would bear it. What if I had always just *thought* that my family was good, that my people and I, in spite of our struggles and setbacks, were doing our best to follow the path our ancestors laid out for us, and that it was the right path . . . when, in fact, none of that was true? Even in imagining it, a part of me wanted to scream out that it was wrong, that my people *were* good.

And maybe Nev had that part of himself too. Screaming inside at the lie he'd believed.

I reached out, but only grazed his shoulder with a finger before my hand dropped. It was all I could do, all I could allow myself. I couldn't do more with Arjan missing. "I'm . . . I'm sorry, Nev."

A laugh caught in his throat as if it had been strangled. "You shouldn't be sorry." He closed his eyes and leaned his forehead against his raised arm, his breath fogging around him. "Only me. And I'm so very sorry, Qole."

He also looked more tired than I'd ever seen him, as if he'd been carrying a burden as heavy as this ship for a long time. One his father had placed on his shoulders and wouldn't let him set down. He looked miserable, in fact.

He should be sorry, but not miserable. It wasn't entirely his fault. He was a Dracorte, but he was not his family. If he'd never found us, maybe we'd all be in a similar situation, no matter what, only with the Treznor-Nirmana family torturing Arjan instead of the Dracortes, and with me still teetering on the edge of madness. But if the Dracortes had never studied the Shadow affinity of people like us in the first place, then the Treznor-Nirmanas would never have known to cut us open to investigate it. And if the Dracortes hadn't sought all the resources in the galaxy that had never belonged to them . . .

But how far back did I want to take it? How much could I put on Nev's shoulders, when he was clearly trying to do things differently from the rest of his family?

Besides, if I'd never come with him, I would never have

gained even the glimmer of hope—much fainter now, but still flickering—that someday Shadow wouldn't have to drive me, my family, and others like us to insanity and death.

And I never would have gotten to know him.

For a second, my throat was too tight to speak while I looked at Nev's bowed head and the snowflakes collecting in his hair.

"I really didn't mean to get on the ship back in Dracorva, you know," he murmured, not looking up at me. "I was only supposed to get you on board and then stay to find Arjan and face my father, whatever the consequences. But I failed at even that."

The thought of him staying, even to help Arjan, and of never seeing him again, sent another bolt of panic through me, in spite of myself.

I took a breath and forced the words out, the words I had to say to save my brother—whatever the consequences. "You can still help us. I know I'm asking a lot, but . . ."

He looked up at me now, his silver-gray eyes heavy. "It's the least I can do. No . . . actually, it's the most I can do, but it's the least you deserve. And this way, I still get to face him, and you stand a chance of getting Arjan back. Although, I warn you, it's only the slightest chance."

I swallowed. "I know. But I have to try."

"We'll probably all die."

"I know," I repeated, the words echoing hollowly inside me. I hugged myself tighter.

He nodded, as if he'd just been making sure, and dropped his arms, causing a gust of snowy air to swirl around him. "In any case, once we return, I won't be coming back out."

My chest went tight as an airlock. "What?"

"After this, I'll be of no good to you. Either I'll be dead, or

I should stay as far away from you as possible. I don't belong—I don't *deserve*—to be in your life. I wanted to help you, and yet I've only hurt you in the worst imaginable way." He smiled, but it was so bitter it hardly seemed like a smile, more like a grimace. So different from how he smiled when I'd first met him. "I also wanted to help my family, but all I've done is betray them." He laughed, a sound that was also so different from the one I was used to. "How is it that I've made myself miserable trying so hard to make people happy, and yet I still haven't succeeded?"

It was odd: I'd always thought Nev was far happier than he had any right to be. That his happiness was a product of his privileged upbringing—privilege that had been gained by standing on the backs of others. And yet it made me sad to watch him lose something I realized I'd begun to appreciate.

Both my sadness and my appreciation surprised me. But then, his happiness wasn't about wealth, I knew now, even if wealth inevitably colored it. It was more about the sense of humor and hope with which he engaged the world. It was humor and hope that many in *my* world still had. I didn't—for good reason—but only now did I realize this was something I'd craved without knowing it, like food or water after a long day of fishing during which I'd forgotten to eat or drink.

I missed it now, when I could hardly stop thinking about everything *else* I'd lost: my path, my family, my world. Nev's happiness gave me hope for my own. And if not for the possibility of happiness, why else was I trying so hard to get back everything I'd lost?

Maybe I was already lost, and I was only trying to get Arjan back. And yet, just like I couldn't give up on my brother, part of me didn't want to give up on myself, either.

Nor did I want Nev to give up on *himself.*

"Maybe you're trying in the wrong ways," I said. "You can't always know what's right for everyone."

He looked up in surprise at the gentleness of my tone.

"You've trained for so long—*been* trained—to be a king, but maybe acting like a king isn't always the best thing to do. Instead of making decisions for people," I continued, "you have to support them with the resources you have in doing what *they* think is best for themselves. They won't always be right, but neither are you, and you have the power to do greater harm. Or greater good."

His lips parted and his eyes widened, like I'd just said the most bewildering thing he'd ever heard. When he began to nod slowly, I had to fight off the utterly irrational and idiotic urge to take his face in both hands and kiss him.

Instead, I told him what he needed to hear. I gave it to him like a gift, even though the words could have been bitter, even though I didn't feel like I had very much to give.

Not that it would be the easiest gift to receive.

"*Greater good . . .* one of your family ideals, hey?" I didn't bother to hide my accent. "It doesn't have to be a lie. It is right now, but you can make it truth."

Nev's beautiful features twisted, wringing my stomach at the same time. I knew there were more than tears of sadness and loss in his eyes. They were probably tears of realizing and relief too, but it still hurt to see.

"How can an unhappy person expect to spread joy?" I whispered, not trusting my voice. "Be happy again, Nev. What would it take to make that happen?"

He blinked at me, looking like I *had* actually kissed him, or maybe kneed him in the stomach. Or both at the same time.

I didn't know the answer for myself, or if there was a chance for me to ever be happy again. But maybe he had a chance.

It took him a moment to respond, afterward. He gazed out over the landscape as if seeing it differently now, his eyes as shiny as melting ice. "You're right. Perhaps I'm not like the drones, stuck in an obsolete destructive pattern without purpose. That's my family. And I don't have to do as they do anymore."

His eyes snapped back to me, the silver-gray irises suddenly sharp and clear.

Purposeful.

"Drones." He laughed, as genuinely as ever before, and my stomach did a flip at the sound, defying the gravity that weighed me down. "I know exactly how to get into the citadel . . . and maybe even how to get back out again."

XIX

THE MIST PARTED, SWIRLING, AND THE *Kaitan* BURST OUT OF THE clouds that clung to the mountains above the Dracorvan plains. For the second time in as many days, Dracorva spread before me in all its glory, the spires of the citadel shining in the sun.

My emotions were profoundly different this time. Rather than dizzying heights of excitement, an accepting calm filled me. I knew what I had to do, and so it had to be done. Glancing at Qole in her captain's seat, her face serious and focused, I wondered if this was how she always felt.

I turned back to the viewport in front of us, a brighter glint of sunlight catching my attention. From the spires of the citadel, a starfighter flitted out, darting this way and that before the pilot found his course and rose to meet us. Another fighter dropped out of a spire to join the first as it passed, and then another, and another. In less than a minute, I had lost count as their number filled the sky in front of us and the weapons-lock klaxon started.

"For someone who was a peaceful fisherwoman just a couple of weeks ago, I think I'm beginning to get used to that sound," Telu observed over the comm.

"*Kaitan Heritage,* you are in violation of royal airspace, are harboring known fugitives, and have kidnapped Prince Nevarian Dracorte." The latter assumption was generous of them, but what followed was less so. "Proceed to Containment Block One immediately, or you will be disabled and boarded."

Qole and I glanced at each other and she raised her eyebrow. I nodded, and with an almost imperceptible adjustment on the controls, she put the *Kaitan* into a near-hover.

"Now, Eton," she ordered.

In the turret, Eton locked his own weapon systems onto the lead fighter, and I didn't have to hear it to imagine the warning that sounded off in the pilot's helmet. *That'll wake them up.*

As we had hoped, the starfighters slowed to nearly hovering themselves. I doubted they were eager to attack the ship they knew carried the royal heir, traitor or not, and I was sure there was a great deal of uncertainty about how to proceed.

I pressed the inter-ship comm button at one of the empty stations on the bridge. "Thank you for your suggestion. This is Prince Nevarian Dracorte. Please listen very carefully to what I have to say."

I paused and took a deep breath. If Telu had been successful, this wasn't only broadcasting to the fighters in front of us, but to every comm channel in Dracorva that she could get us on. And what I was about to say would be treason, pure and

simple. I could still go back, right now. I would face consequences, but it would be possible.

Looking at Qole, her gaze fixed on me, I realized I had no
desire to go back to the way things had been.

"There is a man from Alaxak being held prisoner in my
family citadel. His name is Arjan Uvgamut, and he came here
to help us of his own free will." I paused again, my chest con-
stricting. "Now, through no choice of his own, he is being
detained as the subject of inhumane experiments.

"We all believe that we stand for something greater than
ourselves. I know that every one of you is loyal to my family.
But cruelty isn't an ideal any of us believe in. And his family is
here, now, and they are willing to lay down their lives to bring
their brother home, just as you would for yours." I glanced at
Qole. Her eyes were staring straight ahead, bright with un-
spilled tears, and her knuckles were white on the controls.

"So today you have a choice, and it will be one of the most
important you ever make. You can let us pass, and the systems
will know that the Dracortes do not stand for cruelty, that we
are true to our ideals, and that we believe in justice, not expe-
dience. Or . . ." Now it was my turn to clench my fist so hard
my knuckles turned white. "You can fight me. But if you fight
me, ask yourself what you are standing for. And be prepared
to face the full consequences, because we will not hold back."

I turned off the comm, my heart beating faster. I'd just
told the world that I was prepared to hurt the people who had
served me, who had grown up with me, who had raised me.
That I believed my betrayal was justified.

Father had felt his betrayal of our ideals was justified too.
But Qole had made me see the true meaning of those ideals.
I had to act on what I believed was right and leave others to
choose their paths for themselves.

Those men could choose; I had just given them that chance.

Arjan's ability to choose had been taken away by my family. And it was high time we gave it back.

The *Kaitan* tilted, and we plummeted toward the starfighters below.

"Remember, everyone," Qole said, "they'll probably only try to disable us because Nev is on board. Eton, get their attention and keep it. Hang tight, it's going to be a rough run." She jerked her head at me. "You should get to your station."

The gravitational dampeners hummed and rattled as they desperately fought our descent. I moved to my own station on the bridge, strapping myself in. Qole was right, they would probably use photon guns that were dialed back, chipping away at us until we were forced to land. *Probably.*

Like a swarm of insects, the starfighters filled our viewport and a hail of energy bolts lanced out toward us.

The *Kaitan* was already corkscrewing out of the way before the fighter pilots had even finished depressing their triggers. Timing it perfectly, Qole brought us under the formation and drove for its center.

I heard the grating roar of Eton's mass driver, the shriek of photon interference, and was thrown against the back of my seat as Qole swept us away toward the citadel.

"Nev, I need eyes. Are they buying it?"

I scanned the feeds that were normally used for Shadow fishing. "Affirmative, Captain. We've got a dozen very angry rapier-class fighters about to chew our engines apart."

"One of our aft stabilizers is disabled." Basra's voice was calm as always, but there was an edge to it. "I'm routing more power to the others, but I don't know if they'll handle the strain."

Qole rolled out of the sweep and climbed straight into the

atmosphere above the citadel, the *Kaitan's* engines howling at maximum thrust. "Telu, this would be the perfect time. They aren't paying attention."

"Hold on, Captain, there's a tiny glitch. Two more seconds."

"*Glitch*—you were supposed to be ready!" Eton yelled, his voice almost drowned out by the continuous bellow of weaponry. "*We're* going to be a glitch in another second!"

Qole idled the engines and the *Kaitan* looped around in the sky, juking to avoid the fire directed at it as we pointed straight down.

"Your two seconds are up," Eton growled.

"Drink it in," Telu replied smugly, and through the viewport of the *Kaitan* I saw what she meant.

The citadel and the mountains were spread in vivid sunlit relief before us. Smoke trailed from a spiraling starfighter that Eton had somehow managed to shoot down.

And then the drones arrived, scores of drones. Mining drones, transportation drones, drones covered in trees and vegetation, decommissioned so long ago I couldn't recognize the models. They streamed underneath us, descending from the mountains straight toward the citadel in a terrifying river.

"Great Collapse," someone—maybe me—breathed over the comm.

"Yes," Qole hissed as she poured power into the engines. "Telu, you are the best."

I couldn't argue. Telu had spent a lifetime learning how to temporarily reroute drones during Shadow runs, something others would go to the Academy to learn. But to deploy a script ordering so many at once, of such a variety, onto a single task, was on an entirely different scale of skill. Now it was a question of her ability to thwart the efforts of the royal security team as they attempted to override her programming. Given her muttering about encryption and hashes, I didn't envy them.

I had scant seconds to appreciate the thought as we hurtled downward, the drones rushing up toward us with terrifying speed. At the last moment, Qole brought the nose of the *Kaitan* up and we were in the flood of drones, weaving in and out of them.

I ignored every screaming part of me that had been trained to stay well away from them, and focused on the task I had been given. "The Air Guard is right behind us," I reported, "but they're thoroughly confused. No one has yet been foolish enough to . . . Ah, never mind. They're shooting."

Sure enough, one of the starfighters decided to take a crack at us and hit a drone instead. In a flash, it was upon him, tearing into the aircraft. It had ripped its wings off as if it were a fly by the time another fighter came to the rescue. The new arrival unloaded a string of plasma torpedoes and blew the drone to bits before he registered the screeching order to stand down. But by then it was too late.

The drones reacted with escalating violence to any damage done to another, and in the space of seconds, we were passing through a maelstrom of fighters and drones engaged in a furious firefight. The image of the young guard that Eton had killed rose in my mind unbidden, and I wondered how many other people might die in this battle. I pushed the thought down, somewhere deep. Now was not the time.

Qole deftly threaded the *Kaitan* through the chaos, and for a moment we were in the clear, heading toward the Atrium. Plumes of dust were rising nearby, where drones were burrowing into the mountainside, churning up rocks and soil as they labored to reach the ancient shafts once again. They'd only keep at the task for as long as Telu kept hacking their signals and sending them refreshed orders to do so.

"I think we have a clear shot—" I was cut off when the *Kaitan* lurched and slewed, tossing us in our harnesses.

"Tractor beam," Qole said grimly. "One just locked onto us."

I hadn't worried too much about those, not in this chaos. We'd been dealing with starfighters, not the big destroyers that were equipped with them, and the latter still had to be fast enough to catch you within a relatively close range. Which, apparently, they had been.

"Right, listen up." Qole eyed the feed that showed us slowly drifting toward the hull of the giant, wedge-shaped ship that my family favored. To think there had been a time when the sight of destroyers had reassured me. "Eton, I want you to fill the air with every last bit of ammunition left in the mass driver. Give the tractor beam something to chew on. Basra, jettison everything in the hold and on my mark, divert all power outside of navigation to the engines."

"Is that wise?" Basra asked. "If I do that, life support and gravity dampeners will go offline."

Qole ignored him, her eyes hard, watching a feed of Eton firing at the destroyer. The flecks of mass filled the air, slowed, and then spun off along the beam. I knew I should have been focusing entirely on my duty to scan the info feeds, but I couldn't help glancing up at her periodically. If pure determination were enough to break us free, there wouldn't be a tractor beam in the galaxy that could hold us.

I looked back at the feeds. "Qole, fighters are incoming." Tension crawled up my spine. I suddenly understood that following a leader was fine in concept, but trusting your life to the cryptic word of another person was nothing short of nerve-racking. How many of my family's followers had felt the same tension as they followed Dracorte commands?

"Mark." Qole gave the order, and the lights went out. The only thing that remained was the glow of the console and the blinding glare of the *Kaitan's* engines on overdrive as she strained against the grip of the destroyer's tractor beam. Debris began to tumble toward the port side of the ship as planetary gravity took over. No doubt our oxygen and heat were offline as well, but we were in Luvos's atmosphere, and besides, before long, we wouldn't need either of those things. Either we'd be dead or . . .

Slowly, agonizingly, we began to creep away. It was a victory of sorts, but in my heart I knew that would never be enough. Those starfighters were almost on us, and they would take us apart.

Qole wrenched the controls, and the *Kaitan* twisted in the grip of the destroyer. She wrenched again, and we thrashed like a caught fish. With the screech of tearing metal, the entire ship shuddered, something gave way, and we were free.

None of us cheered. I knew what Qole had just done: she had ripped a part of the *Kaitan*—a part of herself—clean off.

For a moment, we flew toward the spire, and then our momentum slowed. I realized the familiar rumble of the engines was gone. The *Kaitan* was all but dead in the air, and we were about to go into a free fall.

"Ancestors, let this work," whispered Qole, her hands flying over the console in front of her. Then she grasped a lever I had never seen her use before and engaged it.

As the *Kaitan* fell through the sky between the spires of the citadel, I stared in awe as the boom used for Shadow fishing swept to a new position. From it, a shimmering metallic web unfurled, flapping in the air until it snapped tight.

The lights flicked back on in the bridge, artificial gravity returned, and the ship flitted into the latticework of the citadel.

I wanted to shake my head in disbelief, scream for joy. A solar sail. Virtually unused now, it had been the primary method of propulsion for the natives of Alaxak until traders had brought more advanced engines to the planet. Somehow, I'd forgotten about this bit of history that was now saving our lives.

"Telu, pick a drone for me," Qole instructed. "Same as we did with that asteroid our first season together."

Telu sounded uncertain. "We had Arjan to make the call when we should . . ."

"You get the drone, I'll make the move. It's time to end this." Blackness crept into Qole's eyes as she spoke, and I felt the pressure in the cabin change.

The *Kaitan Heritage* swept through the spires of the citadel, pursued by starfighters from every direction. Photon blasts sliced through structural work, and plasma missiles left scorched holes in the citadel itself as the Air Guard threw everything it had in an attempt to stop us.

Not one hit landed.

Climbing, spinning, diving, Qole made the *Kaitan* dance like a kite in the wind. Hurtling impossibly close to the structures around us, we spiraled down through a honeycomb of supports in a stomach-churning drop that I was certain would make me throw up over the dash.

"Drone bearing zero, thirty-one, twenty-eight," Telu announced.

Starfighters scattered in every direction as a massive mining drone dove straight for the root of the mountain. It passed them, and from their vantage, the *Kaitan* must have vanished.

Impossibly, Qole had latched us on top of the drone itself,

and we crashed into the Atrium like a planetoid, utterly demolishing it. Plasma torches flared to life as the drone began boring straight down through the palace grounds as though it were made of paper, not stone and steel.

It should not have been possible to peel off the drone into the interior of the citadel. It shouldn't have been possible to do that at the exact moment the drone hit the abandoned hangar we'd escaped through, right before it refreshed its own orders and gave up on its mission, blasting back out into the chaotic sky.

It shouldn't have, but Qole did it. The *Kaitan* scattered a million sparks into the air as it slid across the floor of the decimated hangar. Container units, power couplings, vents, everything blew apart before us until Qole brought the ship to a halt. I sat back in my chair, trembling hands scraping back through my hair.

We'd made it. We were inside the citadel.

———

With the exception of Telu, who remained at her station to try to keep the drones on task, we gathered in the hold, armed like a military platoon. This was entirely thanks to Eton, who distributed fusion grenades, photon rifles, plasma pistols, and even knives, along with instructions that none of us could possibly remember.

But it was what he was wearing that really tipped the scales from "ragtag group of rebels" to "dangerous military force." He had nothing less than two plasma cannons strapped to his back, attached to a frame that stretched up from either shoulder. As a finishing touch, a shield emitter circled him, protecting his entire body from any sidelong attacks.

"What in the Unifier's good name are those?" I pointed at the plasma cannons. "And how did you even get them? They're usually mounted on interceptor-class fighters."

Eton's expression was the deranged, murderous cousin of a smile. "This is Verta. I made her to punch holes in things that need more holes."

"You need something left for there to be a hole," I said incredulously.

"And what about your secret weapon, Basra?" Qole asked, unfazed by Eton.

"It's launched. It'll take a bit of time to detonate, so to speak. But we shouldn't wait around for it. So, in the meantime . . ." Basra hefted a photon rifle as if he knew how to use it. I had no idea *how* he knew.

"Um, guys." Telu's voice filtered in over the comm. "Can Verta punch holes in that?"

We spun to look at the feed showing the outside of the ship, and my heart sank. A sea of troops surrounded us.

"That makes no sense," I protested. "They couldn't have known how we were going to get here, or even that we would."

"Does it matter?" Basra said coldly. "They're here." He flipped the safety off his rifle, and it began to hum with deadly purpose. "If Arjan is on the other side, we go through them." He wore an expression on his normally impassive face that I couldn't begin to place.

"That's all well and good," I said, "but if we drop the ramp, they have enough firepower to take us all down, even Eton."

Eton opened his mouth, but stopped. I understood why when I felt the hair standing up on the nape of my neck.

I turned around to see Qole standing, hands clenched in fists, all-black eyes staring at the feed. "They can't stop us."

"Qole . . ." I searched for the words. "Dying in an attempt

is one thing, but it presumes some small chance of success. Dying as a gesture simply means my family will get everything they want."

"Not entirely true," Basra said. "If we die, my secret weapon still detonates. They won't get everything, trust me."

"Still, we don't have a way of getting through that army."

Qole spoke as though she hadn't heard me, as though she were someplace far away. "They can't stop us. There's Shadow nearby. It's everywhere."

She suddenly gasped in pain, bending over. Eton and I moved to help her, but the next instant she was back up, her black eyes staring through us.

"No, I don't care," she snarled, as if at someone else. "I'm using it. I'm using it!" The pressure in the hold changed again, and a metal plate crumpled on one wall as though something heavy had hit it. Qole gasped for breath like a drowning woman.

I opened my mouth to call her name, to reassure her, to ask her to stop, but nothing came out. Whatever she was going through, distracting her with pleas for sanity would do little good.

Even so, I could barely rein myself in as she clutched at herself and staggered sideways. I couldn't see her face, but I realized that the light reflecting on the floor underneath her had a purple sheen.

Her head snapped up suddenly, and the blackness in her eyes was gone. They were alight from within with the purple of burning Shadow.

Eton and Basra stepped back, but I stayed rooted to the spot. It wasn't that I was unafraid, or that I even understood what was happening. I didn't. I had no frame of reference for this, any of this. I was betraying my family, killing my own people, and watching a friend fall apart.

All I understood was that she was on a journey far more difficult and painful than she—or I—had ever been on. All I could do was stay with her, and be a witness.

For the briefest of moments, Qole lifted into the air, her hair fanning out around her as though she were underwater.

The entire world contracted on her, and all sound ceased to be. I staggered but could neither hear nor feel, and the next moment pure energy radiated out from her in a shock wave, a purple corona of force. Sound came rushing back into my ears; they were ringing. Qole fell to her knees on the floor.

At first, I thought that nothing had happened. Then I realized that all the troops outside the ship were simply gone.

A trickle of ice ran over my skin. Whatever had just happened was exponentially more extreme than anything else I had seen Qole do so far. From the feed, it looked like she had snuffed out the lives of an entire platoon through solid walls.

Our way was open, but at what cost?

"Is she okay?" Eton asked huskily, obviously dazed as well.

I'd reached down to see if I could help her up when rivulets of purple light began seeping through the ship's vents.

Qole knelt, pressing both palms to the floor. The glowing runnels traced their way to her fingertips, where they disappeared with a pulse. Her fists tightened, and the metal peeled back under her fingernails.

I tried to swallow, but my mouth had gone dry. "Qole, should you be drawing on that much Shadow?"

She lifted her face to me, and her eyes were shockingly clear. "I have to. I can feel Arjan nearby." She smiled ruefully. "Nev, I'm sorry, I need to do it again. . . ." She winced, took a deep breath, and her eyes went pitch black.

Purple fire drifted from her fingertips as she stood. Her face was so calm it was almost devoid of emotion, and she spoke with a certainty I had never heard her use in the grip of Shadow. "I am going to go get my brother. Nev, I'm leaving you, Eton, and Basra here to defend the ship and Telu while I'm gone."

I opened my mouth to protest: What if she passed out? Was she even in control?

But Qole was ablaze, not just with Shadow, but with a resolve that brooked no disagreement. Besides, she could apparently vaporize people. My blades would do Eton and the ship more good, especially since the guards would be less inclined to blow up the *Kaitan* with me standing in front of it.

It was nevertheless with a sinking feeling that I nodded. "Understood. Just . . . come back." It sounded foolish out loud, but it was all that was repeating in my head.

Please come back.

"I'm going too." Basra stepped forward, his voice and face carrying the same peculiar quality I had noticed earlier, and it dawned on me that he was angry.

No, it wasn't anger. Fury. Qole trained her black gaze on him, and he returned it without blinking.

"I'm coming with you to find Arjan," Basra insisted. "No royal family, no captain, and no friend will stop me." He walked toward the hatch and slammed the pad that opened it. "And then, after I've killed whoever has hurt him, I'm coming back with him."

I felt the absolute certainty of his words. With a groan, the ramp lowered, and Basra stalked out.

"Okay." Qole glanced back at us in a flash of darkness, and her hand grazed mine so quickly I almost wondered if I'd imagined it. "Be careful, I didn't get all of them."

She followed Basra into the murky gloom of the hangar and was gone.

Eton and I only took a moment to collect ourselves. I checked that both Disruption Blades were ready in their sheaths on my back, then hefted a photon rifle, while he tested the straps of Verta.

"Are you ready for this?" I asked him, turning for the ramp.

"Are *you*?" Eton bit back.

His eyes flashed from deadly serious to surprised as I held out my hand. "Whatever happens, it has been an honor."

His grip came just shy of crushing my hand this time—probably only so I could still use it. He smiled, and it was oddly genuine. "Don't make me regret meeting you more than I already do."

I shook out my fingers and took up my rifle, and with that, we strode down the ramp.

———

Qole and Basra were nowhere to be seen in the wrecked expanse of the hangar. It was disorienting to walk across the same floor that I had dashed across with Solara just last night.

Solara. The first time we'd ever worked together on something, and now I might never see her again. Or Marsius. Or my parents.

I scanned the ruined girders that outlined the gaping hole where the entrance to the rest of the palace had once been, like the crooked teeth of some monster. The drone had already redirected itself and flown out of the citadel, so I wondered why none of the starfighters had followed us down—perhaps they had been fooled by Qole's incredible disappearing act.

"See anything?" I called to Eton, feeling uneasy. Qole had said there were others here, and I disliked not knowing where.

Instead of an answer, the whining spit of one of Eton's plasma cannons echoed across the hangar. By the time I ducked and spun, the air had filled with the flickering blasts of a firefight.

Our attackers poured into the hangar from a far corner, a full platoon, running in a low crouch and obviously intending to pummel us into submission with overwhelming numbers and force.

I knew that segmented armor, those mirrored visors, the smooth precision of their movements: Bladeguards. But not just Bladeguards. Their blue and silver armor meant that they were the Home Guard, the elite personal entourage of my immediate family. They were the best the Academy had to offer, as skilled with conventional weaponry as they were with a blade. Their presence typically meant one of my family members was here, but I had no time to wonder now that all that firepower was now trained on us.

The blue bursts of photon rifles pitted the floor and the *Kaitan* as they found their range. Ignoring me, the blast marks began to trek steadily toward Eton. Energy shield or no, that many would overwhelm him soon.

Or they would have, if he hadn't returned fire with the force of a volcano. His twin cannons spat in alternating bursts, each hit leaving gouges that gleamed with molten edges. The kickback would have leveled a smaller man but, muscles taut, Eton steadily strafed back and forth, disrupting the concentration of their firepower. Stray shots that hit his shield flickered and went out like raindrops on a fire. A maniacal glee entered Eton's eyes.

"That's it, you insect sonzabitches," he taunted. "Not so fun when someone in your weight class picks on you, is it?"

One of his blasts caught two guards, and their body parts tumbled in different directions. Another blast leveled the container two others were attempting to hide behind.

But they were Bladeguards, and instead of scattering, they rolled out of the way into new crouches, bringing their weapons to bear. Another Bladeguard appeared in the doorway, in armor I didn't recognize. Heavier and thicker, it was a dirty bronze-blue with a cloak attached at the shoulders. A hard rectangular helmet with three long vertical slits glared at us.

Whoever it was, they were an effective leader. The figure made a quick motion, and the Bladeguards reacted as one, even as they split in two. Half of them surged forward, and the rest . . . turned and ran straight for the wall behind them.

"Eton!" I shouted. "They're going to use mag-gloves to get above you!"

Sure enough, with the grace and intent of spiders, the Bladeguards scaled up the hangar walls at a shocking pace. That was the beauty of mag-gloves: they not only magnetized the user to whatever surface they wished, they disrupted his gravity as well, making climbing even easier. The Bladeguards fanned out and reached the ceiling in seconds.

"Keep those on your side suppressed with your rifle," Eton shouted back. "I'm going to take care of everyone else."

Take care of them he did. With nimble manipulations of the controls in his hands, the arm of one cannon came to life, unhinging from its position and swiveling to point toward the ceiling. The rate and type of fire changed; the plasma blasts became smaller, less powerful. But they left in a furious stream that was almost uninterrupted. The other cannon continued its barrage on the troops on the floor, and somehow, Eton kept both cannons aimed and firing at once. He moved like a dancer, not the walking embodiment of death and terror. Laughter began to escape from deep in his chest.

I suddenly recognized him. That light in his eyes, that impossible grace, the crazy laugh. I couldn't believe I hadn't seen it before——but I'd been so young at the time. Teveton Gregorus had been all over the media in the years prior to my time in the Academy as one of the most gifted and iconoclastic students. The crags in his face and his graying facial hair had helped hide it, but still. He had been a celebrity for his genius in battle simulations. He'd disappeared after graduating, and I'd always wondered what had happened to him. Everyone had thought he was going to be a hero.

Instead, he was here in a damaged hangar, single-handedly fighting off a squadron of the most elite troops in the systems—troops that could have been his comrades in arms. He was a hero, just not in the way anyone had expected.

I did my best to defend him. The rifle felt heavy in my hands, and guilt tore at me. No one was shooting at me, and yet I trained the glowing sight of my weapon on human beings I no doubt knew by name. Still, I fired, hitting arms and legs, trying to disable them and knock them off the ceiling. As they crawled on, faster than I could track, I realized it was a fool's game. Heart pounding, I took deadly aim, trying to convince myself this wasn't real.

I had never taken a human life before. Now that the time had come, how could I possibly bring myself to do it? Could I really cross that line, or did I simply think I could because I'd watched others do it?

I began to fire. Some Bladeguards were mowed down by Eton, their shields and armor futile against his barrage. Some fell to my shots, dead or alive, I didn't know.

But one made it through.

He dropped from the ceiling above Eton, his blade flaring. He landed directly on Eton's shoulders, and yet the big man stayed standing. As his knees flexed, his hand flickered and his subcompact whipped up to the Bladeguard with impossible speed, firing as it went. But the Bladeguard brought his sword up just as fast to shield his face. The white band in the middle disappeared in a brilliant burst as the photon blasts hit it . . . and just as it turned blue.

Squinting in an attempt to sight the attacker, I found his blade melted to nothingness. But it had done the job; Verta's cannons winked offline, as did Eton's other weapons.

Everything happened at once. The Bladeguard leapt away, throwing a knife at Eton, just as Eton tossed a grenade high into the air. Reacting without thought, I fired straight into the Bladeguard's chest.

The grenade went off, blue lightning cracking out in a single sharp blast, my vision disappearing in the brilliance.

I didn't feel a thing. I blinked to clear my eyes.

The Bladeguard lay sprawled out on the floor, dead, the hole in his armor smoking, while Eton, with a grimace, pulled the dagger out of his leg. He fell to his knees. Blood immediately began to pool on the ground beneath him.

The grenade had been an EMP. It had fried every other type of weapon and device in the hangar, including the mag-gloves of the Bladeguards, who now rose from where they'd fallen—some stiffly, others only halfway, but still too many.

That is, it had fried every type of weapon except one.

Lines of light flickered across the darkened expanse. One, then two, then thirteen, gleamed to deadly life.

This was it. The moment where I learned how far I would go for what I believed in—for whom I believed in.

"Eton." I dropped my rifle and brought my hands around my back. My blades appeared in my grip in twin flashes of light, flaring in answer to the ones around us. "It's my turn now."

XX

QOLE

SHOUTS ECHOED BEHIND BASRA AND ME, MORE VOICES THAN just Nev's and Eton's, followed by gunfire, but I didn't turn back. If I hadn't already been used to the sensation of things tearing me apart both inside and out, leaving them behind with the *Kaitan* would have brought me to my knees. As it was, I felt a distant twinge, gritted my teeth against it, and tried to focus a different sort of sense, on what I could feel rather than see.

Arjan. He was close, somewhere in these labyrinthine halls and rooms. I hadn't been able to feel him before through all the Shadow muddying my perception, but I'd cleared a lot of it out.

. . . Along with wiping out many, many lives. I couldn't think about that, any more than I could think about abandoning my ship and half my crew to whatever was behind me. I had to find Arjan. He was all the family I had left.

No, that wasn't true, because the crew was my family too. Nev . . . Nev was also more than a friend to me, more to me than I even wanted to admit to myself, especially now that I was leaving him.

But Arjan was my only remaining kin, and our blood was apparently a rare and endangered substance. I didn't care how many people wanted it or how much; nobody was going to take my brother from me while I could still draw breath. I would gladly die to get him out of here, and I would take Arjan into oblivion with me before I abandoned him to further torture.

Oblivion. It almost sounded nice right now, like a peaceful, never-ending nap. My ancestors believed our spirits returned to the Shadow grounds around Alaxak when we died. I wondered if mine could make it back there if I was killed on the other side of the galaxy, or if I would just drift on the wind, lost. Or if there was only bottomless darkness waiting for me once I closed my eyes for the last time.

My vision shuddered, rippling like a dark pond. The walls seemed to be flexing and pressing in on me, and only the Shadow I'd drawn inside me seemed to keep them, or me, upright. I knew Shadow existed in my flesh and bone, but I'd never pulled *more* of it into my body before. I wasn't sure how I'd done it, or what would happen to me once I let it go.

I might just kill myself before anyone else could. But so be it.

Basra walked with the same air of finality, the photon rifle held ready in his hands. He clearly knew how to use it. As a trader, especially one with his skills, I imagine he'd gotten himself into some sticky situations. I'd always sensed something capable and unflinching in him, something dangerous. I'd been expecting his relationship with Arjan to drive the two of us to conflict, not into an alliance against one of the most powerful royal families in the galaxy . . . and likely a suicide pact.

If Nev couldn't be at my side walking into this with me—and he only wasn't because he was guarding my back, my ship, and the rest of my crew—then Basra was the next best option. I was grateful to have him, whether or not his "secret weapon" amounted to anything. He felt like a secret weapon himself, here with me now.

"Thank you," I said, as we slipped down a darkened hallway. Only one light flickered at the end, sending spastic pale flashes over the expanse. The walls were cracked, and not just in my mind. I wasn't sure if the drone had done such damage or if I had. In any case, Arjan was in this direction.

"Just focus," Basra murmured, "and find him. Then it will be me thanking you."

I was focusing so hard that I nearly walked into a pair of guards as we turned a corner.

Basra's rifle was up so fast that a burst of white-hot light hit one in the chest before I could blink. The guard went down in a sizzling heap while the other whipped up his rifle.

I was faster than Basra this time. I flicked my fingers in his direction, and then the man was crawling in purple fire. He opened his mouth to scream, but the flames dove in before he could make a sound. His eyes fell away first, then the rest of him, until all that remained was black dust and silence.

"So that's what happened to all the others," Basra remarked without feeling, and then stepped over the man he'd killed.

No, woman. Her blank eyes stared at the ceiling as if in

surprise. I wasn't sure why *I* was surprised, other than the fact that most of the troops we had faced had been men.

The walls shifted around me again, and I leaned against one of them, trying to get my breathing under control. "That was a woman," I said, mostly just to hear my own voice and make sure it was still there—that I wasn't dissolving in Shadow like the man had.

"All the same to me," Basra said, only pausing a moment while I regained my feet, and then he continued down the new stretch of hallway.

We had less time before the guards found us this time. Either they had heard the rifle shot, or they were responding to the much greater commotion far behind us. We hadn't been too subtle with our entrance, after all. Five of them raced around the next corner.

"Down!" I shouted, seizing Basra's collar and dragging him to the ground as energy blasts went zinging over our heads, crackling in the air and raising the hairs on the back of my neck.

I put out my other hand to brace my fall. One second, it was just my skin against the stone floor. The next, purple fire rippled around my fingertips and lanced down the hall. There were screams this time, and even Basra flinched at the sight of the inferno at the other end.

But when we passed the very spot a moment later, he stepped over a single charred boot and the fragile remains of a charcoal rib cage—all that was left of the five—just like he had the other guard, with his eyes straight ahead. Nor did he flinch away from me when I stumbled and caught his arm to steady myself. I distantly appreciated it.

There wasn't much else he could do to help me, though, since the floor was shifting and splitting under my feet. Basra didn't seem to be having problems with it, so it was obviously all in my head.

"How are you holding up?" he murmured.

"Not . . . well," I gasped. "I'm hallucinating. I don't know how much more I have in me."

His cool, slender hand found my cheek, bringing my gaze to his. "Just a little bit farther, Captain. You can do it. I know you can." His eyes were filled with so much warmth, suddenly, with belief in me. The gesture felt motherly.

I swallowed and nodded. "He's close." I took a shaky step away from him, and even closed my eyes. Behind my lids, I could see other shapes in the darkness, instead of only feeling them. The collection of light that was Arjan was only another few hallways down. But it was odd; there was interference, and not just from what remained of the citadel's huge caches of Shadow. There were other lights, frameworks, like Arjan's. They were weaker, but I could sense them.

I leaned up against a thick metal door that hid one of them. "Basra, I think there's someone . . . someone like me and Arjan in here."

"We'll free them on the way back, if we can," he said with barely a glance. "Save your strength. Arjan needs it."

With a grimace, I straightened. He was right.

When we came to Arjan's hallway, I stopped Basra with a hand. I didn't recognize any other aspect of it; it looked the same as all the others. They'd moved him from wherever the both of us had been held before. These rooms were still intact.

"He's . . . he's here," I whispered, without getting too close to Arjan in my mind. I didn't want his pain to affect me. I needed to focus.

"Any guards?"

I squeezed my lids tighter shut. "I can't tell. I can only see others like me. I would have to reach out with Shadow, use it as my eyes, and leave my body . . . and I don't know if I'd be able to find my way back to myself if I did."

Basra lifted his photon rifle. "Let's try the standard approach, then." Before I could stop him, he leaned into a crouch, aimed around the corner, and fired two rounds. There were shouts, and he pulled back, flattening himself against the wall. "Five outside the room—four now. I missed one."

Several crackling shots, accompanied by the squeak of boots over the floor, answered his volley. They were coming.

This was it. I had to do this. I shoved Basra behind me and, acting on instinct, lifted my arms. A stream of fire rose between my hands, then flared into a wall that I sent ahead of me as I stepped around the corner.

Energy shots rippled against the flaming barrier like they were extinguishing themselves in strange, purple liquid. Then the wall of fire began to hit the bodies. Agonized faces shone through like specters—teeth here, flaring nostrils there, wide holes where eyes had been—before they vanished. When the flames dropped, we were alone in the blackened, smoking hallway.

Basra only coughed and wiped his watering eyes on a sleeve. I doubted he was crying over anything other than smoke irritation. My knees threatened to buckle.

"Think you can manage the door?" he asked.

We were close, so close. I could manage.

But it wasn't as fast as I would have liked. The flames didn't come as quickly when I reached for them, and for a moment, the line of fire flickered and almost winked out as I staggered. The door eventually caved in, a glowing, molten outline around it. Still, it took long enough that whoever was behind it was able to prepare themselves.

Rubion Dracorte II stood behind a table, from which he'd dragged Arjan. My brother was barely standing, still hooked up with needles and tubes to whatever equipment they were using to monitor him—only his restraints appeared to have been hurriedly removed. His one eye rolled in his head.

Basra made a strangled sound next to me, but I couldn't turn from Arjan.

The sight of him still took my breath away, even though he didn't look much worse than when I'd last seen him. I'd been drugged and half delirious then. Even if I was half delirious now, his wounds were perfectly clear, sharp enough to feel like cuts in my own skin. I actually saw my skin peeling away, but I didn't think anyone else could.

"Arjan," I rasped.

Rubion held a plasma pistol up to Arjan's head. "We don't have to do this, Miss Uvgamut."

"Oh, we do," Basra murmured, sighting Rubion through the doorway along his own rifle. "And she's not the only one you have to worry about." He took a step toward the doorway.

"And I'm not the only one you have to worry about," Rubion rejoined.

Basra barely dodged the Disruption Blade that came singing along the other side of the door. I realized it hadn't quite missed him when I saw red begin to seep along his sleeve. A little slower, and he would have lost an arm. He would have lost his head too, if I hadn't engulfed the Bladeguard in flames.

I didn't have the strength to char the man to ash, and he fell to the ground screaming. Basra silenced him with a photon blast. Even the motion of pulling the trigger cost him, judging by the wince that twisted his face. The stain was spreading, blood beginning to drip from his sleeve, but he didn't lower the rifle.

In fact, his mouth twitched in a half smile. "Never play your hand too early," he said.

Rubion hardly paid him any mind. He was looking at me with a hungry light in his eyes. "So, this is what you can do." His reasonable tone was as perfectly smooth as before. "How about we all lower our weapons, you step inside, and we—"

Basra barked a laugh. "You want to try to bargain with me? Fine. How about you shoot the other Bladeguard in there, and then we'll talk."

I had no idea how he knew, but it was obvious he was right from the look on Rubion's face. He glanced to the side with a disappointed twist to his lips. "Lower your weapons and stand down," he said to someone I couldn't see.

"Tell them to kick the weapons into the center of the room," I said. Never mind that the room was flowing and cracking so much, like molten earth, that I wasn't sure I would even be able to see them.

Rubion hesitated, the pistol still against Arjan's head, and then nodded. The dim shape of a gun and then the white gleam of a Disruption Blade skittered across my vision.

"What if there are two swords?" My voice sounded too drunk for my liking, though there wasn't much I could do about it. "Nev has two." A hazy memory surfaced of him wielding one in either hand.

Rubion blinked in surprise. "Blademasters are rare among Bladeguards. Nevarian is the youngest in an age—I assure you, it's not commonplace."

"He's telling the truth," Basra said without hesitation, and stepped into the room. Drips of blood trailed behind him.

"How do you know?" Rubion said with a sleek, raised eyebrow.

"I learned to read faces like yours when I was five," Basra

said, keeping the rifle trained on him, obviously assuming I'd handle the unarmed Bladeguard if he—she—made a move. She stood still in her segmented armor, arms folded behind her back, as she'd been ordered.

Rubion sneered at Basra. "And just who do you think you are?"

Basra's smile returned. He'd flipped on his emotional switch again, because his eyes were filled with nearly malicious pleasure as he stared at Rubion over the table. "You, Dracorte, might know me as Hersius Kartolus."

Without losing his sighting down the barrel, he lifted one hand from the rifle—his uninjured one, even—shook up his sleeve, and curled up his fingertips to press his wrist. A design appeared along on his forearm, which then went a step further to project itself in a glowing holograph, hovering a few inches over his skin. It was like a double helix, all glittery blacks and blues, but with each end looped closed instead of left open.

I had no idea what the name Hersius Kartolus meant, but I'd seen holo-tattoos like these. They were often licensed for use by one particular individual, often for life, and sometimes against their will in the case of prison inmates. It was meant to prove Basra was somebody . . . I just didn't know who.

Rubion did, though. The effect was instantaneous. His jaw slackened and his eyes popped. He was stunned . . . and quite possibly terrified. "You . . . *That's* you?" His eyes roved the design, as if counting the number of overlapping spirals in the lineup. There looked to be around a dozen.

"Yes, and believe me when I say I will wreck you and your family beyond belief."

"Wait, what?" I slurred, swaying. I had to reach for the wall to support myself. The Bladeguard tensed but didn't move. "What does all this mean?"

Basra didn't respond. To me, anyway. "That is, unless you release Arjan Uvgamut. I assure you, it's in your best interest. Your *family's* interest."

That didn't sound right. Maybe *this,* a name and a tattoo, was somehow Basra's secret weapon. But I had seen his anger, and I knew he wouldn't just let Rubion walk away after merely threatening him.

Rubion's fingers tightened on Arjan's shoulder. "No, Hersius, this boy and girl are the only things working in my family's interest right now. If only you knew what we could do with them, I'm sure you'd be on board. With your resources—"

"Resources?" I asked, glancing at Basra.

"You didn't even know who you had on your ship?" Rubion graced me with his attention again, if only in the form of a disdainful glance. "Hersius Kartolus is richer than the Great Unifier. A financial genius. He has major investments in every royal family, including *significant* stock in Dracorte Industries, never mind the top five commoner corporations in the galaxy."

"How . . . ," I sputtered, glancing at Basra. "You're only a few years older than me!"

"And you're the best pilot in the galaxy," Basra murmured. "Give me some credit."

Rubion smiled at Basra like he knew yet another thing I didn't. And he was right. "That's the half secret that isn't widely known beyond certain circles. The name Hersius Kartolus has existed for hundreds of years, possibly dating back to before the Great Collapse. Whoever is the current Kartolus finds a pupil to train, a rising star to take his—or her—place as the sun around which so many revolve. I haven't known any other Kartolus but the Twelfth."

He hesitated, then spoke directly to Basra again. Not that his eyes had ever left him. "And now I meet the Thirteenth.

My father, Axandar, told me the Twelfth was considered young when he gained the name in his middle years. If you didn't have the mark, I would never have believed. Even with his ill health, you must be very skilled indeed for the Twelfth to have considered you ready."

There wasn't quite insinuation in the words, more of a question.

"You have no idea," Basra said shortly. "Now, as you know, my time is rather valuable, so what'll it be?"

"Allow me to make you a counteroffer." Rubion's eyes practically glowed with eagerness from across the table. Arjan's one remaining eye was shut. The other socket still gaped. I couldn't stop looking at it.

My vision pulsed. Whoever Basra was, I didn't care. We needed to end this before either I collapsed or my fury wiped us all out.

"I can't imagine one that could interest me," Basra said. "And I have a pretty good imagination. Outside of Arjan Uvgamut, who will already be coming back to me with less of him than there was before, I don't need anything."

"I will give you Arjan without fuss if you incapacitate his sister—with maybe a shot to the knee so you don't cause too much damage—and then join me."

Basra laughed outright, the most disdainful laugh I'd ever heard in my life.

"You don't understand," Rubion insisted. "With my research and your resources, we don't even need my family. This isn't about them. This isn't about wealth and power either, though we will have that beyond even *your* wildest dreams. It's about what we could do with her abilities. If you join my enterprise, we will be *gods.*"

I glanced at Basra in alarm. As someone who usually appreciated a good offer, I wasn't sure how he could pass up one like that. Even as someone who claimed to have everything.

But the rifle didn't waver. He only said, "I'm not interested in godhood, I'm afraid."

I released an unsteady breath and shook my head at Rubion. "I don't know what you think this is, but it's not godhood. No one can do what I'm doing for long. I don't know how I'm still alive. You're an idiot if you think—"

"You're an idiot if you think all I want to do is play with fire," Rubion said, tossing his head at me in dismissal. "Your abilities are only a stepping-stone to something greater."

I blinked, too surprised to be angry. "To what?"

"The portals."

Now Basra blinked. "Impossible."

Rubion's eyes grew even brighter now that he had Basra's interest. "Not impossible. You see, the myth is that Shadow caused the Great Collapse of the portals. But I know the truth. Shadow has something to do with the portals, yes, but quite the opposite of common belief."

"You're stalling," Basra said.

"Wrong—"

"Prove it," Basra nearly snapped, the pain he was suppressing audible in his tone. "Show me something I haven't seen yet, because so far, your bluffing is textbook."

Rubion glanced up at the cameras, and with deft flicks of his wrist, he shot them out with his plasma pistol.

The Bladeguard started. "My lord—?"

Without a moment's warning, he shot her in the head. His pistol was back against Arjan's temple and his eyes on Basra before she even finished crumpling to the ground. I jumped in shock, but Basra never flinched, his aim steady on Rubion.

"You asked me to shoot the other Bladeguard, but you

probably didn't expect I would, did you? How does that work for getting your attention? No one to overhear now," Rubion added, as an afterthought.

Basra hesitated, and my breath caught as he said, "I'm listening."

"You see, Shadow didn't collapse the portals. A refined version of Shadow is what *ran* the portals. Scientists had a special Shadow affinity from working so closely with them for so long, and they were the ones who kept the portals open."

"You're telling me . . . ," Basra said, and couldn't finish. I could barely complete the thought in my own mind.

Someone with the right knowledge, and the capability, could reopen the portals. Reconnect our galaxy to the rest of the universe. It was an idea that people would kill for, die for. That people would do *anything* for. And the capability—that belonged only to me, and to Arjan.

I was watching Basra now, almost as closely as I was Rubion.

"We could reverse the Great Collapse," Rubion said in practically a whisper. A whisper in my brother's ear, even if he was talking to Basra. "Everything will open."

The blackness in my vision surged with rage.

Basra raised his head from the rifle a fraction, and Rubion lowered his pistol an equal fraction, his finger relaxing on the trigger.

My hands balled into fists. I didn't have much strength left, but I had to do something now, especially if Basra—

Basra pulled his trigger and took off half of Rubion's head—the half farthest from my brother.

Arjan collapsed onto the table with Rubion, but before he could follow him to the floor, Basra shouldered his rifle, leapt over the table, and caught his shoulders. I'd lunged to do the same, but the floor had shifted, making me lose my balance.

Basra shoved Rubion's body away. "That," he said, his lip twisting in disgust, "is how you bluff. I told you I wasn't interested."

He'd nearly had me fooled. I could barely keep up with him, all that he supposedly was, or even wrap my unraveling mind around the fact that Rubion was dead.

"Captain," he said, snapping my attention away from all the bodies on the floor that still seemed to be moving, muscles flowing and limbs twitching in unnatural ways. "Can you please find something for Arjan to wear?"

I glanced at my brother and then quickly away. The white towel that had been around his waist had slipped off. I stumbled toward the cabinets lining the room and lurched against the counter. Keeping one hand on it for support, I wrenched open cupboards and drawers until I found a blue medical gown.

Basra had already unhooked all the needles, tubes, and cables from Arjan's limbs by the time I made it over to them, and he helped me maneuver the gown over Arjan's shoulders, especially since I had to grip the steel table to keep from falling over myself. I tried to ignore Rubion's gaping skull at my feet. The half of his face that was still intact seemed to be smiling up at me, torn lips moving as if continuing to whisper his secrets.

The portals ... If he'd been telling the truth, that could change everything, change the galaxy ...

But Basra was right. Next to Arjan, it didn't matter.

I still felt useless compared to Basra's bustle. He checked a miniature infopad he'd untucked from a pocket, scrolling through a list as he maneuvered around the room. Searching through cabinets, he scooped everything from bandages and tape to injectors and glass vials into an empty containment bag. He was assembling his own medi-kit, I realized. Before I could offer to help, he secured the bag over his shoulder with the rifle and bent for Arjan.

We both looped one of his arms around our necks. I tried to avoid touching the wounds in his skin as best I could. They were plastic-sealed against infection, but they still hurt him. He groaned as we hefted him, his head lolling.

"It's okay," Basra said, his voice softer, more feminine, than I'd ever heard it. "We're getting you out of here."

Our lumbering walk was painfully slow. Basra and I had to drag Arjan between us, and my own legs kept trying to buckle. Sometimes it felt as if Basra were carrying the two of us, if only with moral support.

"Keep going, a few more steps," he kept murmuring, even while he left his own blood spattered behind us. "We're almost there."

We weren't almost there. We had seeming light-years of hallways to follow, and I didn't even know what would be waiting for us when we got back. Even if I still had my ship, my crew—*Don't imagine otherwise,* I told myself—I had no idea if either the *Kaitan* or I could actually fly. In spite of the damage she'd taken, the ship was probably in better shape than me. One thruster was entirely down, another nearly there, but between it and the solar sail, we could maybe limp far enough off-planet to engage the Belarius Drive. But I didn't know if I could fly us that far. And there was no question that Arjan couldn't.

There was also no chance of me helping whoever was trapped on the opposite sides of the many doors we passed. They were people with Shadow affinities from other planets, perhaps insane or only weak, who'd no doubt been tortured like Arjan. And yet I had to leave them. I could barely walk, let alone break them free.

At least no other guards seemed to be coming. Maybe we'd killed them all. There were too many corpses already, and we seemed to be dragging them with us. Out of the corner of my eye, whenever I turned, I could see half-faced Rubion and the two Bladeguards, one burned and the other trailing brains, clawing along the floor behind.

"Basra," I breathed at one point, "are those bodies following us?"

He cast a glance over his shoulder. "No, Captain."

I would have laughed that one of the richest, most powerful people in the galaxy was still using my formal title now that I knew *his,* but I had other things on my mind. Or rather, nightmares from out of my mind, come to haunt me.

"I can hear them," I said. "I can see them. The walls are collapsing."

Basra's wary eyes were on me, now. "You can do this. Just a little bit farther."

I almost laughed in despair then, but the sound died in my throat. Because he was right. We rounded another corner, and the massive, ruined space of the hangar opened around us with the late red sunlight filtering through the cavernous hole we'd torn. But if I'd hoped we'd left the nightmarish scene behind, I had been wrong.

Near the battered, hulking shape of the *Kaitan,* Nev stood over Eton. Eton was on the ground, holding his leg in a puddle of blood. Blood was all around them. Nev was still for the moment, chest and shoulders heaving, swords held out in either hand. His jacket was in tatters, his arms covered in dripping cuts.

Around both Nev and Eton, dozens of bodies lay sprawled

and twisted, radiating out as if the two of them were bombs that had detonated.

At least they were still alive, though they looked nearly as finished as Basra, Arjan, and I were. But then I heard the unmistakable pounding of boots from the opposite end of the hangar.

Armor and weaponry glinted in the bloody sunlight, and I heard the shouts for us to put down our arms. None of us listened. Nev raised his blades and Basra his rifle, leaving me to support Arjan. Even Eton fumbled for a gun with sticky red hands, and Telu appeared on the ramp with a pistol in one hand and a knife in the other.

She waved for me to hurry toward the ship, but I couldn't abandon the others like this. Besides, I didn't think I could carry Arjan all that way on my own. I tried to reach for the last of the Shadow still lurking in the caches below, but it slipped away from me. So did my balance. I slid to the floor, dragging Arjan with me.

I couldn't help my gasp. "I can't. I can't." I closed my eyes. I didn't try to seize the Shadow again, or force it away like I usually did. I simply surrendered.

Lights danced in the darkness behind my lids, and I thought I heard whispering—beckoning me to oblivion.

XXI

TIRED. I SHOULD HAVE BEEN FEELING PAIN, OR FEAR, OR ANGER. And I suppose I did, but I simply felt more tired than anything else.

As the first two of the newly arrived Bladeguards reached me, we engaged in a rapid-fire series of cuts and thrusts, my blades working in a defensive pattern to keep them occupied and at a distance. We engaged and disengaged, clashed and retreated twice. It would have been just another day at the Academy if they hadn't been significantly better than most of the students there—and drawing blood. They were willing to hurt me, but none of the wounds were serious.

It was the realization that they wouldn't kill me that set the exhaustion rolling in as we parted, circling.

What's the point? I wondered. How was I supposed to fight and kill someone who refused to kill me? My heart could never be in that, any more than it could be in torturing people for our gain. *It's impossible, anyway. There are too many of them to do anything.* That rational thought intruded as the exhaustion set in further.

"How about you gentlemen put your weapons down," I suggested, "and we discuss some more attractive options? I don't want to hurt you."

They didn't answer. One kept his blade at cross angles to me, and I realized they had been maneuvering me so one of them could get closer to Eton.

They don't have to hurt me to kill everyone else. Anger flared somewhere deep in my chest. It wasn't about me; it never should have been. I wasn't defending myself, I was defending my friends, who at no point had done anything to deserve any of this. My exhaustion vanished.

Clarity descended upon me. I brought both blades together in the fastest spin of my life, and the Bladeguard nearest Eton lost his head. A moment later, the body toppled.

I'd made the choice to fight against my family before, but now it was time to defend family. Not my royal family, but the one that needed me most.

"Run," I snarled, strength coursing through every fiber of my being.

The Bladeguard nearest me did not flee. He swung his blade at my legs in what was meant to be a debilitating slash.

I spun again, blocking it with both swords, and kicked him in the helmet, staggering him. This time, I didn't hesitate, and he lost both hands for his effort. Nor did I stop to see what else happened to him. I ran, blades out to my sides, straight at the next enemy.

When I had been four, my father had taught me how to punch. When I had been five, I began to train with a blade. When I had been thirteen, I fought off my first group under the tutelage of Devrak.

There are four principles to fighting multiple assailants, Nev: First, control your environment.

The guards might at some point choose to fight me with deadly force for survival, but I would never be the priority target—that was everyone on the *Kaitan*. I had to keep the attention of eleven attackers on me long enough to let the others board the ship and make their escape.

"I'm coming for you!" I shouted at the door, where their commander had been. "You're going down, along with this entire hangar!" A bluff, but then, I had been taught how to manipulate by my mother from my earliest years. These were the Home Guard, defenders, and I was threatening their leader with destructive force.

Their reaction exceeded my wildest hopes; they converged on me in a swarm as I charged. In seconds, they would overwhelm me.

Second, become the unexpected. At the last possible moment, and at a dead run, I fell to my knees in front of them, letting their blades whistle over my head. As I slid under them, I brought my twin swords in sweeping arcs to either side.

The edge of my blades caught, cutting armor and slicing flesh. Wounded, but still mobile, Bladeguards leapt away from my attack. I rolled onto my feet and was upon them.

Third, use your attackers. Parrying blows on either side, I stepped between two guards and stabbed behind me, using my full weight. I drove the points home, pushing them into the others. My blades flickered out and spun, spraying droplets of blood onto their masks as I slashed and parried, feinting attacks from one to the next as I moved through them, never exchanging more than a blow before assaulting my next target. I used them against one another, and when I countered, I countered for the kill.

I should have been short of breath, I should have been ready to collapse, but instead I moved with surety and speed. They would not touch my friends. *Fourth, destroy their pillars. Pick the strong ones off one by one.* Armor chipped, glass splintered, and the ring of steel echoed in the hangar. First one fell, then another.

"*Run,*" I hissed at them again, beyond caring whether they listened or not. I remembered Eton and, as I might at a royal ball, I sidestepped and ducked between attacks to turn, trying to spot where he was.

Telu was struggling to drag him to the *Kaitan,* but that wasn't what made my breath catch. Qole and Arjan were down on the ground, with Basra standing guard above them. They'd made it . . . but running toward them were two Bladeguards. The rest attempted to bar me from either returning to the *Kaitan* or heading for Qole.

"Stop!" I shouted, the words coming unbidden to my mouth. I reared back and snapped my body forward, sending both my Disruption Blades streaking toward their targets, embedding them with deadly accuracy into the backs of both runners.

Before they had even finished falling, I launched myself into a flying kick that dented and spun the helmet of the guard in front of me. Unarmed, I turned back to my attackers, one arm out far in front of me, the other in a fist close to my face in the classic defensive position of the Academy.

They didn't hesitate. I sensed a deadlier purpose to them now. I still didn't know if they would actually kill me, but they were certainly willing to put the medical facilities of the citadel to the test.

I weaved between two slashing attacks, jumped back from a stab, and then moved into the opening. I slammed a sword-arm away, then grasped it as I brought my elbow into the owner's chest. He stumbled, and I kicked at the next Bladeguard, aiming for the sword hand before snapping my foot up to the helmet instead, all in the same motion. My second target dropped. I returned to the first so quickly that he never had a chance to recover, and barraged him with elbows and fists until the knife edge of my hand found his throat twice. With a horrible rattle, he fell. Now I had a clear window for my little trick . . .

Four Bladeguards remained, and they paused, forming a wall between me and their commander, who had appeared in the far doorway. They were obviously reconsidering their tactics against me, and I knew I didn't have much longer before the effects of the EMP blast wore off and weaponry started coming back online. When that happened, the crew would be dead.

"Not while I draw breath," I rasped, responding to my own thought.

"You're unarmed," one of them finally spoke. "Stand down."

That seemed to break the wall of silence, because another one spoke. "You killed my friend, traitor. For that, you'll pay in blood."

I stretched both hands out to my sides.

With a hum, my Disruption Blades dislodged themselves and flew through the air, directly into my waiting grasp. I'd designed the mag-couplings in my sleeve cuffs when I was fifteen. Temporally coded to the magnetic fields in the Disruption Blades, they had enough power for a single use. This kept their circuitry simple enough that they were immune to all but the strongest of EMP blasts, unlike the complex gravity disruptors in the Bladeguards' mag-gloves. Yet another example of how I'd been practically engineered to be an innovative leader. I'd also been taught all my life how to be a warrior-prince for my family. And now I was bringing it all to bear against those who had made me this way.

I smiled, although there was no mirth in me, only fury. "Then don't send your friends to kill the innocent."

Disruption Blades clashed, grated, sparked, and clashed again faster than I could think. I pictured Qole before a Shadow run. Eyes bright, radiating purpose and calm, moving on instinct, memory, and pure focus. I channeled her, sinking into my body. My blades wove a pattern in the air over and over, the lights blurring into a permanent streak. I made my stand there in the wreckage of the hangar, in the cavern underneath my ancestral home, and fought four of my own elite guard to a standstill.

I didn't remember how they fell, or how fast, and I wouldn't have been able to recount how I'd done it. My next memory was of me descending on their commander in his rust-blue armor and cape, leaping at him with unbridled rage and bringing both swords down in an overhead blow meant to remove his arms.

My blades hit his with jarring force. His weapon was larger, broader, than most. It wasn't meant for fencing, or quick work. It was meant for crushing armor and disabling spaceships.

Our blades ground together to the hilt, sparks trailing, and

I brought my face to the slitted visor of the helmet. "Stand down," I growled. "This is your only warning."

The visor flickered, then folded away into itself, revealing Thelarus Dracorte. My king. My father.

Time slowed as I attempted to understand what I was seeing. I knew those deep-set eyes; I had memorized every line on his face, knew every expression that it held.

Or so I thought. The mixture of pain and anger in his eyes was unprecedented.

I hadn't seen him in armor since I was a child, so that was almost new. But he'd grown up with the same training I had, and he had many more years of experience. Far more battles.

"No, son, this is your warning." Father advanced on me, pushing against my blades with his, and I stumbled back a step, disengaging. "As your father, I ask you to drop your weapons before this goes any further."

I didn't lower my guard. "No." It was the first word that came to me, the expression of everything that had been boiling inside me since the last time Father and I had talked. "I drop my weapons, and then what? You kill the useless ones and torture the rest? Why are you even here? Where's Devrak?" I had been deathly afraid that it would be him in the armor, but this was a thousand times worse.

Thelarus lowered his own sword and, with a click, it attached to his hip. I recognized it now, even though I hadn't seen it in years, either. It was the blade he had used before he was king, when he'd fought against pirates in the outer reaches. It had been given a name—Beadvar, the Shipwrecker. "I'm here to clean up your mess personally, since even Devrak isn't entirely aware of the extent of our research." Devrak would never have condoned the torture of innocents, and Father knew it. Anger laced his clipped words. "A much better question might be what you think you are hoping to accomplish here."

I shook my head. "I don't want to fight you. I don't want to fight anybody. But I'm not going to let you hurt anyone on the *Kaitan* again."

"Your delusion is assuming you have any say in the matter." He stepped toward me, but I didn't step back. He stopped, almost touching my blades. "All you've done is brought dishonor on your family, disaster on your people, and death to your friends. You've accomplished nothing else." He took another step, and pressed himself against my blades. "Now, as your *king,* I command you to lay down your weapons."

I felt the twinge of a lifetime spent listening to that voice and obeying. But I had already struggled with my choices, and they were made.

I pushed back against him, my blades grating on his armor, but my father didn't move, and my frustration spiked. "You taught me to never lay aside my duty to this family, which I learned all too well at my Rendering. Now you say I dishonor our family? Who took someone against their will and tortured them? Who lied to his son his entire life? You've dishonored everything, everything that you raised me to believe. You've *forsaken* your duty." I was shouting at him now. "So, no, I'm not putting down my weapons, not by your command, because you haven't earned the right."

Lightning flashed in my father's eyes. He stepped back, and I never even registered how his sword appeared in his hands. It came at me, and on pure instinct, I brought a blade up to answer it. The weight of his weapon took mine to the floor; he shifted, trapped it there with his foot, and hammered his sword back up against my other one. Both were wrenched from my hands at the same time, and he slammed his hilt against my unarmored chest. I wheezed and staggered, falling almost as much from shock as from the blow. I had just been disarmed like a child being relieved of a toy.

"Earned? Leadership isn't bestowed; it is a decision!" Thelarus growled. The lines on his face deepened, and he stood tall, blade pointed down at me. "A ruler doesn't dabble in sentiment. A ruler sacrifices. You would kill a hundred to save one you care for? The selfishness is staggering."

I suddenly became aware of cuts and bruises on me I had no memory of receiving, and at the rate I was bleeding, I'd probably pass out soon. On top of that, new troops were spreading into the hangar, weapons up and aimed. *So much for fighting everyone off. Maybe I can stall them.*

I climbed to my feet wearily.

"You say *sacrifice* a lot. Sacrifice of what?" I asked. "Somewhere, Father, you lost sight. You focused on the practical measures to accomplish our ideals. The big picture." It was my turn to walk toward him, and I stopped with the point of his blade almost touching my chest. "But in the end, that means your ultimate ideal is the success of our family. What kind of choices do you think you make when that is what drives you? Choices that benefit us, or benefit others? Are you really so arrogant as to think those are one and the same?"

Father's face didn't change, but he didn't stop me either. What if I could reach him with my words? Surely there was some part of him that had to know this was true.

"Do you know what you taught me? You taught me to make the lives of others better. *Do you think their lives are better?*" I shouted without warning, stabbing my finger at the ship behind me. My world had shrunk to this, just my father and me, and everything I had ever felt boiled in my veins. Love for this man, love for my family, and a raging despair that it had come to this. "Of what use is the big picture to them? Your big picture is made of billions of single lives, and you'd look each of them in the eye and say they deserve to die, when you yourself give up *nothing*?"

I took a ragged breath and stepped back with my hands spread out. "Father, don't you think that when stealing and torturing is what saves our family, the true sacrifice would be to let our family fail?"

For the briefest of seconds, pain flickered across my father's face, before it was replaced with the king's stony expression once more. He put away his blade.

"The ship of your terrorist comrades is surrounded, there are fighters outside this hangar, and drone security has, thankfully, reset the drones to their master program," he informed me without a trace of emotion. "If you fight, we will incapacitate you. If your ... 'friends' ... fight, they will be killed. You are unwell and will be taken to the infirmary to be treated. I will visit you there when you've at least partially returned to your senses."

What am I supposed to do? I looked over my shoulder, at the *Kaitan*.

Telu and Basra had Arjan on a blanket they were using as a makeshift stretcher. His wounds looked hideous, and I didn't even know if he was alive. Eton's leg was hastily bandaged, if still bleeding. Even though he could hardly walk, he was trying to help Qole up. She was on her knees, her eyes closed, her face drawn, as if she were waging some internal battle. The sight of her stabbed through me, and I wished I could go to her ... but my place was here, between my father and her. The crew was battered, hurt, and yet, they'd made it back to the ship. They had defied all odds, and an entire royal family. The least I could do was defy a king.

I turned back and shook my head. "Don't you see? It's not about winning; it's about doing the right thing."

Thelarus shrugged his shoulders and raised his hand. "Watch the consequences of your choices."

This was it. He was going to give the order, the troops would attack, and everyone would die. Except for me, and I would no doubt go to an asylum for the rest of my days, or until I was somehow reprogrammed. I closed my eyes for a second. *Congratulations, Nev, you're out of ideas.*

"Thelarus Dracorte, there is a warning signal on your comm that just went off. It's there because you receive an alert when any significantly drastic market action occurs."

Basra's voice sounded in my ears, and even in my bedraggled state, I managed to start. His ability to sneak up on me was uncanny.

I had no idea what he was going on about, but Father stayed still, watching as Basra walked past me.

Something was different about him. Drying blood matted his clothing on one side, but that wasn't it. Instead of his customary slouch, instead of all the little ways he faded into the background, Basra was standing straight, his shoulders square and arms clasped behind him. He exuded the confidence and posture of an executive in a boardroom, not a fugitive in front of a firing squad.

"How do you know that?" Father narrowed his eyes.

"Because that's how every industrial head has their alert system configured, and you are the head of Dracorte Industries. Now, let's not waste time on obvious trivialities. I have something much more important to tell you."

Basra stopped and cocked his head to one side. "I am Hersius Kartolus the Thirteenth. You know who I am, you know what my resources are. What you also might know is that for the past week—since our delightful run-in with your moral equivalents, the Treznor-Nirmanas—I have been purchasing Dracorte products from every broker I know across the systems. Minerals, mostly, the same minerals that constitute the majority of your sales and revenues. And Shadow, of course."

I blinked. "Pardon?" Perhaps blood loss was playing with my hearing.

Father, on the other hand, seemed to be hearing just fine. What was more, he seemed to grasp what Basra was saying. His face was still made of stone, but he lowered his arm slowly. "You're bluffing," he said.

Basra's voice could have cut metal with the matter-of-fact edge it possessed. "Feel at liberty to check your comms, or the feed you no doubt have on your visor."

Shockingly, Father actually activated his visor, which reassembled itself over his face. Seconds later it deconstructed again. His eyes were angry, his face gaining color.

"You think this is a good idea? To make me angry before your arrest?"

"Your Majesty." Basra steepled his fingers in front of him, and the way he said "Majesty" stripped it of any distinction outside of formality. "I think we both know that you have outstanding military and judicial capabilities, but your mind has never taken to industry like your father Axandar's. Allow me to explain."

I looked around, trying to make sense of what was happening. The troops were spreading across the hangar, slowly moving farther out and surrounding us. These weren't Bladeguards, and they were obviously somewhat taken aback at the devastation before them. Bodies littered the ground, and blood pooled in score marks and gouges left by the firefight.

In the middle of all this, Basra was talking about the markets? His claim to be Hersius Kartolus—the Thirteenth, no less? There had somehow been *thirteen*?—was beyond absurd. I could buy that he worked for Kartolus, but I'd seen the man myself several years ago, and Basra was most definitely not him.

"First, there is a news article being leaked, with some remarkable footage from the *Kaitan,* stating that there has been a massive incident at the Dracorte citadel, thanks to an inability to control your mining drones any longer. Second, for the past hour, all the minerals I have purchased are now selling as fast as they can. When traders see a product being unloaded so quickly, they inevitably think something is amiss and follow suit. A few who are more intelligent, or just particularly well informed, might take the opportunity to buy instead. Such as, say, the Treznor-Nirmana family. Third, when news begins to spread of your drones running amok on your own homeworld, coupled with the Treznor buy-out, your investors will simply panic. They'll think you've lost faith in your product, and they will lose faith in you. I'm sure Treznor will be happy to snap up what they sell, and watch you struggle to repay your debt to them in the allotted time frame . . . a task you and I both know was to be challenging in the best of situations. Shall I continue?"

Father's breath had become labored. Something in his face twitched. "You just signed your own death warrant."

Basra gave him a pitying smile. "Now, you know as well as I do how concerned the public already is over your ability to maintain control of your drones. The events of the past hour will be a disaster, but with my push, they shall be completely catastrophic. Should you detain or kill us, these events I have described will proceed as planned. The only way they will stop is if my biometric signature gives the order from the good ship *Kaitan* in orbit. What's more, should my compatriots and I be allowed to safely leave the warm embrace of your hospitality, I will personally initiate a buyback. Your stock value is unlikely to return to its current level, but it should recover substantially." He paused and added thoughtfully, almost to himself, "Since I'll be purchasing more of the product back at a lower rate, I might stand to make something on the transaction. Everyone will win."

Thelarus stared at Basra, not with venom, but with calculation, the way a duelist might assess their opponent. "It's a quality bluff, but you know as well as I do any attempt to devalue our product on that scale will look like blatant manipulation. No one will truly believe we don't have confidence in our own product. Besides, you could have made these claims *without* crashing your ship into my citadel and getting yourselves in a dire predicament. I smell desperation."

Basra nodded agreeably. "That's true, on both counts. Unless, of course, it's not a bluff, since the sell orders have all come from within your royal citadel within the past hour." He flicked a thumb, and a small communicator, designed to jack into a larger system, flew through the air. Father instinctively caught it. "Dracorte family members attempt to secretly unload stock, hackers uncover their fingerprints all over the sales. I can see the headlines now. It will be the financial scandal of the century . . . and the ruin of your family."

Silence filled the hangar, broken only by the steady dripping of blood from one of my hands to the floor. Everyone stood in a stillness that felt jarring and eerie compared to the recent havoc.

It was easy to imagine that Basra was simply concocting a

fantastic tale. I knew he was gifted; I knew that only the best came out of the financial corporation he'd been indentured to. How he'd ended up with Qole was a baffling mystery. But that didn't begin to explain why Father was now taking him seriously. Basra had said he could hit my family where it hurt most, and that he'd been doing some shopping during our journey to Luvos . . . but that was like comparing pole fishing to a Shadow run if *this* was what he'd been up to.

Even if Basra was somehow telling the truth, I still couldn't imagine Father agreeing. To allow the crew of the *Kaitan* to simply leave after everything that had happened was unthinkable.

Except . . . there was something Father valued more than his pride.

"Are you thinking of what is best for the family right now, or your ego?" I asked softly.

Thelarus Dracorte took a deep breath. In the dimming daylight, I saw some of the rage leave his face. He didn't look at me but kept his gaze fixed on Basra.

"Leave," he said curtly. He finally glanced at me. "You too. Get out." Without another word, he turned and strode back toward his troops.

In numb shock, I stared after Father as he left. He never looked back. Not once.

XXII

QOLE

CLOSING MY EYES WAS LIKE SHUTTING OUT THE ENTIRE WORLD AND waking up in a different place. I could no longer hear Basra, Telu, or Eton, who'd all been speaking to me—or shouting at me, in Eton's case. I couldn't feel my body in the darkness, or see anything other than distant specks of light. Even though I seemed to be floating, I knew I was in a precarious place, perched on an edge, about to fall.

Had I finally gone mad? Was I dead? Or just on the brink of one of those things?

The lights moved closer, tentatively. With them, I felt a choice coming on. Did I push them away, try to maintain control of myself with an unbendable grip, and force this out of my life? Or did I seize those sparks, unleash the power, and try to control *it*?

And yet reaching toward either option felt like leaning out over that drop. There was only the illusion of choice. Both paths would bring me to the same edge:

Insanity. Death. But maybe there was a third option.

Peace. The word moved through me like a whisper, a trickle, an ocean. Peace, not oblivion. Oblivion was an end. A fall. Peace was a path. Maybe another path I could take.

Peace. Open.

The thoughts occurred to me as the lights gathered around me again. They outlined my toes, my fingers, my feet, my hands. I felt my body coming back to me. This time, I didn't shy away, or lash out, both of which were my first impulses—the two paths I'd been following my entire life.

Embrace.

Yes, I thought. *That.*

My arms reached out, but not to shove or to seize. I opened them and enfolded the light.

The flash was blinding, but not jagged and jarring. It was a warm flood, and I realized my eyes had opened. I also realized I was holding something a lot more solid than the imaginary, insubstantial lights. *Someone.*

I blinked and pulled away to find bright, silver-gray eyes staring back at me. We were on our feet, our faces a finger-width apart. He must have dragged me up, and I'd apparently thrown my arms around him.

"You're awake," Nev said. He cleared his throat. "We need to go."

The rest of the world came crashing back down around me with far less gentleness. The hangar looked like the bottom of a dark pit into which we'd all fallen. Bodies were strewn everywhere, melted gouges and blast holes were splattered with blood, and the dying daylight dripped more red from the mangled bones of the roof and the shattered ceiling of the Atrium above.

We were no longer surrounded. At the far end of the hangar, several guards remained, holding rifles and swords at the ready. But they weren't coming after us. Nev's own blades were sheathed on his back, and the rest of the crew had already made it up the ramp into the *Kaitan*. Basra and Telu were carrying Arjan between them on a blanket, making their way up the stairs from the hold, toward the bridge. The makeshift medi-kit was still looped over Basra's shoulder, though the rifle wasn't. Eton followed, dragging himself slowly up after them, his leg stained red even through the fresh bandages. He clearly needed to be stitched, and was probably making his way to the bridge's medi-kit behind the others. He only had one pistol in his hand, which, for him, barely counted as being armed.

"But . . . how?" I said, too stunned to let go of Nev. I didn't understand why we weren't being shot at, or at the very least stopped.

"Basra. He convinced my father to let us leave."

"How?" I repeated.

"I'll explain later. Like I said, we need to go."

He reached up to take one of my hands, repositioning it around his shoulder to support me. But we took only three steps toward the ship before I realized I could walk, and that Nev was the one who needed help. I looped his arm around my shoulder to support *him*. His jacket was tattered and wet. He wasn't soaked with quite as much blood as Eton, so I hoped that meant none of his cuts were serious. We had too many injuries to deal with already.

But it wasn't only a practical concern. Imagining him seriously hurt made my breathing quicken, my chest constrict. It was like thinking of Arjan being as injured as he was—someone who mattered so much he felt like a piece of myself.

Arjan . . .

I couldn't think about my brother yet. I had to focus on getting us out of here, so I could think about him later.

As Nev and I hit the ramp and started stumbling our way up, it finally caught up to me, what he'd said: *We. We need to go.*

"You . . . ," I said, both my feet and my words stuttering once we reached the top of the ramp and stepped into the hold. "You're coming with us?"

Nev gave me a crooked smile, one that looked nearly broken, but not quite. "This is where I belong now . . . if you'll have me."

As if to punctuate the impossible thing he'd just said, he hit the button to raise the hatch. It ground closed behind us, sounding worse for wear, but at least it sealed with a hiss. He slipped away from me, managing to stand on his own, even if he looked unstable. Purpose had come into his eyes, his face, and his body responded to it, if slowly. He moved for the stairs to the bridge.

"I'll check the ship's systems to make sure we're airtight, and I think between the solar sail and diverting power to the one thruster—the one that's nearly offline, but not quite—you can lift us . . ."

He glanced back at me and stopped, trailing off. I hadn't moved. Something was bright and warm in my chest, so bright it was almost hot, stinging my eyes.

"Sorry," he said, misreading my face. Or maybe he just didn't understand my expression, whatever it was. "I don't mean to usurp your authority . . . Captain. If you have another idea—"

I shook my head. "No, that's exactly what I was thinking."

"Then . . ." He looked unsure. Afraid, almost. "What's wrong? Is it all right that I'm here? I can—"

I shook my head again. Swallowing, I tried to find my voice. "I'm glad you're here. And please . . . call me Qole."

Relief washed over his face, dragging a smile with it. He looked lost and then found. The expression didn't stick around; it was there and gone before he nodded. "Qole . . . I'm going to check our status and make sure you're ready for takeoff."

"I'll be right there."

He bounded up the stairs, tapping into some hidden reserve of energy that I certainly didn't have. Once he'd gone, I dragged my hands over my face, feeling wetness on my palms. I ran them back through my hair, squeezing my eyes closed, trying to banish the rest of my tears. I had to captain, to pilot a ship that would probably try to fall out of the sky at the first available opportunity, and I couldn't very well do that while crying.

Other than tears and tiredness, though, I was okay, for the moment. I seemed to have struck some sort of deal with the power that possessed me, even if it was all in my own head. For now, it seemed to be holding. I wasn't insane, or dead.

At least, not yet. I didn't know how long that would last.

The bridge was in organized chaos when I arrived. Arjan lay on a makeshift bed of blankets on the bench, Basra bustling efficiently over him, surrounded by infopads. He'd no doubt chosen the bridge to commandeer any help he might need, but I wasn't sure what we could do that *they* couldn't.

I spotted at least three different faces video-comming with Basra at the same time. They looked like a variety of doctors from different systems, and I couldn't imagine how much these comms had to be costing. Basra was following their instructions to the letter, cleaning, bandaging, jabbing injector tubes into Arjan's neck, only speaking to ask questions or for clarification. He was deferential, and I had a hard time reconciling this image of him, nursing my brother, with the person he'd been in the lab . . . and evidently in the hangar, afterward, when he'd faced down Thelarus Dracorte.

Eton had less attention, sitting on the floor next to an open medi-kit, but he was managing. Telu was helping him stitch the glaring, weeping slit in his leg when she wasn't fetching or holding something for Basra. Instead of taking any of the injector tubes meant for Arjan, Eton clutched an open bottle of white liquor in one hand, which he poured in equally liberal amounts over his wound and down his throat. Nev was both checking the ship's systems and occasionally calling advice to Telu over his shoulder. He'd clearly been trained to field-dress battle wounds.

No one snapped to attention when I walked in, and I was glad. They were already doing what needed to be done. In spite of how battered we all were, we were still a good team.

I slipped into my chair and checked the feeds. It took only a few pieces of information for me to know for sure that the *Kaitan* could fly.

"I'm getting us out of here," I said, and took up the controls.

We had an escort, of course, consisting of the Royal Dracorte Air Guard and several of their destroyers. But like the guards in the hangar, they didn't touch us. They only watched and waited. They were patient, at least, because we were slow. The *Kaitan* struggled to gain every bit of altitude, climbing as if crawling up a cliff face, with only one partially working thruster and a solar sail to power her. But she rose.

The city of Dracorva was still grand, if injured, as it fell away beneath us. The only drones in evidence were those that had been blasted into blackened craters of wreckage. Several towers were blackened as well, others broken. Smoke billowed in thick streams from a few places still burning.

Nev didn't look at it, either down through the viewport or on any of the feeds. Maybe he couldn't. He focused on my face instead, leaning against the dash and filling me in on what had happened in the hangar. He murmured the details as we made our way up through Luvos's atmosphere, quietly so as not to disturb Arjan. My brother was no longer groaning. Basra had given him something that had rendered him unconscious but continued working over him. Eton hissed occasionally as Telu finished his stitches and then tightly wrapped his thigh with a thick compress.

Once she finished with him, she moved over to Nev, interrupting him only long enough to command him to take off his jacket. He smiled, bemused ... and no doubt loopy from blood loss, I realized, when the thing hit the floor with a wet smack. Telu immediately set to work cleaning and bandaging the cuts lacing his arms like gory latticework, working quickly to stop the bleeding.

He shrugged with red arms at both Telu's and my alarmed expressions. "These would have been deeper, or would have cost me limbs and life, if my father's guards hadn't been holding back." His tone grew grimmer as he finished the story, explaining what had happened between him and his father, and then Basra.

According to Nev, Basra—or Hersius Kartolus the Thirteenth, apparently—would call off his full-scale financial assault of Dracorte Industries before we engaged the Belarius Drive ... but only the second before. Otherwise, if he did it any sooner, I had no doubt our alarm systems would blare once again, alerting us to a weapons lock. Based on the state of Nev's arms under his new bandages, I suspected they would try to blow us to dust even with the king's heir on board.

My suspicions were confirmed when a hard voice cut over the inter-ship—and planetwide—comms.

"Attention, lawful citizens under the stewardship of the Dracorte royal family. Your king, Thelarus Axandar Rubion Marsius Dracorte, will now be making an official announcement of grave importance."

If that voice had been hard, it was nothing to the one that came next. It didn't sound anything like the man I had met in that ornate sitting room. Thelarus had acted like a king then, but I could still imagine him as Nev's father. There was nothing to balance the king in his voice, now. Nothing of a father.

"I hereby announce the formal disavowal and disinheritance of Nevarian Dracorte. He is my son, my heir, and your prince no longer, and may make no further claim to the other names of his ancestry. His own actions brought this ruin upon him, first and foremost, but it is by my hand finished."

We all froze, looking at Nev in shock. He blinked, as if the news hadn't hit him yet.

Thelarus's voice fell like another powerful blow. "I hereby banish him from the planet Luvos, and if he ever sets foot upon it again, he will be executed for treason. His life is my gift of my mercy, the final mark of what he once meant to me, but if he should lose it at another's hands, it will be of no importance to us, the Dracorte family. He may keep the Dracorte name only in remembrance of his shame and dishonor. His fate is now the Great Unifier's to decide."

Even though the ship had remained airtight, it still felt like the oxygen had been vacuumed out into the upper atmosphere. Nev looked winded, his hand scraping over his face and mouth, fingers parting to reveal his eyes. His eyes were terrible.

"As a result," Thelarus continued in a pitiless tone, "it is both my duty and honor to announce Solara Ysandrei Rezanna Verasia Dracorte as my heiress. Upon my death, she will be bequeathed all titles, domains, and assets belonging to me, and with those, the Throne of Luvos and all the responsibilities that sitting it will entail. May she someday rule wisely, honorably, and with unwavering loyalty to her family."

Nev's eyes closed on the last words, and the comms fell silent.

We were all quiet for a moment, except for Basra, who'd mostly ignored the whole thing and returned to questioning and listening to the doctors. Even Eton was looking at Nev with some measure of pity, though maybe only because his gaze was glassy and the liquor bottle half empty.

Then Telu shrugged and slapped a last piece of tape on the end of Nev's bandages, making him wince and open his eyes. "We all knew it was going to happen anyway, hey? This is just a formality, the bit that everyone else sees—the rotten frosting on top of the scat-cake, if you know what I mean."

I was about to tell her that she maybe wasn't helping when Nev straightened from his perch on the dash. He smiled, though it wasn't cheerful. It was the opposite of cheerful.

"I think Eton wants to bake me that cake," he said. He stepped away without looking at me, heading off the bridge.

"Nah," Eton said from where he sat with his back against the wall, his words lazy and swooping, a bit like how the *Kaitan* was trying to fly. "Not really, not anymore. Maybe. Anyway, you saved me . . . but let's be honest"—his voice dropped—"you didn't do it for me."

Nev paused and met his stare. Something passed between

them, and then they both glanced at me. I turned in my seat and looked fixedly back out the viewport, hiding my flush. Stars were nearly visible through the last of the atmosphere now.

"I'm pretty sure *I* saved you," Telu grumbled, maybe to ease the tension, "by keeping the Air Guard busy with drones so they didn't blow you to bits." She hesitated. "Then again, you saved me while I was still on the ship hacking those drones. And Qole saved us before that by vaporizing an army. And Basra saved us all *after* that ... I guess we all sort of saved each other, so stop taking all the credit, hey?"

I was an idiot. Because, in spite of everything we'd been through—in spite of my ship and my crew being practically held together by bandages, my brother unconscious on the bench behind me, our distance from our enemies not yet great enough to engage the Belarius Drive—my focus drifted as I pictured the look in Nev's eyes. My heart started beating faster.

But then Nev left without a word, taking my childish hopes with him. I was doubly an idiot. Because not only was the young man who made my heart pound from a different world and a royal bloodline he could trace back before the Great Collapse, but I'd just helped him get exiled *and* disowned.

That didn't keep my thoughts from churning as I brought us farther and farther from Luvos. Maybe I was *triply* an idiot, because I didn't shut them down. But closing myself off hadn't done me much good in the past. It might have hurt me, as much as unleashing myself without restraint had. Maybe I just needed to stay ... open. To look for balance, not extremes.

Besides, my family was as old as Nev's, if not as royal, and my history as rich. And if there was *one* aspect of all this I could look at in a positive light, it was that Nev wasn't quite as royal anymore. Maybe we had somehow found a patch of common ground after we'd *both* ruined each other's lives.

Eventually, the Air Guard starfighters and destroyers held back, giving us enough space to engage the drive, though not enough that they couldn't try to torpedo us into particles if we didn't deliver our end of the deal.

"Basra?" I said. It felt odd for a second, giving an order to someone who was apparently richer than the Great Unifier. But then, it was still just *Basra*. I'd have to get to know this other side of him later. "Do your thing. We're ready."

Without looking away from Arjan, he swiped a finger over one of the infopads. "Done," he said.

I didn't wait to verify. I punched the button for the drive and was relieved to find that at least one thing on the ship still worked right. The stars melted around us. In moments, the *Kaitan* had left Luvos light-years behind, along with the Dracortes.

All except for one.

———

After making sure Telu had set the proper coordinates, receiving Basra's assurances that Arjan was stable for the time being, and helping Eton to his quarters to rest, I made my way alone into the hold. There, I found Nev.

His bandaged arms were braced on either side of a viewport, red already seeping through the white in some places. It would take some time, but they would heal. I didn't know about the rest of him, though, as I watched him staring out at the weeping stars. As I knew from experience, losing your family was a hard thing to weather.

But I hadn't lost all of my family. I'd gotten my brother back against impossible odds. The thought made my breath catch in my chest. I hadn't let the relief crash over me yet. Arjan was alive. He was hurt, but those injuries—even his eye—didn't weigh anything next to his life. I was nearly dizzy with joy simply to still have him. We'd deal with the rest later.

Meanwhile, Nev had lost more than he thought possible.

And yet, he'd chosen this, chosen *us,* even before he'd known he was exiled and disowned. Somehow, that made me able to reach out to him. I threaded my fingers through his, where they lay splayed on the wall. As he straightened in surprise, I took his hand in mine.

Nev blinked at me. And then, before I knew what was happening, he pulled me into him, his mouth hungry, his lips firm and warm against mine. I tilted my head back in breathless response, my arms wrapping around him. For one moment, neither Shadow, nor crew, nor family, nor anything else existed. Only us. This was the answer to the question he'd asked about what I wanted most for *just* myself—my hidden, desperate dream come to life, while all my cares and responsibilities faded away.

His chest rose and fell against my own. We were both breathing rapidly, and I was dizzier than ever. Maybe it was because of how tightly we were holding each other, as if something would try to tear us apart. His arms, for being injured, were quite strong.

In the end, it was that practical detail that made me pull away. "Your cuts . . . ," I said. And then I suddenly didn't know what else to say.

I would have pulled away entirely, but he kept a firm hold of my hand. Our hands hung between us, linked, bridging the gap, and we both looked at them like we didn't know what to do.

Still, neither of us let go.

"Where are we headed?" Nev asked.

"Alaxak. Are you okay with that?"

He nodded.

"You . . . you don't have to stay, once we get there." The words hurt to say, but I had to.

"I know," he said, and I held my breath. "But I want to."

I exhaled and said in a rush, "I don't even know what we'll do once we get there."

He glanced up at me, smiling. "We'll Shadow fish, I imagine. We all need to make a living, after all . . . even me, now." He grimaced. "You don't even have a net, never mind functioning thrusters. I was supposed to pay for the damages to your ship, but all my assets have likely been frozen. I took some money with me, though it's nothing like what I had."

"Frozen money for a frozen planet," I said, unconcerned. "Basra told me that he managed to save some of what you had, somehow. He didn't explain, and I didn't ask, but it might be enough."

I meant enough for him to live, to do whatever, without having to work on my ship or anywhere, but he said, "Well, then, at least I can pay off some of my debt." His smile returned, but it was still pained. "I hope you'll let me work off the rest."

The words were so loaded, it would have taken hours to unpack everything in them. All I could do was nod, for now.

"You realize . . ." Nev paused. "You realize my family might still try to come after you, or me. If they do, Basra could try to sink Dracorte Industries again, of course, but any attempts on our lives might not be directly linked to them. There are plenty of assassins and bounty hunters who do work for the Dracortes, never mind those who could be sent by other families."

For some insane reason, I still wasn't worried. I couldn't

get over the simple fact that we were all alive. Beyond that, everything was unimportant. "I won't let them hurt any of us. There's so much Shadow on Alaxak that I can use if—"

I tried not to start when Nev rested his forehead against mine. His breath was warm on my face. "I have no doubt . . . but at what cost to you?"

"I . . ." I hesitated, and then said truthfully, "I don't know. I don't know if, or when, all this will catch up to me."

His hand tightened in mine, tugging me closer, his forehead nudging mine. "I'm not just going to leave you to this. I promised. I promised to help you figure out your Shadow affinity, how to use it safely. I haven't forgotten." He chuckled, once. "And now that we're not all about to die, it has moved to the top of my priority list, just short of breathing."

Now *I* couldn't breathe again. But if I'd thought that was bad, he then kissed my forehead. It was like he'd dropped a bomb on my skin. A tingle spread in a radius out from his lips, racing over my scalp and down my spine. I couldn't believe he could just *do* something like that, and the ship didn't grind to a halt, or the planets stop spinning, or the stars burn out.

His arms came around my shoulders like nothing had happened. I couldn't help leaning into him, resting my cheek against his chest.

"I know," he began, "that everything just changed for the both of us. A lot. Everything is different. But perhaps . . . perhaps we can figure it out together. I'm ready to face these changes."

My own arms snaked around his back. Next to him, almost anything seemed possible. Even the impossible.

It was time to find that balance, that peace, I'd been looking for all my life. My lips parted, and I breathed into his shirt.

"Me too," I whispered.

ACKNOWLEDGMENTS

This book went through a unique process in its birth, and as with anything, there are a number of people and entities that made its very existence possible.

First—and this always gets stuck at the end—thanks to our respective life partners for initially thinking this was a terrible idea and then being ridiculously supportive. We essentially stopped being humans while writing, and somehow they didn't lose their tempers while cohabiting with sleepless grouch golems. Not only that, they both eagerly devoured and then critiqued the manuscript. Margaret Adsit, thank you for your unflinching recommendations on chapters, and, Lukas Strickland, thank you for calling it like you see it. We love you both.

Second, a big thank you to Alex Miller, Michael's brother, for being there for the initial brainstorming on the snow-swept drive to the airport that kick-started this entire adventure. As for Deanna Birdsall, AdriAnne's mom—if there's a missed apostrophe in the entire thing, it's because we put it in after her incredible proofreading. Dan and Pam Strickland, AdriAnne's parents-in-law, somehow found time to be early readers and to lend us kind words. Chelsea Pitcher, awesome author and friend, gave us a thorough critique and was an early cheer-leader. And to our friend and Michael's coworker, Logan Bean, who patiently wondered why Michael was sleep deprived and then happily volunteered as a test audience when he found out, thank you. Thanks so much to all of you.

It goes without saying (but we will anyway): many thanks to our agent, Kirsten Carleton, who has proven a combination of contract warrior, story connoisseur, and all-around cool. And then there's Kate Sullivan, our amazing editor at Delacorte Press, who was (and will continue to be) a virtual shepherd to our book, and left truly hilarious comments in the margins while she was at it.

We also want to thank the real, live fisherwomen and lady captains (all of them pilots too) who were such an inspiration when uniting Qole: Anna Hoover, Thorey Munro, and Amanda Zharoff, you are badasses of epic proportion. Thanks especially to Anna for vetting parts of the manuscript and providing feedback.

Last but not least, Michael would like to thank God, and AdriAnne would like to thank the god of beer.

This book was written in Alaska, Wisconsin, Hawaii, and Washington. It was written on windswept beaches and sunny beaches, in snowy forests and forests of people. It has traveled thousands of real and digital miles and has fueled untold sleepless nights and our wildest imaginations. So to each and every one of you who helped make this possible, we are more thankful than these puny words can say.

ABOUT THE AUTHORS

Michael Miller and AdriAnne Strickland met in their home-town of Palmer, Alaska, where they agreed on books 99 percent of the time, and thus decided to write together. They grew up on Lord of the Rings, Russian folktales, the Ender Quartet, the Little House on the Prairie books, and *The X-Files*. Michael grew up off the grid in a homestead in Alaska and ironically now works very much on the grid in IT and Web development. AdriAnne grew up in Nevada and now spends her summers as a commercial fisherwoman in Bristol Bay, Alaska, and the rest of her year writing. This is their first book.